Mariah Stewart is the *New York Times* and *USA Today* bestselling author of twenty-six novels and three novellas and has been featured in the *Wall Street Journal*. She is a RITA finalist in romantic suspense and the recipient of the Award of Excellence for contemporary romance, a RIO Award for excellence in women's fiction, and a Reviewers' Choice Award from *Romantic Times Magazine*. She lives with her husband and two daughters amidst the rolling hills of Chester County, Pennsylvania.

D0532893

Home Again

Mariah Stewart

piatkus

PIATKUS

First published in Great Britain in 2012 by Piatkus,
an imprint of Little, Brown Book Group
This paperback edition published in 2012 by Piatkus

A CIP catalogue record for this book
is available from the British Library.

ISBN 978-0-7499-5835-0

Typeset in Bembo by M Rules
Printed and bound in Great Britain by
Clays Ltd, St Ives plc

Papers used by Piatkus are from well-managed forests
and other responsible sources.

MIX
Paper from
responsible sources
FSC
www.fsc.org   FSC® C104740

Piatkus
An imprint of
Little, Brown Book Group
100 Victoria Embankment
London EC4Y 0DY

An Hachette UK Company
www.hachette.co.uk

www.piatkus.co.uk

For Blanche

Acknowledgments

I've lived all my life in small towns: That's the rhythm I understand best. My first seven books were a reflection of the towns I grew up in and later lived in, from Hightstown, NJ, to Marion, MA, to Lansdowne, PA. I'm happy to be returning to my roots with The Chesapeake Diaries, set in fictional St. Dennis, MD, which is a composite of all the small towns I've known and loved over the years. Grateful thanks to Loretta Barrett, Kate Collins, and Linda Marrow for wholeheartedly encouraging and supporting my return to those feel-good, relationship-oriented, family-centric books I used to write.

Thanks, also, to the wonderful team at Ballantine Books, who have so enthusiastically supported this effort, especially Libby McGuire, Kim Hovey, and Scott Shannon. I always hesitate to name names, because I inevitably forget someone who should be remembered, so while I offer my sincere thanks to everyone at Random House for all they do, I want to say a special thank-you to the marketing and publicity teams (with special thanks to Kristin Fassler, Alison Masciovecchio, and Quinne Rogers); the art department's Scott Biel for the beautiful, eye-catching covers that capture the spirit of this series; everyone in the sales department; the long-suffering production department, for hanging in there with me; Kelli Fillingim in editorial; and Andrea "The Decimator" Sheridan (who smites the pirates).

Grateful thanks to the lovely and gracious Grace Sinclair, who I met at the Country Meadows Retirement Village in Hershey, PA, for loaning her name to the author of the diaries that serve as the Greek Chorus to these books. Last but, Lord knows, never the least, the home-town girls, especially Cathy Lanning Simmons and Eileen Griggs McGillan, who make going home such a pleasure, and the Friday Club of Hightstown for inviting me to visit and for making me feel so welcome (with special thanks to Dale Snyder Grubb).

Home Again

July 13, 1983
Diary ~
Another sunny summer day in sleepy St. Dennis. Spent the morning at the Inn helping the housekeeping staff wash the bed linens, and the afternoon washing the lunch dishes and trying to keep my children out of trouble. Oh, the glamorous life of an innkeeper on the Chesapeake Bay!

Oh—one exciting thing did happen! Over the weekend, Beryl Eberle—the fabulous actress Beryl Townsend, for anyone in St. Dennis who's been under a rock for the past quarter century—came back and opened up her family's home as if she intended to stay awhile. I was at the market early in the week and overhead one of the clerks mention that Beryl— Berry, to those of us who have been lucky enough to have known her forever—had called in an order that morning and he was getting ready to deliver it, and just which of those big old houses out on River Road was hers? (I was able to tell him, of course.) There was a time when she and my cousin Archer were sweet on each other, but she's a huge movie star and he's a country lawyer, so anyone could tell that was going nowhere.

Anyway. Berry's nephew Ned had a fatal heart attack and died very suddenly two weeks ago. Berry, of course, dropped everything and flew from California straight to New Jersey, where Ned lived with his family. Berry is taking Ned's children for the summer. Imagine Berry—who never had a child of her own, and, as far as I know, never missed the experience—having full responsibility for a seven-year-old boy and an eleven-year-old girl for the rest of the summer. Yes, I *said full responsibility: It appears that while Roberta did bring the children to St. Dennis, she returned to New Jersey—alone—the following morning.*

Word has it that Berry had to back out of a movie she was to begin filming to spend the summer here with her grand-niece and -nephew. While many in town have expressed surprise over this, I do not. Berry adored Ned—he was clearly her favorite of her siblings' children. It should be an interesting summer.

~ Grace ~

P.S. I spotted the children with Berry at the park today. The little boy has hellion written all over his face; the girl looks lost and sad and is very quiet. Berry will have her hands full this summer, no doubt about that.

Prologue

July 18, 1983

EVERYTHING in Dallas MacGregor's life was wrong and she wanted to die. At least if she died, she'd be with her father, and the taunts of these hateful people wouldn't matter. Her mother had promised her a summer of fun with lots of new friends at her great-aunt's beautiful house by the beach, but she'd lied. She'd lied about everything.

There was no beach here, no ocean, just the Bay, and the river, neither of which had what a girl from New Jersey considered a proper beach, so that was lie number one. Lie number two: She hadn't had a minute of fun since they arrived here in St. Dennis. Lie number three: The kids here all hated her and called her names like Pudge and Chub. And her great-aunt Berry's house was like a museum. All the furniture was old and stiff and uncomfortable and there was only one small television, which her great-aunt rarely turned on except to let Dallas's little brother, Wade, watch *Mister Rogers' Neighborhood* or *Sesame Street*. What fun was there in any of that?

Dallas threw herself down on the riverbank and sobbed. Even if she died, no one would care. Why, she could walk right into that river and drown and it would probably take weeks before someone missed her. Yeah, no one would

3

even realize she was gone until her mother came at the end of the summer to pick up her and Wade.

Except maybe Wade. He'd probably miss her some.

The thought of her little brother missing her—maybe even crying for her—made her cry even harder. He was only seven, and he still didn't really understand that his father wasn't coming back or why. For that matter, neither did Dallas.

It was bad enough that her father had died, but dying so suddenly, without even having been sick, had denied his family the chance to say good-bye. Ned MacGregor's heart attack, at age forty, had come totally without warning. Dallas had gone to the viewing and the funeral with her mother's sister, Lynette, who'd flown up from Florida as soon as she'd heard, but the still man in the wooden box surrounded by flowers didn't look anything like her father, even though everyone said it was really him.

Maybe that had been another lie.

And then to have her mother send her and Wade away for the whole rest of the summer ... why, that all but made them orphans. Unwanted and alone like Anne Shirley, in *Anne of Green Gables*. Her eleven-year-old's sense of drama awakened, she would now be Dallas of ... of ...

Did Aunt Berry's house have a name? She wasn't even sure what a gable was, so it was hard to tell if the house had any of those.

Dallas sat up and wiped the tears from her face with the backs of her hands. Her arms wrapped around her knees, she stared out at the river, feeling immensely sorry for herself. She just wanted someone to tell her why her father

4

had been taken from them, and why her mother seemed so far away even before they left home to come here, and why she'd left her son and daughter in St. Dennis when she returned to Dunellen where they lived.

Her father had always told her that the only stupid question was the one you didn't ask when you didn't know, but what if you ask and no one has an answer that makes any sense? Her mother certainly hadn't made any sense when she told Dallas she just wanted "you kids to have a good summer and enjoy yourselves." Obviously another lie.

Dallas began to sob again, so loudly that she didn't hear the girls who had parked their bikes under the trees and were creeping up behind her.

"Look at the crybaby, crying like a baby." One of the girls stood in front of Dallas, her fists on her hips, her face an ugly mask of derision. "Do you do anything but cry, little baby?"

"'My daddy died, boo-hoo,'" one of the others mocked, rubbing her eyes.

"Maybe you should be riding that bike instead of sitting around," the girl to Dallas's left taunted. "Maybe you wouldn't be such a pudge."

Dallas's stomach clenched, and for a moment, she was afraid she'd throw up. She tried to think of something to say that would make them shut up and go away, but there were five of them and only one of her, and humiliation had clouded her mind and cut off all hope of coming up with something smart or clever to say.

"Go away," was the only thing she could think of. "Just go away and leave me alone."

5

"Who's gonna make us?" The girl who was standing behind Dallas poked her in the back.

"Maybe I will."

The boy had come out of nowhere, but he walked up the riverbank with a fishing rod in one hand and a bucket in the other. "Brooke, why don't you take your stupid friends and just get lost?"

"Or what, Grant?" A girl with dark blond hair in a long ponytail stepped out from behind Dallas.

"Or maybe I'll toss this bucket of worms on you." The boy held up the bucket.

"You wouldn't dare." She smirked.

He did.

The girls screamed, swatted the worms away, and ran for their bikes. When the girl who'd issued the dare reached the trees, she turned around and called back over her shoulder in a singsong voice, "Grant's in love with Pudge!" and the others took up the chant.

The boy ignored them and sat down next to Dallas on the ground. For a long time he didn't speak. When he did, he said, "You ever been fishing?"

Still so embarrassed she dared not speak, she shook her head no.

"Come on down by the water." He stood. "If you want to, that is."

Dallas couldn't tell him that all she really wanted was to go home and have things be the way they used to be, with her mother and father and brother, so she didn't say anything. He walked down to the river's edge and sat on the bank and threaded a worm onto the hook that was hanging from the rod's line. He turned to look over his shoulder before casting the hook out into the river with a flick of his wrist. She sat and watched while time and again he reeled in the line, only to put another worm on the hook to replace the one that was missing, and cast back out again.

"Why do you keep doing that?" she called to him.

"What?" He half turned. "I can't hear you. Come down here if you want to ask me something."

She hesitated, then looked behind her and found the taunting chorus had disappeared. She got up and joined him. "I asked you why you keep putting more worms on that hook and throwing it back into the river."

He shrugged. "I figure something out there must be eating the bait but is smart enough to avoid getting hooked. Maybe it'll get careless and take the hook one of these times."

"Maybe you'll keep losing your worms."

"Maybe. Plenty more where they came from."

They sat for a few minutes in silence, then he asked, "How old are you?"

She looked up into his eyes. "Eleven."

"You're small for eleven. I'm almost twelve."

"Maybe you're big for almost twelve," she said, and he smiled, the ends of his mouth turning up.

"I am. Everyone says so."

"What's your name?" she asked.

"Grant. What's yours?"

"Dallas," she told him. "Dallas MacGregor."

"You're Miss B's niece, aren't you?"

"Grand-niece," she corrected him. "Aunt Berry is my dad's aunt." Her throat constricted just to say the word "dad." When it passed, she asked, "Do you know Aunt Berry?"

"Everybody knows her. She's a famous movie star. She's the only famous person who ever lived in St. Dennis."

He looked down into her face and stared at her for a moment, then said, "You do know that she's a famous movie star, don't you?"

"Of course. I'm not stupid." She frowned. "She's my aunt. Great-aunt."

"No one thinks you're stupid," he told her.

"Those girls do," she said softly.

"Those girls who were here before?" He shrugged. "They don't know anything. None of them do."

"Do you go to school with them?"

"Uh-huh. They were all in my class this year." He reeled in the line and started over.

"Why were they mean to me?" she whispered.

"They're mean to everyone. Especially Brooke."

"Are they mean to you?"

He laughed. "Like I would care."

She wanted to thank him for making himself a target for her sake, but couldn't figure out the right way to say it. *Thank you for making them stop calling me names?* It just sounded dumb so she didn't try.

"Why did you chase them away?"

"Because I hate it when people are mean and say mean things for no reason at all."

They sat in silence again. Finally, Dallas heard herself say, "My father died. He had a heart attack and died while I was at camp."

"I know."

8

"Everyone says I'll see him again when I get to heaven, but I don't know where heaven is. People say it's up there"—she pointed toward the sky—"but if they've never been there, how would they know?"

"I don't think grown-ups know as much as they pretend."

"Where do you think heaven is?"

He shrugged his shoulders. "I don't know. I think it's wherever God wants it to be. He doesn't have to tell us where."

She thought this over and it made sense. It was the first thing that had in weeks.

"I think I'd better get back to Aunt Berry's," she told him after a while. "She might start to worry."

"I'll walk you back." He started reeling in the line.

"You don't have to, but thanks."

"I want to. Besides, I'm done fishing for the day."

"But you didn't catch anything yet," she pointed out.

"I didn't really expect to." He secured the hook to the rod and picked up the bucket. "I just like to come and sit by the river sometimes. Fishing's just an excuse to be here."

She walked off to get her bike then returned to the path that followed the flow of the river, and joined her new friend. They were almost to Berry's house when he said softly, "My little sister died in April. She was only four, and she was sick for a really long time."

Dallas was so stunned that at first she couldn't speak. When she finally found her voice, she said, "I am so sorry."

"Yeah." He nodded solemnly. "So am I ..."

★

From downstream on the riverbank, Grant had watched the small army of girls descend on the unsuspecting new kid who'd been sitting by herself for the past twenty minutes or so. Grant had been on his way to a point about a hundred yards beyond where the girl sat when he'd heard her sobbing as if her heart was about to break. Not wanting to walk past her, because that would likely embarrass her to have someone see her crying like that, he'd set up to fish where he'd been when he first heard her. The sound of her weeping had made him sad: it would make anyone feel sad for her. Except those bored and stupid girls who decided that they'd have a little fun at her expense.

One thing Grant Wyler had no tolerance for was mean.

Not that he'd ever borne the brunt of it. He was the biggest kid in the class and the most popular, partly because he didn't have an ounce of mean in him. He'd always taken up for the underdog, and anyone in grade school who had a lick of sense knew that on any given day, anyone could be the dog on the bottom. So it made good sense to be nice to Grant—he was everyone's ace in the hole.

He'd seen Brooke Madison cut down other kids for no reason other than she could, and he didn't think it was fair that the new girl couldn't even sit and have a good cry without being bullied.

Grant had known why Dallas was crying—he knew that her father had died not long ago and that she'd been sent to St. Dennis because he'd heard the grown-ups talking. He'd heard his parents talking about how the sudden death of Ned—Dallas's father—had nearly broken Berry Eberle's heart: He had been the favorite of her late sister's children. For a while, back when Ned was a boy, he'd spent so much time in St. Dennis with Berry, there was speculation that he was not her sister Sylvie's son, but Berry's. Grant's parents had pooh-poohed the story whenever they heard it repeated, but there was still the slightest wisp of doubt in some circles.

Not that any of that mattered to Grant, though he suspected it might matter to Dallas if she ever heard the gossip. What did matter was that after he'd sat down next to her, she'd looked up into his face, and the minute he'd looked into those strange-colored eyes, he'd felt a little zip inside, and he knew that she was going to be something really special in his life. He didn't know how he knew, but since his sister, Natalie, died, he'd had a number of these moments where things just happened and he knew to pay attention to them.

On instinct, he'd offered her his friendship, and she'd accepted. When it came time for her to leave, he'd walked her back to Miss B's big house on River Road, then walked himself the rest of the way to his home on the opposite side of town. He went into the backyard, where his mother was working in her garden. Since Natalie died, she spent most of her time out there alone.

When his mother asked him what he'd caught, he'd told her honestly that he'd been dropping his line in a place where he figured he wasn't going to catch much of anything. It was hard to explain to anyone why he wanted to be around the river, but his mother seemed to understand without him telling her that that was where he felt closest to Natalie, because it was quiet there and he could be alone with his thoughts. He figured that was pretty much why she spent so much time tending her garden. Then he told her about the girls teasing Dallas and how he'd thrown all but a few of his bait worms at them.

"You threw a bucket of worms at Brooke Madison?" His confession had stopped his mother in her tracks on her way into the house from the garden.

"She was being really mean to this other girl, calling her names and getting the other girls to tease, too," Grant said defensively. He wanted to add, *Like the way some kids used to tease Natalie when we took her to the library or the park after she lost her hair*, but he couldn't get those words out.

"I've raised you better than that." Shirley Wyler had poured herself a glass of water and took a few long sips.

"Mom, if you'd have heard them, you'd have thrown the worms, too."

"Well, I can't yell at you for coming to the aid of someone who needed your help." She smoothed down his hair where it had been sticking up. "Any idea who the girl was? Is she new in town?"

"Her name is Dallas."

"Berry's grand-niece?"

He nodded.

His mother took another sip of water, then poured the rest into the sink.

"That girl's had a real hard time these past few weeks. You know what it's like when you lose someone in your family." Her voice dropped and her eyes misted. "And to be sent away from home before she's really had a chance to deal with it . . . well, who knows what her mother was thinking? I'd give anything for one more day—hell, one more hour—with Nat, but I guess we're all cut differently.

Anyway, it's good that Berry was there to take in the girl and her brother."

"She looked really sad, Mom."

"I'm sure she is sad. I'm proud of you for sticking up for her, but tossing the worms ... We should probably talk about that part. But the rest of it ... you did the right thing."

Grant had wanted to tell her something else, about how looking into Dallas's eyes had made his heart beat a little faster, but he held his tongue. Maybe she'd make too much of it. One of the reasons why you didn't tell your mom everything was that you didn't know who she was going to repeat it to. But on her way back outside to her garden, she'd stopped in the doorway and turned to look over her shoulder.

"You know, you've probably made a friend for life, Grant," his mother told him.

He nodded. He knew. He wasn't sure how, but he knew.

May 2010
Diary ~

I saw Steffie Wyler the other day and the bags under her eyes were deep enough to carry mail. She says she's already hired three more high school kids to work at Scoop because, well, doesn't everyone want ice cream on a hot summer day? I'm afraid I committed a bit of a faux pas, however. You see, I saw her dancing with young Wade MacGregor at Beck's wedding and it looked to my seasoned eye as if they were . . . well, let's just say "interested in each other" is the most polite way I can think of to describe it. But when I asked if she knew if he'd be back in St. Dennis anytime soon, she darn near bit my head off with a short and snappy "How would I know?" I suppose if I really wanted to know I could ask Berry what she hears from her nephew.

Speaking of Berry—I saw one of those tabloid papers in the market that said her grand-niece, Dallas, had just wrapped up another movie. Well, I'm delighted to see she's so successful— I've always been fond of the girl. But there's a bit of scandal brewing, if those rags are to be believed: There were photos of her husband with yet another "mystery" woman! Of course, there have been rumors about him for years—Berry says that she'd put nothing past him because he is totally without scruples. He and Berry never did get along—she's seen through him from the very start. I certainly don't know what Dallas ever saw in the fellow—oh, he's handsome enough, if you like that Hollywood type, but Berry says he's all style and no substance. She swears that the day Dallas filed for divorce from that man was the first time Berry had set foot in a church in almost thirty years. Hopefully, she'll be able to say a final good-riddance-to-bad-rubbish before too much longer.

You know, you never see pictures of Dallas with other men, or read tawdry stories about her. She's always had much too much class for such shenanigans.

Well, they do say opposites attract . . . though only the good Lord knows why.

~ Grace ~

P.S. As a newspaper owner myself, I cannot conceive of carrying such rubbish in my paper. Why, the day I'm tempted to print trash in the St. Dennis Gazette *is the day I hang up my notepad, and you can take that to the bank!*

Chapter 1

AT the precise moment Dallas MacGregor was picking up her son, Cody, from his pricey summer day camp out near Topanga State Park, the home video starring her soon-to-be ex-husband and two of the female production assistants from his latest film had already been uploaded to the Internet. By the time she arrived at her Malibu home—she'd stopped once on the way from the set of her latest movie promo shoot to pick up dinner—the one-thousandth viewing had already been downloaded.

The phone was on overdrive, ringing like mad, when she walked into her kitchen.

"Miss MacGregor, you have many messages. Two from your Aunt Beryl." Elena, her housekeeper, cast a wary glance at Cody and handed her employer a stack of pink slips as the phone continued to ring. "About Mr. Emilio . . ."

"Would you mind answering that?" Dallas slid the heavy paper bag onto the counter. "And why are you still here? I thought you wanted to leave today by four?"

"Yes, miss, I . . ." Elena lifted the receiver. "Miss MacGregor's . . . oh, hello, Miss Townsend. Yes, she's home now, she just arrived. Yes, I gave her the message but . . . of course, Miss Townsend . . ."

Elena held the phone out to Dallas.

"It's your great-aunt," she whispered.

"I figured that out." Dallas smiled and took the cordless receiver from Elena. "Hello, Berry. I was just thinking about—"

"Dallas." Her aunt cut her off sharply. "What the hell is going on out there?"

"Not much." Dallas paused. "What's supposed to be going on?"

"That numbskull you were married to." Berry's breath came in ragged puffs.

She was obviously in a lather over something. Not unusual, Dallas thought. At eighty-one, it didn't take much to rile Berry these days.

"What's he done now?" Dallas began emptying the bag, lining up the contents on the counter.

"Not *what* as much as *who.*" Berry was becoming increasingly agitated.

"Mommy." Cody tugged at her sleeve. "Why are all those cars out there?"

"Berry, hold on for just a moment, please." Dallas glanced out the side window where cars were lined up on the other side of the fence that completely encircled the gated property, cars that had not been there five minutes ago when they drove through the gates. It wasn't unusual for paparazzi to follow her home, but she hadn't noticed any cars tailing her today. She raised the blinds just a little, and saw more cars were arriving even as she watched.

"I don't know, Cody. Maybe the studio put out something about Mommy's new movie. Maybe we should turn on the television and see."

"No!" Elena and Berry both shouted at the same time.

"What?" Dallas frowned and turned to her house-keeper, who stood behind Cody. She pointed to the child, then raised her index finger to her lips, their silent code for "not in front of Cody."

Keeping a curious eye on Elena, Dallas asked, "Berry, why don't you tell me . . . ?"

"Are you saying you don't know? Seriously? You haven't heard?"

"Heard what?"

"That idiot ex of yours—"

"Not ex yet, but soon, please God . . ." Dallas muttered. "And it's long been established that he's an idiot, so anything he's done should be viewed with that in mind."

"—managed to get himself filmed doing . . . all sorts of things that you will not want Cody to see . . ." Berry was almost gasping. "And with more than one person. It was disgusting. Perverted."

"You mean . . ." Dallas's knees went weak and she sat in the chair that Elena wisely pulled out for her.

"Yes. A sex tape. Not one, but *two* young women. I was shocked. Appalled!"

"Wait! You actually *saw* it?"

"Three times!" Dallas could almost see Berry fanning herself. "It was vile, just vile! You know, Dallas, that I never liked that man. I told you when you first brought him home that I—"

"Berry, where did you see this?"

"On my computer. There was a link to a site—"

"Hold on for a moment, Berry." Dallas put her hand over the mouthpiece and turned to Elena. "Would you mind cutting up an apple for Cody? Cody, go wash your hands so you can have your snack."

After her son left the room, Dallas took the phone outside and sat at one of the tables on her shaded patio.

"Dear God, Berry, let me get this straight. Emilio made a sex tape and it was put on the Internet? Is that what you're telling me?"

"Yes, and not just any sex tape. This one had—"

"Wait a minute; they allowed you to download the whole thing?"

"No, no, not all of it, just a little peek. You had to pay to see the whole thing."

"And you did? You paid to watch ..." Dallas didn't know whether to laugh or cry. The thought of her elderly aunt watching Emilio and his latest conquests burning up the sheets—and paying for the privilege—was horrifying and crazy funny at the same time. "Wait—did you say *three times?*"

"Yes, and it was—"

"Berry, why did you watch it three times?"

"Well," Berry sniffed. "I had to make sure it was really him."

The rest of the evening went downhill from there.

Dallas made every attempt to remain calm lest Cody pick up on the fact that she was almost blind with anger at the man she'd been married to for seven years.

Seven years, she repeated to herself. Seven years out of my life, wasted on that reprobate. The only good thing to come out of those years was Cody—and Dallas had to admit that she would have weathered a lifetime of Emilio's amorous flings and general foolishness if she'd had to in order to have her son. When she filed for divorce eight months ago, following the latest in his long line of infidelities, Emilio hadn't even bothered to beg her to reconsider: they'd done that dance so often over the years that even he was tired of it.

She managed to have a normal evening with Cody and ignored the cars that parked beyond the protective fence. They had a nice dinner and watched a video together, then Cody had his bath and Dallas read a bedtime story before she tucked him in and turned off the light.

It wasn't until she went back downstairs, alone, that she permitted herself to fall apart.

There was no love lost between her and Emilio. She'd long since accepted the fact that he'd married her strictly to further his own career as a director. For a time, she'd remained stubbornly blind, insisting that her husband be signed to direct her movies, and for a time, she'd been equally blind to his affairs. Lately it occurred to her that she well might be the last person in the entire state of California to catch on to the extent of Emilio's indiscretions.

For the past five years, she and Emilio had battled over the same ground, over and over until Dallas no longer cared who he slept with, as long as it wasn't her. Looking back now, she realized she should have left him the first time he'd cheated on her, when the tabloids had leaked those photos of Emilio frolicking with a pretty up-and-coming Latina actress on a sunny, sandy beach in Guatemala when he'd told Dallas he was going to scout some locations for a film he was thinking about making, but it had been so much easier to stay than to leave. There was Cody to consider: Emilio had never wanted the child, but Dallas had hoped—for Cody's sake—that he'd come around. Besides, Dallas's schedule had been so hectic for the past three years that she'd barely had time to read the tabloids. She'd had the blessing—or the curse—of having had wonderful roles offered to her, roles that she'd really wanted, so she'd signed on for all of them, and had gone from one set right onto the next, leaving her time for nothing and no one other than her son. It had only been recently that Dallas admitted to herself that perhaps she'd been deliberately overworking herself to avoid having to deal with her home situation.

Well, avoid no more, she told herself as she dialed her attorney's number. This time, Emilio had gone too far. When the call went directly to voice mail, Dallas left the message that she wanted her lawyer to do whatever had to be done to speed up the divorce.

"And oh," she'd added, "we need to talk about that custody arrangement we'd worked out . . ."

While she waited for the return call, Dallas logged on to the computer in her home office. She searched the Web for what she was looking for. The link to the video appeared almost instantaneously, along with a running tally of how many times the video had been watched—all thirteen thousand, four hundred, and thirty-one viewings. Her stomach churning, she clicked on the link and was asked first to confirm that she was over eighteen, then for her credit card number.

"Great," she murmured. "For the low, low price of nineteen ninety-five, I can watch my husband . . . that is, my soon-to-be ex-husband, perform daring feats with his production assistants."

The video began abruptly—"What, no music?"—and while the lighting could have been better, there was no question who was the filling in the middle of that fleshy sandwich. As difficult as it was to watch, she forced herself to sit through it, commenting to herself from time to time ("Emilio, Emilio, didn't anyone ever tell you to always keep your best side to the camera? And, babe, that is decidedly *not* your best side.").

When the phone rang before it was over, Dallas turned off her computer and answered the call.

"Hey, Dallas, it's Norma."

"Thanks for getting back to me right away." Dallas leaned back in her chair and exhaled. Just hearing her attorney's always cool and even voice relaxed her.

"I just got in and I was going to call you as soon as I kicked off my shoes." Norma Bradshaw was not only Dallas's lawyer, she was also her friend.

"So you heard . . ."

"Is there anyone in this town who has not? So sorry, Dallas. We knew he was a colossal shithead, but this latest stunt even beats his own personal best." Before Dallas could respond, Norma said, "So we're going to want to see if we can move the divorce along a little faster. We'll file a motion to revise those custody arrangements we'd previously agreed to."

"You read my mind."

"I'll file first thing in the morning. If nothing else, I think we should ask for sole custody for a period of at least six months, given the circumstances, which of course we'll spell out for the judge in very specific terms."

"Would it help to know that that little forty-two-minute production was filmed in his house? The same one Cody and I moved out of just eleven months ago because he refused to leave?"

"Really?" Norma made a "huh" sound. "Are you positive?"

"I picked out that furniture," Dallas replied. "Along with the carpets and the tile in the bath and the towels that were dropped around the hot tub."

"That was really stupid on his part. Now you can say you don't want Emilio to have unsupervised custody because you don't know who will be in the house or what they'll be doing. Or who might be filming it." Norma paused. "How are you doing?"

"On the one hand, I feel devastated. Humiliated. Nauseated. On the other, I feel like calling every reporter who chastised me for being so mean and unforgiving to poor Emilio when our separation was announced and yelling, *'See? I told you he was a jerk!'*"

"Anyone you want me to call for you?"

"No. I'm not making any statements to anyone. This is strictly a no-comment situation if ever there was one."

"You know you can always refer people to me."

"I'll have Elena start doing that tomorrow. Thanks."

"How did Cody react?"

"He hasn't. He doesn't know what's going on."

"You didn't tell him?"

"Of course not. Why would I tell him about something like that?"

"Do you really think you can keep him from finding out? Isn't he in camp this summer?"

"He just turned six. He's only in kindergarten." Dallas frowned. "How many of the kids at his camp do you think caught Emilio's act?"

"They could hear their parents talking, they could see the story on TV. It made the news, Dallas."

"I don't think it's going to be a problem." Dallas bit a fingernail. "At least, I hope it won't be. But if he hears about it, I'll have to tell him . . . something."

"Well, good luck with that. In the meantime, if you think of anything else I can do for you, you know how to reach me." Norma's calls always ended the same way, with the same closing sentence. She never bothered to wait until Dallas said good-bye. She just hung up, leaving Dallas to wonder just what she would tell Cody if he should hear something.

She didn't have long to wait to find out. When she arrived at camp the following afternoon, the Cody who got into the car was a very different child from the one she'd dropped off earlier that morning.

"How was camp, buddy?" she asked when he got into the car.

He looked out the window and muttered something.

"What did you say?" She turned in her seat to face him.

"I didn't say anything."

"Well, how *was* camp? Did you have your riding lesson today?"

He shook his head but did not look at her.

Uh-oh, she thought as she drove from the curb. *This doesn't bode well . . .*

"So what did you do today?" she asked.

25

"I don't want to talk."

"Why not, baby?"

"Because I don't and I'm not a baby," he yelled. He still hadn't looked at her.

Oh, God. Her hands began to shake and she clutched the wheel in an effort to make them stop.

She did not try to engage him in conversation the rest of the way home, and once they arrived, she drove in through the service entrance at the back of the property to avoid the crowd that was still stalking the front gate.

"Those cars out there, they're all there because . . ." Cody said accusingly. "Because . . ."

It was then that Dallas realized he was crying. She stopped the car and turned off the ignition, then got out and opened his door. She unbuckled his seat belt but he made no move toward her.

"Cody, what happened today?" When he didn't respond, she asked, "Does it have something to do with your dad?"

"They said he did things . . . with other ladies. Justin's big brother said his dad saw it on the computer and he heard his dad tell his mom." Huge, fat drops ran down Cody's face and Dallas's heart began to break in half. "Justin's daddy said my daddy was a very, very bad man. The big kids said he . . . they said he . . ." He began to sob.

Dallas had never felt so helpless in her life. She got into the backseat and rubbed Cody's shoulders, then coaxed him into her arms. How could she have been so naive as to think he wouldn't hear something from the older kids at camp? And how could she possibly explain his father's actions to her son?

26

"I'm never going back to camp, Mommy. Not ever. Nobody can make me." He hiccuped loudly. "Not even you. I'll run away if you try."

"All right, sweetie." Silently cursing Emilio for his stupidity and his carelessness, Dallas held her son tight, and let him cry it out. "It's going to be all right . . ."

But even as she promised, Dallas wondered if, for Cody, anything would ever be right again.

Chapter 2

DALLAS sat in the leather seat of the private jet and pulled off the dark wig that had kept her signature platinum hair under wraps. She tossed her dark glasses onto the seat across the aisle and looked to the cabin where her friend, Jessie Krane, stood conversing with the pilot and Cody. Moments later, Jessie strolled down the narrow aisle. A former child star, now in her fifties, Jessie was still one of the industry's most recognizable faces. Dallas often said she could only hope that her career and her popularity would last as long as Jessie's had.

"They'll take you to BWI," Jessie told Dallas. "From there, you'll have to find your way home on your own."

"I know the way." Dallas tried to smile, but her bottom lip was trembling. "Jess, I don't know how I can thank you enough for what you're doing for me. Loaning me your plane—"

"I'm not going anywhere for a while, so at least the pilots are getting a day out of it. For which you're paying their premium rates plus the fuel, I might remind you."

"Still, not everyone would offer."

"Everyone doesn't know what you're going through like I do," Jessie said. "And everyone doesn't love you like I do."

"You're a great friend," Dallas told her.

"I'm merely repaying a very small part of what I owe." Jessie sat on the edge of a seat facing Dallas. "Last year, when Peter left me for that trashy little bimbo and she started giving interviews right and left, talking about how my drinking caused my daughter to turn to drugs—"

"Jess, no one who knows you believed any of that. Even Courtney doesn't blame you for her problems."

"There were a lot of people who *don't* know me who *did* believe it, who did blame me. And there were plenty of others who reveled in the sideshow." Jessie swallowed hard. "You were the only one who spoke out, the only one who went on the talk shows and spoke with reporters about what a lie that was—"

"I wasn't the only one."

"You were the first, the most visible. The most vocal. My custody of Courtney could have been reversed. I have my daughter because of you."

"Not because of me. Because you're a good mother." Dallas added, "A great mother. And a great friend."

"I know what I know. And I know that your testimony influenced the judge. I only wish I could do more for you right now."

"Are you kidding? You're giving us a way out of L.A. that lets us leave anonymously. The thought of having to walk Cody through the airport and stand in those lines where anyone could say anything that he could overhear, where reporters could harass us ..." Dallas shivered. "I couldn't face it, Jess. I couldn't bear to have Cody walk that gauntlet. Thanks to you, we didn't have to."

"Sweetie, I know what it's like to be harassed, to have

my kids harassed. I know how tough these last few days have been for you."

"Tougher for Cody. He's too young to have to deal with this kind of nonsense."

"I'm sure some time away will be good for him. For both of you." Jessie looked critically at Dallas. "Any thoughts on how long you might be gone?"

Dallas shook her head. "I'm not thinking that far ahead. We'll have to see how things go and how long it takes for this thing to die a natural death. I have no work lined up until late fall, and Cody's school doesn't resume until the second week in September, so we have time."

"What will you do with yourself until then?"

"Relax. Spend time with Cody and my great-aunt." Dallas smiled wryly. "Maybe even work on that screenplay I've been thinking about writing for the past three years, if we stay long enough."

"Well, from what you've told me, there won't be much else to do in that little town of yours."

Dallas laughed. "Berry says it's changed a lot in just the few years since I last visited, so we'll see."

Jessie leaned over and tilted Dallas's face into the sunlight.

"When was the last time you slept?" she asked. "You could hide a family of four in the bags under your eyes."

"Oh, thanks for that."

"Merely observing."

"Another reason to be grateful for the private plane."

"So how long has it been since you slept?" Jess repeated.

"I've had a lot of details to attend to these past few days. A lot of packing to do . . ."

"With any luck, you'll sleep from coast to coast." Jessie stood. "I see the copilot has arrived. That's all we've been waiting for. They'll be taking off now."

She leaned over and kissed Dallas on the forehead.

"You'll let me know what else I can do for you, and you'll call me when you're ready to come back and I'll send them"—she nodded in the direction of the cabin— "back for you. Easy out, easy back in."

"You're the best, Jess." Dallas rose and hugged her friend.

"Don't I know it?" Jessie smiled and called to Cody, who was lingering in the cabin doorway talking to the pilot. "Come give your Aunt Jess a hug, Cody. You'll be taking off any minute now, so you need to find a seat."

"Aren't you coming, too?" Cody made his way down the aisle and hugged the woman around the waist.

"Goodness, no. I have things to do." Jessie steered him to a seat and helped him strap in.

"What kind of things?" Cody asked.

"All kinds of very important things. Meetings. Lunch. Take the dogs to the groomers. Get my nails done." She ruffled his hair, then went to the front of the plane and tapped on the open door. "Your passengers are ready whenever you are. I'm getting ready to leave, so come lock up after me."

The copilot followed her to the door, where Jessie turned and blew a kiss.

"Keep in touch. Eat lots of those Chesapeake blues for me," she added before disappearing down the steps.

"What are Chesapeake blues?" Cody asked his mother.

"Crabs that come from the Chesapeake Bay," she told him. "They're very famous, because they're very delicious."

"Will Aunt Berry have some of those?"

"I'm certain of it. Especially this time of the year. The crabs are big and especially sweet by the middle of the summer. Maybe we'll even catch our own. Remember I told you how the river runs right past the back of Aunt Berry's property?"

Cody nodded thoughtfully. "I don't really remember being there, though. I only remember the pictures."

"You were only three the last time we visited, and we didn't stay very long that time. Maybe some things will come back to you when we get to St. Dennis."

"How do things come back to you?" He leaned his chair back and rested his head. To Dallas, he looked so small, and so sleepy, and so uncertain.

"Well, sometimes you remember things that you don't even realize you remember." Dallas leaned her chair back, too, and nodded to the pilot, who appeared in the doorway to see if they were ready to take off. He disappeared back into the cabin, closing the door behind him. "Sometimes your mind will connect one thing to something else that you know." She thought for a moment. "Remember when we went to see the ice-skating show last winter? The skaters all skated to music. Then a few weeks ago, in the car—"

"—we heard that song and I said, 'Hey, they were playing this song when the guy who was dressed like a pirate skated at the show!'" Cody sat up, excited at the memory. "You mean, like that?"

32

"That's exactly what I mean." Dallas smiled. "You heard the song, and you remembered the pirate skater. We say, 'the song came back to you.'"

"The song came back to me," he said softly, as if trying on the phrase for size.

The engines on, the plane began to taxi slowly to take its place in line on the runway.

"Mommy, what will we do at Aunt Berry's besides catch crabs and eat them?" he asked a moment later.

"Well, we'll probably go out onto the Bay in boats and maybe swim in the river." Dallas paused, wondering if the recent efforts to clean up the New River had been successful. There had been a time, in her youth, when the water in both the Bay and the river had been too polluted for swimming. "And we'll go to the park, and we'll see whatever there is to see in St. Dennis since the last time we were there. Aunt Berry tells me there are lots of new shops and several new restaurants, even a new park. Oh, and she said there's an ice-cream place down near the docks now."

"I like ice cream." Cody's eyes began to close.

"So do I." Dallas looked out the window and held her breath as the plane began to move, then picked up speed. From past experience, she knew she wouldn't exhale until the plane made it off the runway. When they lifted up, she sighed and closed her eyes, too, thinking it would be wonderful if they both slept for a few hours. She had a feeling Cody hadn't slept much these past few nights, either.

"Will there be kids at Aunt Berry's?" he asked.

"No kids at Berry's house, but there are kids in St. Dennis."

"Will I go to camp?"

"I imagine that any camps there are in town might have started by now, but we'll see."

"Can I have a dog?"

"A dog? Why a dog?"

"Because you said when we weren't living in the white house anymore, I could have a dog."

The white house was their rented temporary home, so named because most of the furniture, carpet, and walls were white.

"But we'll be going back, Cody. What would you do with the dog then?" She glanced out the window, and with equal parts of relief and regret, watched the city below grow smaller and smaller. "We couldn't just leave it."

"Maybe Aunt Berry would want a dog," he said hopefully.

"I don't recall that Berry ever had a dog, even when I was little."

"Then we'd take it home with us and we'll go live someplace that isn't white. I saw a thing on TV. They let dogs on airplanes. Besides, Jessie wouldn't care if we took our dog on her plane."

"I don't think Berry would be happy if we brought a dog into her home, Cody."

"Why?"

"Well, because they shed and sometimes they make a mess. I don't know that Berry's housekeeper is looking to add to her workload."

"We could get a good one, one who doesn't make a mess or shed."

34

"We'll have to discuss this with Berry, sweetie. After all, it is her house, and we're going to be guests there."

Cody reflected on that for a moment. Probably, she thought, trying to come up with a way to get around Berry.

"How long are we going to stay there?" he asked.

"I haven't decided yet. We'll have to see."

"Will I go to school there?"

"I wasn't thinking quite that far ahead."

"Is there a private school there like the one I went to at home?" His voice was starting to fade.

"I don't know. We'll find out when we get there."

A moment later, a shadow crossed his face and he asked, "Do you think the kids there will be mean to me? You know, about Daddy, like the kids at camp were?"

"I doubt the kids in St. Dennis have ever heard of your dad, Cody."

"Really?" He opened his eyes and stared at her. Obviously this was a concept he'd not considered.

"I don't imagine people in St. Dennis spend much time worrying about what people in L.A. are doing." She could only hope. "They don't make films the way people at home do. They do other things to make a living."

"Like what?"

"Like, they catch crabs and oysters and fish to sell to restaurants all over the country. Some people build boats, and—"

"Does Aunt Berry have a boat?"

"She used to. I don't know if she still does."

"That would be fun, to have a boat." He closed his eyes again.

35

Dallas watched her son settle back and begin to drift off to sleep. She looked down through the darkness on the city she'd called home for so long and found its lights fading far below. There was a knot in the pit of her stomach that throbbed painfully at the thought of all she was leaving behind. She'd come to L.A. as a twenty-one-year-old, fresh out of college, with dreams of becoming not only a star, but a serious actress. No casting couches for her. Uh-uh. She'd make it on her talent or she wouldn't make it at all. She was well aware that it had been her looks that had gotten her an agent who'd been able to help her land those first small roles. It wasn't long before the platinum blond with the lavender eyes and the long legs was noticed. Even as a fledgling, she'd been gutsy enough to turn down parts she'd considered frivolous, choosing to wait for those that had some substance, and she'd made a promise to herself to never take her clothes off on-screen. For her, that was the line that she wouldn't cross, and she never had.

When she finally got what she considered her big chance, she made certain that she knew every line perfectly, that she was always early to the set, that she never made anyone wait for her for any reason. She was the very definition of professionalism. When the director from that film found his current project stalled and over budget due to the antics of one of his stars, he remembered Dallas, and offered her the role. She soon earned a reputation for being as dependable as she was beautiful, and oh, yes, this young woman could act. All through her career she kept to her standards, never causing a studio to lose money or to have any regrets in having hired her. She never engaged in the sort of high jinks that so many young stars seemed to be involved in or caused a distraction on the set. Through hard and consistently good work, she earned the right to be regarded as a serious actor. Over the years, her name was always at or very near the top of the best or favorite or most beautiful lists. She'd won prestigious awards as well as the respect of her colleagues. Now, her thirty-eighth birthday closing in, she was at the very top of her game.

She couldn't deny, even to herself, that it hurt to leave her life behind, even for a little while. But it was hurting Cody too much to stay in the eye of the shit-storm that had taken on a life of its own over the past few days and showed no sign of going away anytime soon. She could always go back, but he wouldn't always be six and needing her the way he needed her right now. She loved her work, but loved her son more than anything in the world. In the end, the decision to leave town had been an easy one.

Poor Cody. He'd been so unhappy and anxious, and true to his word, had cried bitterly at the suggestion that he return to his day camp. That was when Dallas decided it was time for a little getaway, just her and Cody. Berry's had always been her go-to place when she needed to heal whatever was broken. When she'd called Berry to propose a visit, her aunt had readily agreed.

"Anita comes tomorrow," Berry had said, speaking of the woman who'd been her part-time housekeeper for over thirty years. "I'll have her open your rooms and change the sheets."

Dallas's eyes grew heavy, and she felt herself begin to

drift off. Just before she fell asleep, she thought she heard Cody whisper, "Maybe it won't be too bad there . . ."

The car Dallas had ordered in advance was waiting for her when they arrived at BWI, and she loaded the bags into the cargo area. She'd thought about tucking her hair back into the dark wig, but decided not to bother. No one would be expecting to see her in Baltimore, she theorized, and anyone who might recognize her would probably think she was someone who merely looked like someone else. She put on her dark glasses, pulled her hair back into a ponytail, and put her theory to the test.

She'd been correct. No one gave her a second glance— at least, until she reached the car rental kiosk and had to hand over her driver's license.

"Really?" the woman behind the counter squealed after a triple take. "You're really Dallas MacGregor?"

Dallas nodded, then whispered conspiratorially, "Yes, but I'd really appreciate it if you'd keep it to yourself. My son and I are trying to have some quiet time away."

"I understand," the wide-eyed woman replied, then began to gush. "Oh, my God. I've seen every one of your movies. You're my favorite actress. I even voted for you in last year's America's Favorite Actress poll."

Dallas smiled and glanced at the woman's name tag. "That award meant a lot to me, Dawn. Thanks so much for voting for me."

"Oh, my God, wait till I tell my mother." Dawn giggled, then recalled her promise. "Oh. Right." She made a zipping gesture across her lips.

"Well, I guess you can share with your mom," Dallas

whispered, knowing there was no way this woman was not going to tell her mother and everyone else in her calling circle. Dallas could almost hear the calls go out the minute she drove off: *Okay, she asked me not to let on that she was in town, so you can't tell anyone, but guess who just rented a car from me!*

Dallas added on a car seat for Cody, signed autographs for Dawn, her mother, and her best friend, Colleen, then strapped her son into the back of the SUV and headed for the Bay Bridge. Cody didn't say much until they were crossing the Chesapeake. Then he craned his neck to look out the windows.

"Mommy, what are those birds? See the little island down there? Do the birds live there?"

"They look like some sort of gull," she replied. "I don't know if they live there. They might just be fishing for their dinner out there on the water."

"There are lots of boats down there." His face was as close to the glass as he could get.

"There sure are." She glanced out the side window. "All kinds of boats. It's summer, remember, and in the summer, lots of people come to the Chesapeake Bay to vacation."

She lowered the windows, hoping for a whiff of the Bay. What she got was a hot blast of early evening air.

Cody stretched his arm to stick his hand out the window. "It's hot."

"Want me to close the windows and turn the air-conditioning back on?"

He shook his head. "I like it. The water's all sparkly and pretty."

It *was* pretty, with the sun just beginning to set gently behind them and the water morphing gold and orange in its wake, fingers of light glowing on the waves and touching the sails as they turned in the wind. She adjusted the mirrors against the glare, and checked the outside temperature. The thermostat read eighty-seven degrees, so it must have been blistering there on the water when the sun was high, Dallas mused. She recalled days from childhood summers when it had been hot as blazes from the morning straight through till the sun set. She and her brother, Wade, would take Berry's rowboat onto the river, trying to keep close to the shady banks. Sometimes they just drifted, hanging strings over the side of the boat to catch crabs, chicken parts tied to the end to lure their prey to feast. When there was a nibble, they'd ease the string upward slowly until they could see what was hanging on to the bait. If it was a big enough crab, one careful scoop of the net would bring it home. Small ones would be released to grow bigger and fatter for next year. Whenever interviewers asked how she'd had the patience to wait for the roles she wanted, Dallas always said that she learned that fine art while crabbing on the New River when she was barely in her teens.

There were other things she'd learned in St. Dennis when she got to be a little older.

She smiled to herself, remembering all those summer nights when she was fifteen, sixteen, seventeen, eighteen. Remembering Grant Wyler, her first and only real summer love.

Berry had mentioned several times that Grant had gone to veterinary school, just like he'd always planned, that he'd married a girl he met in college and had at least one child that Berry knew of. Well, good for him, Dallas thought. He deserved to be happy.

"Mommy, I'm talking to you." Cody kicked the back of her seat.

"I'm sorry, sweetie. What did you say?"

"I said, are we almost there?"

"We'll be there soon," she assured him. Once on the Eastern Shore, she knew they were less than an hour from St. Dennis.

A few minutes later, Cody asked, "Where are all the big, tall buildings?"

"Well, there aren't any."

"How come?" He frowned.

"I suppose because people don't really need them here. There aren't as many people living here as there are in Los Angeles or in New York. Remember when we went to New York last year?"

He nodded solemnly. "There were lots of big, very tall buildings in New York."

"Lots of big, tall buildings because there are lots of people and not so much space for them to live and work. So they have to build up to make room for their apartments and for their offices."

"'Cause there's more room in the sky than on the ground?"

"Exactly."

Cody continued to trail his hand out the window as the highway narrowed to two lanes, and the strip malls gave way to fields, opening and closing his fist as if catching and releasing the muggy air.

They stopped at a gas station attached to a convenience

store where Dallas bought them each a bottle of water and used her iPhone to call her aunt to let her know where they were.

"Berry said we're only about a half hour from St. Dennis and we'll be there just in time for dinner," Dallas told Cody as she drove from the small parking lot. "I guess you're hungry."

Cody nodded but fell silent.

They drove past weathered barns and through several small towns, past an old mill, and a farm with a sign that read MINIATURE HORSES, FOR SALE AND FOR STUD. Corn shot up in straight rows in fields that ended right at the shoulder of the road, and they passed more than one farm stand that advertised tomatoes, green beans, melons, peaches, and fresh-cut flowers on large hand-lettered signs. They stopped at one and bought produce to take to Berry's and a bouquet of colorful summer flowers—zinnias in every shade and some fuzzy blue flowers on long arching stems that fascinated Cody.

The small bridge she crossed over was as familiar as if she'd driven over it yesterday. Dallas knew that just beyond it, on the right, would be the first of the marshes. On her left would be the old Madison farm. As she passed by, she checked the name on the mailbox. H. MADISON was barely visible in faded, thin black letters, but it still proclaimed ownership. Brooke Madison had been her rival for the heart of the boy they'd both loved back in their high school days. It had killed Dallas at the end of every summer to leave, to go back home to New Jersey knowing that Brooke would still be around, sharing classes with Grant and probably going to all of the same parties and social events. She wondered where Brooke was these days. Berry had never mentioned her.

She made the turn onto River Road and slowed so she could drink in the sights. The houses in Berry's neighborhood looked much the same as she remembered them. On big lots that sloped down to the river, with carriage houses or barns—some with both—and wide porches, tidy lawns and colorful flower beds, the imposing old homes were all approximately of the same vintage. All were still well kept, which spoke as well of their new young owners as it did of the older residents who'd never left their family homes.

Dallas slowed on her approach to Berry's, to savor that first view of the main house that had been built by an ancestor over two hundred years ago. She was just about to point it out to Cody, just about to tell him how the original section of the house was even older than that, when he asked, "Are we almost there?"

"We are here," she told him as she eased into Berry's winding driveway and followed it around to park near the back porch.

"There's the river, just like you said, Mommy!" Cody was out of his car seat and running across the yard in the direction of the river before the key was out of the ignition.

"Cody, hold up." Dallas opened her car door and called to him, but he was already closing in on the dock.

"Well, for heaven's sake, Dallas, let the boy wander a bit." The back door flung open and Beryl Eberle—stage name Beryl Townsend—glided onto the porch.

Eighty-one years young, but looking at least ten years

less, Dallas's Great-Aunt Beryl had been a star in her own right once upon a time. She'd never lost her sense of timing or failed to make a memorable entrance. Her once blond hair was now snowy white, but her blues eyes still sparkled and her figure was still trim. Dressed in white gauze capris, a matching tunic, and white mules studded with large faux gems, she posed momentarily at the top of the steps before descending, both arms open to her grand-niece.

"You look frightful, darling." Berry's arms wrapped around Dallas.

"Frightful?" Dallas grimaced as Berry embraced her.

Berry stood back and held Dallas at arm's length. "Bags under the eyes, skin pale," she observed. "And possibly a bit too thin."

"But *frightful*, Berry?"

"All right, sweetie. We'll go with exhausted," Berry announced. "Is that better?"

"Anything is better than frightful."

"Nothing that some restful days and nights and some time in the sun can't cure."

"I always heard that sun exposure isn't good for your skin," Dallas replied. "That it ages you prematurely."

"Does this face look prematurely aged?" Berry asked. Without waiting for an answer, she said, "I get my twenty minutes every day without sunscreen, which you need to do for vitamin D. Do I look as if I've aged prematurely?" she repeated.

"You look wonderful, as always, Berry."

"Of course I do, dear. And you're here now, and we'll take good care of you and soon you'll look wonderful again, too. Now, I need to see my boy."

"Who at this moment is a little too close to the water." Dallas handed her aunt the flowers and set off for the dock.

"Lovely colors, dear, thank you." Berry laid the bouquet on the steps then hastened to keep up. "The child does know how to swim, doesn't he?"

"He's taken lessons but he's never been tested."

"Well, he has to be able to swim if he's going to be staying here on the river, Dallas. We can't be worried about him falling in and drowning."

"There's a pleasant thought for our first night here."

Dallas stepped onto the wooden deck and walked the length of it to where Cody lay on his stomach trailing his fingers in the water.

"Cody, you're not showing very good manners. You didn't even say hi to Aunt Berry," Dallas chastised him softly.

"Hi, Aunt Berry," he said without looking up.

"Cody, that isn't . . ." Dallas began but Berry dismissed her with a wave of her hand.

"What's down there, Cody?" Berry asked. "What do you see?"

"There are lots of little tiny fishes," he told her. "See there? By the pole?"

"The pole is called a piling, dear," Berry told him. She looked over the side of the pier. "Look here, Cody, there's a crab near this one."

"Where? I want to see." He jumped up and followed her pointing finger. "Is that a Chesapeake blue crab?"

The crab took off, scurrying through the sea grass and disappearing in a blink.

45

"Ah, there's a lesson learned," Berry said. "Soft voice, slow movements when you're trying to observe something in nature."

"The crab heard me under the water?" Cody narrowed his eyes.

"No doubt it did, but I believe it was your shadow falling on the water that frightened it away. Creatures like crabs and small fishes are always alert for danger from something bigger that might want to eat them, but yes, that was one of our famous Chesapeake blue crabs."

Cody knelt slowly, and inch by inch, approached the end of the dock and peered into the water.

"Much better, child." Berry turned to Dallas. "He is quite the quick study, isn't he?"

Dallas laughed. "Very quick."

Berry tapped him on the shoulder. "Well, then, Cody, come along inside and let's see if you're as quick to learn how to eat one of those Chesapeake blue crabs."

He looked up at her as if confused. "Do you eat them a special way?"

"Oh my, yes. There's a special technique to opening the shells." She stood and she took his hand and led him up the gentle slope toward the house. "Perhaps tomorrow, your mother and I will teach you how to catch one. Assuming, of course, that she remembers . . ."

Chapter 3

DALLAS awoke the next morning in the same room she'd slept in every summer night in St. Dennis since she was twelve. Before that, she and her younger brother, Wade, had shared a room at the end of the hall, but on her twelfth birthday, Berry had moved her into a room of her own. Overlooking the river, Dallas's turret room was furnished with antiques and had an alcove with a cushioned window seat where she'd spent many a rainy day reading or writing in her diary about her one true love, and many a night when she'd stared up at the moon and imagined herself in his arms. She'd sighed many a dramatic sigh and shed many a teenage tear in that alcove. If she sat too long in the window seat, she could almost believe that some of that young angst had somehow survived the years and lingered on in that room, absorbed into the wallpaper and the overstuffed chair in the corner, neither of which had changed over the years.

As Dallas rose on this first morning in St. Dennis, the only thing on her mind was breakfast. She'd been promised pancakes and bacon, and since there were no photo shoots to worry about for a while, she was going to *eat*.

She walked to the window and opened it, then leaned

down to take a deep breath of fresh, smog-free air. She rested her hands on the wide windowsills and looked out toward the Bay, where sunlight caught the arc of gentle waves and gulls swooped gracefully across the sky. Below on the dock, movement caught her eye, and she pushed the curtain aside to get a better look.

Berry, dressed in a black top and yoga pants, was practicing tai chi on the dock. Cody, by her side, was trying his best to mimic her movements. Dallas couldn't help but smile as she watched the two of them together. A few minutes later, still smiling, she let the curtain drop back into place and headed for the shower.

"Ah, you're up!" Berry beamed when Dallas strolled into the kitchen, her hair still damp around her face. "Cody and I were just discussing flies."

"Flies?" Dallas frowned as she helped herself to coffee from the old-fashioned silver service that Berry kept on the counter.

"Oh, you remember the flies, dear. Those horrible greenhead flies, and those nasty stable flies that eat us alive in July and August." Berry turned her back to flip a pancake on the griddle, and Cody turned to his mother with a questioning eye. Dallas nodded—*Yes, Berry was telling the truth, the flies could be vicious*—and took a seat at the table across from her son.

"Depending, of course, whether the breeze is blowing from the Bay, or from land." Berry glanced over her shoulder. "You want the breeze from the Bay, Cody, like this morning. Otherwise, during fly season, you could be snatched up and simply carried away by a swarm."

Cody shot a glance at his mother, who shook her head—*No, that couldn't really happen.*

"We all have scars here and there from those beastly greenhead buggers who bite and positively *rip* the skin to get at your blood." Berry finished with a flourish.

Dallas nodded again. "Sad but true."

"How big are these flies?" Cody frowned.

"Oh, they can grow as big as half an inch," Berry assured him.

"How big is that?" he wondered.

"Over in the cabinet there by the door, second drawer from the top on the left side"—Berry pointed—"you'll find a small tape measure. Bring it over to your momma and she'll show you what half an inch looks like."

Cody did as he was told, and Dallas pointed out the half-inch mark.

"That doesn't look so big," he said.

"Darlin', in the world of flies, that is one big sucker. And don't let's even talk about the mosquitoes we've had this year. You go outside, you put on some of that spray I have. Won't help against the flies, but it will keep the mosquitoes away." Berry placed a full plate of pancakes on the table and removed the empty one. "Dallas, I'm so happy to see you eating. You're way too thin."

"I'm happy to see me eating your pancakes, Berry."

"Well, there's bacon there, too, so you help yourself," Berry said as she reached for the ringing phone on the kitchen wall.

"Wow. Dinner last night and breakfast this morning," Dallas observed. "When did you become such a cook?"

"Since I got hooked on the Food Channel," Berry noted, and answered the phone.

"Why doesn't Aunt Berry's spray help against the flies?" Cody asked his mother.

"Because nothing much does," she replied. "These are some tough, wily flies."

"Did you ever get bit?"

"Many times. Berry isn't exaggerating. Those flies are downright mean. Fortunately, here where we are on the point, we get many more days when the breeze from the Bay blows the flies inland." Dallas pointed out the window. "Oh, and see those birdhouses on the poles along the side yard there? Those are purple martin houses. A lot of people think those birds help by eating mosquitoes and flies."

"And for my money, they do," Berry remarked as she hung up the phone and turned to Dallas. "That was Grace Sinclair on the phone. She wanted to know if it was true that you were in town."

"I knew word traveled fast around here, but that's impressive. How could she have heard so quickly?"

"She said Tom Roth was just passing by when you turned into the driveway yesterday, and he was pretty sure it was you."

"What passes for news around here . . ." Dallas grumbled. "How is Gracie these days?"

"Still hanging on to that weekly paper of hers." Berry brought her coffee to the table and sat next to Cody. "I hear she's doing quite well with it these days, since St. Dennis has had such a rebirth, what with all the tourists coming through all the time. The paper is free, but she takes paid ads from all the local merchants who want to make sure the visitors know where to find their shops, what specials they're offering, what's doing in the town that week, that sort of thing. And of course, her son, Daniel, is doing very well with the Inn." Berry paused to take a sip of coffee. "You remember the Inn at Sinclair's Point, don't you?"

"Sure. I used to play tennis out there with ..." She bit back the name. "With friends when I was in high school."

Berry smiled to let Dallas know she wasn't fooled.

"I don't recall you playing tennis with anyone other than Grant Wyler, dear." Berry stirred her coffee. "Did I tell you he's back in St. Dennis?"

"Yes. I think you might have mentioned it." Dallas refused to bite. *Only about forty times.*

"He bought Dr. Evans's vet practice when the old man retired last year," Berry continued.

Dallas grinned in spite of herself. That "old man," Dr. Evans, was probably a good five years younger than Berry.

"And I heard he opened a rescue shelter for small animals."

"What kind of small animals?" Cody's head shot up.

"Oh, dogs and cats, mostly, I believe," Berry told him.

"Why do they need to be rescued?" he asked.

"I suppose because they are animals whose owners either don't want them or can't keep them for some reason." Dallas chose her words carefully. She knew that many of the animals in such shelters had been rescued from high-kill shelters. "The shelters take them in and try to find new homes for them."

"Maybe we could find a dog for us there." Cody

51

looked across the table at his mother. "You said I could have a dog."

"No, Cody. I did not." Dallas placed her cup carefully on the saucer. "What I said was—"

"Oh, every boy should have a dog, dear," Berry interrupted.

"I don't recall that Wade had a dog when he lived here," Dallas said.

"I don't recall that Wade ever asked." Berry ran a bejeweled hand through Cody's hair. "But now that I think about it, a small dog—perhaps one of those pretty, fluffy little things—might be nice. A white one, I think. A lapdog . . ."

"When can we go?" Cody jumped up from his chair.

"Cody, for heaven's sake, we only just arrived here yesterday," Dallas reminded him. "Let's get unpacked first and settle in, give us all time to think this over. We talked about this, remember? A dog is a big responsibility. They have to be fed and walked—"

"I can feed it! I can walk it! I can be responsible!"

"—and they have to be cleaned up after, as well. In the yard, if you catch my drift."

"I can do that! I will do that!" Cody was wide-eyed at the prospect.

"As I said, let's settle in before we go making decisions that we will have to live with for a long time." Dallas watched her son's face. He rose from the table and started toward the door, then stopped, turned around, came back, and picked up his plate and his juice glass. Without prompting, he stood on his tiptoes to rinse everything at the kitchen sink. Then he opened the dishwasher and put in the plate and glass. He returned to the table and picked up his knife and fork, and took them to the dishwasher as well.

Dallas met Berry's amused eyes across the table as they watched.

When Cody had finished, he turned and said, "Thank you for breakfast, Aunt Berry. May I be excused from the room? I'd like to go upstairs and unpack and put my clothes away now."

"You may, my sweet boy." Berry nodded.

"Who was that child? He looks so much like my son," Dallas whispered, "but he's so well mannered. So polite. So thoughtful. And putting his clothes away without being told to? Unheard of."

"He's a boy who wants a dog." Berry laughed softly. "A boy who is proving how responsible he can be."

"Berry, I hate to impose on you . . ." Dallas began.

"I don't see it as an imposition. I do get lonely here sometimes," Berry admitted. "A dog might be a nice companion."

"You still have your housekeeper . . . ?"

"Oh, yes, but she's only here during the day, and lately, she's only been coming once or twice each week. It might be nice to have a little dog around at night to sit on my lap while I watch TV or read." She tilted her head and added, "I did tell you, did I not, that almost all of my movies are available now on DVD?"

"No, you didn't, but that's wonderful. Now another generation will be treated to the dramatic genius of Berry Townsend."

"Don't forget, I played several comedic roles as well. And I must say, I was brilliant in all of them."

53

"I know that you were." Dallas knew this was no idle boasting on her aunt's part. "Your performance in *Miss Lafferty's Lover* inspired my own in *Tell Me True.*"

"Really, dear?" Berry looked flattered and very pleased. "You won several important award nominations for that role, I recall."

Dallas nodded. "It was my first attempt at comedy. The critics didn't think I could pull it off, coming right on the heels of *Silver Mornings.*"

"I was so proud of your work in that film. You deserved the awards, the accolades." Berry's eyes took on a dreamy cast. "It reminded me of my performance in *The Long Last Look.*" Berry sighed. "I just loved those tearjerkers."

"Do you ever miss it, Berry?"

"Miss Hollywood?" Berry raised an eyebrow, then shook her head. "No. I am proud of every film I ever appeared in, but I don't think I'd want to be working again."

"What if the perfect role came along?"

"At my age? Ha." Berry shook her head. "It's not likely. We'll just be content to look back on my body of work as it stands."

"So, no regrets, then?"

"Oh, I have regrets, my dear, but none relative to my career. A life without some regret is probably a life that wasn't lived to its fullest."

It was on the tip of Dallas's tongue to ask what regrets her aunt did have, but the phone rang again.

"Dear me, it's going to be one of those days, isn't it?" Berry said as she rose to answer it. "I suppose the word is out."

"Sorry," Dallas told her.

"Don't be, dear." Berry patted Dallas's shoulder as she passed by. "We could use a little excitement around here right about now. It's been a dreadfully dull summer . . ."

Dallas spent most of the morning putting clothes into the old dresser that had served this same purpose for her for many years. Earlier, she'd opened all the curtains and the shades to let light flood in, but soon the sun would be beating down, and by midafternoon, the room would be stifling hot despite the central air-conditioning Berry had had installed when she moved back to St. Dennis for good. She changed into shorts and a T-shirt and slipped into sandals and headed down the steps.

At the landing, she found Cody staring up at the portraits that lined the wall all the way from the second floor to the first, and continued from there throughout the center hall.

"Who's that?" He pointed to a painting that hung above him.

"That, I believe, is my great-great-uncle, Lloyd Worthington Eberle." Dallas stood back to admire the man in the full-dress uniform of the Confederacy.

"Is he related to me?"

Dallas nodded. "He'd be your great-great-great-uncle. Or that could possibly be four greats back, I don't remember. To each generation going back, you add one more great."

"Like Aunt Berry is your *great*-aunt and my *great-great*-aunt?"

"Exactly like that."

"She is a *very* great aunt."

"She certainly is." Dallas smiled. She'd often thought that very same thing.

"That lady there." He pointed to the next portrait. "She looks like Aunt Berry."

"Sweetie, that *is* Aunt Berry."

"Why is she holding a snake?" Cody looked closer.

"She played Cleopatra once in a movie when she was very young," Dallas explained, "and she liked the costume so much that she had her picture painted in character."

Throughout her career, Berry had had her portrait painted in the characters of all her favorite roles. It had confused the hell out of Dallas and Wade as children because those portraits were hung on the walls interspersed with those of real relatives.

"How about that one? Is that Berry, too?" Cody moved on to the next frame.

"Helen of Troy," Dallas told him.

"And that one?"

"That's great-grandmother Lorelle Stevens."

"She sort of looks like Aunt Berry," he noted.

"There is a resemblance," Dallas agreed.

"That one? She's wearing a funny hat." He pointed to a woman in a black gown.

"That, my love, is Mary Tudor," Berry announced from the bottom of the stairs. "One of my greatest roles. I was a *magnificent* Bloody Mary."

"When I was little, I thought she was an ancestor," Dallas said. "I told everyone in school that we were related to the Queen of England."

"Merely an accident of fate that you were not, dear. If my great—I'm not sure how many *greats* Aunt Hermione would be—if she'd been less cautious, well, who knows . . . ?"

"I don't remember a Hermione." Dallas went down the steps to join Berry.

"Oh, she was quite notorious in her day. She was said to have . . ." Berry glanced at Cody, who was leaning over the rail at a point midway between the landing and the first floor and hanging on every word. "To have kicked up her heels a time or two. She was quite the scandalous girl in her day."

"Do we have a portrait of her?" Dallas looked around the hall.

"Unfortunately, no. But I've no doubt that she was quite glorious." Berry leaned closer to Dallas and whispered, "Family lore says she left some very steamy memoirs. I've never seen them, but at one time, a distant cousin in the UK claimed to have had them in her possession. Wouldn't they make a juicy little read?"

Berry was in one of her nostalgic moods. There was every chance that by dinner, she'd be in costume if any still fit her and delivering lines from any one of her favorite roles. Dallas's mother had been annoyed as hell whenever Berry decided to relive her glory days, but Dallas and Wade had loved it.

"Marie Antoinette," Dallas murmured, remembering.

"So sorry, dear, but I won't be doing her again," Berry announced. "After all these years, moths finally got into the box and ravished the wig. Sadly, I had to toss it. And try finding an authentic reproduction these days."

"Pity." Dallas bit back a smile.

"Indeed." Berry watched Cody attempt to slide down

57

the banister. "Dear me, no, child. You're going to land smack on the newel post." She pointed up to the top of the steps. "Try going from the top. The round post at the landing makes for a much better stop."

Cody did as he was told, and found the ride sufficiently satisfactory. He repeated it several times.

"So ..." Berry turned to Dallas. "What's on your agenda for today?"

"I don't really have one. I'm thinking I'd like to lay low for as long as I can."

"No, no, that's impossible, dear. That cat has left the bag. You can't stop word from getting around. I suspect that by tomorrow, the photographers will have invaded. The best you can do at this point is hope there's still enough time to build a solid defense."

"A defense? Against reporters? Photographers? Paparazzi?" Dallas scoffed. "There's no such thing."

"Wrong, dear. You forget that this is a small town. You have to make it work for you."

"I'm all ears," Dallas told her. "How do I do that?"

"Hide in plain sight, as they say."

"I don't understand."

"There are only two types of people in St. Dennis, Dallas. There are tourists, and there are townies. Tourists are free game—townies are off-limits." Berry started toward the kitchen and Dallas followed. "You used to be a townie. You have to remind people of that while there's still time."

Berry poured two glasses of iced tea and handed one to Dallas.

"What are you suggesting I do?"

58

"Make yourself very visible. Let people see you, talk to you. Act like you belong here. Shop in our shops, eat in our restaurants. Remind them that you are one of them. Get them on your side."

"You seriously think that parading around town and making nice with the local folks will keep the tabloids away?" Dallas took a sip of tea. It tasted exactly the same as she remembered, with just a hint of lemon and mint.

"Of course not. But the more you try to hide, the more effort they'll put into trying to find you. It's a game, you see. If you're out in the open, accessible, acting like you belong here, the attitude in town to outsiders is going to be, 'Move along, nothing to see here.' When reporters do show up, no one will talk about where you're staying or where you shop or what you do or take money to take pictures of you lying on the dock in a bikini."

"It wouldn't be hard to find out any of those things, especially when it's no secret that you're my aunt and this was once my summer home."

"True enough. But no one is going to be looking for Beryl Eberle, which is how I'm known here. 'Beryl Townsend, the actress,' has no listings." Berry sighed dramatically. "Even at the height of my career, I could come and go here as I liked. Why, last year when *Beautiful Dreamer* was rereleased as a tribute to David Gaston and his last and greatest role and there was an upsurge in interest in *moi* and so many photographers descended on St. Dennis looking for me, there were no ambushes."

"I saw lots of photos of you walking the streets of St. Dennis, Berry," Dallas reminded her.

"All on my terms, my dear. No one took a picture I

didn't want taken." Berry took a seat at the table. "When I got a heads-up that someone from this rag or that was in town asking about me, I got myself together and went into town on a casual errand. I was photographed going into the bookstore and into the coffee shop—you have to try their iced lattes—and several other places. The photos were taken on my terms and the photographers left town thinking they'd caught Beryl Townsend off guard and unsuspecting. Of course, I looked lovely in every shot because I planned it that way." She took another sip of tea. "So if you don't want anyone snooping around hoping to find you with no makeup and looking like a fright, my advice is to get yourself out there today and make nice. Become part of the community again, and the community will protect you. Every time a photographer or reporter leaves his card with someone in St. Dennis, that phone on the wall is going to ring to let us know."

"Well, it's certainly a novel approach," Dallas said thoughtfully. "And I suppose sooner or later we will have to go into town. Might as well make it today and test your theory."

"Good. Get dressed—something casual, but nice. Put on a little makeup—not too much, mind you—and we'll go to Captain Walt's for lunch." Berry stood. "After that, we'll get ice cream, then we'll walk up to Charles Street and stop at some of the shops that are new since your last visit. By the time we come back home, everyone in St. Dennis will be buzzing about how nice it is that Dallas MacGregor hasn't forgotten where she came from."

"You really do think this is a good idea, don't you?"

"Dear, when J. D. Salinger died, there was an article in

the paper about how his neighbors and friends in that little New Hampshire town where he lived protected him from outsiders. They were quite proud of never having given him up to the curious." Berry paused in the doorway. "Just as my friends here in St. Dennis have always protected me. I'm certain they'll offer you the same courtesy if you give them the chance."

"Well then, give me fifteen minutes to get ready." Dallas glanced out the window and saw Cody kneeling at the edge of the river, the water lapping up over his thighs in the waves generated by a passing boat. He was soaking wet from his shirt to his bare feet. "Better make that thirty . . ."

Chapter 4

"WELL, now, that wasn't so difficult, was it?" Berry leaned on Dallas's arm as she stepped from the threshold at Captain Walt's onto the wooden boardwalk. "Lunch was delicious and Walt and Rexana were thrilled to see you. All in all, it was worth the hour, don't you agree?"

"It was very nice to see them, too. I always liked Rexana, and I'd forgotten how wonderful their food is. So no, it wasn't difficult at all, and very definitely worth the hour." Dallas allowed her aunt to continue to hold on as they walked along the dock. "Berry, are you having trouble keeping your balance or are you hanging on because you're playing the part of an old woman today?"

"Hush your mouth, Dallas MacGregor." Berry straightened her back and stuck out her chin. "I was just thinking that I must look somewhat stately—perhaps even *elegant*—strolling along the Bay like this."

"Stately, eh?" Dallas mused. "It must be the hat."

"It is quite something, isn't it?" Berry touched the wide brim of the white straw from which a profusion of white roses spilled over.

"Oh, it's something, all right."

"Mind your manners," Berry admonished.

"Is that the ice-cream store?" Cody, who'd been

skipping ahead, turned and pointed to the small structure near the end of the boardwalk.

"It is." Berry nodded.

"What does the sign say? One what?" he asked.

"It says, 'One Scoop or Two.' That's the name of the shop," Berry told him. "Although most of the time, people from St. Dennis call it simply Scoop."

"Scoop," Cody repeated. "That's a fun name."

"I agree." Berry nodded. "And it's a very fun place. The owner makes her own ice cream."

"You said we could have ice cream for dessert," Cody reminded his mother.

"Yes, I did. Would you like it now, or later?" Dallas asked.

"I would like it now." Cody took off for the shop. Still on his best behavior, he turned and added, "Please."

Cody was already at the door and waiting when Dallas and Berry arrived at Scoop. Outside, several tables were clustered, their umbrellas open against the afternoon sun. Inside, round tables that could seat four were placed by each window, and two long coolers ran the length of the building. There was an old-fashioned cash register on a granite counter sitting atop an antique dresser, and the walls held brightly colored drawings of ice cream in cones and in small dishes that appeared to have been drawn by childish hands.

Dallas and Berry stood near the door and read that day's flavors from a chalkboard.

"Oh my, there are almost too many choices," Berry declared.

"They had me at peach pecan." Dallas sighed. "That sounds like perfection."

"That certainly does." Berry continued to scan the board. "But pineapple coconut macadamia fudge ripple sounds positively sinful."

"Cody, would you like me to read the board for you?" Dallas asked.

"No, I know what I want." He went directly to the case and pressed his face to the cold glass.

"Go ahead and place your order, then." Dallas touched his shoulder as she joined him at the counter.

"I would like one scoop of chocolate and one scoop of strawberry, and one scoop of—"

"Whoa. Hold it right there." Dallas laughed. "Two scoops is a lot. Three is out of the question."

Cody stuck out his bottom lip as silent pronouncement of his displeasure.

"Pick two, buddy," Dallas told him. She stretched her neck to address the blonde woman whose face was hidden by the counter. "While he's deciding, I'll have one scoop of peach pecan, please."

"Excellent choice," the woman behind the counter said. "I just made it this morning. Bowl or cone?"

Dallas debated. "I'm going for broke here. Might as well put it in a cone."

The blonde scooped the ice cream into a cone, then stretched over the top of the case to hand it to Dallas. The woman's eyes widened when she realized who she'd just served. Before she could react, Berry stepped up to the counter.

"Dallas, you remember Steffie Wyler."

"Steffie? You're Steffie Wyler? Little Steffie?" Dallas's brows rose in genuine surprise. "I never would have recognized you. The last time I saw you, you were just a cute little girl, and now here you are, all grown up, and positively gorgeous."

Behind the counter, Steffie Wyler blushed to her roots.

"All grown up, gorgeous, and quite the entrepreneur, dear. Steffie owns Scoop, and she makes all her ice creams herself."

"You make up the flavors yourself?" Dallas asked.

Steffie nodded, still apparently too flustered to speak.

"How do you know how to do that?" Dallas pressed her.

"I . . . I don't know, I just look at what fruits are available, in season, and try to think of what might taste good together."

Dallas licked a bit of ice cream that had started to ooze onto her cone.

"This is amazing. Seriously delicious." Dallas meant every word. It *was* seriously delicious. "I'd say you found your true calling in life. I could become addicted." She turned to Berry. "I highly recommend the peach pecan."

"Oh, dear, and I had my heart set on the pineapple coconut . . . whatever." Berry frowned.

"Have a scoop of each," Dallas suggested.

"I couldn't . . ."

"Of course you could." Dallas smiled at Steffie. "Make them small scoops so she can't complain too much."

Steffie served Berry, then rested her forearms on the counter and asked Cody, "Have you decided yet?"

Cody nodded.

"What's it going to be?" Steffie asked.

"Chocolate and strawberry," he told her solemnly.

"Would you like to try the chocolate peppermint?" Steffie asked. When he nodded, she gave him a sample spoonful.

"Yum." His face lit with pleasure. "I like that."

"One scoop of chocolate peppermint and one of strawberry?" she asked.

"Yes, please." Cody added, "On a cone, please."

"Maybe you should try a dish," Dallas suggested, but Cody shook his head. She mouthed the words *small scoops* to Steffie, who complied. Dallas went to the cash register and took her wallet from her bag preparing to pay, when a young girl of perhaps twelve appeared at the register. Steffie stood behind her and showed her how to enter the sale.

Dallas smiled at the girl, who looked away quickly.

"Dallas, this is my niece, Paige." Steffie met Dallas's gaze. "My brother Grant's daughter."

If Dallas was caught off guard, she did her best to hide it. "How nice to meet you, Paige."

"Hi." Paige never took her eyes from the register.

"Dallas is Miss Eberle's niece, Paige. She used to spend all her summers in St. Dennis," Steffie explained.

"I *know* that," Paige muttered rolling her eyes. "Then she went to Hollywood and became a big movie star. *Everyone* knows that."

"Is your father all settled into his new clinic, Paige?" Berry ignored the girl's rudeness.

"Yes," Paige replied.

"Cody, Paige's father is the veterinarian in St. Dennis," Berry went on.

"Do you have a dog?" Cody asked.

"We have three," Paige told him in a flat, too-bored-to-be-bothered voice.

"Three dogs? You have *three dogs*?" Cody's jaw dropped at the thought of it. "Wow. You are really lucky."

Paige shot him a look over the top of the cash register, then seemed to soften when she saw how young he was.

"My dad brings in the dogs from the shelter that no one wants to adopt. He said it's not good for them to stay in the shelter for too long because they get sad," she told him. "But he has lots of really nice dogs—really good dogs—at the shelter. If you're looking for one, you should go and see if there's one you like."

"Could we, Mom? Could we go take a look?" Cody begged, his ice-cream cone held at a precarious angle.

"We need to talk to Berry about that." Dallas reached over and righted his hand.

"Berry said she wanted a small fluffy dog that could sit on her lap," Cody reminded her excitedly. He turned his small face up to Paige and asked, "Are there any small fluffy white dogs that could fit on Aunt Berry's lap?"

"I help my dad with the animals in the shelter, so I'll be there later and I can look for you." Paige smiled for the first time since they'd engaged her. Up until then, Dallas had seen no trace of Grant in Paige, but there, in the smile that turned her mouth up on the left just slightly more than on the right, she saw the girl's father, and remembered how that smile had set her world on fire, once upon a time.

"You get to help?" Cody's eyes were shining with a combination of awe, envy, and admiration. "Whenever you want?"

"Sure. I help out every day."

"Wow. You really *are* lucky." He tugged on his mother's arm. "Mom . . ."

"It's a big decision," Dallas reminded him. "One we can't make right now, especially since we haven't decided how long we're going to stay in St. Dennis. Let's get ourselves settled before we do something that important."

"Okay." Cody's disappointment was obvious but he chose the high road and didn't argue. A point in his favor, Dallas noted.

"Whenever you're ready, you get your mom to bring you to the shelter." Paige addressed Cody but still had yet to really look at Dallas.

Dallas knew he was dying to press her, but to his credit, he simply told Paige, "Okay."

"Steffie, it was great to see you again," Dallas said, ushering Cody toward the door. "I know we'll be back soon. I have a feeling Scoop might become one of our very favorite places in St. Dennis."

"I hope so." Steffie waved and turned her attention to the customer who'd just come into the shop. "Come back anytime."

"There, now," Berry said when they were outside. "That was worth a stop, too, wasn't it?"

"Besides the fabulous ice cream, yes. I was glad to see Steffie. I remember her as such a precocious little thing." Dallas smiled at the memory. "So nice to see how she's grown up and has her own successful business. Her family must be very proud of her."

"Of course they are." Berry walked along the boards. "Where would you like to go now?"

"I don't know. How many places am I supposed to visit today?"

"Maybe just a few shops on Charles Street." Berry paused. "But I think I might like to drive up and park in one of those little lots so I won't have to walk so far. The heat is starting to get to me."

"Are you all right, Berry?" Dallas's eyebrows knit in concern. She couldn't remember a time when the heat of summer had prevented Berry from doing anything.

"Of course I am. It's just a long way to walk in the hot sun if you don't have to. And since the car is close by, I don't have to."

Berry had driven her old Mercedes sedan, telling Dallas, "I'll drive, dear. We don't want any of the tourists to know what car is yours, or you're liable to be followed every time you venture out on your own."

"I thought you said someone already saw me when I drove into the driveway yesterday."

"Oh, that was Tom. He's probably already forgotten that he saw you," Berry had assured her. "Besides, he's an old friend. He wouldn't give you away."

They returned to the car, and Berry drove to Charles Street, where she found a parking spot in a lot behind Book 'Em. They went into the bookshop through the back door, and Berry reintroduced Dallas to the owner, Barbara Noonan, who had, once upon a time, been Berry's next-door neighbor and who now lived five houses away.

"Barbara, do you remember my grand-niece, Dallas?" Berry smiled, knowing Barbara often bragged about how well she knew the family.

"Of course." Barbara beamed, and with a smile, excused herself from the customer she was assisting, who did a triple take when she saw Dallas. "I heard you were here for a visit. And this is your little boy . . ."

And on it went for the next hour, from Book 'Em to Bling, the upscale women's boutique a few doors down, where Dallas was introduced to Vanessa Keaton.

"Her brother is our wonderful chief of police. He was married just recently to a lovely girl. They had the most beautiful wedding," Berry noted while Dallas looked through a colorful pile of T-shirts. "Oh, but you must remember Gabriel Beck, Dallas."

"Of course I do. And you did tell me about the wedding." Dallas smiled at Vanessa. "Please tell him I said hello and congratulations when you talk to him."

"I'll be sure to do that." Vanessa beamed, and Dallas was pretty sure she'd be relaying the greeting by phone the minute Dallas left the shop.

A few minutes later, she'd selected several pairs of shorts and a few matching tops, then it was across the street to Cuppachino. They ordered lattes that were every bit as good as Berry promised, and chatted with Carlo, the owner, and several of the patrons.

"Berry, I see you dragged Dallas in for an iced latte." Grace Sinclair waved from a table near the front window.

"I didn't have to be dragged," Dallas told her, and without hesitation, went to the table and leaned over to hug the older woman. "How are you, Miss Grace?"

"I'm very well, dear." Grace smiled broadly.

"You look wonderful. Cody, come meet Miss Grace."

70

Cody stood shyly behind his mother. "Miss Grace is a dear friend of Aunt Berry's and mine . . ."

After twenty minutes in the coffee shop, where Dallas did her best to ignore the whispers among the startled patrons, Dallas gave Grace a good-bye hug after promising an exclusive piece about her recollections of her childhood summers spent in St. Dennis for Grace's newspaper.

"No more, Berry," Dallas pleaded when they reached the sidewalk. "Let's leave a few shops to visit another day."

"All right, dear." Berry led the way back to her car. "I'm sure that by now, phone lines all over St. Dennis are simply abuzz. You did very well, Dallas."

"Oh, it wasn't an act. Actually, I enjoyed myself." They'd reached the car and were settling in, the doors open momentarily to let the hot air trapped inside the sedan to escape. "I can honestly say that there wasn't one person I saw today that I wasn't genuinely happy to see."

"I'm glad to hear it." Berry smiled, obviously pleased. "Sincerity always plays so well."

For Berry, all the world really is *a stage*, Dallas mused as they drove back to the big house overlooking the river, and it probably always would be. Dallas had no doubt that if she had given her aunt any encouragement at all, they'd still be up on Charles Street, shopping and chatting and renewing old acquaintances that would, as Berry insisted, offer some protection once word spread that she and Cody were in St. Dennis.

It's already out there, Dallas reflected after she'd tucked in Cody that night. She'd not been oblivious to the number of cell phones and small cameras that had been directed

71

her way that afternoon while she was on the sidewalk or in the shops. While they'd been in Cuppachino visiting with Grace, every now and then she saw the flash of a camera, but pretended not to notice. The only concession she made to the picture takers was to keep Cody between her and Berry, so he'd not appear in any of the shots. So far, no one had approached her, and no one had made a big deal out of her presence, so maybe there was something to Berry's theory.

We'll see, Dallas thought as she pulled on an old favorite nightshirt that she'd earlier found in the bottom drawer of her dresser and tossed into the washer after dinner. She told herself she wanted to wear it just for old times' sake, but she knew it was more than that.

She wanted to feel the way she used to feel in this house, to remember the sure belief that the whole world was waiting for her, that she'd grow up to be a huge star and that her life would be beautiful, filled with success and love that would last forever and happiness that would never fade. Well, she had become a big star, that much came true. But as for the rest of it, well, some part of her still wanted to believe that it could all still happen. Her divorce would be final soon and she'd be free to move on. She hoped she'd be wiser in her next relationship.

Assuming, she thought wryly, that there'd be such a thing. How do you know who you can trust not to cheat on you?

Dallas sat in the dark on the window seat and looked out on the night. The moon rose high and full, and she couldn't help but think back to all those summer nights she'd sat right there, dreaming of the glorious days she just knew were waiting for her. Mostly, she'd been waiting for Grant Wyler to appear on the lawn under the window.

"Hey," he'd call up in as loud a whisper as he dared.

"Hey, yourself." She'd raise the screen and sit on her knees and lean out the window as far as she could without falling. "What are you doing here?" she'd ask, even though she knew.

"Came to see you, what do you think I'm doing?" Even through the dark, she'd sensed his smile, and a little thrill ran through her, every time.

Dallas sighed at the memory. Those days had been filled with innocence and exploration, of love that had yet to be tested but was nonetheless true. She'd never forgotten the girl she'd been then, or the first boy who'd won her heart.

Back then, it had been easier to trust. She hadn't yet learned that people weren't always as they seemed, that marriage wouldn't always guarantee happiness, and that true love didn't necessarily last forever.

It had been odd this afternoon in Scoop, seeing his daughter, searching for traces of him in her face, and wondering—in spite of her resolve not to—what the woman he'd married was like.

"Stef, slow down, will you?" Grant Wyler tucked the phone against his shoulder and skimmed the patient chart of the Chesapeake Bay retriever who at that moment shivered with trepidation in the vet's waiting room. "Who was where . . . ?"

"Dallas MacGregor." Steffie was all but out of breath with excitement. "In my shop. Eating my ice cream."

"Oh." Dallas was in town? He'd been caught off guard, and for once, couldn't think of anything clever to say.

"She is so gorgeous," Steffie gushed. "And she didn't have much makeup on and she was dressed just like anyone would be. Nothing fancy or too frou frou, you know? She's staying at her aunt's house. I guess all that scandal about her husband got to be too much for her. At least, that's what they're saying on TV."

"What scandal?"

As if he didn't know, as if he hadn't seen the tabloid headlines in the market just that morning. He'd tried to write off those long-ago summers, and rarely, if ever, permitted himself to dwell on what he'd had then that he couldn't have now. Which was not to say that he'd forgotten, or that his subconscious didn't bring her back in dreams now and then, particularly after seeing her face—once so familiar—on TV or on those occasions when he took himself to the theater and sat in the dark, watching her, bigger than life, on the silver screen. He may have been able to convince everyone else that she was a forgotten chapter in the book of his life, but he knew *that* for the lie it was. He suspected that Steffie might know it, too.

"What scandal?" Steffie snorted. "Where have you been for the past week?"

"I've been busy," he said. "Spaying dogs and cats, setting broken bones, worming puppies, and picking up strays on the highway. Nothing important."

"Dallas's husband—could be her ex-husband by now—made a sex tape with two young chickies and it's all over the Internet. I read it was the single most downloaded video last week."

74

"Did you watch it?"

"Me? Hell no. That is just so not my thing." The note of disgust in her voice was loud and clear. "Ugh. How could you even ask me that?"

"I guess that's tough on her, huh?" He didn't know what else to say.

"She doesn't look any worse for it, though, I gotta say." Steffie sighed. "Grant, she was so nice. She said I'd grown up to be . . ."

She paused, and Grant asked, "You grew up to be what?"

"Gorgeous. She said she thought I was gorgeous." She sighed again. "Dallas MacGregor thinks I'm gorgeous."

"Yeah, well, she doesn't know you like the rest of us do."

"You jerk." Steffie laughed. "Leave it to my big brother to burst my bubble."

"All right. You're okay."

"I'm not just *okay*, buster. I'm *gorgeous*. Who are you to argue with Dallas MacGregor?"

"No one, apparently."

"My point."

"Listen, Stef . . ."

"I think she grows even more beautiful as she gets older, you know? Even without being all made up the way you see her in the magazines or on TV, she's just so beautiful. That long pale hair and those eyes. Her eyes really are lavender-colored, you know that? I guess she doesn't need all that—"

"Good for her." Grant cut her off, remembering all too well the exact shade of Dallas's celebrated eyes. As if

75

anyone who'd stared into them could forget. "Look, I have a—"

"You can judge for yourself," Steffie told him. "You'll be seeing her soon enough."

"What do you mean, I'll be seeing her . . . ?"

"Did I leave out the part about her little boy wanting a dog and Paige telling them about the rescue shelter?"

"Yeah. You were too busy remembering how gorgeous you are."

"Well, she didn't seem to think it was a good idea, but he looks like the type of kid who knows how to get around his mom, so I'm guessing you'll be seeing her sooner than later."

"Great. Thanks for the heads-up. Gotta go, kid."

Grant disconnected the call. He hadn't seen Dallas since he was eighteen, except on the screen, both big and small, and he wasn't sure he was in any big hurry to see her now. At least, not in the flesh. He'd be hard-pressed to admit it, but he'd seen every movie she'd ever made, going alone to see those first films in which she'd had small parts mostly to prove to himself that she couldn't possibly be that good an actress and to reassure himself that she'd only gotten those roles because of her looks. Surely she'd be just a flash in the pan, and she'd be back in St. Dennis one of these summers, her tail between her legs, and he'd be waiting for her. He *had* waited for her, for longer than he wanted to admit.

As time went on, and she proved to him—and to everyone else—that she was more than just a pretty face, he'd been drawn back to the theater every time she had a new release. He'd sit in the dark, a hollow pit in his stomach, as he watched her, so much larger than life, and heard her voice, which sounded exactly as he remembered it. He'd even bought all of her movies, first on video, then on DVD, and sometimes, late at night when he couldn't sleep, he'd watch them, even now. Not as an obsessed fan, but as someone who'd truly loved her once, when she had belonged only to him, and he couldn't help but wonder what could have been. He considered that his sad little secret.

He was grateful for Steffie's call. He'd have been flustered if he'd run into Dallas on the street, and it would have been awkward. He often wondered what he'd say to her, should the day come when their paths crossed again, and as many times as he'd thought about the inevitability of that happening, he never was able to even fantasize how that conversation would go.

"Dr. Wyler, Evelyn Jenkins is on the phone." Joanie, his receptionist, burst through the door. "Her old shepherd was hit by a car over on Canal Road and she's panicked. She thinks his leg is broken and she doesn't know what to do."

Reality pulled the plug on his fantasy, and he snapped into action.

"Tell her to keep him quiet, not to move him, and I'll be there in"—Grant stole a look at the clock on the wall—"four minutes." He grabbed his emergency bag and hurried out through the back door. "Go ahead and do the exam on the retriever that's in the waiting room. It's a well checkup so there shouldn't be any urgency there. I'll be back as soon as I can ..."

Diary ~

What a lovely summer it's turning out to be! The weather is perfect, the Inn at Sinclair's Point is doing record business, and tourists continue to flock to St. Dennis. Though I must admit that there have been days when we—that is, the regular early-morning crowd that gathers at Cuppachino—have arrived to find that our table has been hijacked by tourists! Carlo says he tries to keep the table clear for us, but sometimes he's so busy that he doesn't notice that it's been taken until it's too late. The bottom line is that we just have to get into town sooner and stake our claim if we want that front window table. Which of course we do—how else could we keep up with everything that's happening on Charles Street?

Speaking of happenings: Berry's grand-niece, Dallas, is visiting with her son, who is—anyone with eyes can see—the absolute apple of Berry's eye. I saw them in Cuppachino the other day, and I must say, Berry's pride in her family is justified. Dallas is still the sweet girl she was when she first came to town—she's promised me an exclusive interview for the Gazette. The sad truth is that Dallas's sorry excuse for a husband made an S-E-X tape with some young chickies and it's been all over the Internet and has been downloaded about a million times! I can't bring myself to watch it, though Berry says she did to make sure it was, in fact, Emilio, whose real name, rumor now has it, is actually EUGENE!

Berry says the divorce is imminent—it's merely a matter of sorting out the details and the judge signing his name. If Dallas is hoping to recover from this sorry state of affairs, she's come to the right place. I happen to know one eligible young man who's carried a torch for her for years. But if she's interested, she's going to need to stake her claim quickly. She's not the only former St. Dennis girl who's come back following a heartbreak who has a history with the young man in question. Of course, I made Berry fully aware of the situation. She knows what she must do.

You know, that woman is eighty-one if she's a day, and she looks ten years younger. Which would make her my age. Except that I know for a fact that she isn't. I'm wondering if she's found some sort of secret the rest of us don't know. Like directions to the Fountain of Youth. Only half kidding, but if she had found such a thing, surely she'd have wanted to look younger than seventy-one. I know I would!

~ Grace ~

Chapter 5

"HOW come people are so mean to animals sometimes?" Paige leaned on the counter and watched her father examine one of two kittens that someone had placed in a paper bag and tossed out the window of a moving pickup. Fortunately, a young boy on a bicycle saw one of them fall from the bag and had the presence of mind not only to get the license plate number of the truck, but to gather up the bag and its frightened little contents and pedal directly to the vet clinic, the bag safely carried in the basket of his bike.

"Why are people sometimes mean to other people?" Grant completed his exam and passed the kitten to Paige. "She looks okay. Nothing's broken. She's probably a little sore, though, so hold her gently, and see if you can get her to eat something."

Paige cradled the kitten in her hands. Almost immediately, the kitten snuggled close to her body and mewed softly.

"But why would someone do something like that, Dad? If they didn't want the kittens, why didn't they just bring them to the shelter instead of trying to hurt them?"

"Baby, if I knew the answer to that, I'd be the smartest man in the world. People do stupid, thoughtless things every day, and very often there's no understanding why."

Grant knelt down and picked up the other kitten, who protested loudly. "Oh, are we hurt or are we just mad at the world? Let's take a look at that back leg . . ."

"Well, I'm glad Chief Beck arrested the guy who was driving the truck," Paige said. "I hope he puts him in jail forever."

"*Forever* might be a little longer than the law allows, but I was glad to see Beck took it as seriously as he did." Grant gently felt the tiny animal's leg. "This little guy might not be as lucky as his sister. I think I'm going to want an X-ray here. Paige, will you go out front and get Mimi and ask her to come in here and give me a hand?"

"I can give you a hand," she replied. "I've watched Mimi take a lot of X-rays. I can do it."

"I know, sweetie. But right now I want you to hold on to that little one. See how she's calmed down since you picked her up?"

He looked up at her and smiled. She wanted so badly to help, to please him, so that he'd let her stay beyond the summer. He saw her resolve in everything she did. He'd tried to explain to her that the decision wasn't his to make, that her mother was expecting her back in Camden Lakes at the end of the summer for the start of the new school year. If it were up to him, she'd stay in St. Dennis and go to school here, but his ex-wife, Krista, insisted that in this time of big changes in her life, she needed the comfort of the familiar. Therefore—in Krista's opinion—it would be best for Paige to return to her own room in the home she'd grown up in, in a neighborhood where she knew everyone, and attend her old school, with the kids she'd known since first grade.

Grant couldn't say with any certainty what was best. All he knew was that his daughter wasn't ready to deal with her mother's new relationship, and that she wanted to stay with him in St. Dennis. While he wasn't one to encourage avoidance, he did think that giving Paige a little more time to adjust wasn't likely to hurt anyone.

"I saw her today," Paige told him from the doorway. The tone of her voice left no doubt that her words were meant to give him a poke, a small way of retaliating for not giving in to her and letting her help with the X-rays.

"Saw who?"

"Your old girlfriend."

He refused to take the bait. "I had a lot of girlfriends in my day. Which one are you referring to?"

"Dallas MacGregor."

"Oh, right," Grant said with what he hoped would come across as cool nonchalance. "Steffie told me she was in Scoop this afternoon."

Paige snorted. "Steffie told everyone in town that she was in Scoop today. I think Steffie was more excited than you are. She's really pretty. REALLY pretty." Grant knew Paige was waiting for a reaction. "Even prettier than she is in the movies."

"Dallas always was a pretty girl."

"Well, you'll see for yourself." She smirked.

"I'm sure I'll run into her sooner or later while she's here."

"It's gonna be sooner."

He glanced up at her. She was still smirking.

"Her little boy wants a dog and I told them about the shelter. So, sooner, not later."

"Steffie did mention that. That's good. We have lots of dogs to choose from. Maybe they'll find one they like and give it a good home." He pointed to the door. "Get Mimi, please."

He'd already reconciled himself to the fact that she might show up at the shelter one of these days. Well, that would be okay. And if she wanted a dog for her son, a shelter animal was a good choice. It wasn't any big deal.

Oh, who was he kidding? His heart was beating a little faster at the mere thought of her being in the same town.

Good to know he'd matured so much since he was fifteen, he thought drily. Though if his heart was the only part of his anatomy that had an involuntary reaction when he saw her, he should probably count his blessings.

"You wanted me, Grant?" Mimi Ryan downed the last bit of coffee from a cardboard cup and tossed it into the trash. "Paige said something about a young cat with a broken leg?"

He nodded. "I'm not sure it's broken, but it's pretty tender. I think we need to take a look."

"I'll take care of it." She pulled a pair of glasses from the case that rode in her back pocket and slipped them on. "Ginger Messick called to find out when she could pick up her dachshund."

"I'm going to want to keep him one more day."

"She's only going to be home till six." Mimi pointed to the clock. It was 5:55. "You go on and call her. Janelle's still here. We can take care of the kitten."

"Thanks. Let me know what's what with our little friend here." Grant handed over the injured animal and went into his office.

The Messicks' dachshund had had a tumor removed the day before and needed another day of peace and quiet, something Grant knew it wouldn't get in the Messicks' home. With four young boys and an equal number of girls, he suspected that no one got much peace under that roof. He made his phone call, then went into the break room to grab a cup of coffee. The pot was empty, so he made another. They had hours tonight until eight, so he knew the brew wouldn't go to waste. He sat at the table, his legs stretched out in front of him, and remembered why he wanted to buy new chairs. The ones they had were damned uncomfortable. He took a small notebook out of his pocket and started to write a reminder, but found he already had done so almost three weeks earlier.

"So much for writing things down," he muttered.

That was another reason why Paige should probably go back to her mother for the school year. He was so busy these days that he was having trouble keeping track of things. Grant's days at the clinic were long, and he couldn't foresee them getting any shorter. And then there was the shelter, and the animals there that needed tending. He knew that Paige cherished the time they spent together, tending to the homeless dogs and cats that had been brought to him or that he'd found. But the number of animals they'd taken in was increasing by the week, and he'd already had to hire extra staff just to feed and exercise them during the day. How in the world could Paige keep up with homework and school activities and her time at the shelter? Grant knew his daughter well enough to know that she'd cut back on sports and she'd skip studying for a test before she'd skimp on her time with the animals.

They'd done all right together this summer, he reminded himself. Better than all right. They'd done damn well. Father and daughter had made out just swell, thank you very much.

Yeah, that nagging little voice replied, *but summer comes without the responsibilities of the school year. Study time. After-school activities. Homework. Class trips.*

He didn't like the idea of her leaving any more than Paige did, but Krista was probably right. Paige probably would have a more structured home life back in Camden Lakes. At least until summer came around again.

But damn it, he was going to miss his girl. She was growing up so fast. By next summer, she'd be going into junior high, and from there, it was a just a short hop to high school. Why, before he knew it, she'd be leaving for college. Blink, and she'd be grown up, an adult. Next thing she'd be wanting to get married. Or, God forbid, live with some guy.

The coffeemaker beeped to let him know the coffee was ready. He snapped out of his funk, got up, and poured himself a cup. He took the first slow sips while leaning against the counter, trying to conjure up the face of the guy his little girl would be moving in with, sharing an apartment with. Unconsciously, Grant's teeth began to grind.

If he hurts her, I may have to kill him . . .

"Daddy, Mimi said the little guy doesn't have a broken leg." Paige stuck her head in through the open door. "She said he's just very sore and maybe hurt his muscles. Can I take him to the shelter and feed him?"

"Did you feed his sister?"

Paige nodded. "She took several droppers full of baby kitty food and some milk and some water. I could give Smoky the same."

"Smoky?"

"I named them Smoky and Misty." Paige grinned. "'Cause they're both gray."

"Very clever. Okay, go ahead and take them both to the shelter and find a warm spot for them." He set his cup on the counter. "But first come here and give your dad a hug."

She eyed him suspiciously as she crossed the room. "Why?"

"No reason. I just want to hug you." He paused. "Do I not hug you often enough that you think I need a special reason?" He tried to remember if he'd hugged her the day before.

"Nah. I was playing with ya." Paige returned the hug, then looked up into her father's face. "You're thinking about how much you're going to miss me when I'm gone."

"Well, yeah, but college is a long way away."

"College?" Paige rolled her eyes. "You are so weird sometimes."

She skipped off to get the kittens and take them to the shelter, which was housed in a barn that stood behind the clinic and across the drive from their house. Grant finished his coffee, rinsed out the cup, and headed for the lobby to see if his six-fifteen appointment had arrived. He'd deal with the specter of his grown-up child some other time.

★

Dallas sat on the rough wooden deck of Berry's old dock, her bare feet skimming the water below, a glass of wine in one hand and her iPhone in the other.

"You are good, you know that, don't you?" Dallas told Norma after hearing all the attorney's news.

"I'm the best. That's why you willingly pay my totally outrageous hourly rate," Norma said merrily. "I've filed all the appropriate papers with the court. Now it's up to the judge to decide whether or not Emilio should have access to his son right now."

"What if Emilio denies everything?"

"I obtained a copy of his now-infamous video on DVD and attached it to my submission. Emilio's attorney is well aware of the fact. I doubt they'll put up too much of a fuss." Norma paused. "But I should tell you he's trying to raise a bit of a stink about you taking Cody out of the state without telling him."

"I'm the custodial parent. I don't have to tell him." Dallas thought it over, then asked, "Do I?"

"No. Under the terms of the original agreement, the only time you'd need to communicate Cody's whereabouts would be if it was Emilio's weekend to have him, or if you're taking him out of the country."

"But you are asking that his visitation rights be revoked, right?"

"As we discussed. It's all in the emergency motion I filed with the court. I'll email a copy to you so you can look it over. We'll use the hearing that's coming up to go over the property agreement. If he wasn't being such an ass over the distribution, we'd be done with this by now. That's the only thing that's hanging up the divorce."

"But I told you that Emilio had a weekend coming up . . ." Dallas frowned. The last thing she wanted to do was fly Cody back across the country next week.

"He won't be permitted to have it. Besides, if the rumors I'm hearing are true, Emilio will be in rehab by then."

"Rehab?"

"For his alleged addiction to sex."

"Oh, dear Lord," Dallas muttered. "Can this get any more sordid?"

"Of course it can, sweetie. This is Hollywood." Norma laughed, then signed off in her usual fashion.

Dallas tapped her fingers on the side of her glass. How was she going to explain this latest development to Cody? What was she supposed to say? "Daddy needed to go away so he could learn to keep it in his pants"?

She took a few minutes to check her email and listen to messages—none of which she felt like returning at that moment—then slid the phone back into her pocket.

She heard laughter from the lawn, and looked up to see her son struggling to carry a folded beach chair across the grass.

"Cody, do you need a hand there?" she called to him.

"I can do it," he called back.

"Just watch the end of the deck so you don't trip."

"I can see." He carried the chair onto the dock and pushed her hands away when she tried to help him open it. It took him a minute, but he finally was able to set the chair upright. "It's for Aunt Berry," he explained. "She wanted to come and sit with us by the water."

"That was nice of you to carry the chair for her."

He shrugged off the compliment and lay on the deck on his stomach.

"There are little fishies down there," he whispered. "They look all silvery."

Dallas peered over the edge slowly. "I see them darting around."

"Did you used to watch the fishies when you were six?"

"You bet I did. Your Uncle Wade and I used to take his boat out and—"

"Uncle Wade has a boat?" Cody's head shot up. He looked longingly toward the old carriage house. "Is it in there?"

"I'm pretty sure Wade sold it before he went away to college. But Berry might still have his rowboat."

"I'll ask her. She's out front talking to the bookstore lady." Before Dallas could open her mouth, Cody had popped up and taken off.

He streaked across the grass as if he hadn't a care in the world, a sharp contrast to the boy who'd boarded the plane from L.A. Maybe he'd needed the change in scenery as much as she did.

Dallas rested back on her elbows and stared at the cattails that grew along the bank on the opposite side of the river, thinking how nothing ever changes here. The river looked the same; it even smelled the same. She took great comfort from the realization that no matter what happened anywhere else in her world, this place—this dock, this river, this house—was always here waiting for her. She couldn't imagine a time when it might not be, refused to even consider such a thing. She folded her hands behind her head and closed her eyes, and listened to the gentle lapping of the river against the stones along the bank.

"Shhh. It looks as if Mommy's napping," Dallas heard Berry whisper to Cody a few minutes later.

"No, she isn't," Dallas told them. "She's just relaxing."

"Good. You could use some rest. You're looking way too tense." Berry sat in the chair that Cody had set up for her.

"I suppose tense is a step up from frightful." Dallas sat up.

Berry smiled. "Yes, and it took less than twenty-four hours. Imagine how much better you'll look—and I daresay, feel—after you've been here for an entire week."

"We get to stay here for a whole week?" Cody asked.

"Who knows? Maybe even more than a week," Berry said.

"Yay. This is way better than camp," Cody told his mother. "Aunt Berry thinks there might be a rowboat in there." He pointed at the carriage house. "But she thinks it might have a hole in it. She thinks it might have . . ." He turned to Berry. "What did you say it might have?"

"Dry rot, dear. We'll have a look in the morning. It's getting dark, and we won't be able to see a blessed thing in there. Besides, the bats will be coming out soon, and—"

"Bats?" Dallas frowned and looked skyward. She'd forgotten about the bats.

"Well, yes, dear, they have to come out and eat sometime, you know." Berry tapped Cody on the shoulder. "They eat mosquitoes. Why, just the other day, I read that bats can eat up to a thousand of them in one hour. Imagine how many more mosquitoes we'd have to swat away if we didn't have bats to eat them."

"I have a book about a bat." Cody hung on the back of

90

Berry's chair. "She's a baby fruit bat and her name is Stellaluna. She gets lost and has to live in a nest with some birds."

"I would love to read that book." Berry patted his hand. "Did you happen to bring it with you?"

"No, I didn't bring any books." He appeared suddenly saddened at the realization.

"Perhaps tomorrow we'll see if Barbara has the Stellaluna book in her store. If not, we'll try the library. Remind me when we go inside to give you a little notebook and a small pencil to put in your pocket. Every time we think of something we want to do while you're here, you can write it down."

"Auntie Mame," Dallas muttered just as her phone began to ring. She peered at the caller ID before answering it. She recognized Emilio's number and debated whether or not to let the call go to voice mail. She hadn't spoken with him since the scandal broke and some perverse part of her wanted to get in a few licks. She couldn't help herself. She left Berry and Cody to their discussion of bats, and walked to the end of the dock.

"Hello, Emilio."

"Where is he?"

"Where is who?" She walked across the yard, her eyes peeled for the bats she just knew were lurking nearby, waiting for her.

"You know damned well who. Cody. My son. Elena said he was with you but she wouldn't tell me where you are."

"If you recall our agreement, I do not have to consult you before taking him anywhere I want."

"I need to see him, Dallas."

"I don't think he wants to see you right now. Because of you and your antics, he's refused to go to day camp."

"Ridiculous. What do I have to do with him going to camp?" Emilio scoffed.

"It seems your film debut was all anyone at camp wanted to talk about. The older kids called you names and teased Cody about ... well, about what you were doing with someone other than Cody's mother, and how it was all right there on their computers for anyone with a credit card and about forty-five minutes to kill."

"Little bastards. I hope you told him to bloody their noses."

"Dear God," she murmured. Aloud, she said, "He's only six years old. And you know I've never condoned violence."

"You should be teaching him to stand up for himself, not run away."

"I repeat, he's only six."

"Well, at the very least, I hope you complained to the camp administrators. They ought to kick those little bullies out."

"I guess it would be foolish of me to expect that you'd take some responsibility for this yourself."

"Why? I didn't choose the camp. You did." His voice took on that self-righteous tone that made her blood boil whenever she heard it. "Maybe you shouldn't have sent him to a camp with such mixed age groups. Maybe you should have chosen a camp that only takes kids his own age."

"Maybe you should have used better judgment. Maybe you should have checked to make sure the camera wasn't running before you started your threesome." Dallas paused. "Or was it your camera?"

"Of course it wasn't my camera," he snapped. "If it had been one of my cameras, the resolution would have been so much better."

"What's the purpose of this call?" Dallas rubbed her right temple. She felt a wicked headache brewing.

"I want to see my son. I'm going away for a while."

"Ah, yes. The ever-popular sex addiction cure."

Emilio ignored her. "I want to see him before I leave. He'll wonder where I am. He'll be upset . . ."

Dallas laughed out loud. Was he serious?

"Isn't it a little late to start thinking about how Cody feels? And why in the name of all that's holy do you think he'll be upset if he doesn't see you for . . ." She bit her bottom lip. "How long does it take to cure one's sex addiction, anyway? Generally speaking."

"I can see you're not taking this seriously, Dallas." Self-righteous turned haughty. "Hypersexual disorder is every bit as serious, every bit as debilitating as drug addiction, as—"

"Oh, spare me. You are no more addicted to sex than you are to peanuts. You're grabbing at the only excuse you can find to try to excuse your abominable behavior. You can sell that story to the tabloids, bud, but I'm not buying it."

"Sex addiction has been recognized as a legitimate disorder."

"By some. And I'm sure that it's valid for some people. For you, it's just an attempt to legitimize your disgusting behavior. You're jumping on that bandwagon because you think it will make you look sympathetic instead of sleazy.

93

You're using it because 'sex addiction' is currently more socially acceptable than 'immoral horn dog.'"

"I didn't call to talk about me, I called to talk about Cody."

"Oh, please, Emilio. It's *always* about you."

The silence on the line was so complete, Dallas thought he'd hung up on her.

"I'll meet you anywhere you want. Someplace public—your choice."

"Ah, of course. Public so that you can alert the media and they can send reporters and cameras and get all those touching close-ups of you saying good-bye to your little boy before you go off to wherever it is they're taking you. Wouldn't that go a long way toward rehabilitating your image? I can see the lovely shot of you and Cody on the cover of every celebrity rag." She knew Emilio well enough to know that was exactly what he had in mind. "I don't think so."

"So are you saying I cannot see my son before I go away?"

"I think it's best for him that he doesn't see you for a while. This whole incident has been very upsetting to him."

"All right. I can try to understand your reasoning, even if I don't agree. I guess my reunion with my family will have to wait until my treatment has been successful."

"What family? There is no *family*. Our divorce is all but final." She gritted her teeth.

"Oh, but once I've completed my treatment, I'll be a different man. You'll see. Once I get this monkey off my back, I can be the man you married—"

"You cannot seriously think for one second that I would have any interest in you after everything that's happened over the past five years. With or without the monkey, I'm done." She could barely believe what she'd heard. "Here's the best advice I can give you: whatever shred of self-respect you might still have? Hang on to it and don't put yourself in the position for me to have to remind you and the rest of the world what an all-around shit you really are. You go ahead and get yourself straightened out so that you can make your big comeback. I really don't care what you do. But don't bring me or Cody into it. If you do, I will be forced to let everyone know exactly what I really think of you and this little charade of yours. Have a little dignity. Save face."

"I'll have my lawyer call your lawyer," he said stiffly.

"That's the only intelligent thing you've said since this call began." She hung up a split second before she knew he would be doing so.

Dallas sat on the back steps and tried to get her blood pressure under control with breathing exercises she'd learned in yoga and a few sips of wine. She was still sitting there when Berry and Cody joined her as the evening hung on to the last bit of light. Dallas knew that Berry would know that something had upset her, but she wouldn't ask in front of Cody.

"Aunt Berry's going to give me a glass jar to collect lightning bugs in," Cody announced.

"Oh, but then they'll die," Dallas protested.

"Not if I let them go before we go into the house," he told her.

"Why not just catch them in your hands—gently, of

course—then watch them unfold their wings and fly away?" Dallas suggested.

Cody considered this.

"Try it and see." She set her glass on the step between her feet, then opened her palms to show him. "See, your hands would be open, like this. You close them quickly around the bug—be very careful not to squash it, though. Give it a minute to rest itself, then open your hands, and watch. It's so much more fun to watch them fly than it is to see them just sitting or crawling around in a jar. Plus, you can count how many lightning bugs you've caught and let go."

He nodded—that made sense to him—then took off to catch and release.

"I don't recall you letting the lightning bugs fly away unharmed when you were his age," Berry said as she lowered herself to the top step. "I seem to recall you and Wade both catching bugs in jars and leaving them."

"We were young and didn't know any better. Before I'd developed a conscience about such things." Dallas looked over her shoulder at her aunt. "Besides, I always punched holes in the top and I always let them go the next morning before it got too hot."

"True."

Because Dallas knew Berry was dying to ask, she said, "That was Emilio on the phone. He called to try to set up a meeting with me and Cody before he goes away for his rehabilitation."

"Drugs again?" Berry raised an eyebrow.

"No. Sex addiction." Dallas let that hang in the air for a moment.

Berry laughed. "Surely, he isn't serious."

"Oh, he's serious, all right. And quite indignant about it, too."

"Knowing Emilio, the only thing he's trying to rehabilitate is his reputation. How like him to use the malady du jour as an excuse for his very bad behavior."

"That's exactly what I said. He's trying to stir up sympathy so that, once he's 'cured,' everyone will forget what a jerk he is."

"Surely no one's memory is that short." Berry tsk-tsked. "He'll go off in a blaze of camera lights, portraying a tragic, solitary figure. The man who lost it all. No wife, no children, to bid him adieu and Godspeed." Berry sighed dramatically. "Surely you didn't agree to meet him? Or to let him see Cody?"

"No, of course not." Dallas shook her head, then asked, "Do you think I did the right thing?"

"Absolutely. Good Lord, what else could you have done? Invited him here to St. Dennis? Rushed back to the coast with Cody to allow him to use the two of you to gain sympathy? Don't second-guess yourself. He isn't worth it. The sooner your divorce is final, the better off you and Cody will be." Berry paused. "You didn't tell him where you were, did you?"

"No, but I'm sure he'd be able to figure it out after he's called every one of my friends and realizes I'm not with one of them. And he is smart enough to know that if the tabloids aren't reporting that I'm in this hotel or that, at this one of our houses or the other, I'm probably not in California. And where else would I go but here?" Dallas shook her head. "I'm sure he remembers that this was always my refuge."

"Well, if he comes here, we'll deal with him."

"He won't waste the time. He said he's leaving in a few days."

"How long do you suppose he'll stay?"

"I don't know. I suspect it would have to be at the very least a month, if he's trying to make this appear at all credible."

"Credibility is exactly what he's after. I'm sorry, dear. I know these past few years have been very difficult for you." Berry squeezed Dallas's shoulder. "But you know, he was never right for you. You need someone stronger, someone whose feet are on the ground. Someone who understands what it means to be a real man."

"Well, now listen to you." Dallas forced a smile. "Aren't you a font of advice."

"I've been around the block a time or five." Berry smiled coquettishly. "I'm sorry that your marriage didn't work out, and that Emilio is exactly what I thought he was. You and Cody are better off without him. I doubt you'll ever regret divorcing him, but I do believe you'd regret taking him back." Berry looked out toward the Bay. "And there are few things sadder than regrets when it comes to matters of the heart."

"Odd," Dallas observed. "That's the second time since we've been here that you mentioned regrets. I don't remember that you ever admitted regretting anything in your life, Berry."

"Mom! Aunt Berry!" Cody ran to them, his cupped hands held out in front of him, a huge smile on his face.

"I got one! Want to see? We can all watch it fly away together . . ." he called as he dashed across the lawn.

"Yes, dear, bring it here, and we'll admire it before you let it go," Berry told him.

"Here it goes . . ." Cody opened his hands and waited for the insect to fly off. When it had disappeared, he turned to Berry and said, "I'll bet you'd be real good at catching lightning bugs, too, Aunt Berry. Maybe almost as good as me."

"Now, that sounded like a challenge, young man." Berry rose and made her way down the steps, the sparkly stones on her sandals catching the light. "Let's just see who can catch the next one. Starting now . . ."

Dallas watched the old woman and the small boy hunt lightning bugs in the faded light.

There are few things sadder than regrets when it comes to matters of the heart.

Dallas knew that, throughout the years, Berry had been romantically linked with this leading man or that director. She tried but couldn't recall any one man in particular having been a part of Berry's life for any real length of time. Certainly she'd never had gentlemen in her home when Dallas and Wade were visiting. A curious Dallas wondered who Berry looked back on with regret. Perhaps one day soon, she could persuade Berry to bring out her old scrapbooks, and see if she could ask the right questions that would lead her to the answer.

Chapter 6

BERRY was right, Dallas decided as she set out on foot toward St. Dennis's commercial center. Using the morning hours for shopping was better than waiting until the afternoon. For one thing, the morning hours were cooler, the tree-lined streets offered shade, and the breeze off the Bay was crisp. Once the sun rose high in the sky, it would beat down on the bayside town unmercifully.

The other good thing was that the shops were less crowded, which meant she'd run into fewer tourists who'd be elbowing each other when she passed by.

"Hey! Isn't that . . . ?"

It had taken the media exactly three days to find her, and since then, she'd been photographed from every possible angle. Whether professional photographers or tourists wielding digital cameras or cell phones, she figured she'd been good for a half mile's worth of four-by-six photos if they were all placed end to end. But no one had really bothered her or harassed her, and several people had so shyly and politely asked if they might have their picture taken with her that she couldn't bring herself to say no, as long as Cody wasn't photographed. So far, she suspected that some of those photos had found their way onto their owner's Facebook pages, but she hadn't seen them surface anywhere else. Everyone had respected her wishes about Cody not being included in the pictures. She drew the line at having her son's photo taken by strangers. You just never knew.

But Berry had also been right about the residents of St. Dennis accepting her as one of their own, and that had given Dallas particular satisfaction. When camera crews from a network entertainment program showed up in town, suddenly no one had much to say about Dallas. As her aunt had predicted, discreet phone calls gave them quiet notice, so that Dallas could decide whether to come into town, or not. No one had given away the location of Berry's house, though she realized it wouldn't be too difficult to find for anyone who knew that Beryl Townsend, the great star of the 1940s, '50s, and '60s, was her great-aunt and that the family name was Eberle.

Not so hard to discover for someone who took the time to dig into Berry's bio, Dallas knew. As yet, no one had, but it could well be just a matter of time before she awoke one morning to find paparazzi parked along River Road. But Dallas understood that the less she made of her presence here, the less everyone else did, too.

And that was just skippy, as far as Dallas was concerned. Since arriving in St. Dennis, she felt everything around her slowing down, as if the earth itself were spinning a little slower. The days seemed longer and more pleasant, the afternoons spent languidly relaxing on the dock or in the hammock in the shade of Berry's ancient oak tree. Dallas had become a regular at Book 'Em, gobbling up the latest mysteries and romances and memoirs the way a starving woman would attack a buffet. For years, she'd read nothing but scripts and entertainment magazines and movie reviews. She'd forgotten what a wonderful world there was to be found between the pages of books. She read quickly, and once finished, the gently read books were donated to the local library. In the week since she'd been in St. Dennis, Berry had taken five new bestsellers to the library on Dallas's behalf. The books had been gratefully accepted, since funding for new purchases had been cut.

Every day felt like a holiday, something to be savored and celebrated. She awoke each morning to the sound of the breeze blowing through the long thin branches of the willows, birds gathering in the pines along the side yard, or boats heading to the mouth of the river and the Bay beyond. She'd shower, have a leisurely breakfast with her son and her aunt, and then there'd be hours to do as she pleased, to read or to take walks, swim in the river or simply lie back on the grass and let her mind wander through the clouds that floated high over the Chesapeake. There seemed no reason to think about how long they might stay. That she'd found some bliss here was all she needed to know for now.

And Cody, it would seem, had found his own bliss. He and Berry had gotten into the habit of heading to the library in the mornings for the children's story hours. Every day her son had returned bubbling over, eager to tell her about the book the librarian was reading to them, or the book Berry checked out for him, or the kids he'd met that morning. Dallas had never seen him so engaged in any activity.

Just like a normal, happy boy, Dallas had told her friend

Laura, the night before on the phone. They'd been young starlets together, though their career paths had taken different turns.

"Of course he's a normal happy boy," Laura had replied. "Why are you so surprised?"

"I guess because he's so different here," Dallas told her. "He's . . . I don't know, lighter. More lighthearted. More like a little boy than a . . ."

"A clone of every other kid in Hollywood?"

"Yeah. That, too, but he's more engaged, less serious. Even before Emilio's latest escapade, I felt Cody was too serious for a six-year-old."

"Well, look at the way things have been for the past few years, babe. His mom and his dad were rarely together, and when you were, you were arguing. Dad's picture was in the tabloids almost every week. Cody may not have been able to read, but he sure as hell had eyes to see that the woman his father was cozying up to on the magazine covers was not his mother. Kids absorb hostility. They soak up your anger and your unhappiness like sponges." Laura hesitated, then added, "Plus, you've been working like a fiend for the past three years. You've gone from movie set to movie set, location to location. How much time did you really spend with Cody last year?"

"Jeez, Laura." Dallas frowned. "If I felt like being kicked around a little, I'd call Emilio."

"Sorry, sweetie. I didn't mean to come across so harshly." Laura sighed. "I've just gotten real sensitive to this sort of thing since, well, since Alissa and Kevin had all those problems last year. We've been spending a lot of time together, just the three of us. They were more deeply affected by the divorce than either Paul or I had realized. And I've put off the wedding to Brock indefinitely. I've come to the conclusion that the kids need more time to adjust. One of the things that came out in our therapy sessions was that they were bothered by the fact that I could leave their father and take up with someone else so quickly. While the situation is far from being that simple, it's made me stop and reevaluate a lot of things in my life."

"Wow. All that from Laura Fielding."

"I know," Laura said wryly. "The ditzy blonde bimbo actually has a brain. Who knew?"

"Anyone who knows you knows that the roles you've played are not who you are."

"True enough, but I've been typecast for so many years, no one thinks I can pull off a more serious role."

"They said the same thing about Marilyn Monroe," Dallas said pointedly. "One word, my friend: *Niagara*."

"I keep reminding myself of that, but I haven't worked in months." Laura sighed again. "All those stupid films I made when I was younger . . . I should have followed your lead and refused to take my clothes off. I even went brunette, but it seems like I can't buy a part in a legitimate film these days."

"Have faith in yourself. The right role will come your way."

"I hope you're right, Dallas. It's been hell on the ego to be turned down for so many projects, but on the plus side, I've had time with my kids and we're really getting to know each other. I can honestly say I like them both, and I think they like me a lot more now."

"Good for you. It sounds as if you're getting it all together."

"I am. *We* are. Look, I have to run. I'm taking Alissa to dinner and then we're going to a movie. We go once a week now, just the two of us. Honestly, I've learned more about my daughter in the past two months than I have in the past thirteen years. Paul's taking Kevin to dinner and a ball game. We're actually almost a normal, happy family, now that we're divorced. Go figure. Hey, give my love to Cody, okay?"

"Will do."

Laura's words stayed with Dallas through the night and into the next day.

Like Laura, Dallas was learning things about her child she'd somehow missed before, like the fact that he liked to take his time to observe new situations before he participated, or that in social groups, he needed to understand everyone else's role before he decided on his own. What she had always perceived as shyness was actually Cody's way of taking his time to study a situation and observe before joining in. She saw that he liked to try new things but was cautious, wanting to know how all the parts worked and fit together, whether the new thing was a toy or a social situation. Like when they dragged the old canoe out of Berry's carriage house and down to the river a few days ago. Cody had wanted to know where everyone would sit and how the paddles were handled and how they made the canoe go before he wanted to take it for a spin. She'd always known he was clever and curious; she just hadn't realized how deep his curiosity went.

Working at a job you love was a good thing, she'd concluded, unless it crowded out everything else. While she'd tried to balance work and motherhood over the past few years, in retrospect, she had to admit she hadn't done nearly as well as she could have. Laura had been right about that. She'd made three films back-to-back-to-back, leaving her little time for anything else, including Cody.

But for now, for as long as they were in St. Dennis, life was better. Life was good. And whatever lessons they learned here could be taken with them when they returned to L.A. She still hadn't given much thought to when that might be. There hadn't been a reason to plan. Part of the whole holiday ambience was just going with the flow.

Like now, having the morning to herself to walk into town and shop. She followed River Road to its end at Queen Anne Street, then walked three more blocks to Charles. Six blocks up Charles, the business district began with the bank on one side of the street and a small grocery on the other. The closer she came to the center of town, the closer the shops were to each other, until every house on the last two blocks had been converted into a shop or a restaurant. It was interesting, she thought, that so many homeowners had either sold their properties or converted their first floors into shops when St. Dennis had been "discovered." She passed by several Victorian-era homes where she'd played as a child, or where friends of Berry's had once lived. Walking the streets had made it all familiar to her again.

Dallas crossed the street and went directly to Bling. She

opened the door and went in, the little bell tinkling to announce her, and found herself alone.

"Hello?" she called. "Vanessa?"

She heard a muffled giggle from the rear of the shop, and seconds later, Vanessa emerged from the back room, her hands smoothing her skirt, a tall, ruggedly good-looking man walking close behind her.

Ah, that explains the giggle, Dallas mused.

"Hi, Dallas." Vanessa smiled even as a blush crept from the open collar of her cotton shirt to her hairline. "Ah, have you met Grady?" She gestured to the man who was approaching the counter where Dallas stood. "Dallas, this is Grady Shields. Grady, meet Dallas MacGregor."

"Good to meet you." He extended his hand. "I'm a huge fan."

"Why, thank you." She shook the hand he offered. "It's nice of you to say."

He turned back to Vanessa and kissed her on the side of her face. "I'll see you soon."

"Be careful, you hear? And take something that shoots real bullets. In case of bears." Vanessa watched Grady walk to the door. "And call me before you leave, okay? And when you get back."

"Will do." He winked and was out the door.

"He's a wilderness guide." Vanessa turned to Dallas. "He takes people into the mountains in Montana and they hike and they camp and shoot rapids and all sorts of stuff that could be dangerous. He's taking a party out on Friday into some remote area and they're staying for five days."

"I'm sure he knows what he's doing."

"Yes, but there are bears in those mountains. And wolves." Vanessa looked worried. "You never know . . ."

"If he's experienced, he'll prepare for those things."

"Oh, of course he will. I know he will." Vanessa waved a hand as if to dismiss her own thoughts of doom and gloom. "I just can't help it. I imagine these scenarios and my mind just takes flight."

"Well, if you don't mind my saying so, he's one great-looking guy."

"He is, isn't he? Best guy, ever." Vanessa beamed, the sparkle returning to her eyes. "Now, what can I get for you today? We have some new short skirts, if you're interested."

"I was hoping to find a pair of these shorts in khaki." Dallas stepped back to allow Vanessa to see what she was wearing.

Vanessa's eyes narrowed. "Didn't you buy those in khaki last week?"

"I did, but we—Cody and I—were rummaging around in Berry's carriage house last night and I got the pocket caught on a nail and ripped a good-size hole in them."

"That sounds like something I'd do." Vanessa sorted through the stack of shorts on display near the counter. "Here you go. I think these are your size."

Dallas looked at the ticket. "That was my size last week, and it may be my size today, but I'm afraid another few weeks of eating the way I've been doing and I'll be coming back for a larger pair."

Vanessa laughed. "We do have some pretty good restaurants, especially if you like seafood."

"Last night for dinner at Captain Walt's, I ate seven

steamed crabs—seven!—and a whole order of french-fried sweet potatoes. Polished it off with a slice of that ridiculously fabulous sponge cake with the fudgy frosting."

"The nine-layer job?" Vanessa grinned knowingly.

Dallas nodded.

"Smith Island cake." Vanessa nodded. "There's nothing else on the planet quite like it."

"You can say that again. I've been eating like there's no tomorrow, and there's no gym to work it off at."

"There's a gym out on the highway," Vanessa told her. "Though you probably wouldn't want to go there. It gets pretty crowded. You'd have no privacy there."

"I'm hoping that all the walking I'm doing will make up for it. I haven't even driven my rental car since I got here." Dallas placed the shorts on the counter near the cash register. "I will take these, but I think I'd like to see those skirts you mentioned. And maybe the sundress you have in the window. The coral one."

"The skirts are right here. The dark denim ones are especially cute." Vanessa led Dallas to the display. "The sundresses in your size are along the wall—that pink-and-gray number is nothing short of adorable—but I'm afraid we don't have designers. Not the labels you're used to, anyway."

Dallas smiled at her. "They don't need designer labels, they're darling. I think I want to try on the coral one . . ."

Two pairs of shorts, one of the dark denim skirts which Dallas agreed were in fact especially cute, and two sundresses later—the coral and one that had pink-and-gray swirls on the skirt—Dallas left Bling with two of the shop's signature brown-and-pink bags over her arm. She stood at the corner and waited for the light to change, a contented smile on her face. She and Berry had agreed they'd meet at Scoop at eleven-fifteen. Dallas was a few minutes early, but she didn't mind. It gave her a little extra time to sit on one of the benches and watch the boats out on the Bay.

Strolling along Kelly's Point Drive on a summer morning, she could almost imagine herself as the girl she'd once been, a shy, pudgy, lonely, sad eleven-year-old that first summer they'd stayed here, the one that followed her father's death. She remembered how she felt coming to Berry's that first time. They'd arrived in the middle of the night during a summer storm, her mother having gotten lost several times during the drive from New Jersey. The house had loomed large and dark and oh so spooky against a sky that was continuously split by lightning and rocked by thunder. She'd been too terrified to get out of the car. Wade, who was seven, had slept through it all. She'd been confused and didn't really understand why her father had died and left them and had thought Berry a very strange person and Berry's house a haunted mansion. She was certain that her first night in that house would be her last. Surely some terrible creature would slink out of the dark to do her in.

But Dallas had survived that first night, and every night thereafter. Berry had won her over with charm and humor and love, and before too long, the house had become home to her and her brother. She'd wept at the end of the summer when they left to return to a house that didn't seem at all like home anymore. With her father gone, the light had gone out of their family, leaving her mother bitter and angry. It wouldn't be until Wade was in junior high school, when their mother met her second husband, Antonio, on a winter trip to Florida to see her sister, that Roberta MacGregor found something that made her forget the bitter hand she believed she'd been dealt. The following summer, the summer when Wade left for college, Roberta had flown to Argentina to marry her polo player, and she'd never come back, not for either of her children's college graduations or for Dallas's wedding. To celebrate the birth of her only grandchild, Roberta had sent a case of champagne and a sterling-silver rattle engraved with Cody's name and date of birth. If either Wade or Dallas felt her loss, neither had ever expressed it, even to each other. It had taken Dallas years to understand that what she'd perceived as her mother's rejection was really Roberta's way of putting behind her the loss that she'd never been able to accept or understand any more than her children had. If Roberta had found love and peace of mind with her new husband, Dallas could only wish her well. She was beyond judging and many steps away from being hurt by the situation. Roberta was simply Roberta, and that was that.

A police car was heading out of the municipal building's parking lot as Dallas strolled down Kelly's Point Drive. The cruiser slowed as it passed her, then stopped, and the driver's window rolled down.

"Dallas MacGregor, is that you?"

Puzzled, she walked toward the car, then smiled when she recognized the man behind the wheel.

"Hey, you need to be careful. I heard impersonating a police office was a chargeable offense." She rested an arm on the car door. "How are you, Beck?"

111

"Great. I heard you were back." The town's chief of police put the car in park. "I was planning on stopping out at your aunt's place to say hello, see how you were doing, and here you are."

"I'm here and I'm doing fine. Congratulations on your marriage, by the way. Berry showed me the pictures she took at the wedding of you and your beautiful bride. Berry said she's an absolutely lovely person. I'm still trying to figure out how you got so lucky."

"Believe me, so am I." Beck grinned. "You'll meet Mia if you hang around St. Dennis long enough. How long are you planning on staying?"

"I haven't decided yet. I've been enjoying myself too much to give serious thought to anything this past week."

"Well, that's a good sign, then. You enjoy yourself, you're more likely to stay a little longer this time than you did the last few times you were here." He paused, then asked, "How long's it been, anyway?"

"Three years, I think."

"Well, whatever it's been, it's been too long. Good to see you, Dallas." He put the car into drive. "You need anything, anyone bothers you, you have problems with any of the tourists, you give me a call, right? Berry has my home number and my cell."

"You give out your private numbers to everyone in St. Dennis?"

"Nah. Just the special ladies." He smiled, and she understood he'd been keeping an eye on Berry.

"I appreciate that, Beck. Berry's always been so independent, I forget how old she is and how alone she is here."

"You'll be in for a tongue-lashing if she hears you used the O-word and her name in the same sentence," Beck reminded her. "And she's not alone, Dallas. She has an entire community looking out for her. But for the love of God, don't let her know anyone's keeping tabs on her. Heads would roll."

"My lips are sealed." Dallas stepped back to allow the car to pass. "But thanks, Beck. I do appreciate it, and I appreciate you letting me know."

"Berry's a legend in St. Dennis, Dallas, you know that. She's a treasure." He rolled up the window as he eased the cruiser on by.

Dallas waved and continued on down the road toward the Bay and Scoop, thinking how life sometimes took the oddest twists and turns. She remembered the summer when Gabriel Beck just sort of appeared in town, a sullen boy in his early teens who seemed to have it in for just about everyone who had the misfortune of crossing his path. It wasn't long before she and the entire town heard that he'd been dumped off by his mother on the front porch of his unsuspecting father, Hal Garrity, who at the time was the chief of police. Back then, Beck was a wild child, the kid who bordered on bad but who never seemed to cross that line. Somehow, he'd gone from being as close to juvenile delinquent status as any kid in St. Dennis ever had, to a respected officer of the law and a man beloved by his town, even by those who'd been plagued by his adolescent antics. Dallas was happy to see that life had turned out so well for Beck. She'd always liked him and his dad.

That's how it is in places like this, she thought as she took a seat on a wooden bench at the end of the path that looked out on the Bay. *People look after each other.*

It had never occurred to Dallas that Berry needed looking after, but she was pleased to know that someone cared enough to keep tabs. A lot of someones, she suspected. It was comforting to know that Berry would be checked up on after Dallas and Cody returned to California. Berry's ego aside, it was clear that she wasn't as strong as she'd been the last time Dallas had visited. The concept that Berry was, after all, human, and susceptible to the effects of time just like everyone else, was a foreign one. Dallas never thought of Berry as anything but hale and independent. If anyone could live forever, surely it would be Berry.

It bothered Dallas to think about a day when there'd be no Berry in St. Dennis, in her life.

Some other day, she told herself, and pushed the thought aside.

It was hot sitting in the sun and she was getting a little cranky waiting for Berry and Cody.

"Well, how dumb am I to be sitting right outside an air-conditioned ice-cream parlor while I complain about the heat?" she muttered. She picked up the bags from Bling and her shoulder bag, and went inside.

"Looks like someone's been shopping." Steffie was leaning on the counter near the cash register.

Dallas smiled and held up the bags. "I could really lose my head in that place."

"Vanessa would be delighted to hear that."

"The woman has fabulous taste. If Bling was in California, I'd be there every day." Dallas paused near the menu board. "What do I want today?"

"I think you want something light but fruity and refreshing. Maybe the lemon meringue. It's brand-new. Want a taste?"

"Sure."

Steffie grabbed a plastic spoon from a cup and opened the freezer case. The spoon disappeared for a moment, then reappeared, a pale yellow confection mounded in its bowl. She handed the spoon over the top of the case to Dallas.

"Oh, man, that is truly heaven." Dallas sighed after she'd licked the spoon clean.

"I just made it this morning. It has homemade lemon curd in it."

"Sold. I'll have two scoops." Remembering the meal she'd had the night before, she added reluctantly. "No, better make it one. In a bowl, please."

"How 'bout one generous scoop?"

"You're the devil, aren't you? The real one, the one who leads us into temptation . . ."

Dallas reached up for the bowl just as the door opened behind her. Expecting Berry and Cody, she glanced over her shoulder, ready to admonish them for being late.

"Grant," Steffie called from behind the counter, "you're just in time to say hey to Dallas."

"Hey, Dallas," he repeated as if on autopilot.

"Grant." Dallas forced a smile and hoped it didn't look as forced as it felt. "How are you?"

"I'm good. Thanks." He put a friendly hand on her shoulder, as anyone might do when greeting an old friend. "You're looking good."

"I'm good." She nodded and tried to ignore the fact

that, beneath her shirt, her skin was starting to warm at his touch.

"I heard you were in town." Was he avoiding eye contact? Or was she? Either way, Dallas was okay with that.

"Since last week." She nodded again, then told herself to stop. "Bobble-head" was not a good look for anyone.

"My daughter said you might be thinking about getting a dog." His hand slid away—across her shoulder and down her back—as he walked past her to the counter. She relaxed slightly and exhaled a breath she hadn't been aware she'd been holding.

"My son would like a dog, but there's been no decision yet."

"I'm sure Paige told you we have lots of adoptable dogs at the shelter." He turned to his sister. "How 'bout a double chocolate malt with a dabble of raspberry and some chocolate sprinkles?"

"Oink," Steffie muttered, and Grant laughed good-naturedly.

He'd always been like that, Dallas recalled as she took a seat at a small table just inside the door. He'd always laughed easily and had a great sense of humor. Maybe that's why she'd never forgotten what his laughter sounded like, or the way his mouth turned up when he smiled. Or the way he—

"Hey, Mom!" The door flew open and Cody burst through.

"Whoa, pal." Dallas put an arm out to reach for him. "Take it easy. And quick, catch the door before it bangs against the—"

The door hit the wall.

"—wall." She jumped up to grab it and pull it back. She held it while Berry came inside, then closed it quietly. "You owe Steffie an apology, Cody."

"I'm sorry I let your door bang." Cody didn't look the least bit concerned but he sounded sincere. One out of two wasn't bad, when you were dealing with a six-year-old.

"I forgive you," Steffie told him solemnly. "Now come over here and sample this new flavor and tell me what you think of it." She dipped into the case. "It's chocolate chip fudge."

"Sorry to be late, dear." Berry sat her handbag on the chair next to Dallas's bags from Bling. "The story hour ran late, and . . ." Behind her dark glasses, her eyes scanned the shop. A huge smile spread across her face when she saw the man leaning against the counter. "Why, is that Grant Wyler?"

"Just waiting here for you, Miss B." Grant put down his bowl of ice cream and crossed the floor in two strides to plant a kiss on Berry's cheek. "How's my favorite pinup?"

"Oh, dear, I can't believe you found those old photos on the Internet." Berry blushed prettily. "You'll never let me live that down, will you?"

"Are you kidding? I printed them out," Grant teased. "On glossy paper. Poster size. Got 'em hanging on my walls at home."

"Oh, you do not." Berry pretended to be flustered.

"Oh, I certainly do. Just the other day, I was thinking I'd have one made a little bigger for the waiting room at the clinic."

"Grant Wyler, you're just . . . naughty." Berry laughed coquettishly.

"I've been called worse. Actually, I believe I've been called worse by you."

"Never, dear boy." Berry shook her head.

"What can I get for you?" Steffie addressed Berry.

"I'll come up there and take a look." Berry went to the case to look inside. Grant followed and grabbed his bowl of ice cream from the counter where he'd left it. When he returned to Dallas's table, Cody was right behind him.

"Grant, this is my son, Cody Blair. Cody, this is Mr. . . ." She corrected herself. "Dr. Wyler. He's Paige's father. Do you remember Paige?"

Cody nodded. "You're the veterern . . . vetererarian."

"Veterinarian," Dallas corrected.

"The dog doctor." Cody looked up at Grant and extended his little hand. "It's nice to meet you."

Dallas smiled. It was always a surprise when your child remembered the manners he'd been taught. Her smile faded when Grant reached a hand to take Cody's. Dallas remembered those hands . . .

"It's nice to meet you, too, Cody," Grant was saying as Dallas's heart began to speed up just a little.

"You have lots of dogs and you give them to people who want them."

"I run a shelter where we take care of dogs that are waiting for new homes. Cats, too," Grant told him.

"Mom said maybe I could have a dog," Cody said. "Maybe you have a dog for us."

"Maybe I do. That's up to your mom."

"Actually, it's really up to Berry, since it's her house we'd be bringing a dog to." Dallas tried to focus on a freckle in the middle of Grant's forehead but she couldn't help but meet his eyes. He held her gaze for a long moment before she blinked and looked away. Blue eyes. So very blue. She'd written a poem about his blue eyes when she was sixteen. It had been embarrassingly bad. She blushed at the memory.

Cody scrambled off his seat and ran to the counter, where Berry stood talking to Steffie.

"A dog's a big responsibility." Dallas cleared her throat. "I don't know if Cody's ready to take on that kind of responsibility."

"Taking care of a pet is a great way to learn responsibility." Grant leaned on the back of the chair that Cody had vacated and brought himself eye level with Dallas. "But of course, it's up to you. And your aunt."

"We need to give it some more thought, but thanks. If we decide to take on a pet, we'll be sure to come to you first." Even to herself, she sounded stiff and formal.

"Good. I think it would be great for your aunt to have a dog in the house with her." He loaded ice cream onto his spoon and raised it to his mouth, then licked the spoon clean. "A dog would make a great companion for her."

"I don't know that Cody would want to part with it when we leave." She tried to look away, but couldn't. She remembered that mouth, those lips.

"When do you suppose that's going to be?" Grant asked as another spoonful of ice cream headed for his mouth. Dallas fought hard against remembering the many places where that mouth and those lips and those hands had been, once upon a time.

119

"I haven't really thought about it." She sat riveted to her chair, visions from her past dancing merrily in her head. *Shoo*, she demanded. *Go away. Go away now.*

Grant appeared to be about to say something else when Cody bounced back to the table.

"Aunt Berry is thinking about it," he announced gleefully. "She said she would think about it today and she's going to talk to you some more." He pointed at his mother. "So you should talk now."

"We'll talk when we get home, Cody." Dallas could feel Grant's eyes on her. She looked up at him and tried to project calm, tranquillity. *Which is where being an actor comes in*, she mused. "Do we need to call first, if we wanted to pursue a dog through your shelter?"

"A call is always a good thing. Gives us a heads–up, a little time to look over the dogs that might be contenders." Grant pulled his wallet from a back pocket and a business card from the wallet. He scribbled something on the back with a pen he took from the counter next to the cash register and handed the card to Dallas. "Now you have all my numbers. The clinic, the shelter, my house, my cell." He looked down into her eyes and added, "You can find me anytime you want me."

"Good to know." Dallas tucked the card into her pocket.

Berry approached the table with a generous scoop of peach ice cream balanced on top of a sugar cone.

"Delicious," she declared after taking a nibble. "And doubly so since I don't have to obsess about my weight anymore."

"When did you ever obsess about your weight?" Dallas

snorted. "I don't recall you ever having a problem with your weight."

"Perfection doesn't come without a price, dear," Berry said breezily.

"You've always been perfect in my eyes, Miss B," Grant told her.

"You know, Grant, if I were twenty years younger . . ." Berry flashed a smile.

Dallas cleared her throat.

"All right, thirty years younger . . ." Berry paused, then waved her hand. "Oh, never mind."

Dallas laughed and grabbed her bag from the floor. "I say we leave it right there."

"Probably for the best," Berry agreed, then tapped Grant on the shoulder. "We'll let you know what we decide about the dog, dear."

"I gave Dallas my numbers, so you can call anytime," he told Berry.

"A fluffy white dog," Cody said with emphasis on the color. "Aunt Berry would like a fluffy little white dog."

"I'll see what we can do for her," Grant assured the boy.

"We'll be in touch," Dallas told him as they headed for the door.

"I'm counting on it." Grant held the door, and closed it behind her after she passed through.

Chapter 7

"WELL, that was fun." Steffie leaned on the counter after the door closed with a click.

"What was?" Grant turned to her, his face as impassive as he could make it appear while his heart was beating out of his chest.

Steffie laughed. "You are so not a good actor."

"What are you talking about?"

"Please." She rolled her eyes and lowered her voice. "'Here are all my numbers. Now you can find me whenever you *want* me.'"

"You're a jerk." He grabbed a few napkins from the holder on the counter and left the shop, his sister's "Love you, too," trailing behind him.

He walked down to the water's edge and watched the sailboats out on the Bay while he finished his ice cream, and tried to get his thoughts straight.

That he would run into Dallas while she was in town had been a given. St. Dennis wasn't so big that they wouldn't have bumped into each other at some point if she stayed for more than a few days. He'd known this and had mentally prepared himself for the day when it happened. At least, he thought he had.

He'd told Paige that Dallas had always been pretty, but

pretty didn't tell the whole story. Her physical beauty was one thing, and yes, she'd had that for as long as he could remember. When he looked at photos of her when she was in her teens, he could see the beautiful woman she'd one day become. But there was something more there, something he'd never been able to define. Charisma didn't quite say it, though that certainly was a factor. It was something more fundamental, something that even as a teenager he'd felt, something that pulled him to her like the moon pulled the tide. Back then, he'd believed that it was fate, pulling them together, making them inevitable for then and for forever.

Until, of course, that last summer, when she'd come late to St. Dennis and stayed only two weeks because she had summer theater back in New Jersey and needed to get home in time to audition for the female lead in *Romeo and Juliet*. That had not been the first he'd heard of her acting ambitions. Berry had run a summer theater group for the kids in town for years, and he'd joined to be with Dallas, even though he had no talent and she always won a leading role. But that summer—the summer she'd only stayed for two weeks—had been the first time he realized just how serious she was. He'd never felt he had a rival for her affection, had been confident he could ward off any guy who tried to come between them. But her love of acting had been something he hadn't counted on, something he never had understood and probably never would. In the end, he'd had to admit it was something he'd never be able to compete with. He'd believed he was her first, her only love. Realizing he was wrong had hurt more than anything else he'd ever experienced, and the hurt had lasted

123

for a very long time. Even now, he couldn't recall anything that had given him more pain than having to admit, at eighteen, that the girl he loved—the girl who'd sworn she'd always love him—was out of his life and wasn't coming back.

It still stung to remember how it had all unraveled.

"What do you mean, you're not staying for the summer?" he'd asked, shocked when she told him that she'd be leaving after two weeks.

"I have an audition," she'd told him excitedly, "for a summer theater production. It's for *Romeo and Juliet*, one of my favorite plays."

"I don't believe this."

"I can hardly believe it myself. Me, playing Shakespeare." Dallas had positively beamed. "Wish me luck, Grant." She'd paused. "You do wish me luck, don't you?"

"Sure," he'd replied sourly. "About as much luck as I'm gonna have for the rest of the summer."

"Oh, don't be that way," she'd pleaded. "It's hard to explain how important this is to me. It's what I want to do, not just this summer, but always. I want to be an actress, Grant. I want to make movies and be a star. A *for real* movie star."

"Swell." He'd rolled his eyes.

"Isn't there anything you want more than anything else, Grant?" She'd grown very serious. "Isn't there something that means more to you than anything else?"

"Yeah, and I'm looking at it."

"I don't mean a person, I mean something for your-self." She paused as if collecting her thoughts. "Something that frees you up inside to be yourself, that makes you know that's what you were born to do."

"No." He shook his head. "I don't feel that way about anything except you."

"You will someday," she'd told him solemnly. "You'll find something that you want to do forever, and you'll be so good at it that you'll know it's meant to be."

"I thought we were meant to be, Dallas."

"Well, we are. But we have to do something with our lives. We have to have goals."

His only goal that night had been to get her out of her shorts and her T-shirt, but he'd had the good sense to know that wasn't what she wanted to hear.

"Isn't there something you know inside you were born to do?" she'd asked.

"Yes," he'd replied without hesitation. "I was born to love you, Dallas."

"I love you, too," she'd assured him. "I always will. And I'll be back, I promise. And you can come for a week to visit. I already asked my mom, and she said it would be okay if it was okay with your mom."

All these years later, Grant's cheeks still burned when he recalled how that visit had turned out. The only week he could take off from his lifeguard job was smack in the middle of Dallas's rehearsals for her play. He'd spent the entire week watching the guy who was playing opposite her smugly gloat as he monopolized her time. Grant had wanted nothing more than to beat the crap out of him. By the end of the week, he returned to St. Dennis knowing it was over, even while he insisted to himself that it would never be over between them.

Maybe he'd been right, back then, if the way his heart had thumped and his pulse raced and his head swam when he first saw her in Scoop meant anything.

He wondered if any of it meant anything at all.

It was funny, but after she left that last summer, he'd told himself that he'd been wrong about her, about them. He'd rationalized that it had probably only been something sexual in nature that had bound them, and for years, that's what he kept telling himself. But twenty minutes ago, he'd walked into Scoop, and there she was, and he'd felt it all over again. That *ping* to his heart, that *zap* to his nerves felt exactly the same as it had almost twenty years ago. He felt that same sense of having been bewitched that he'd felt the first time he'd met her. Back then, he'd looked into her eyes and had fallen hopelessly in love. There was no doubt in his mind that Dallas MacGregor could still in fact lead a man to distraction, that gazing into her eyes would be like looking too long at the sun.

And that, he warned himself, was something he needed to avoid.

Yeah, right. Let me know how that works for you.

Grant tossed his empty ice-cream dish into the tall trash receptacle at the end of the path and headed back to the clinic for his afternoon appointments.

"So, Dallas." Berry sat on one of the new Adirondack chairs. At her direction, the deliverymen had placed the chairs right at the edge of the lawn, where they could sit and look out at the Bay beyond the river's mouth. "I think that went well today."

"What went well?" Dallas sipped her after-dinner

126

coffee and stretched her legs out in front of her. "Oh, wait. Is this going to be about running into Grant? Because if that's what you're wanting to talk about . . ."

"Why, Dallas, what makes you think I want to talk about Grant?" A mischievous glow danced in Berry's eyes.

Dallas glared at her aunt.

"Though I was wondering if you were all right about seeing him."

"Of course I was all right seeing him. Why wouldn't I be?" *Other than the fact that my palms sweat every time I think about him. Or that I've been deliberately not thinking about him since we left Scoop.*

"Oh, I don't know." Berry shrugged. "Maybe because he was, at one time, the center of your life."

"I was very young then," Dallas said from between clenched teeth. "That was decades ago."

"They say that your first love is the one you always compare others to," Berry mused. "How did Emilio stack up?"

"Berry . . .," Dallas warned.

"Oh, all right, dear. But you have to admit that he's grown up awfully nicely. He was always a handsome boy, but my goodness, he's grown into an exceptionally good-looking man."

When Dallas fell silent, Berry prodded her. "Admit it, Dallas. You know you agree with me."

"All right. Yes. Grant's grown up to be a very handsome man. Are you happy?"

"Almost."

"Berry, he's a married man. And I would never, ever—"

"Not anymore."

"What?"

"Didn't I mention that he was divorced?"

"No, you did not."

"I was sure I had . . ."

"I would have remembered."

"Really?" Berry's face brightened.

"As I would any of my old friends."

Berry laughed out loud. Dallas chose to ignore her.

"That's what you wanted to talk about?" Before Berry could respond, Dallas said, "Anything else you want to know?"

"I think that will do. For now."

Out on the dock, Cody was doing one of his favorite things, lying on his stomach and gazing into the water, the bottoms of his bare feet white below his now-tanned legs.

"He's having such a good time here," Dallas noted. "He loves everything. Even the bats." She smiled. "I can't remember when I last saw him having so much fun."

"He reminds me so much of Wade, when he was a little boy," Berry reminisced. "Always around the water, always catching bugs and frogs and finding baby birds and such. I swear that boy lived for the summer."

"We all did, back then."

"Oh, yes, dear, even I looked forward to having you both here. I never scheduled work for the summers so I didn't have to miss a day with the two of you. Of course, you both did keep growing older, and once you became teenagers, you had other interests. But when you were little, you were both all mine."

Dallas turned to Berry, whose face was beaming with memory.

"Remember the theater we had in the old barn?" Berry glanced at the empty space where their barn had once stood. "We'd put on a different play every month. None of them very good—I have to admit that after having watched your debut performance I'd have bet against you ever making it as an actor."

"Rapunzel." Dallas remembered. "Was I really that bad?"

"Dreadful, even considering your young age. I am happy to say that you've since redeemed yourself. And of course, by the time you were in high school, it was obvious that you were born to be a star."

Dallas laughed. "I remember being onstage and completely forgetting my lines. I had such stage fright."

"I'm glad you've managed to overcome it, dear."

"Actually, I never have. I don't like to perform live. A few years ago I was offered a role in a play that was to open on Broadway, but just the thought of it made my stomach churn."

"Well, then, I suppose we're lucky that you've found film more to your liking. I always did, too, though I had my share of stage triumphs," Berry confided. "Once done, a stage performance is . . . well, it's *done*. Gone forever. Unless of course it's filmed, but then it's no longer live. I prefer that my performances be available to the ages."

"Mom! Aunt Berry! Look out at the Bay!" Cody called excitedly. He was jumping up and down and pointing out toward the horizon, where a schooner was sailing across the water, driven by the wind in her sails. "Isn't it cool? Isn't it pretty?"

"It is, indeed, Cody," Berry called back to him, and Dallas walked down to the water to watch with him.

"It's a reprer ... repo ..." Cody looked up at his mother. "What's the word?"

"Reproduction."

"A *reproduction* of an old ship." He pronounced each syllable carefully. "Berry told me about it, and at the library one day Mrs. Anderson read us a story about a schooner that used to sail right out there for real."

"You're really enjoying the story group at the library, aren't you?" Dallas ruffled his hair. She knew one day he'd become an age when he'd no longer tolerate such displays by his mother, but for now, he accepted such gestures in the spirit in which they were made.

"It's neat, Mom. Every day we read a new book and then we get to talk about it. I wish we had it in California."

"They have children's hours at the libraries there, too. We can sign you up when we go back."

The joy drained from his face as quickly as water seeped from a sieve.

"It wouldn't be the same. The kids wouldn't be the same." He turned his face, but not before she saw the look of disappointment.

"What's different about them?" Dallas sat on the grass near where he stood.

"The kids here are nicer. They aren't mean."

"You mean about your dad?" she asked softly.

He nodded. "No one knows about that."

"And you like that? That you're sort of anonymous here?"

130

"What does that mean?"

"It means that they know your name is Cody, but they don't know that your dad makes movies and your mom acts in them."

"Some of the kids know that you're a movie star but no one seems to care much." He paused. "Except Mrs. Anderson. She knows Aunt Berry, and she said she knew I was Cody and that I was your son. Berry asked her not to talk about it to the other kids, and she didn't."

"You said that some of the kids knew, though. How'd they know, if Mrs. Anderson didn't tell them?"

Cody shrugged. "They just knew."

"Is that okay with you?"

"Sure. It's no big deal. The kids are more fun. Things are different here."

"You said that and you gave one example, that they're not mean about your dad."

"They're not mean about most things. Not when kids mess up when they're reading or when you . . . when *some* kids don't know stuff. And they don't talk about their moms and dads all the time and where they go and what they do. They talk about other stuff. Fun stuff."

"I see."

The first lightning bug of the evening flashed at the end of the dock, and it caught Cody's eye. He sped off to catch it, the conversation apparently over as far as he was concerned.

"Careful," Dallas called after him. She watched as he stalked the insect, which flew out over the water. Cody turned back to the grass and went on the hunt. Dallas returned to her chair and sat with a sigh.

"What was all that about?" Berry waved her hand to the place where Cody and Dallas had been chatting.

"Cody was talking about the story hour at the library."

"Oh?" Berry sat up straight. "Is something wrong? He always seems to enjoy it so much."

"He does. He loves it."

"I thought he did. Well, he always says he's having fun there. And he interacts with the other children nicely, and they all seem to like him. He seems as if he's almost making friends."

"Almost?" Dallas frowned.

"He seems to be holding back, as if he's afraid to get to know any of the other children too well. It's as if he's afraid to make friends." Berry paused again. "I overheard the little boy he sits with every day invite him to come to his house to play one day next week, but Cody immediately declined. When I asked him why, he said he doesn't know if he'll be here next week."

"He hasn't asked once," Dallas murmured aloud.

"What's that, dear?"

"Cody. He hasn't asked when we're going home, not even one time. Apparently because he thinks it's going to be soon and he doesn't want to know."

"Will it be soon, Dallas?"

"I don't know. Do you think not knowing bothers Cody?"

"I think it would be most helpful to him if he knew he'd be here for another week or however long you plan to stay." Berry appeared to be choosing her words carefully. "There was talk this morning about a party at the library next Thursday for the official dedication of the new children's wing, and all the others signed up for an activity. Cody wanted to leave before it was his turn at the sign-up board."

"I really hadn't thought about how long we'd stay," Dallas admitted. "I didn't think it would matter. For the first time in three years, I don't have a schedule to keep and I'm enjoying having some free time. It's been such a pleasure to not have appointments and meetings and rehearsals."

She thought of the screenplay she'd been wanting to work on. And there was that wonderful book she'd read earlier in the week, the one that was just screaming to be made into a film. What might she do with that, if she gave herself the time to work on it without other distractions?

"I don't mean to push you into staying or going, though I will readily admit that I love having the two of you here. I'd be delighted if you'd stay ... well, for however long. I would never interfere in your life or in the way you raise your son. But you did ask ..."

"Yes, I did. You know I value your opinion. It hadn't occurred to me that winging it this summer, while liberating for me, might not be the best thing for Cody."

Dallas thought for another moment, then asked, "You really think he's making friends at the library?"

"As I said, he and another little boy sit together every day. They share books with each other and laugh together the way little boys do. There's a little girl there who sometimes sits with them. Yes, I'd say he's making friends. Or at the very least, would like to."

Dallas tried to recall the last time Cody had referred to another child as his friend, or the last time he'd been asked to play at another child's house. Or the last time he'd asked to have another child over to play after school. Birthday party invitations didn't count. His school had an "invite one, invite all" rule in place, so he'd been invited to many parties over the past year. Though now that she thought about it, he hadn't been overly eager to attend any of them. And there'd been that invitation she'd found stuffed in the bottom of his book bag toward the end of the school year that he said he'd forgotten about ...

"I've had an idea for a screenplay," Dallas told Berry. "Had I mentioned that?"

"You may have said something about it."

"And the novel I finished reading on Tuesday ..." Dallas continued to think out loud. "I keep envisioning it as a film. It has two very strong female characters. They're just marvelous women—a woman and her middle-aged granddaughter—and I keep seeing them, big as life, on the screen. I've been toying with the idea of buying the film rights." She left out the part about how she saw Berry in the role of the older woman.

"Oh?" Berry turned to her, interested.

"I think I'd like to work at maybe adapting it, writing the script myself." Dallas looked at Berry for a reaction.

"I do like the sound of this."

"I'd only do it if I thought I could do it really well."

"Of course you'd do it well," Berry assured her. "Why wouldn't you?"

"I've never attempted anything like this before. Actually, until I had this one idea for a film, I never even thought of doing such a thing. Then I finished reading this amazing book, and I can't get the characters out of my head. I keep seeing them, hearing their voices. Berry," she added in a hushed voice, "it would make a magnificent film."

"Then call Norma and have her pursue the project, dear. What's the very worst that can happen? The author says no and you don't make a deal. Otherwise, what do you have to lose?"

"Nothing." Dallas stood, every nerve ending tingling. "You're right, Berry. I have nothing to lose. And if I'm successful in buying the rights, I can work on the screenplay right here."

"Here?" Berry asked cautiously.

"We could stay for the rest of the summer here, couldn't we?"

"Of course you could, dear." Berry was trying hard to contain herself. "Why, we could set up that third-floor room for you to use as an office . . . or, no, no. We'll take the library on the first floor and you'll use Grandfather Eberle's desk. Wouldn't the old man be proud?" she mused.

"First I have to see if I can get the rights," Dallas reminded her.

"And if you cannot?" Berry's smile began to fade. "What then?"

"Then I will go back to writing the original screenplay I was thinking about before I read *Pretty Maids*. Actually, I think I should start on that right away. Who knows how long it might take to obtain the rights to the novel."

"Are you certain that's what you want? I didn't mean to influence you."

Dallas shook her head. "I've been wanting to do

something like this for a long time. It just hadn't occurred to me that I could do it here."

"I'm delighted. I won't say I'm not happy that you're not going home."

Dallas looked at the big house with its gables and turrets. "This is really the only home I have right now. The house we've been in is rented and it's never felt like home. There are other houses we bought over the years but they're all tied up in the divorce. To tell you the truth, I don't want any of them. I don't have any happy memories of any of them. Actually, now that I think about it, I don't really have happy memories of any place except here."

"You're welcome to stay for however long you'd like. But I do think you should let Cody know what your plans are. He needs to know." Berry paused. "You did say the rest of the summer?"

Dallas nodded. "I think we both need a break."

"Dallas, are you sure . . . ?"

"I'm sure, Berry. There's nothing for either of us back in L.A. I don't have any work lined up, though my agent emailed me last night and told me she had a ton of scripts for me to read. I can read them here as easily as I can there." Dallas laughed. "Better actually, because I won't be tempted to run out for lunch and pick up on the latest gossip and who's doing what with whom, or get lured out to parties I don't really want to go to or to see people I don't really like. Cody's school doesn't start until the second week in September, so we can stay through the end of August and go back after Labor Day. We should probably give ourselves at least a week to get ready for school."

Berry sat back in her chair, a smile lighting her face. "The entire rest of the summer! I never dared hope you'd be with me that long."

"This is your last chance to change your mind. Once I tell Cody, it's a done deal."

"Well, then, go tell the boy. I'm sure he'll be as happy as I am."

Dallas got out of her chair and leaned over her aunt and kissed her on the forehead. "That will make three of us."

Chapter 8

AFTER supervising Cody in the old-fashioned claw-foot tub, Dallas tucked him into Wade's old twin bed for the night. At odd moments it struck her how strange it was that this was her child, her son, not her little brother, that she read to each night. Cody did favor Wade in some ways, Berry was right about that. She glanced down as she began to turn a page in the latest favorite book, and realized that Cody was sound asleep. She hadn't thought it possible that he'd fall asleep at all, since he'd gotten so excited over the prospect of spending the rest of the summer in St. Dennis.

"The whole rest of the summer?" His eyes had widened at the thought. "All of the summer?"

"Well, we'll have to leave sometime to get you ready to go back to school, but we'll stay until right after Labor Day. I think I'll see if we can make arrangements to fly back on the Tuesday after Labor Day."

"When is Labor Day?" he asked.

"It's always the first Monday in September, but offhand, I don't know the date this year. Let's go take a look at the calendar." They went into the kitchen and opened the pantry. Dallas pointed to the large wall calendar that Berry had tacked up on the door. "See, here we are, in July. And we will stay here through the whole rest of the month of July, and the whole month of August. Here's Labor Day. September sixth. We'll go back the next day. September seventh."

Cody moved the step stool under the calendar and stood on it to touch the days.

"Wow, that's a lot of days." He turned his face up to hers, and the joy was unmistakable. "I can go to all the stuff at the library. I can do lots of stuff."

"You can do lots of stuff," she agreed.

"Yay!" He hopped down from the stool. "I'm going to tell Berry that we can stay until September—" He stopped and turned around. "What day did you say?"

"We'll leave on September seventh."

"September seventh," he repeated as he ran from the room. "September seventh . . ."

She couldn't remember ever having seen Cody so happy. It reinforced her decision to stay. Perhaps he'd needed that little bit of stability even more than either Berry or she imagined.

She kissed the top of his head, turned off the light, and tiptoed out of the room and down the stairs.

The first floor was quiet, and she wondered where Berry had gotten to. The faint sound of voices drew her to the front of the house, and in the dim light, she saw Berry at the foot of her driveway talking to someone. She was just about to open the door to join them when the phone rang. Dallas all but ran to the kitchen to grab the phone from the wall before it could wake Cody.

"Eberle residence."

"Dallas? It's Grant."

"Oh. Hi." *How brilliant*, she thought. *How original. How . . . juvenile.*

"Hi. Is your aunt around?" he asked.

"She's here but she's out front. I can run out and get her if you don't mind holding on for a few minutes."

"When she comes in, just tell her that there's a dog here at the shelter that might be right for her." He paused, and she could hear his breathing, soft and steady. "That is, if she's still thinking about adopting one."

"I honestly don't know what she's thinking," Dallas replied, "but I can tell her when she comes in and she can call you back."

"There's no real hurry. The dog has only been here for a few days, but she's a really special dog, so who knows how long she'll be around." He paused. "I don't know why I didn't think of her before."

"Got it. I'll let her know."

"You have my numbers, right?"

"Ah, no, I don't think I . . . oh. The card." She reached for her bag and pulled out her wallet. The card was right where she left it, in the slot behind her driver's license. "Yes. I have it."

"Great. I'll wait to hear from you. I mean, from her. About the dog."

"I'm sure she'll be in touch." Dallas walked to the back door and looked out at nothing in particular, then back to the counter, then to the windows.

There was a silence that neither of them seemed able to break, but neither made a move to hang up. For a split second, Dallas was sixteen again, standing on this very spot, holding this very phone, and pacing from the back door to the counter to the windows. Just as she was doing now.

Déjà vu all over again, she mused.

Finally, Grant said, "So. How's it feel to be back in St. Dennis after all this time?"

"It's great. It feels great."

"You said it's been a few years since—"

"Yes. Three. I think it's been three. But I didn't stay very long that time. I got called home for work. The town sure has changed a lot since I was able to spend any time here."

"Yeah, it's changed a lot since when I moved away, too."

"The changes look like they'll be good, though. I mean, I heard that the new shops and the restaurants are big attractions for tourists."

"It's all good for the town. Tax dollars and all."

She nodded, then remembered he couldn't see her. "Right," she said. "I guess your sister's doing well."

"Steffie had the right idea at the right time. She makes a great product—you know she makes all her ice creams herself?"

"Berry told me. I'm really impressed with what she's done in that old shack. I seem to remember that it didn't look like much, back when we were kids."

"It wasn't. That's the old picking shack where my grandmother and my aunts used to pick crabs. You know, steam them and then pick the meat out for shipping to restaurants."

"I do remember that. I remember trying it one time during camp." Dallas laughed softly at the memory. "I

141

wasn't very good at it. I cut my fingers so many times on those hard shells, I was dismissed."

"There is a knack to it. They say you need to be born on the Eastern Shore to know how to do it properly." Grant cleared his throat. "Dallas, listen, I don't know if this is the right thing to say or not, but I heard about . . . well, about the trouble you've had, and I just want to say how sorry I am that you and your son are going through this."

"Thank you, Grant." For some reason her throat threatened to close. She hadn't been expecting that.

"I mean, the guy is obviously a moron. Any guy lucky enough to—" He stopped. "Sorry. I'll just let it go at sorry."

Another silence followed. She wondered about his wife, and what had happened there, but couldn't bring herself to ask. Instead, she simply said, "When did you move back to St. Dennis?"

"Almost a year ago. The old vet in town was ready to sell his house and his clinic right at the time I was at a point when I had decisions to make, so it seemed to be the best solution to several problems. The price was right, the facilities were good, although I had to do some major updating. I'm still working on the house but the clinic is up-to-date. We use the old barn for our rescued animals, so it's all worked out nicely."

"There are several shelters in the area where we live in California. I didn't realize there were so many abandoned animals that needed rescuing."

"The animals aren't all abandoned. Some of them come from high-kill shelters, places where people dump their

142

animals or puppies from unwanted litters. You know, your dog gets out of the yard and the next thing you know, she's giving birth to a litter of puppies on the kitchen floor. You don't want the puppies, or you give away as many as you can find homes for, don't want the rest, they go to a place where they're overrun with animals and can't keep them beyond maybe forty-eight hours. If they can't find a home for the animal quickly, well, they put them down."

"They do that to puppies?" Dallas frowned.

"Unfortunately, yes. So sometimes we get word of a litter that's at another shelter and about ready to be put down, or we get a call about some really nice animals that are on the short list, and someone's sending a van to wherever the animals are and they'll bring some back and try to find homes for them."

"What happens if you can't?"

"We only have a few that have been here since we opened that we haven't been able to place. A couple of the cats seem to prefer staying in the barn. The dogs . . . well, they followed Paige home, somehow, so they moved into the house with us."

"That's nice," she said. "I mean, that's really nice that you do that."

"Well, we've got a few good dogs, so it's not been a hardship."

Dallas heard the front door close and Berry's sandaled feet cross the hardwood floor of the foyer.

"Grant, hold on," she said. "Berry just came in."

She put her hand over the mouthpiece and called to Berry: "Grant's on the phone. He wants to know if you're still thinking about getting a dog."

"Of course I am. Why wouldn't I be?" Berry smiled and reached for the receiver. "Were you finished, dear?"

Dallas nodded and handed off the phone. She sat at the table and tried to pretend she wasn't listening to the conversation. When Berry hung up, Dallas said, "So you're going to go look at this dog, are you?"

Berry nodded and leaned back against the counter. "Grant said it's an especially nice dog. We can see it tomorrow at four."

"Did you ask him what kind of dog?"

"No, but I do recall that Cody told him I'd like a nice lapdog. A fluffy little white one, I believe we decided on. I'm guessing that's what he has for me." Berry smiled. "Won't Cody be thrilled when he wakes up tomorrow morning and finds out that we not only have story hour in the morning, but we're going to look at a possible dog in the afternoon."

"Ummm." Dallas nodded.

"What's that 'ummm' for?"

"I'm just afraid that Cody will get overly attached to the dog and not want to leave it."

"This is a good way for him to prove how responsible he can be with a pet, dear. And when you get home, you can let him get one of his own. Let's just wait and see how it goes. Why, maybe we'll come home with two dogs, one for him and one for me." Berry went to the back door. "There's a storm coming. Just look at that lightning out over the Bay."

Berry stood and stared out at the darkening clouds for a long moment. When she turned to close the door against the breeze, Dallas saw a shadow fall over her aunt's

144

face. But when she turned, her smile was bright and her voice chipper. "Well, dear, I think I'll go up to my room now. I'd like to write a few notes tonight and I don't want to be up too late." She flashed the smile that once lit up the silver screen and melted many a heart.

"Good night, Dallas. I'll see you in the morning. Tai chi at dawn, you know." Berry stopped halfway through the doorway. "Perhaps you'd like to join us? It's very relaxing. It helps you get in touch with your most peaceful self. It's a means to find enlightenment. It helps to activate and energize your inner core." She grinned and added, "It also lowers your blood pressure and keeps you limber, which is mostly why I do it. And of course because I do look so good doing it."

"You certainly do." Dallas laughed. She blew Berry a kiss. "Have a good sleep."

"Will you lock up before you come upstairs?"

"Sure. I'll be down here for a while, though. I want to make some notes about the screenplay. I'm going to call Norma and talk to her about my new plans."

"Excellent. No reason to put it off . . ." Berry's voice trailed away as she climbed the stairs.

Moments later, Dallas heard the floorboards overhead creak just a little as Berry crossed her bedroom floor. Another minute, then the chair that sat next to Berry's desk scraped lightly across the floor. Dallas went out onto the back porch and leaned on the railing. A flash in the sky was followed by a rumble of thunder. Overhead the clouds had gathered in a low dark mass and would soon dump their burden on the earth below. The air was electric and expectant and redolent with a combination of salt

145

and ozone and the roses from Berry's garden. Once the storm began, she'd go back inside, but for now, she wanted to watch the changes in sea and sky. It had been so long since she'd seen lightning work its way across the Bay.

There was so much on her mind tonight. There was the film she wanted to do—just talking about it to Berry had fanned the flames of her enthusiasm. The more she thought about it, the more realized that she wanted it as badly as she'd ever wanted a part in a film that she believed in. But this was different, it was bigger, and she ached to do it. It was three hours earlier on the coast; she could still get Norma before she left the office.

And then there'd been the news that both she and Grant were here in St. Dennis, both unencumbered. Well, that might not be true, as far as he was concerned, she really shouldn't make that assumption. Just because he looked at her the way he used to didn't mean he wasn't involved with someone else. Funny how things worked, though, how after all these years . . .

Her phone, which she'd left on the kitchen table, began to ring, and she went back inside to answer it.

"Norma," she said as she activated the call. "I was just getting ready to call you. I have a project I want to talk about. But you go first. What's up?"

"What's up is your divorce is this close to being final. The only hang-up is still the property settlement. As you know, there's quite a bit of valuable real estate at stake here."

"I don't want any of it. Emilio can have it all."

"Are you crazy? Uh-uh. I'm not letting you give away millions of dollars. Let's walk through this."

"I really don't want it. Emilio picked out all of those houses except the one in the Canyon, and that's where he made that damned video. Do you really think I want to ever go inside that place again? Or the one in Palm Springs, where he took that little Brit singer he was playing with last year? I never really stayed in the Manhattan apartment, and I've only been to Florida three times." Dallas frowned. "I don't have happy memories of any one of them, frankly."

"Then we'll tell him we want to sell them all and split the money evenly."

"He isn't going to want to do that. He loves his little palaces."

"Then we'll split them down the middle. He gets two, you get two."

"All right, but then you'll sell my two, okay? I took with me everything that mattered to me when I moved out with Cody. Our clothes, his toys, and some photographs. I don't care about the rest of it."

"I'll see what I can work out with him."

"If he balks, if he gives you a hard time, you tell him fine, he can keep them all except the apartment in New York as long as when each one is sold, half of the sale price goes into trust for Cody."

"Dallas . . ."

"Norma, by most standards, I've made an obscene amount of money over the past ten years. Yes, Emilio did spend a lot of it those first few years. But I've invested most of what I've made since the day I realized what a jackass he is. That was five years ago. I've amassed enough to keep Cody and me very comfortable for a very long time. And I'll offer to not seek child support to keep my investments."

"I guess now's the time to tell you that Emilio has asked for alimony."

Dallas fell silent, then said, "Would he drop that if I offered him all of the properties? On the condition that I mentioned, though, that once sold, half the proceeds go to Cody."

"He might." Dallas could hear Norma's pen tapping on the receiver as she thought over this proposal. "You really want this divorce through now, don't you." It wasn't a question.

"I want it over and done with as quickly as you can make it happen."

"I'll talk to Emilio's attorney and let you know what he says. Frankly, I can't see him turning it down. He's a fool, but he isn't stupid." She thought that over. "Well, yes, he is stupid, but his attorney isn't. So let me see what I can do."

"There's something else I want you to look into for me." Dallas told her how much she'd loved the book *Pretty Maids*, and her ideas for bringing the story to the screen.

"Wow, what a great idea. I read that book. I can see the story as a film. You have casting in mind?" Norma chuckled. "Like, your aunt as Rosemarie and you as Charlotte? That would be brilliant."

"Berry would make a perfect Rosemarie," Dallas agreed. "Once I started thinking about it, I couldn't imagine anyone else in that role. But as for Charlotte, I actually have someone else in mind for that part, someone who I think would be amazing."

"Who'd be more amazing than you?"

"Let's see if we can get the rights, and then see if we can line up a studio. Then we'll talk casting . . ."

Dallas closed up the house, locking all the doors and windows, and went into the library and switched on the overhead light. The storm had blown in and the rain now lashed at the windows and the wind bent the willows over and sent their branches flapping, those long thin leaves outstretched like long arms rustling on both sides of the river. Earlier, she'd counted the number of weeks she had left in St. Dennis, and had come up with seven whole weeks and part of another one. If she worked every day, there'd be time enough to write her original work and possibly start on the script for *Pretty Maids*, if she was lucky enough to get her hands on it.

She sat at her grandfather's large walnut desk and turned on the small lamp that sat on one corner. The chair was oversize, having been selected for a man of much greater stature than she, and the top of the desk was bare except for a small calendar, a round penholder of worn brown leather, and a faded photograph of her grandparents—Duncan MacGregor and his bride, Sylvie—on their wedding day. She picked it up and studied the faces of two strangers, people she'd never met but had heard so much about. Most of her father's family died before Dallas was born. Berry and her twin sister had been the youngest of their generation, Dallas's father one of only three children in his.

She went upstairs and got her laptop and brought it back to the library. She turned to plug it in to recharge the battery, and noticed the row of photos on the bookshelf behind her. She was surprised to find a picture of her and Emilio on their wedding day. She reached for it, then pulled her hand away as if not wanting to touch it. The picture caught the newly married couple on their way out of the church, Dallas looking deliriously happy next to her handsome groom, who looked, she decided, nothing short of smug. Not happy in love, just ... smug, as if he knew he'd scored big by marrying one of Hollywood's most popular and most beautiful stars. Also, Dallas recalled bitterly, one of Hollywood's highest-paid actors.

Yeah, you really hit the jackpot, didn't you, you creep?

Her eyes burned for her younger self, who'd believed she'd found the man who would make her happy, the man who'd father their houseful of children. Since the scandal broke, her energy had been focused on protecting Cody, on shielding him from the fallout from his father's actions as best she could. Even this trip to St. Dennis had been planned with him in mind. She hadn't permitted herself to dwell on her own feelings of betrayal and loss. Even though she'd known for years that Emilio was a serial cheater, she'd never really mourned what could have been. The blow to her pride when the stories of his infidelities began to circulate had been nothing compared to what she'd felt when she first heard the rumors that he'd married her only to further his career. Having him fall out of love with her was one thing; learning that the love had never existed was something else entirely.

Live and learn, girl. Live and learn.

What was the point of dwelling on what was or wasn't there? It was done, and she was moving on to the rest of her life and very happily leaving Emilio behind. She

150

opened her laptop and began to make notes on the original idea she had, but her mind kept wandering back to *Pretty Maids*.

There'd be no harm in playing around with a few scenes. If her offer was declined, she'd delete them. If Norma was successful in making it all happen, she'd be that much further ahead. She started by making some notes to herself about the characters as she understood them and the setting as she saw it, then began the first scene. Before long, she was lost in the story, seeing and hearing the characters as they came to life on her computer screen.

By the time Dallas turned off the computer at 3:20 the next morning, she had the first scene written and revised. The sense of awe she felt—at fleshing out the two remarkable women in the book and making them real, at having taken the first steps toward bringing their story to the screen—took her breath away like nothing had since she'd seen the first of her own film performances on the night it opened in a small theater in a suburb of L.A. She'd slipped into the back row alone and watched, wide-eyed, as her image first appeared. It had been a very small role in a very small film, but it hadn't mattered. It had been hers, and she'd been filled with pride in the good job she'd done.

She'd gone alone because it had been a moment too big to share with casual acquaintances. When she left the theater, she headed right back to her tiny apartment and called the one person she knew who'd understand. Berry had already turned in for the night but had been delighted at the call and full of encouragement and pride, as Dallas had known she would be. For Dallas, the night had been nothing short of magical.

Tonight's work had filled her with the same sense of accomplishment and joy. She read the completed scene over and over, and each time, she rejoiced, knowing that the magic was there. She hooked up her printer and printed out the scene and turned off the lights. Tomorrow she'd go to the office supply store outside of town and pick up some supplies: more paper, more ink, some notepads, some file folders. She snapped off the hall light and walked up the steps, past the portraits of her ancestors and those of her costumed aunt. She fell asleep across her bed, the credits rolling in her head: *Screenplay by Dallas MacGregor, adapted from the novel written by Victoria Seymour* . . .

Chapter 9

DALLAS was already behind closed doors in the library when Berry and Cody came back into the house from their morning tai chi. Berry knocked before opening the door, then poked in her head.

"Pardon the interruption, dear, but we're wondering if you're going to join us for breakfast."

"I'm just having coffee," Dallas said without taking her eyes from the computer screen.

"There are peaches and some yogurt in the fridge if you get hungry later. Cody and I are going to eat and go to the library."

Dallas nodded, and Berry began to close the door quietly, but Cody slipped through and bounded into the room.

"Mom, we're going to go to the library right after breakfast 'cause I want to be there early." He threw himself onto her lap, forcing her to back away from the keyboard. "I can write my name on the activity paper for next week and I can tell Logan that I am going to stay here until September seventh."

"Who is Logan?" Dallas leaned back in the oversize chair and ran her fingers through her boy's hair.

"He's my friend at story hour." Cody squirmed away

153

from her hand. "And I can't wait to see what happens next in the story Mrs. Anderson is reading to us."

"Sorry, Dallas," Berry told her from the doorway. "I was trying not to disturb you."

"It's fine, Berry. I was going to have to stop soon anyway to run to that office supply store to pick up a few things I need."

"Do you have a list? Cody and I can stop after the library and pick up whatever you need so that you can continue working. I could tell by the look on your face when I opened the door that you were totally absorbed in whatever it is you're doing."

Dallas smiled. "I spoke with Norma last night. She's going to contact Victoria Seymour and see if we can negotiate the film rights for *Pretty Maids*. But I'm so excited about the project that I decided I'd just start working on a possible screenplay. You know, in case it works out, I'll be that much farther along with the project. And yes, I was totally absorbed in it. It's such a wonderful story. You really should read the book."

"I'll see if Barbara has another copy. I'm curious to see what it is about this story that has you so enthused."

"I'll be very interested to know what you think of it. I think the characters are absolutely ... well, read it and we'll talk about it."

"I'll stop at Book 'Em between the library and the office supply store. Go ahead and make that list for me." Berry waved Cody to the door, and shut it behind them, leaving Dallas to work on her new project.

It seemed like no time at all had passed between the moment Dallas handed Berry her list of supplies and the second she heard the back door slam to announce their arrival back home. She glanced at the digital clock on her computer and was stunned to see that almost three hours had gone by.

"We have your stuff, Mom." Cody pushed open the door and carried a plastic bag directly to the desk. "I have pens and a stapler and paper clips and boxes of ink."

"Thank you, Cody." Dallas pushed the chair back and reached out for the bag, but her son went past her to dump the contents of the bag onto the desk.

"See? Pens with blue ink and some with red, like you wanted. And this box has big paper clips in it." He held up a box with the picture of a big clip on it. "And these are pencils. I had to show Berry the kind you like best."

Dallas picked up the package of mechanical pencils. "And you're exactly right. This is the kind I like best."

"Dear, I had no idea you had such a thing about refillable lead pencils." Berry came in with a box of file folders on top of a box of computer paper. Dallas got up to take the load from her aunt.

"I have it, Dallas. I'm not a weakling, you know. I'm just going to drop them right here." The boxes landed with a *thud* on the worn Oriental carpet. "There is another box of paper for your printer in the car, but my arms aren't long enough to carry more than one at a time."

"I'll get it. Thank you so much for picking up everything for me. I really appreciate it." Dallas stood and stretched. "I got quite a bit done on the second scene."

"Why don't you go get that other box from the car, and use this as your break? Anita came to clean this morning, and she made some of her delicious chicken salad for us to have for lunch. I'd love to sit out on the back porch to eat. Last night's rain cooled things off quite nicely, and there's a delightful breeze off the Bay, so we're not only cooler and less humid today, but we're bug-free as well."

"How could anyone turn down an offer like that?" Dallas saved her work and closed the program.

Twenty minutes later, they were enjoying lunch on the small back porch that was just wide enough for the wicker table and six chairs. Dallas was distracted, still thinking about how best to write her scene, but Cody chattered away. Finally, Berry tapped her on the arm and said, "You're a million miles away, dear. Why don't you go back to work until it's time to go to see Grant."

"See Grant?" Dallas blinked. Was she going to see Grant today?

"To see the dog he called about last night, remember?" Berry prodded.

"We're gonna get a dog! We're gonna get a dog!" Cody sang out at the top of his lungs.

"Perhaps, child. We'll see." Berry turned back to Dallas. "You can get another few hours of work in. We'll give you ten minutes' heads-up before it's time to leave." She studied Dallas for a moment. "You might want to think about changing into something that doesn't say 'working at home and don't give a damn how I look' quite so loudly. And a little makeup might help, while you're at it. You have circles under your eyes and look as if you haven't slept in several days."

"I was up until three working," Dallas admitted. "But I don't know that I need to go with you today."

"Of course you do, dear. What if we can't decide between dogs? We'll need you as the tiebreaker."

"You have a point. And I suppose a little cleanup before I leave the house is in order." Especially if she was going to see Grant. Not that it mattered, but, still … "A twenty-minute heads-up would be appreciated, Berry. Thank you."

Dallas stood and held the door for her son, who was suddenly helpful again, as he appeared at her elbow carrying the basket of rolls from lunch and the salt and pepper shakers. He smiled at her angelically, and she glanced over her shoulder at Berry and rolled her eyes. Berry laughed, and followed them into the kitchen.

Berry sat on the porch and thumbed through the day's mail while keeping one eye on Cody, who was crabbing off the dock with a raw chicken neck tied to a length of string. Earlier he announced that today he would catch crabs. He was doing okay luring them to the bait, but still hadn't mastered the art of scooping them up with the net, so the bucket he'd prepared with cool water and seaweed held no crabs. So far he'd lost five big ones, he'd told Berry mournfully, because he wasn't fast enough to catch them before they saw the net coming and disappeared into the eelgrass.

"The only way to learn is to practice," Berry had told him, and he'd nodded, determined to perfect his technique.

Berry set aside the magazines and the small pile of envelopes, and watching Cody's efforts, offered a simple prayer of thanks for the unexpected blessing she'd so recently received. Dallas's call out of the blue, asking if she and Cody could come for a visit, had been nothing short of a miracle. Berry had hated to admit, even to herself, just how lonely she'd been. *Lonely* always sounded so needy. But if the truth were to be told, there was no denying that she was paying the price for the years of independence she'd enjoyed when she was a much younger woman, the woman who had had the world by the tail and had enjoyed every last moment of her fame and stardom.

At a very young age, Berry had been drawn to Hollywood and had conquered it. Over the years, she'd tired of the game, yet she'd gone back time and time again, even when there'd been nothing left to win. It had taken years for her to realize that there really was nothing for her there, and several years beyond that to understand that, sadly, there was precious little for her in St. Dennis, either. Any chance she'd had for real happiness with the things that truly mattered, she'd squandered. Too late she'd learned that a man—even one who claimed to love you more than anything else on the face of the earth—could only wait for so long before he'd give up, and move on to someone who was there for him.

She sighed heavily. That was all in the past now. The man she'd loved—and learned too late had a limit to his patience—had moved on, and in time, so had she. If she thought of him now and then, if her ears perked up at the sound of his name, if her heart beat faster if she thought she caught a glimpse of his proud head towering above others in a crowd—his hair now as white as her own— well, that was hers to deal with, hers to own.

She wished she'd known how best to warn Dallas of the consequences of confusing illusion with reality (was there anything sadder than believing one's own press?). She'd been simply beside herself when Dallas had announced she was going to marry Emilio. Berry had known the first time Dallas brought him to St. Dennis to meet her that he was a snake. There was a certain sort of man who should never be trusted, and Berry recognized at once that Emilio was just such an entity. Berry had picked up right away on something that apparently eluded Dallas: Emilio didn't love her. So for Berry, it had been loathing at first sight, and in spite of her efforts at cordiality for Dallas's sake, Emilio knew exactly how Berry felt about him. There had been no crisis on his latest film, as he'd claimed, that had forced them back to Hollywood days earlier than they'd planned. He'd disliked Berry every bit as much as she disliked him, and couldn't wait to be out from under her roof.

Berry often regretted not having told Dallas how she'd really felt about him, but other than having made some vague comments like, "Dear, are you sure you've known him long enough?" or, "Why the rush to the altar?"— well, how did one tell a loved one that the person they're set on marrying is a cad? And God knew, Berry had had enough experience with cads in her day to know one when she met one. Emilio had been and always would be unworthy of Dallas, and that was the bottom line. It had given Berry no satisfaction to have had her fears confirmed. She'd have given anything to have spared Dallas the pain and the humiliation of these past few years.

Yet to Berry's eye, Dallas seemed to be holding up well

enough, but then, that would be expected. On the Eberle side, Dallas came from a long line of women who knew how to rise from the ashes. Berry had not been the least bit surprised when Dallas declared she was going to write her own screenplay; she'd never been one to sit in the corner and wait for something to come to her or for someone else to make things happen for her. Berry was willing to bet everything she had that by the end of summer, Dallas would not only have completed her work, but would have found backing for it.

Of course, Berry reminded herself, by the end of the summer, Dallas and Cody would be gone.

Yes, there is that.

"Aunt Berry, look! I caught one!" Cody held up his net in triumph. "Come see!"

Berry smiled and set aside the mail and went down the cobbled path to the dock. She peered into the net.

"He isn't very big, is he?" Cody noted.

"Well, no, he isn't very big," Berry agreed, "and *he* isn't a *he.*"

"He's not?" Cody frowned. "How can you tell?"

She pointed at the crab's claws. "See how the tips of her claws are bright red?"

Cody leaned closer, then nodded.

"Hold the net up higher so I can show you something on her underside."

Cody did as he was told.

"See how this part of her abdomen is shaped like a V? The males—we call them jimmies—have a T shape there. When she gets older, this shape will round out more and look more like a bell."

160

"She isn't very old, then?"

"Not very old, and not very big. And since the crabs have to be at least five inches in length—that would be this way"—she showed him how to measure from side to side on the shell—"I'm afraid we're going to have to let her go back into the river so she can grow a little bigger."

He studied the crab for a long moment, then said, "It's okay, Aunt Berry. There wouldn't be enough for all three of us to eat from one little crab. We should let her get bigger and catch her next year. By next summer, I'll be much better at this."

"I'm sure you will, Cody."

Berry squeezed her eyes closed for a second or two. How cavalierly the young could look forward a whole year without considering what might come between now and then. She could only pray that she'd be here come next summer, and that fate would arrange for Cody and Dallas to be here with her.

"Is it time to go see the dogs yet?" Cody asked.

Berry glanced at her watch. "Almost. Put the net away and we'll go see about your momma."

"Can I leave the bait down there? In case some hungry crabs come by?"

"Just loop the string around the top of the piling . . . yes, like that. That way, when you come back, your string will still be there."

Cody tied the string and raced with the net to return it to the carriage house. Watching him made Berry revisit her earlier mental diatribe against Emilio. Because of Dallas's marriage—however ill-fated it may have been— they had this marvelous boy, and nothing, not even

Emilio's piggish behavior, would ever make Berry wish that wedding had never taken place. The man may have been unworthy, but the child he had fathered was a most precious gift.

"Why don't you go up to your room and clean up a bit," Berry suggested, "while I get your mother."

"Okay." The excited boy ran into the house and up the back steps.

Berry knocked on the library door to let Dallas know it was time to stop working and get ready to leave. Thirty minutes later, the three of them were seated in Berry's sedan and were on their way. Cody sat alone in the backseat and chatted for the entire time it took them to drive across town.

"Well, it looks as if Grant has quite the operation here," Berry observed when she'd parked the car in the lot behind the clinic. "I've passed by many times, but I've never driven up the lane. Of course, I've never had a pet before, so there'd been no reason."

They got out of the car and Cody took off running toward the clinic door.

"Cody, stop. I don't think the animal shelter is in the same building as the clinic," Dallas called to him.

"What?" He stopped on a dime.

"I think Grant . . . Dr. Wyler said that the shelter was in the barn," Dallas explained.

"That's back there?" Cody pointed to a large structure that sat opposite a Federal-style house.

"That's the barn, all right." Grant came out through the double doors in the back of the building that housed the clinic. "You ready to look at some dogs?"

"Uh-huh!" Cody jumped up and down.

"Follow me, then." Grant turned to Berry and Dallas. "You sure you're ready for this, Miss B?"

"Of course. Lead the way."

Grant offered her his arm and Berry took it. "The terrain is a little uneven and goes slightly uphill. We don't want to see you tumbling down."

"That would be a sight." Berry winked at Dallas. "Come along, dear. Let's take a look at this dog that Grant thinks might be perfect for me."

Dallas trailed behind slightly, and Berry thought she was probably taking stock of the grounds, since that's what Berry would have done. The house was nicely landscaped and well sited on the property. The clapboard on one side of the front door showed signs of having had the paint recently scraped off. A ladder leaning against the house on the opposite side was evidence that the scraping was still a work in progress.

"Having the house painted, dear?" Berry asked as they passed by the front walk on their way to the barn.

"Once I get all the old stuff off, I'll paint," he replied. "Dr. Evans and his wife maintained the house well in terms of the structure, but there's been no painting or any other cosmetic work done in, oh, I'd say thirty years, at least."

"You're doing it yourself?" Dallas asked.

Grant nodded. "In whatever spare time I get, yes."

They arrived at the door of the barn, where Cody waited impatiently.

"You can go on in," Grant called to him. "Paige is in there getting ready to walk some of the dogs."

Cody disappeared immediately into the barn, and Dallas, Berry, and Grant followed moments later.

"Dad, I can't get her to come out of her pen." Paige met them at the door. "She just won't come. And she hasn't eaten all day."

"Let's see." With Berry still on his arm, Grant went to the third pen from the door and stooped down to look at the yellow dog inside.

"What's wrong with her?" Berry asked. "Is she sick?"

"She's depressed," Grant told her.

"Dogs get depressed?" Dallas joined them.

"Sure. Dogs have feelings, they have emotions, and they show them, like people do. A depressed dog looks sad, like this one does."

Berry peered into the pen. "Why is she depressed?"

Grant stood. "Did you know Leona Patten? She lived out on Kent?"

"I believe we'd met, yes." Berry was still studying the dog that lay on the floor and appeared to be doing her best to ignore the three humans who were lurking outside her pen. *"Lived*, you say?"

"She passed away on Tuesday morning. Ally here belonged to Ms. Patten. Got her as a pup ten years ago. They were inseparable." Grant leaned against the top of the pen. "Ms. Patten had a heart attack and died right there in her house. The visiting nurse found her the next morning. Ally was right by her bedside, wouldn't even go outside until they took Ms. Patten out. I heard the dog tried to go with her in the medical examiner's van."

"So why is she here?" Berry asked. "Leona had family. Why is her dog here?"

164

"Her son lives in Maine and won't be in town until the funeral this weekend. Her daughter, who lives over in Ballard, came to remove her mother's jewelry and lock up the house. She dropped Ally off here on her way back through town."

"Why, that's ... despicable," Berry exclaimed. "No wonder the poor thing's depressed."

"I know, it's a shame, isn't it? Ten years of love and loyalty, and you end up in a pen, tossed aside, unwanted." Grant reached over the side of the pen to scratch behind the dog's ears, but she never looked up. "Poor girl. She's a really sweet dog, too."

"But you said she's only been here since Tuesday," Dallas noted. "She's a pretty dog. Someone will probably want to adopt her."

"At her age, that's not likely to happen."

"What do you mean, 'at her age'?" Berry asked archly.

"The dog is ten years old, Miss B. In people years, that's seventy."

"You mean she'll just stay here until ... until she ..." Berry stared at the dog, which had yet to look at her.

"I wouldn't be surprised if she dies of a broken heart," Grant told them. "She hasn't eaten anything since she was dropped off. Frankly, I don't expect her to last too long."

"Oh, dear," Berry said softly. She bent down as far as her knees permitted. "Ally, you say her name is?"

At the sound of her name, the dog locked eyes with Berry, but her head never moved.

"The breeder named her Allegra, but Ms. Patten always called her Ally."

"What kind of dog is she?" Berry asked.

"Golden retriever," Grant replied.

"I thought they were larger dogs."

"Ally is somewhat small for the breed."

"Aunt Berry, come look at Fleur! It means 'flower.' She's fluffy and white and little enough to fit on your lap! Come see," Cody called excitedly from farther back in the barn.

"In a minute." It took Berry a moment to right herself.

"See? Here she is!" Cody was at her side holding the leash of a small white dog with lots of fur. "Isn't she beautiful?"

"Yes, dear," Berry said, barely glancing at the ball of fluff.

"Paige is going to show me how to walk her. Come watch." Cody followed Paige outside, the little white dog racing ahead.

"Well, it looks as if you've found your dog." Dallas appeared at Berry's side. "She's everything you said you wanted. Small enough to sit on your lap and keep you company at night. A pretty white fluffy thing. Grant said she's a bichon frise, which, he tells me, means 'curly lapdog' in French."

Berry walked to the door and watched Cody run Fleur around the yard. The boy and the dog seemed well suited to each other. Both moved frenetically, round and round in circles with no sign of tiring.

"So, I guess you've made up your mind." Grant came to the doorway. "Shall we wrap her up so you can take her home?"

"Cody does seem to be having a good time," Berry murmured.

"It was love at first sight," Dallas told her.

"Yes, I suppose it was." Berry walked back to Ally's pen. "Grant, how do you suppose Fleur and Ally would get along?"

"Ally gets along with everyone. She's very laid-back."

"What do you say, Ally?" Berry said softly. "Would you like to come home with me now?"

Ally picked her head up.

"Grant, do you have a leash for her?" Berry asked.

Grant already had it in his hand, along with a cream-colored bowl that said ALLY in purple letters.

"You scoundrel, you knew all along I was going to take her." Berry smacked him lightly on the arm, and Grant laughed.

"As soon as you told me you wanted a dog, I thought of her. I tried taking her into the house, but I already have three dogs, and they just overwhelmed her. She just couldn't find a place to be alone. She's a one-person dog, Miss B. She needs someone of her own."

Berry nodded. "Well, then, she's found her someone. Hand over the leash, Grant. Let's get on with it."

"And Fleur?" he asked.

"She's Cody's dog," Berry replied. "We're taking them both."

"Are you sure, Berry?" Dallas asked.

"Absolutely, positively." Berry nodded emphatically. "Fleur looks like a darling dog, but I don't have the energy for so active a creature. She and Cody are well matched. I, on the other hand, well, I'm more of a dawdler than a racer these days. Much like Ally, I would guess." She turned back to Grant. "Is there an adoption fee?"

He nodded and gave her a figure.

"Will you take a check?"

"Of course."

Berry opened her bag and took out her checkbook.

"Berry, let me . . ." Dallas began but Berry waved her off and proceeded to write the check.

"Now, did I see on the sign that this is Page One Animal Shelter?" Berry asked.

"Animal Rescue Shelter, yes to the rest."

Berry finished writing the check and handed it to Grant. His eyebrows rose almost to his hairline.

"Miss B, this is for quite a bit more than the normal fee. For this amount, you could probably take half the shelter home with you."

"It's a fair enough number," she told him. "I have a feeling Ally alone is worth her weight in gold."

"The animals thank you for your generosity." He held up the check. "The adoption fee helps cover the cost of their food and any treatment they might need when they come to us, plus the occasional bag of treats and a new toy now and then."

Grant opened the pen and snapped the leash onto Ally's collar. Immediately the dog walked to Berry and looked up.

"Come along, Ally," Berry said. "We're going to grow old together."

Ally walked to the door with Berry and stepped outside onto the grass.

"Aunt Berry, who's that?" Cody approached her cautiously. "Why do you have that dog on that leash?"

"Because she's coming home with me. Cody, meet my

new dog, Ally." Berry patted Ally's head. "And, Ally, meet Cody's new dog, Fleur."

"Two dogs? We're getting TWO dogs?" Cody's eyes widened. Fleur and Ally sniffed each other.

"One for you, and one for me." Berry smiled.

"TWO dogs, Mommy! Aunt Berry said we could have two dogs."

"So I heard." Dallas stood off to the side, her arms crossed over her chest. "Cody, what is that all over Fleur?"

Cody looked up sheepishly. "I think maybe she walked in mud."

"I'll say she did. She's a mess." Dallas frowned.

"Hmm." Grant joined them outside. "Miss B, is that your nice clean Mercedes over there?"

Berry nodded.

"I'll bet it's got really nice leather seats."

"Lovely light gray ones," Berry replied.

Grant turned to Cody. "It would be a shame to take a muddy dog into your aunt's beautiful, clean car, don't you think? How about if you leave Fleur here so we can get her cleaned up? I'll bring her over after she's all pretty and clean again."

Cody looked uncertain. He glanced from Berry to his mother to Paige and back to Grant.

"I'll give her the bath." Paige patted Cody on the head. "I'm really good at it."

"You sure you'll bring her ...?"

"Promise." Grant walked over to Ally and ran his hand over her fur. "Actually, she could probably use a little cleaning up, too, after lying on the straw on the floor of her pen for the past few days. I'd hate to send you home with a dog that could have fleas."

"I imagine there's a groomer in town somewhere." Berry was momentarily disconcerted. There was no question that there would be no fleas in her house.

"You'd need to make an appointment, and it's late in the day." Grant took both leashes. "Leave them. We'll take care of them and we'll bring them over as soon as we're done."

"Do you offer to do this for everyone who adopts one of your dogs?" Berry asked.

"Nope." Grant grinned. "Only you, Miss B."

"Well then, how can we refuse?"

"What's a good time to drop them off?" Grant asked her.

"Anytime they're ready." Berry smiled, an idea taking hold. "Does seven work for you?"

"Sure."

"Then come at seven, you and Paige." Berry started for her car. "And plan on staying for dinner."

"That's not necessary, Miss B," Grant told her. "Paige and I can eat before we come over."

"Nonsense. Seven it is. Cody, say good-bye to Fleur and Ally and tell them you'll see them in a little while."

Berry walked to the driver's side of the sedan and looked over her shoulder. Ally was exactly what she needed in her life. She'd known it the minute she looked into the dog's eyes. Ally was meant to be hers. Sometimes we don't know what we need until it's right under our nose.

Next to the barn, Grant and Dallas appeared to be deep

170

in conversation. Berry smiled with secret satisfaction. They made such a handsome couple. They always had.

Well, Berry thought, *whether or not Dallas knows it, what she needs is a second chance at her meant-to-be.* Berry was willing to move heaven and earth if necessary to make sure she took it.

Diary ~

Well, I suppose wonders will never cease to happen around here! Berry tells me that not only has Dallas decided to stay in St. Dennis for the rest of the summer (which has Berry dancing on air!). And now I'm hearing that Berry has taken in not one, but TWO dogs! Yes, I said DOGS! Can you imagine dogs running amok in that house, with all those antiques and ancient Persian rugs? Of course, it all makes sense only when one considers that the dogs came from the animal rescue that Grant Wyler runs. The intent, so I understand, was to get a dog for Cody, one that Berry perhaps might keep after the boy goes home, but she left the shelter with an old dog who'd been abandoned by the family of its late owner as well. Who'd have guessed that the old girl—Berry, not the dog—would be such a sucker for a sad tale?

I wouldn't have known any of this had I not been passing by Petals and Posies at the exact moment that Grant was coming out with an armful of dahlias, which he said were for Berry, who'd invited him and Paige for dinner that very evening because he offered to bring the dogs to her. Of course, he said he'd offered to drop off the dogs because they'd gotten muddy or some such thing, but goodness, he's telling this to me with a straight face as if I don't know the real reason he wants to pay a visit to the house on River Road! Ha! As if I don't know why Berry issued the dinner invitation in the first place! This is a situation that definitely bears watching!

Speaking of situations that bear watching, my dear friend Trula is coming for a long weekend next month, and I must plan some fun activities. Trula tells me there's a wedding in the

*future for someone near and dear to her, and she's lobbying to
have the whole thing—ceremony and reception—at the Inn.
Daniel is beside himself at the very thought. I reminded him
once again that if he's going to take on events of that grand
scale, he needs to hire a professional event planner. Specifically,
he should hire his sister. And once again, my counsel fell on
deaf ears. He continues to argue that if Lucy wanted to come
home, she'd do so—and I continue to argue that perhaps Lucy*
would *come home if she had something* to come home to!
*When, I'd like to know, do your children cease to drive you
mad?!*

*Perhaps it's time to prod Vanessa into looking for those
journals of Alice's once again. You'd think that having bought
Alice's old house with the contents intact, the girl would be
more curious about what's in all those trunks in the attic. Berry
says she has notes but the ink has faded over the years and she
can't read them. Sigh.*

~ Grace ~

Chapter 10

"BERRY, are you sure it was a good idea to invite Grant and Paige for dinner?" Dallas glanced back through the passenger-side mirror at the father and daughter as they disappeared into the clinic with the dogs. "And whatever possessed you to take both dogs?"

"The same dog wouldn't suit both Cody and me. He needs a playmate. I need a companion. One of us would have missed out if we'd only gotten one dog." Berry stopped the car at the end of the drive and waited until an oncoming SUV passed before proceeding onto the road. "Besides, as you pointed out once before, it would be very hard on Cody to leave behind a dog he'd become attached to when you leave to go back to California at the end of the summer."

Berry paused, then added, "Dallas, promise me that if something happened to me, you wouldn't send Ally to a shelter."

"Of course I wouldn't." Dallas turned to her aunt. "But nothing's going to happen to you anytime soon. I think you'll probably be around to watch me grow old."

"No one lives forever, dear."

"Berry, is there something you're not telling me?" A concerned Dallas studied Berry's face for a hint.

"Of course not. No need for drama, dear. But it is a proven fact that sooner or later, everyone ..." Berry looked in the rearview mirror, where Cody was hanging on every word. "Well, the old dust-to-dust thing. You know. I only brought it up because of what Grant told us about Ally's owner passing and her daughter immediately discarding her mother's dog. Her mother's *much-loved* dog."

"Maybe she was allergic," Dallas offered weakly.

"I don't care. It was inexcusable. Allergy or no, she could have made some efforts to find another home. Perhaps with the brother who lives in Maine. Or a neighbor." Berry sniffed with indignation. "My feeling is that she didn't want to be bothered. I don't expect such behavior from you."

"Why do I suddenly feel like a scolded fourth grader?" Dallas muttered.

"Sorry, dear. It just upset me, that sweet little creature being tossed aside like that. I know you'd do right by Ally. And by me."

"It's interesting to see you so worked up over this," Dallas observed. "Especially since you've never had a pet of any kind before."

"You don't need to be an animal lover to know right from wrong."

"Well, at least give the woman credit for taking Ally to a place where she'd be kept instead of ..." Dallas remembered that Cody was listening and didn't want to get into a discussion of what "put down" meant. "Well, you know. Or for not just opening the door and letting the dog run off."

"Dallas, you always amaze me." Berry chuckled. "You always seem to come up with some means of making crass people look not so bad."

"Dad always said to look for the best in people. That everyone had some redeeming feature and it was our job to look for it, even when it seemed futile." Dallas smiled. "Especially when it seemed futile, because those were the people who needed our kind thoughts the most."

"You do know where your father got that from, don't you?"

"Where?"

"From my grandmother Priestly. She beat it into all of us at a young age. She always said she never met anyone who didn't have a soul, and we needed to find the best in them." Berry glanced over at Dallas. "Of course, Grandmother Priestly never worked in Hollywood."

The car made a right turn into a parking lot, where Berry eased into a spot under the canopy of a magnolia tree.

"I'm going to pop into the market to pick up a few things for dinner," Berry said. "Why don't you and Cody run across the street to that pet shop and pick up some dog supplies. Food and toys and whatever else dogs like."

"Good idea." Dallas unfastened her seat belt and opened her car door. "What do you think, Cody?"

Cody nodded vigorously. "I think Fleur would like some toys to play with." He unstrapped his belt and hopped out after his mother opened his door for him.

"Berry, you never did answer me about inviting Grant and Paige for dinner tonight."

"What was the question again?" Berry paused on her way to the market.

"I asked if you were sure it was a good idea to invite them. It's five forty-five already and I'll bet you ten bucks that you don't even know what you're going to serve." Dallas stood on the sidewalk, one hand on Cody's shoulder to hold him back from rushing across the street to the pet shop.

"If I hadn't thought it was a good idea, I wouldn't have invited them. I can tell time, so I am aware of the hour. And you owe me ten dollars. Anything else?" Berry stood poised impatiently, about to enter the market.

"I guess not." Dallas bit her bottom lip to keep from smiling.

"Good." Berry proceeded to nab one of the small shopping carts and went through the automatic door.

The rush-hour traffic had mostly cleared out, but there were still some fast-moving cars on Charles Street, so Dallas took Cody's hand as they crossed to the other side. The shop was two doors down. The front window displayed sundresses, bathing suits, and sleeveless T-shirts with KILLER or SECURITY in black block letters.

"Mommy, I think Aunt Berry was wrong." Cody tugged at her arm. He pressed his face to the glass. "I think this is a store for kids."

Dallas took a step back to check the name of the shop. The sign over the window assured her that yes, this was in fact the right place. A smaller sign urged you to come in and ACCESSORIZE YOUR PET!

"Furry kids." Dallas pointed to the sign overhead.

BOWWOWS AND MEOWS—ACCESSORIES FOR LES CHIENS AND LES CHATS.

Cody screwed up his face and asked, "What does that say?"

"It's the name of the store—Bowwows and Meows. *Les chiens* means 'the dogs,' and *les chats* means 'the cats' in French. It says they sell accessories for dogs and cats." She pointed into the window. "See? There are some cute leashes and collars over on the side of the window display."

"Why do dogs need bathing suits?" He was riveted to the spot, staring.

"They don't, sweetie. And they don't really need sundresses or T-shirts, either."

"Jack in my school? His mom came to pick him up one day and she had her dog in the car and the dog had on a dress." Cody turned and looked up at her. "Fleur and Ally don't wear dresses, do they?"

She shook her head. "And they're not going to. Let's go inside to see what things they do have that our new dogs might like."

"Toys, I think." He followed her to the door and went on in when she opened it. "And a bowl for food and a bowl for water."

He went immediately to the rack of collars and leashes and ran his hands over a stream of leashes that were hanging from a wall unit. He held out a bright orange one. "This would be good for Fleur."

"It's certainly bright." Dallas almost had to back away from the horrendous neon shade.

"I like it. I think it would be pretty on Fleur."

"Maybe this green would be better." She held an alternative between her thumb and index finger, but Cody shook his head.

"I like the orange one."

Dallas shrugged. It was his dog. If he wanted Fleur to wear orange, orange it would be.

"And we need one for Ally, too," he reminded her.

"Perhaps something a little more subdued for Ally." *Something that won't give Aunt Berry a headache.* "This red one would be very pretty on Ally, don't you think?"

Cody shook his head. "Aunt Berry's favorite color is purple." He grabbed the purple leash and matching collar. "She would like this one best for Ally."

"Oh, good call. Ally gets the purple." Dallas held up the different sizes and tried to determine which would be best for each dog.

"May I help you?" A woman appeared from behind the counter and began to artfully arrange a stack of canine T-shirts on a round table.

"We're getting a new dog," Cody announced importantly. *"Two* new dogs."

"Well, isn't that wonderful." The woman looked over her shoulder. "What kind of dogs are you getting?"

"A small and white and fluffy for me," he told her, "and a golden one for Aunt Berry. We are rescuing them."

The woman looked over Cody's head to Dallas, then took a second look. "You're Dallas MacGregor."

"Yes." Dallas nodded.

"We heard you were in St. Dennis for a visit." She put down the stack of shirts.

Before Dallas could ask who the "we" might be, the

back door of the shop opened and a boy around Cody's age came in.

"Gramma," he called, "I'm here."

The woman smiled. "I'm out front with a customer, Logan."

Cody peered around the woman, then grabbed his mother's arm and pointed to the boy excitedly. But before Cody could speak, the boy was almost to the front of the store.

"Hey," he called, a big grin spreading across his face. "Cody!"

"Hey, Logan." Cody took off to meet the boy halfway up the aisle.

"Did you see the fishes in the tank?" Logan pointed to a huge fish tank.

"We're buying a leash for our new dogs," Cody told him with equal exuberance as his friend pulled him over to the fish tank. "And a collar and toys, too."

"You got a dog?" Logan looked envious.

"Well, we're getting it—them—tonight. We're getting two!" Cody held up two fingers.

"Lucky duck!" Logan was wide-eyed. "My mom won't let me have a dog because she's allergic."

"You can come to my Aunt Berry's house and play with my dog," Cody offered. "Mommy, Logan can come and play after library tomorrow, can't he?"

Dallas opened her mouth to say something appropriate, like, *As long as Aunt Berry doesn't mind*, when Berry came through the door.

The two boys ran off to the fish tank, and Logan began to point out the different kinds of fish to Cody.

"Dallas, I have fish in the car so we can't dilly-dally," Berry said. She smiled absently at the woman next to Dallas, then smiled with more warmth and said, "Why, Hannah, is that you? For heaven's sake, how long has it been?"

"Five years," the woman replied, and reached for Berry's hand. "It's good to see you, Berry."

"And good to see you, too, Hannah. I was so sorry to hear about Dave . . ."

Dallas's attention drifted to the water and food bowls on a nearby shelf.

"Thank you, Berry. It's been a hard year for all of us."

"Did I hear you'd moved to South Carolina?"

The woman named Hannah nodded. "We turned the farm over to our son when Dave decided to retire. We bought a place in Myrtle Beach and no sooner were we settled in when Dave had that first heart attack."

Berry reached a hand to her. "I do recall hearing about his heart attack. I'm so sorry, Hannah."

Dallas began to sort through the bowls. Maybe the pink one that said PRINCESS in fancy script for Fleur? *Should we worry about the bowl clashing with the collar?*

"Thank you. For years he was fine. Then he had the second one, and, well, that's all she wrote. Sometimes even now it's hard to remember that he's gone." She tucked Dallas's purchases into a bag. "I stayed in South Carolina because it was too hard to face coming back here alone. Then my daughter lost her husband in Iraq two years ago, and she was all at loose ends. She moved in with me for a time, but after a while we both agreed that it was time to come back to St. Dennis. We'd stayed away too long. Brooke had Logan, and with my son here in town, well, it just seemed like the right time to move back."

Dallas held a white bowl with black paw prints in one hand, and a green one with dog bones in the other, when her ears picked up.

Brooke?

She tried to recall if there'd been more than one Brooke in St. Dennis back in the day.

"I'm happy to see you, Hannah." Berry squeezed the woman's arm. "I'm glad you came back."

"I appreciate that. We've only been back a short time. I needed to do something, so I looked around town and found that no one had a place where you could buy fun things for your dog or cat. We'd noticed that all the dogs in the cities were wearing little coats in the winter and little T-shirts, so I thought this might fly here."

"How's that going for you?"

"Sales are brisker with the tourists for the fancy dog clothes—the 'Discover St. Dennis!' tee is especially popular—but local folk seem to like the different collars and leashes and the toys best."

Berry picked up a white tee from the table and read the front of it aloud. "'My owner went to St. Dennis and all I got was this lousy T-shirt.'" She turned to Dallas. "Dear, you might remember Hannah's daughter, Brooke Madison. I believe she was about your age."

"The name rings a bell," Dallas replied with a slow nod.

"Mommy, did you ask Aunt Berry if Logan can come over and play?" Cody was at her elbow pleading.

Berry refolded the T-shirt and turned around. "Oh, it's

Logan from the story hour." To Hannah, she said, "Logan is your grandson?"

Hannah nodded.

Berry replaced the shirt on the table. "Of course Logan is welcome. As long as his mother and grandmother approve, he can come home with us from the library tomorrow."

"That might be a nice change for him," Hannah said thoughtfully. "We're all staying at the farm. There aren't any children his age out that way, so he hasn't really had many playmates this summer. He's been going to the library story hour and to that day camp at the park every other day, but he gets rammy after he's been home for a few hours with no one to play with."

"Do you want to check with his mother?" Dallas came back into the conversation, her arms piled with dog bowls.

"No, I'm sure it will be fine. He's mine in the afternoons." Hannah turned to Logan. "You can stay until four thirty, all right? But when your momma comes for you, I don't want you to be arguing. If you argue, you won't be invited back. Got it?"

"Got it!" Logan and Cody jumped up and down.

"You're still in the same house on River Road?" Hannah asked.

Berry nodded. "We'll have him ready at four thirty."

While Hannah gave Logan last-minute instructions— *listen to Ms. Eberle and Ms. MacGregor, behave, mind your manners, don't be a pest*—Dallas reflected on the irony. The one friend Cody had made in St. Dennis was the son of her old nemesis, Brooke Madison. *Ain't that a kick in the pants?* she mused.

Dallas wasn't quite sure how Berry did it, but at seven o'clock when Grant and Paige arrived with the dogs, the table had been set, wine was chilling, and most of dinner had been prepared except for the fish. Berry had shooed Dallas from the kitchen, telling her, "I work alone, dear. Please don't try to help."

"But, Berry, I could—"

"Leave. Scoot." Berry blocked the kitchen doorway.

For a moment, Dallas had visions of Berry coming after her with a broom. "All right, but if you need any help ..."

"I won't. Now go upstairs and put on something with a little style." Berry pointed up the back steps.

"What's wrong with what I'm wearing?" Dallas looked down at the shirt and shorts she wore. "This is nice."

"Nice, schmice. Go put on one of those darling skirts you bought at Vanessa's and one of those cute T-shirts with the rows of ruffly fabric around the neckline."

"You want me to dress up for Grant." Dallas narrowed her eyes. "You had this planned all along."

"Nonsense, dear."

"Tell me this. If Grant didn't have that shelter, would you have taken Cody to a breeder? Or to a pet shop?"

Berry shrugged innocently. "It was all just a matter of expediency, as far as I'm concerned. Or serendipity, if you prefer. Now go. Leave. I have work to do."

Dallas went up the narrow back stairwell. She stopped in Cody's room to see what he was up to.

"Where are the dog toys you picked up before we left the shop?" she asked.

"Downstairs on their new beds. The dogs might like to see their new toys right away so that they'll know they'll be staying," he explained solemnly. "I have three toys for Fleur and three toys for Ally, remember?"

"Don't be surprised if they decide they like the other's toys better, or if they want to share."

"They can share their toys," he said earnestly. "They can be best friends." He thought about that for a moment. "Best friends after me."

"I'm sure both dogs will be very happy here," Dallas assured him.

"Do you think Fleur will want to stay here when we leave?" His face clouded. "What if she wants to stay with Aunt Berry and Ally instead of coming home with us?"

"I think that Fleur will know who her special person is, and I think she'll be happy as long as she's with you."

Dallas started toward her room to change.

"Mom?" Cody sat on the foot of his bed. "Aren't we lucky that we came here this summer? This is the best time I ever had in my life."

"Better than Disney World?" she teased.

"Better than any place." He nodded solemnly. "Better than anything ever."

"Why do you suppose that is?" she asked.

"Because everything is fun here. Everything is happy."

"Everything is fun here. And I'm so very glad that you're happy." Dallas smiled at her son. "Now, why not go into your bathroom and wash up, then maybe put on a clean shirt for dinner? Paige and Dr. Wyler will be here very soon."

"Okay." He hopped off the bed and went into the bathroom. As she walked down the hall, she could hear the water running in his sink.

And he didn't even argue with me about washing up or changing his clothes, she marveled as she went into her room and closed the door. *What's next?*

She changed quickly into a short denim skirt and a simple light green tee, then took a good look at her face. She never needed much makeup, she knew that, and was grateful. She wasn't a woman to pretend not to know how beautiful she was. But she was smart enough to understand that in the long run, while it might be her looks that opened doors, life had to be about a lot more than a pretty face if it was to have any meaning at all. Unless she was doing a photo shoot, she rarely did more than the minimum. She swiped on a bit of mascara and that was all. The time she spent in the sun had given her skin color, and her lips were naturally pink. She pulled her hair back in a tail and slipped into sandals just as the front doorbell rang.

"Yay!" she heard Cody yell as he ran down the steps. Dallas held her breath, hoping he'd make it to the bottom without falling. When she was sure he had, she went downstairs to join the group in the foyer.

"Fleur might be just a little wet yet," Paige was telling Cody. "She has a lot of fur, so it takes longer to dry."

Cody was on the floor laughing, the dog madly licking his face. When Dallas reached the bottom step, she noticed Ally sitting patiently at Grant's feet, as if uncertain as to where she fit in, or how. Berry came in through the dining-room door and smiled at the scene.

"Well, there is one happy boy with one happy dog," she declared. "Dallas, we should have a camera."

"I have my phone." Paige whipped it out of her pocket

and began taking pictures of Cody and Fleur rolling around on the floor.

"Ah, aren't you just a perfect lady." Berry walked over to Ally slowly. "Just waiting your turn, are you?"

Berry reached out for the leash and Grant handed it over. Leading the dog, Berry walked to the stairwell and sat on the bottom step. The dog sat obediently at her feet.

"Cody, why don't you take Fleur outside and show her around the yard?" Berry said.

"Come on, Fleur!" He tugged on her leash. "Oh! Wait! We got new collars and new leashes for them." He raced into the kitchen, the white dog merrily keeping up. "Mom, can you help me get the new collar on her?"

"I'll do it." Paige followed Cody.

"Well, Grant, I'd say you're two for two here." Berry's hand rested on Ally's head, her fingers scratching behind the dog's ears.

"I'm glad you're pleased, Miss B." He leaned against one of the columns that stood between the living room and the entry hall.

"She is exactly what I wanted," Berry told him. "She'll be a fine companion for me." She looked at Dallas. "Why, I might not miss you very much at all after you leave."

Dallas laughed. "Replaced so easily, and by a dog. My ego is shattered."

"Hardly, dear. And Ally isn't just any dog." At the sound of her name, Ally looked up into Berry's eyes. "No, you're a special girl, aren't you?" The dog turned her head and licked Berry's wrist. Berry smiled. "Dallas, why not take Grant out onto the back porch and pour him a glass of wine? Ally and I will be along in a moment."

"Sure." Dallas turned to Grant. "This way . . ."

She could feel him close behind her as they went through the house to the back porch, not too close, just enough that she knew he was there. She fought back against the memories his proximity stirred up.

"I really appreciate you taking such good care of Berry," she said when they reached the porch. "I know you went above and beyond for her."

"It was my pleasure."

She reached for a bottle of wine and stopped. Looking up at him, she asked, "Red or white?"

"Either. Whatever you're having."

She picked up the corkscrew and started to work on opening the bottle.

"Want me to . . ." He offered to help.

"I've got it, but thanks." *Odd that as close as Grant and I were, I don't know what he drinks except for beer. At least, he used to drink beer. That's about all we could get our hands on back then.*

". . . so I'm really pleased it worked out this way. Win-win, right?" he was saying.

"What? Oh, yes. Win-win. Definitely." She had no idea what she'd just agreed to.

"So how do you feel about it?" He leaned back against the porch rail.

"How do I feel about what?"

Grant laughed, and she knew her cover was blown. "You never were all that skilled at pretending, you know."

She felt her face redden.

"Sorry. I just—"

"No explanations necessary. I was thinking the same thing."

"What same thing?" She poured wine into each of their glasses.

"How strange it is to be here, at your old house, together." He pointed to the lawn, where Cody was tossing a ball to Fleur and Paige was trying to teach the dog to return the ball. "With our children in the yard. That is, your son, my daughter." He took a sip of wine. "Not quite what either of us had planned way back then, but it's the way it is." There was a burst of laughter from the kids and he looked back over his shoulder at the two of them. "Not that either of us would trade what we have for what we might have had." He turned back to Dallas. "I wouldn't change a thing if it meant not having Paige. I suspect you feel the same way about Cody."

She nodded. "His father is one colossal creep, but Cody is the sweetest boy you could imagine. He's everything to me." She took a sip of wine. "But actually, what I was thinking was that I didn't know what you liked to drink, except beer. Assuming you still drink beer."

"I do." He paused. "The reason why you don't know is because you gave me the boot before we were old enough to legally drink."

"I didn't give you the boot."

"Of course you did." He reached out and touched her arm. "It's okay, Dallas."

"It's not okay," she argued, annoyed that he'd brought it up. "You make it sound as if I just dumped you for no reason at all."

"Oh, I'm sure you had your reasons for dumping me."

"No. I mean, no, I didn't dump you, okay? So stop saying that I did. It didn't happen that way."

"That's how I remember it. Maybe your recollection is different, but I remember that last summer, visiting you at your house in New Jersey, and spending every day at your play rehearsal. Most of the nights, too, since Romeo insisted on practicing every waking minute."

"You knew I was going to be in that play. You knew I was having rehearsals that week and that my schedule was going to be tight. If it bothered you, why didn't you wait until the end of the summer?"

"Because I had a job and that was the only week I was allowed to take off. Besides, you said you'd be back in St. Dennis at the end of the summer."

"When I left at the beginning of the summer, I thought I was coming back. I didn't know my mother had made other plans."

"So if I hadn't come that week, we wouldn't have seen each other at all." He stared at her for a long moment, then laughed self-consciously. "I can't believe we're arguing about something that happened twenty years ago."

"You're right." She nodded. "Whatever happened back then, it's in the past. Let's not go back there now. As a matter of fact, maybe we should just start over."

Grant placed his glass on the table and extended his right hand, and she took it. "Grant Wyler."

"Dallas MacGregor. It's nice to meet you."

"Want to have dinner with me on Friday night?"

She laughed out loud. "Well, you certainly don't waste any time, do you?"

The back door opened and Berry came out onto the porch, Ally off her leash and following behind cautiously.

"It looks like a party out here," Berry said. "I'm in the mood for a party, too. Dallas, would you pour me a glass of wine?"

"I have it, Miss B." Grant lifted a glass, filled it, and handed it over.

Berry took an appreciable sip. "Lovely."

"How are you and Ally getting along, Berry?"

"Famously." Berry glanced down at the dog. "She's a real love. Grant, you outsmarted me, but I cannot thank you enough. She's just perfect."

"You're welcome. I can't thank you enough for giving her a good home. She deserves better than she'd gotten this past week."

"Indeed she does." Berry took another sip of wine, then put down her glass. "I need to get dinner on the table or we'll be eating in the dark. Dallas, would you give me a hand?"

"Sure."

"I can help, too," Grant told her.

"You can help by taking Ally for a little walk around the yard." Berry opened the back door, then paused. "I'm thinking of having the entire front fenced, Grant. What do you think?"

"You afraid the dogs will take off?" He stood at the top of the stairs. Behind him the sun was dipping into the water, fingers of light reaching as far as where he stood. It looked like a magic trick, one intended to highlight the man and nothing else. Dallas couldn't look away.

"I'd like to protect them if I could. I know there are

those who like those electric fences, but I'm not keen on them. If the power goes out—and God knows any good storm can knock out all of St. Dennis on any given day—then the boundary is gone. Plus, it doesn't stop other dogs or wildlife from coming into your yard and possibly attacking your pet," she said thoughtfully. "Suppose Fleur and Ally were in the yard, and some big vicious dog came in after them. Why, they couldn't even flee the yard."

"Well, you're right about that. It keeps your dogs in but nothing out. So if that's a concern of yours, a physical fence is probably what you want."

"Any thoughts on who I might call to put one up for me?" Berry asked.

"I'll ask around. I'll find someone for you," he promised.

"Thank you. Now, Dallas, let's get on with it." Berry went into the house, then popped her head back out. "You should probably tell the children that it's time for them to come in and wash their hands."

"I'm on it." Grant went down the steps, then called Ally to follow. The dog did so, though she appeared to be somewhat reluctant.

"She's already your dog," Dallas observed when she went into the kitchen. "She didn't really want to go with Grant."

"I hope she doesn't think he's taking her back to the shelter." Berry appeared concerned. "She can't possibly understand what's going on."

"I think she understands that she's yours now." Dallas picked up the covered serving bowls containing the green beans and the salad and took them outside to place on the table. In the side yard, the kids were showing something to Grant. *In another lifetime, they could have been our children*, she thought before reminding herself that she and Grant had been kids themselves back then. She forced herself to look away from Cody and Paige, who were heading toward the house, Fleur bouncing up and down between them.

"If we have time later, we'll get it out and I'll teach you how to play, okay?" Paige was telling Cody as they came up the steps.

"We have a croquet thing, right, Mom? In there?" Cody pointed across the yard to the carriage house.

"There used to be one," Dallas replied. "I don't know if it's still around."

"It's there." He nodded. "I saw it in a box and asked Aunt Berry what it was and she said a croquet thing."

"Then I guess it's still there. Did you want to play?"

His head bobbed up and down as he opened the back door. "I don't know how, but Paige said she'd teach me." He looked over his shoulder at Paige with utter adoration.

Paige ruffled his hair with obvious fondness and followed him into the kitchen, the white dog still trailing after.

Berry opened the screened door and passed out another serving dish.

Dallas peeked under the cover. "Oh, yum. Brown rice. My favorite."

"It's very healthy," Berry sniffed.

"I know." Dallas grinned. "I wasn't being sarcastic."

"Lucky for you."

Dallas moved a plate slightly to make room for the new dish. "Anything else?"

"No, thank you. I have biscuits but I'm saving them for Cody. He said he'd like to bring something out once he and Paige are cleaned up." Berry looked out across the lawn to the dock. "But you could walk down and get Grant after you take the salad out. The fish is almost ready and I'd like to enjoy it while it's still warm."

Dallas nodded and walked to the river then onto the pier. "Grant," she called to him. "Berry's ready to serve dinner."

"Oh, thanks." He turned away from the water with a half smile on his face. "I was just thinking about the night we took Wade's boat and we—"

"Don't." She held up a hand. "Don't go there. We agreed that we were wiping the slate. That goes for the good times as well as the times that maybe weren't so good."

He nodded slowly but didn't say anything until they were almost to the back steps, Ally at his heels wagging her tail.

"You know, we can pretend that certain things never happened if you want to, but the truth is that what was between us back then was very special. Some things just become a part of you, and no matter what you say, or what you do, they're always going to be there. I'll play along with you because pretending that we have no history together seems to make you feel better somehow, but don't think for a minute that I don't remember." He paused and looked down into her eyes. "I suspect that in spite of your wanting to 'wipe the slate clean,' you remember, too."

He held her gaze for a longer moment than she'd have liked.

"I didn't say I didn't remember," she told him pointedly. "What I'd said was, whatever happened back then was in the past. And the past, as you know, can't be changed."

She might have said more, but Ally ran past them to the top of the stairs, where Berry stood.

"Dinner, dears . . ."

Chapter 11

IF Berry had heard the conversation, she gave no sign. Except, Dallas thought, there might have been just the tiniest bit of subtle satisfaction in her smile when she called them to the table. But all in all, dinner had gone as well as it could have. Cody was so clearly smitten with Paige, he copied everything she did, from the way she held her fork to the way she used her napkin. It was the first time Dallas had seen her son mimic an older child's actions. At least he'd found someone with good manners to emulate, she mused.

Dinner had barely begun when they made the discovery that Fleur was evidently accustomed to being fed from the table, as she begged unmercifully. Berry and Dallas agreed that she'd have to be broken of that, and forbade Cody to slip the little scamp so much as a taste of fish. Ally, on the other hand, continued to exhibit impeccable manners—much to Berry's delight—by curling up next to Berry's chair and remaining there throughout dinner. No begging, no whining. No bad behavior.

"I can't say it often enough, Grant," Berry told him when he and Paige were leaving. "I couldn't be happier with Ally."

"I'm glad it worked out for everyone and that you're happy," he replied.

"Outrageously so," she assured him.

"Me, too," Cody told him. "I love Fleur."

Berry glanced down at the white dog, then looked a little closer.

"What is that around her neck?"

"That's the new collar we bought her today," Cody explained. "Paige is taking the black one back to the shelter and the leash, too, so she can use it for another dog." He knelt down and snapped the new leash on Fleur. "See? She likes it."

"Yes, well, not everyone can wear that shade," Berry murmured. "It's rather . . . well, striking."

"And see? We got purple for Ally, 'cause purple is your favorite color." He shook the contents of the bag onto the floor and proudly held up Ally's new purple accessories.

"Lovely," Berry told him. "It's actually more of a shrieking violet, though, wouldn't you say?"

"I thought the expression was *shrinking* violet." Dallas picked up the new leash and collar and handed them to Berry.

Berry held up the leash. "Shriek or shrink?"

"I see your point." Dallas nodded.

Grant laughed and put his arm around his daughter. "Thanks again for a great dinner, Miss B. We had a great time, didn't we, Paige."

"It was fun." Paige leaned over and tapped Cody on the tip of his nose. "Next time you get the croquet set out and I'll teach you how to play."

197

"Okay." Cody was content with the promise.

"I'll get back to you about the fence," Grant said over his shoulder as he and Paige walked to his Jeep that was parked next to Dallas's rented car.

"Thank you, dear." Berry went onto the porch, Ally at her heels.

"Dallas, I'll be seeing you," Grant called to her just before he got into the car.

"Most likely." She did her best to appear nonchalant, though she was anything but.

"Well, that was lovely, don't you think, dear?" Berry said after waving good-bye to the departing car and coming back into the house. "Grant is still ... well, he's Grant, what more can I say?" She laughed. "And his daughter is delightful."

"Paige is a very sweet girl, yes." Berry had already made it obvious how she felt about Grant and Dallas wasn't going to take the bait. "Dinner was very nice. Someday you'll let me in on the secret of pulling together a meal like that in little more than an hour."

"Easy-peasey, as they say. You call your market and tell them what you want, and they have it ready for you when you pop in to pick it up."

"When did you call the market?"

"While you and Grant were chatting after we left the barn. I went straight to the car, my cell phone in hand. Speed-dialed Jaime at the market, asked what kind of fish was fresh today and what salads he had already made up. His wife makes them all from scratch, you know."

"You amaze me." Dallas shook her head.

"It's my idea of fast food. Now, where did Cody go? It's

time for us to take our dogs out for one last spin around the yard before we all turn in for the night. Would you like to join us?"

"Thanks, but I want to make sure everything's in from the back porch and get the dishes into the dishwasher."

"I appreciate that. I am a bit tired," Berry admitted. "It's been a big day, hasn't it, Ally. Now, let's go find Cody and Fleur and take a little walk together."

Dallas finished loading the dishwasher and turned it on just as Berry and Cody came into the house with their new best friends.

"Mom, I don't think Fleur wants to sleep downstairs on her dog bed," Cody told Dallas.

"Where do you think she wants to sleep?"

"I think she wants to sleep in my room," he said earnestly.

"I think you might be right. Take the dog bed upstairs and put it next to your bed."

He ran from the room, the little dog at his side, pausing to pick up the dog's bed from the hall where he'd left it.

"He is one happy little boy tonight," Berry observed.

"He told me he was happier than he's ever been anywhere. Including Disney World."

"My, that *is* happy." Berry smiled. "Thank you for telling me. That warms my heart. I want nothing more at this stage of my life than for the people I love the most to be happy." She frowned. "Which reminds me. Have you spoken with your brother this week?"

"No. I called him and left a message but he hasn't called back."

"So did I. I wonder what he's up to these days."

"We'll track him down, don't you worry." Dallas kissed Berry on the cheek. "You and Ally go on up to bed. I think I'd like to work for a little bit. I'll close up when I'm finished."

"All right. I'll see you in the morning." Berry bent over and unhooked Ally's leash. "Come along, pup, and I'll show you to our room."

Dallas had just finished in the kitchen, locked the back door, and turned off the lights, when her phone rang.

"Hey, Norma," she said after a glance at caller ID. "What's up?"

"What's up is your divorce. I called Emilio's attorney last night and offered him the deal we discussed. I told him that I'd heavily lobbied against it but that it was your idea and you insisted, and that there was a twenty-four-hour window before the offer went away forever." Norma paused, and Dallas knew she was sneaking a drag from a cigarette that she'd supposedly given up last month. "Because if his client is too stupid to see a once-in-a-life-time opportunity to make a killing in real estate, then he didn't deserve it. Ted—that's Emilio's lawyer—couldn't hang up fast enough. Long story short, he flew to Arizona and talked to Emilio, who apparently isn't as dumb as I thought he was—at least where real estate is concerned. Ted called me from the rehab center and told me to draw up the papers, which I'm doing now. I'll get them to him by messenger in the morning, and I told him I wanted them signed and back in my hands by four tomorrow afternoon because I already told the judge that we were not asking for a continuance of the upcoming hearing."

"What happens then?"

"Then I make my case to the court to have the divorce finalized, Ted agrees on the record to all the terms including the child custody arrangement that you wanted." Another covert drag on the cigarette. Dallas was tempted to tell Norma that she wasn't fooling anyone but decided to let it go. "Knowing this judge and given the package we're bringing is nice and neat, I think it's almost a done deal. The property division was the only obstacle, and you removed that with one swift blow."

"And that's it? We're divorced?"

"I left out a few steps for the sake of brevity, but yes. You'll be footloose and fancy-free." Norma chuckled. "Oh, to be single and gorgeous in Hollywood."

"You *are* single and gorgeous in Hollywood," Dallas reminded her.

"But 'lawyer' just doesn't have the same cachet as 'famous Hollywood superstar.'"

"You do just fine." Dallas smiled. Norma did better than fine. "This is fabulous news. I can't thank you enough for pushing this for me."

"It's why you pay me the big bucks, girl."

"You earn it." Dallas could hardly belive that this ordeal was actually going to come to an end. Other than Cody's visitation with his father, Dallas's dealings with Emilio were going to be limited. "By the way, were you able to get in touch with Victoria Seymour or her agent?"

"Did we not only discuss that project last night?"

"Yes, but did you call—"

"Yes, I called her literary agent, whom she thanked in

the acknowledgments, so it was easy to track her down. The agent is on vacation until next week."

"Did you ask for a number where she can be reached?"

"I asked that she call me as soon as she receives my message, that it's a matter of great importance to her and to her client. She'll call me back or I'll track her down next week. Not to worry. I'm on it, Dallas." Norma paused. "I don't remember you ever being this impatient over anything. Not even your divorce."

"I'm just really excited about the possibilities." Dallas realized she'd been biting a nail, something she hadn't done since she was a child.

"I can see that you are. I started reading it again last night, and completely see the movie in this novel. But I do think you'd make a perfect Charlotte."

"I'm not thinking about starring in it. I'd like to try my hand at directing. I can just see this story unfold on-screen and I want to be the one to do it."

"I will do my best to see that that happens."

"I know you will, Norma. Thanks."

"Don't thank me yet. Wait till we get the rights."

"I have faith in you."

Dallas hung up and realized she was still standing in the darkened kitchen. She closed up the rest of the house, then went upstairs to tuck Cody in. She found him already in bed, under the covers, his head on the pillow—next to Fleur's.

"Sweetie, I don't know that you want her to sleep on your pillow with you."

He nodded vigorously. "I do. And she wants to. See? She's smiling."

"I think she might get too warm under the blanket. She is wearing a fur coat, you know."

Cody shook his head. "She's not too warm. She's just right. I just want to hug her for a while. She's my dog. My very own dog."

"Well, that she is." Dallas sat on the side of the bed and patted the dog's head. "We'll compromise. She can stay there for tonight, because Paige gave her a bath today and she's all nice and clean, but maybe tomorrow night she should try her dog bed."

"If she wants to." Cody snuggled the dog that was clearly eating up the attention.

"How 'bout a story?" Dallas asked.

"The one about Clifford." Cody yawned.

"Clifford?"

"The Big Red Dog. I got to take it out of the library. They let me have my own library card cause I'm gonna be here all summer." His eyes were all but closed. "It's yellow and it says 'Cody Blair' on it."

Dallas looked on the corner of the dresser where a stack of books sat. She found the requested title, but by the time she walked back to the bed, Cody was asleep.

"Big day, indeed," she whispered. "For both of you, I suspect." Fleur's eyes were open and she watched Dallas approach the bed. "That's right, girl. You keep an eye on him. It's going to be your job from now on."

Dallas kissed her son and turned out the light. She left the door partly open in case the dog wanted to roam during the night. She quietly went back downstairs to the library where she sat for a few minutes in her great-grandfather's leather chair and rested her feet on the matching ottoman. The chair's arms were worn in places, maybe those spots where he'd rested his elbows. She imagined him sitting there, his pipe resting in the green glass ashtray that still sat on the square table on the right side. A floor lamp with a silk shade stood behind and to the left of the chair, and she could easily see where a man—or a woman—might relax here at the end of the day with a good book. She'd never met her grandfather, but she'd seen photographs of him, and of course, his portrait hung in the front hall.

She studied the row of bookshelves that ran along the one wall, and got up to take a closer look. On one shelf, several leather-bound albums were stacked and she brought them back to the chair. She was feeling nostalgic and hoped to find some pictures of her father that she might not have seen before, but this particular album was all Berry. Berry in costume, publicity shots from the studio she worked for on that particular film. Berry on the arms of just about every major Hollywood heartthrob of her generation—and a few who came after, Dallas noticed with a smile. She turned page after page, noting, not for the first time, that Berry had been stunning in her youth.

"And right through middle age," she murmured aloud.

She was almost to the end of the album when she came across a loose photo of Berry with a man Dallas didn't recognize. He was tall and blond and extremely handsome, though he didn't have that Hollywood look about him. In all the other pictures, Berry looked very glamorous, her escorts equally so. But in this one, she was dressed casually with not a jewel in sight, her hair loose and soft. This one wasn't taken at a high-powered event or party. She held the photo under the light. Was the background familiar? And the look on Berry's face—just slightly dreamy—as she looked into the eyes of the man wasn't something Dallas had seen ever before. She held on to the photo while she replaced the album on the shelf. Leaving the picture on the desk, she made a mental note to ask Berry about the man tomorrow.

She turned on her laptop and tried to work on the notes she'd started to make on the next scene of *Pretty Maids* and hoped that she wasn't jinxing herself by being premature in writing the screenplay, but she couldn't help herself. The story had wound its way into her head and she knew she wasn't going to be satisfied until she had finished, and she had a long way to go. But she hadn't worked for more than ten minutes before she realized she wasn't going to accomplish much that night.

Instead of the characters' words, it was Grant's that kept coming back to her.

The truth is that what was between us back then was very special. Some things just become a part of you, and no matter what you say, or what you do, they're always going to be there.

Of course, Grant was right. That whole time with him, that part of her life, had been special. It had been a time of exploration and innocence, of learning the rules of love and learning to respect them, of offering her heart for the first time and having it taken and cherished. Grant had been the perfect first love, because he'd loved her whole-heartedly in return. She'd never looked back on that time in her life with regret because there'd been nothing to be sorry about. At least until today, when she realized how much pain she'd caused him when the relationship came to an end. She'd never thought of it as her having dumped him, but clearly, he did. She didn't know how, all these years later, to apologize, how to make him understand that she'd seen the end as something mutual, as they both moved on to college, she to Rutgers, he to UNC.

The following summers were hectic, a combination of work and summer theater and little time for dating or trips to the Eastern Shore. Even Berry had had a busy few years. She'd had to hire a middle-aged cousin to serve as house sitter while she flew back and forth between the coasts during a temporary resurgence of her career because Wade was too young to stay alone and too old for a babysitter. It had been unthinkable to Wade or Berry that he skip St. Dennis and stay in New Jersey those years. To find out now, all these years later, that Grant had believed that she'd simply abandoned him and never looked back caused her heart to hurt. Knowing that he'd harbored those feelings all these years only made it worse.

Her concentration broken, Dallas checked the front door to make sure it was locked, then made her way upstairs.

"I'm taking Cody to story hour, dear," Berry announced after she'd opened the door and peered into the library, where Dallas was busy working on her laptop. "Don't forget that Cody is bringing Logan home with him. I'll give them lunch, but later I do have an appointment for a trim." She raised a hand to the nape of her neck. "I'm feeling a bit shaggy right about now. Oh, and we've taken both dogs out, so they should be fine until we come back."

"Thanks for the heads-up. Oh, Berry, wait. Before you leave." Dallas held up the photo of Berry and the tall, handsome blond man she'd found the night before. "Who is this?"

Berry crossed the room and took a long look at the picture.

"Where did you find this?" she asked softly.

"It was loose in one of the albums I was looking at last night," Dallas told her. "But who is that?"

"Why, it's me, dear."

"Really, Berry? I didn't recognize you." Dallas rolled her eyes. "I meant the man. Who is he?"

"Just someone I used to know," Berry replied blithely.

"Someone you knew from Hollywood? 'Cause he doesn't look Hollywood to me."

"No, dear. I mean, no, I didn't know him from Hollywood, and yes, he doesn't look Hollywood at all." Berry smiled. "Must run. Cody's in the car . . ."

Dallas picked up the photo and studied it after Berry closed the door behind her. Clearly, the photo captured two people who were deeply in love. But who was he, and why was Berry being so evasive?

Dallas stood the picture up against the small pile of Post-its and memo pads. One way or another, she was going to find out who Berry's mystery man was.

Chapter 12

DALLAS heard Berry and the boys come into the house, and had all intentions of going to the kitchen to say hello, but wanted to finish one last sentence. That one sentence became another, which led to yet another, and before she knew it, Berry was at the door.

"I'm leaving to get my hair done," Berry told her. "The boys have been fed and they'd like to crab from the dock, but I told them they had to wait for you. I don't think they're quite old enough to be playing that close to the river without an adult close by." She paused. "Of course, they're not playing, they're crabbing."

"I'll come now. Thanks for feeding them. I meant to come out, but I guess I got carried away with what I'm doing." Dallas stood and stretched. She hadn't realized how stiff she was from sitting all morning in one position.

"Well, I'm sure the screenplay will sparkle." Berry went into the front hall. "Oh," she called back to Dallas, "anything under five inches must be thrown back."

"What?" Dallas frowned as she made her way from the library.

"The crabs, dear. They have to be at least five inches across the top of the shell, or they're not legal to take. Cody knows."

"I'll keep an eye on them," Dallas assured her as Berry went out the front door and shut it behind her.

Ally stood in front of the closed door and listened to Berry's echoing footsteps.

"She'll be back," Dallas told the dog. "Now come on outside and sit with me, why don't you?"

The dog ran to one of the living-room windows and looked out from a perch on an antique settee.

"Down, Ally. Berry loves you, but I don't think she'd be happy to see you sitting where many generations of the family once sat."

One last look out the window and Ally was at Dallas's side.

"Good girl." There was a package of dog treats on the kitchen table and Dallas swiped one as she passed and gave it to Ally. After grabbing a cold bottle of water from the fridge, she and the dog went outside.

"Hey, guys!" Dallas called to the boys, who were patiently sitting on the lawn waiting for her. Fleur was chasing a yellow ball and brought it back to Cody, who gave it another toss.

"Can we crab now?" Cody asked.

"Yes, you may." Dallas moved one of the Adirondack chairs under the tree and sat, Ally in the shade nearby, to watch the boys, who were busy on the dock with lengths of string and two buckets, one large, one small.

"What are you using for bait?" she called.

"Chicken necks," Cody called back, his tone of voice letting her know that that had been a stupid question.

Fleur sat beside Cody on the dock for a while, then joined Ally on the grass under the tree, apparently having decided that the direct sun might be acceptable to small humans, but it was too much for her.

Dallas was called to the end of the dock several times by Cody and by Logan to check the size of the crabs. So far, only three had been judged big enough to keep, and those only marginally. The boys kept water and some eelgrass in the larger bucket, and after almost an hour, with the same three crabs, the decision was made to let the crabs go. Together the two boys carried the bucket to the river's edge and turned it on its side to allow the crabs to scamper off into the water.

"So you're practicing catch and release, I see," Dallas observed.

"No." Cody shook his head. "We let them go because there were only three of them."

"But we caught them and then we released them," Logan pointed out. "Like when you fish and you catch a fish that you shouldn't eat 'cause they're 'dangered and you let them go."

"What's 'dangered?" Cody asked.

"When there aren't many of them left and you catch one and eat one so there's one less," Logan explained, "that means they're 'dangered."

"*En*dangered," Dallas corrected, and Logan nodded.

Cody rolled onto the ground next to Fleur, who scootched away slowly, her way, Dallas supposed, of telling Cody it was too damned hot to be hanging on her.

"I'm hot," Cody told her. "Logan, are you hot?"

Logan flopped on the grass near Cody. "Yeah."

"We need ice cream, Mom. Can we go to Scoop?"

"Yay, Scoop! I love Scoop!" Logan chimed in.

"Sure. Why not?" Dallas picked up her water bottle. "Let's get the dogs inside and give them a cool drink, then we'll go."

The boys ran off, Fleur trailing behind, and Dallas and Ally bringing up the rear. Once the dogs were watered and settled down, Dallas left a note on the kitchen table for Berry and got the boys into her rental car.

"Why'd you leave Aunt Berry a note?" Cody asked.

"So in case she gets home before we do, she won't wonder where we are," Dallas said.

"Why don't you call her on the phone and tell her?"

"Because she might be under the dryer and wouldn't hear the phone ring."

"Under the dryer?" Cody laughed. "Aunt Berry wouldn't fit under the dryer. Not under the clothes dryer!" At which he and Logan fell into fits of laughter.

Six-year-old boys—Dallas shook her head as she drove onto River Road—could possibly be the silliest beings on the planet. The silliness continued all the way to Charles Street and down Kelly's Point and right into the parking lot across from the municipal building. The boys unhooked their seat belts and flew out of the car.

"Don't run into Scoop, you two. Walk when you get there," she called to them, but they were already to the sidewalk.

By the time Dallas got to the ice-cream shop, both boys were already at the counter and sampling the newest flavor.

"Hey, Dallas." Steffie waved as she leaned over the counter to hand another sample spoon to each of the boys.

"Hi, Steffie." Dallas closed the door behind her. "What's new today?"

"Peach melba and chocolate fudge divinity." Steffie grinned. "Which is exactly what it sounds like."

"It sounds deadly." Dallas nodded.

"Exactly." Steffie got another sample spoon of each for Dallas.

"Well, I suppose that would be my entire day's worth of fat and calories," Dallas told her after tasting both. "But so worth it. I'm going with one scoop of the peach."

"Excellent choice," Steffie agreed. "Cone or dish?"

"A dish, please." Dallas turned to the boys. "What will it be, guys?"

"Chocolate fudge . . . what Steffie said." Cody pointed to the new flavor.

"Me, too," Logan told her. "Please," he added.

"Two cones, one scoop each of the new chocolate flavor," Dallas told Steffie, who had just landed a scoop of peach melba into a bowl and handed it to Dallas.

The little bell over the door rang and Dallas turned in time to see Grace Sinclair enter.

"Well, I see I'm not the only person in St. Dennis who's craving something cold and sweet today," Grace declared.

"You should have been in here earlier," Steffie told her. "From eleven until about twenty minutes ago, we were packed."

"It's wonderful that your business is doing so well," Grace said. "How clever of you to have foreseen the need when you did."

Steffie handed the cones to the boys and Dallas stepped to the cash register with her wallet in her hand to pay for them.

"Dallas, I hear you and Berry are to be congratulated on your recent adoptions," Grace noted.

"Word does travel fast here." Dallas smiled and sat at one of the tables along the wall. "The dogs just arrived last night."

"I heard you got a couple of great dogs." Steffie joined the conversation.

"Leona Patten's dog, I heard." Grace studied the menu board. "She's a lovely dog. Just perfect for Berry."

"I guess you were both talking to Grant," Dallas said.

"No, Paige told me this morning." Steffie leaned on the counter.

"I saw Hannah Madison at Cuppachino this morning," Grace said. "Stef, would there be any of the lemon curd left somewhere? I don't see it on the menu board."

Steffie looked in the cooler. "There's enough for maybe a scoop and a half."

"I'll take what you have in there, then," Grace told her.

"Sure." Steffie grabbed a sugar cone and held it up. "Your usual, Miss Grace?"

"Yes, dear, please."

"Paige said you all had a really nice dinner together last night." Steffie scraped the ice cream out of the container and piled it onto the cone.

"Oh?" Grace turned to Dallas. "Did you have dinner with Grant last night?"

"No, no." *Better nip this in the bud*, Dallas thought, *or by this time tomorrow, it will be all over town that Grant and I are dating again.* "Paige and Grant brought the dogs over to Berry's, so she offered them dinner. It wasn't like . . . well, it was dinner, but it was a thank-you dinner. From Berry.

Grant and Paige gave the dogs baths before they brought them over."

Dallas wasn't blind to the look that passed between Steffie and Grace. The one that said, *Doth Dallas protest too much?* Even to her own ear, it sounded as if she had, but it was too late now for her to try to mitigate the impression.

"How nice of Berry." Grace paid for her ice cream and sat across the table from Dallas. The boys had taken a table of their own where they could watch the police cars coming and going from the lot in front of the municipal building just up the road.

"So how does it feel to be back in St. Dennis?" Grace asked.

"It feels fine," Dallas replied, then remembered she was speaking with not only an old friend, but the woman who owned the local newspaper. "Actually, it's great. I've never seen my son as happy as he is right now, and I'm having time to relax and enjoy a real vacation for the first time in . . . I don't remember my last real vacation. One where I wasn't studying a script or negotiating terms for a contract."

Dallas reminded herself that she was in fact doing just that, except the negotiation was for rights to a book and Norma was doing all the heavy lifting. Still, it didn't seem the same.

"How are you spending your time?" Grace dabbed a napkin on the side of her mouth.

"I've been doing a lot of reading these past two weeks." That was certainly true.

"Oh?" Grace appeared interested. "Anything in particular that you'd recommend to my readers?"

214

"*Pretty Maids* by Victoria Seymour," Dallas answered without hesitation.

"I read that over the winter. It's a wonderful story."

"Isn't it? I bought mine at Book 'Em at the beginning of the week and finished it in one day. Barbara has several more copies—or at least, she did earlier in the week. I know Berry was going to stop in to pick up a copy for herself."

"Not willing to share, eh?" Grace teased her.

Dallas hesitated. Should she tell Grace of her interest in the novel and give her some exclusive tidbit she'd be the first to know? Did Dallas really want that information out there before she could get her hands on the rights?

"If I tell you something in total confidence, Miss Grace, can I trust you not to repeat it or to use it in your paper until I give you the green light?" Dallas lowered her voice.

"Of course, dear," Grace whispered in a conspiratorial tone. "You know I'd never break my word."

"I do know that." Dallas patted the older woman on the arm. "Right now my attorney is trying to buy the film rights for *Pretty Maids*."

"For you to star in?" Grace's eyes lit up. "The part of the younger of the two women would be perfect for you."

"I want to write the screenplay and direct it, if I can get the backing."

"I don't recall hearing that you'd done this sort of thing before."

"This would be my first attempt at both," Dallas admitted. "Writing and directing."

215

"I have no doubt you'll be brilliant at both," Grace assured her. "And your secret is safe with me. But once it's official, may I disclose that I knew . . . ?"

Dallas nodded. "Once it's official, you may say you've been sitting on the story."

"Now, you did agree to let me interview you for the paper," Grace reminded her.

"Anytime, Miss Grace."

"How about one day next week? Or will you be leaving before then?"

"Actually, we're staying for the rest of the summer. So any day that's open for you is open for me."

"Really?" Grace's surprise was evident. "Until the end of the summer, you say?"

Dallas nodded.

"That's . . . why, that's wonderful," Grace said. "I'm sure your great-aunt is delighted. I'd still like to do it sooner rather than later, though, so I'll check my calendar and give you a call."

"That'll be fine." Dallas noticed that the boys were finished and getting a bit restless. "I'd better take the boys back to the house before they start getting crazy." She stood. "It's always nice to spend a little time with you, Miss Grace."

"Likewise, dear. I'll give you a call after I get back to the office," Grace said. "Berry's home number?"

"Let me give you my cell number." Dallas wrote it on a piece of paper napkin and handed it to Grace.

"Thank you." Grace tucked it into her purse.

"Come on, boys," Dallas told Cody and Logan, who jumped up, obviously more than ready to leave. "Time to head back to the house. I don't remember what time Logan's being picked up."

"Four thirty," Logan told her. "My mom's picking me up on her way back from school."

"That's Brooke's boy, isn't it?" Grace turned in her seat after the boys had gone outside.

At the doorway, ready to follow them, Dallas nodded. "He and Cody are friends from the story hour at the library."

"Were you and Brooke friends back in the day?" Grace asked.

"Not really." Dallas shrugged. "I didn't really know her."

"I thought not." Grace wore a slight frown. "You know that she lost her husband in Iraq?"

"Her mother mentioned that, yes." Dallas tossed her empty ice-cream bowl and spoon into the trash receptacle near the door.

"And that she's back here to stay now?" Grace looked Dallas in the eye and added, "She's single again."

"Well, yes. She's a widow," Dallas replied, not sure where this was going.

"I heard she's looking for a dog," Steffie said from behind the counter. "She's been spending a lot of time over at the shelter. Guess she still hasn't gotten what she's looking for." She rested her chin in her hand and added, "Whatever that might be."

"Well, then, I wish her luck." Dallas had gotten the message. "Thanks for the visit, Miss Grace. Steffie, we'll probably see you soon."

Stepping outside into the afternoon sun was like being

smacked in the face with a hot towel. She called to the boys, who had walked down toward the marina, and they came running, eager to get home and begin to play whatever game they'd cooked up while in Scoop.

"Logan, you mentioned that your mother's in school," Dallas said as they drove back to River Road.

"Uh-huh." He nodded. "At the community college. She's gonna be a veterinarian assistant."

Logan played with the window controls, sending them up and down. "So she can work with Dr. Grant."

Well, Dallas thought as she pulled into the driveway, *sounds like Brooke hasn't changed much in all these years. Still chasing after Grant.*

She'd just turned off the engine and opened the car door when Berry drove in and parked behind her. Dallas got out of her car and walked over to Berry's. The boys took off for the house to let the dogs out.

"Well, don't you look spiffy with your new do." Dallas opened Berry's door for her.

"I told the girl not quite so much hair spray, but did she listen?" Berry frowned. "Apparently not." She touched her hand to the back of her head, grumbling, "Ridiculous."

"It looks lovely, if that's any consolation." Dallas slammed the car door.

"Really?" Berry was still frowning. "You don't think I look like a tart?"

"A *tart*?" Dallas laughed out loud. "Berry, who says 'tart' these days?"

"I'm eigh . . ." Berry coughed. "A senior citizen. I can say any damned thing I please."

218

"True enough." Dallas put her arm around Berry's shoulder. "But you still look beautiful. Hair spray or no."

"Thank you, dear." Berry calmed down slightly. "How was your afternoon?"

"Fine. The boys crabbed, tossed back the three they caught, and we went for ice cream." Dallas had the house key in her hand as they approached the front door. Inside, the dogs were barking.

"What's the newest flavor?"

"Peach melba and some chocolate fudgey thing. I had the peach, the boys had the chocolate."

"Sounds yummy. I may have to make a trip down there."

"I wish I'd thought to bring you something."

"Nonsense, dear. Standing in front of Steffie's board and reading all the concoctions she's come up with is part of the whole Scoop experience."

Dallas unlocked the front door, and both dogs piled out.

"There's my good watchdog." Berry bent to greet Ally, who danced around her legs. Fleur took off for the yard and the boys, where she was greeted happily.

"Miss Grace was there," Dallas told Berry as they went inside. "We're going to do an interview for her paper one day next week."

Berry put the bag she was holding onto the hall table, then turned and closed the door behind them.

"I stopped at Book 'Em and picked up a copy of *Pretty Maids.*" She took the book from the bag and held it up. "I think I'll get a glass of iced tea and sit outside under the tree and read for a bit."

"I told Miss Grace what I was thinking about doing. With the book, that is." Dallas followed her aunt into the kitchen. "Do you think that was a mistake? I did tell her it was a confidence."

"Grace has never been one to kiss and tell." Berry went straight to the fridge and reached for the pitcher of iced tea she'd made earlier that day. "What else did she have to say?"

"Not much." Dallas thought back on the exchange between Steffie and Grace about Logan's mother. She thought she'd repeat it to see Berry's reaction. "She did mention that Logan's mother has gone back to school. She's studying to be a veterinarian's assistant."

Berry turned slowly and met Dallas's eyes. "Do tell."

Dallas nodded.

"This is the same girl who ran after Grant when you were all children, isn't she?"

"I seem to remember hearing something about that." Dallas turned her back and took glasses down from the cupboard. "I got the impression from Steffie that she still is." She started to pour tea into the glasses. "Still after him, that is. Steffie said she hangs around Grant's clinic quite a bit."

"That doesn't necessarily mean she's chasing after him." Berry picked up a glass and tasted the tea. "Perfect."

"Steffie seemed to think so."

"But for all Steffie knows, Brooke could be there at Grant's request." Berry slipped her feet out of her sandals. "Perhaps it was Grant's idea that Brooke study to become his assistant." She made her way out back in her bare feet.

"Coming, dear?" Berry called over her shoulder.

"I think I'm going to work in the library."

"Do listen for the doorbell," Berry said over her shoulder.

Dallas went into the library, leaving the door open so she could hear the bell. She turned on her laptop and found the place where she'd been working earlier. She typed four or five words, then stopped. She wondered what Brooke looked like these days. Not that it mattered, but still, Dallas was curious. Twenty years ago, she'd been the acknowledged beauty queen in Grant's class. Everyone said so back then. Was she still? Not that it mattered.

She resumed typing, then stopped.

It would make sense for Brooke to come back to St. Dennis after her husband's death. Her family home was here. Hadn't her mother mentioned that she and Brooke both had tried staying in—where had it been? Myrtle Beach?—after both their husbands passed away, but in time they needed to come back here. *Well, of course. It's where their ties are. It all makes sense.*

Dallas typed another few sentences.

What a coincidence, though, that Brooke and Grant both returned to St. Dennis around the same time.

It had been a coincidence, hadn't it?

She supposed there was always the chance they'd been in touch. Maybe he'd heard about Brooke's husband's death and maybe called or sent a card of sympathy. Then maybe they'd corresponded for a while, maybe they even got together a time or two, before . . .

The ringing doorbell brought Dallas back to reality.

"Overactive imagination," she grumbled as she went to answer the door.

Dallas would have known Brooke anywhere. She hadn't changed a bit … from her Meg Ryan curly hair to her off-the-shoulder top and miniskirt, Brooke just screamed "Class of 1990."

"Hi." Dallas fixed her best smile on her face and opened the door. "Come on in."

"Hi." Brooke appeared to give Dallas the same once-over that Dallas had given her.

"The boys are out back." Dallas started to lead the way through the house, then realized Brooke hadn't moved. "We'll go this way. It's faster."

"I heard you were back," Brooke said.

"Well, yes. This is my family home," Dallas said.

"I heard about your husband."

"You and about three hundred million other people." Dallas tried to force that smile again.

"It really sucks. I mean, to be able to turn on your computer and see your own husband screwing someone else." Brooke's eyes narrowed. "It must really suck."

"Yeah, well, it happens." Dallas shrugged and started to turn again.

"And then you have to see it everywhere," Brooke continued. "Every magazine, every tabloid."

It was then Dallas realized that Brooke held a rolled-up newspaper under her arm. She hadn't seen a tabloid or a gossip magazine since she'd arrived in St. Dennis, but her instincts told her exactly what Brooke had in her hand.

"That's not funny, Brooke," Dallas said softly. "I came here to protect my son from seeing that sort of thing. I'll ask you to put it in your handbag now."

"I thought you'd want to see." Brooke unfolded it. The

headline read, THE MANY WOMEN OF EMILIO BLAIR SPEAK OUT!

"I'll get Logan. You can meet him out front." Dallas opened the front door. Brooke simply walked through it without a word.

Her legs shaking, her knees weak with anger, Dallas composed herself enough to go out back and call the boys.

"Do you have your library book, Logan?" she asked with as much calm as she could muster. *Don't take it out on him*, she told herself. *It isn't his fault that his mother's a bitch.*

"I left it in the kitchen," he told her.

"Let's go back through the house, then." Dallas held the door open and the two boys and the now-ever-present dog all but fell through it. Logan picked up his book and the boys headed for the front door.

Dallas stayed in the kitchen, still trying to compose herself.

"Mom, aren't you going to come outside with Logan and say hi to his mom?" Cody called from the foyer.

"I already said hi to his mom."

"But you said it's rude to not go outside when your company is leaving," he reminded her. "You said it was a rule."

Dallas hesitated. She had made that rule. She had said it was rude. At that moment, she didn't care.

But what she did care about was the possibility that Brooke might flash that headline where Cody could see it. Her anger barely under control, Dallas followed the boys onto the front porch and down the steps.

"Did you thank Mrs. Blair for having you?" Dallas heard Brooke say as Logan climbed into the backseat.

"It's MacGregor," Dallas said. "Ms. MacGregor."

Logan's look was one of confusion when he looked up into Dallas's face.

"My mom's name is MacGregor because she's a movie star," Cody explained, and Dallas guessed that was why he thought she'd kept her last name. "No one ever calls her Mrs. Blair. And besides, they're divorced."

Dallas leaned into the car and met Brooke's eyes through the opening between the front seats, as if daring her to hold up the tabloid.

Brooke's face went beet red.

"I'm sorry. Of course, it's Ms. MacGregor." Still looking at Dallas, she said, "Thank Ms. MacGregor for having you."

"Thank you, Ms. MacGregor, for having me." Logan was all sincerity. "And for taking me for ice cream and letting me play all day."

"You're very welcome, Logan. You're welcome back anytime." Dallas broke the stare-down and backed out of the car and closed the door.

"Yay!" Cody shouted. "You can come back anytime!"

"Say good-bye, Cody." Dallas put a hand on her son's shoulder and stepped back from the car.

"Bye, Logan. I'll see you tomorrow . . ." Cody waved until the car rolled onto River Road.

"Cody, take Fleur inside and get her a drink of water. She might be hot from being out here in the heat for so long."

"I'm hot from being out here in the heat, too. I think I need a drink of water, too."

"Go on in, then."

224

"Aren't you coming?"

"In a minute."

"Okay." Cody ran up the steps and disappeared into the house.

Dallas sat on the top step and wondered what the hell had just happened. Her mind still trying to make sense of it, she took the long way to the backyard, around the far side of the house, hoping to avoid conversation with Berry before she cooled off.

Dallas had been the object of gossip and mean-spirited remarks over the years, from one source or another, but she'd never experienced such out-and-out cruelty before.

What, she asked herself, would possess someone to do what Brooke had just done?

Diary ~

Whew! It's been a hectic week! We had an unprecedented number of ads to run in the current issue of the Gazette, *and so many activities and events to cover over the past week, I could barely keep up! Times like this I think perhaps it's time to sell the paper, but then, what would I do with myself? Boss everyone around at the Inn, I suppose. The truth is, I need the paper as much as the tourists need it. I think of "retire" as a four-letter word.*

I ran into Dallas at Scoop several days ago—I really must remember to check my schedule and get back to her about a date and time for the interview she promised me. I did pry several bits of news from her, but nothing I can use in the paper. Except that she's decided to make St. Dennis her summer home till Labor Day. I do know that Berry takes Cody to the library every day for the children's story hour, which Berry says she enjoys as much as Cody does. I'm wondering if Dallas realizes how much she and the boy mean to her great-aunt. I hope she does. Berry has always been spry and lively, but I swear, having Dallas and Cody here has put a little extra zing in her step. I haven't seen her this happy in years. Not since she and Archer . . . well, we all know how long ago that was. I wonder if she's aware that he's now a widower . . .

Anyway. Dallas had her son and Brooke Madison's boy with her at Scoop. They say that Brooke's late husband was a fine young man, but I only met him at the wedding and only remember him as having been quite good-looking and head over heels over Brooke. And of course, he was a hero, having given his life to serve his country. Now, the word according to Steffie Wyler is that Brooke came back to St. Dennis because of Grant—Steffie says Brooke has had a crush on him for as long as Steffie can remember. She says that Brooke's son, Logan, told her that his mother was going to school to learn to be a veterinary assistant so that she could work for Grant. Well, Steffie and I tried to warn Dallas without spelling it out, but perhaps we were a bit too subtle. However, I was not the only person who noticed that Dallas's face turned pink at the very mention of his name. Steffie is of the opinion that Grant has never gotten over Dallas. So—we shall see!

Speaking of confidences: Dallas has sworn me to secrecy, but she's working on a screenplay based on a book for which she's trying to buy the film rights! How exciting! What a story—but alas, my lips have been sealed!

~ Grace ~

Chapter 13

THE question continued to nag Dallas through a mostly sleepless night, and by morning, had morphed from *Why would Brooke have done such a thing?* to *Why is it bothering me so much?* She'd hesitated to bring it up to Berry, because Dallas thought it sounded too much like whining *(Brooke said a mean thing to me)* but in the end, she tossed it out there because she needed to talk about it and the only other person around was Cody.

Dallas recounted the story while she and Berry sat at the table on the back porch, drinking their morning coffee and watching a great blue heron swoop majestically around the river's bend.

"Ahhhh, he's back. I was starting to worry about him. It's been a while since I've seen him. I've missed him." Berry pointed to the bird that was flying six feet above the surface of the water and dead-on down the middle of the river. "The wingspan is breathtaking, don't you think?"

Dallas nodded and waited for Berry to comment on her encounter with Brooke.

"Yes, he's lovely. But, Berry—back to yesterday afternoon," Dallas prodded.

"Oh. Yes. Brooke. The tabloid. Did she say where she bought it?"

"I think she said the market but she didn't specify which one."

"Well, it wasn't Jaime's. I was there myself this week and certainly would have noticed. So that leaves the supermarket and that new convenience store out on the highway."

"What difference does it make where she bought it?" Dallas asked.

"If any establishment that I patronize is carrying that rubbish, there will be words."

Dallas smiled. Who but Berry could command such loyalty?

"But back to the incident. I think the real question is why you're losing sleep over this." Berry finished her coffee and looked with disappointment into the empty cup.

"What makes you think I'm losing sleep?"

"If you had those dark circles under your eyes yesterday, I failed to notice. So unlike me," Berry said drily as she refilled her cup. "But not to worry. I have some wonderful restorative cream upstairs. Make sure you use some before you leave the house again. And make sure when you put it on, you use only a dab on your middle finger." She leaned closer to Dallas to demonstrate her technique. "Dab under the eye, don't rub, and I guarantee—"

"But why make a point of waving that paper in my face? 'Emilio Blair's Women Speak Out!' Or whatever nonsense. As if there are so many of them lined up just dying to talk." Dallas paused to consider what she'd just said, then sighed. "Oh, of course they are, what am I saying? Doesn't everyone want those fifteen minutes they feel they're entitled to?"

"Well, at least Brooke made you aware of the story," Berry pointed out.

"That makes me feel so much better toward her."

"It might come in handy when Norma goes to court. A little more fuel for the fire."

"That fire is very well fueled, thank you. And you sound as if you're okay with what Brooke did."

"Not at all. I'm merely pointing out that you can use this if you need it." Berry rested her head against the back of the chair. "That it was Brooke and not someone else, that's what's bothering you, and you know the answer to the question as well as I do. Brooke has never forgiven you for being the girl who showed up every June and took away the boy she wanted for the entire summer."

"So what is this, junior year all over again?"

"Of course I could be wrong and there could be some other motive."

"What more could there be?" Dallas frowned.

"I suppose you should ask Brooke, dear."

"I'm hoping not to see her again for the rest of the summer."

"That won't be possible. Unless, of course, you're not going to permit Cody to play with Logan again."

"I couldn't do that. I'd never do that." Dallas shook her head adamantly. "Logan is the closest thing to a best friend Cody's ever had. I've never seen him have so much fun with another kid his age, never seen him laugh so much."

"They do appear to be BFFs." Berry glanced at Dallas and added, "That's 'best friends forever,' dear, in case you're a little behind on your pop culture."

"Thanks. I got it." Dallas took a sip of her now-cold

coffee and made a face. "Logan is welcome here anytime. I'm just hoping that Cody isn't invited to play at Logan's anytime soon. I don't trust Brooke not to leave that paper around for Cody to find."

"Well then, you're going to have to make that point very clear to Brooke, or insist that the boys play here all the time, which I don't mind, but it doesn't seem fair to the boys."

They watched a bowrider pass by slowly on its way upriver.

"Well, I think there's more to this than being offended that Brooke's taunting you with more evidence of your husband's infidelity." Berry poured some hot coffee from the pot into Dallas's cup.

"Thanks, Berry." Dallas added cream from a small pitcher. "What's that supposed to mean? What else could there be?"

"We both know that St. Dennis has become a haven for you—just, I might add, as it was for me back in my day. It's your refuge. While all felt like chaos in L.A., once you arrived in St. Dennis, all was calm. You relaxed, you slept better, felt better. The people in town embraced you, protected you. Brooke's action was an abrupt reminder that the chaos continues. You thought you were safe and beloved by all here, and it's upsetting to realize that there may be those who may not wish you well after all."

"Why, Berry, if I didn't know better, I'd think you were a frustrated psychologist."

"Not really. Though I did play one once." Berry's eyes took on a dreamy look. "It was 1951. *Doctor in the House.* I remember it as if it were yesterday. I had the most gorgeous leading man in Franklin Steele. Tragic that he died so young. Drowned off Catalina Island . . ."

Through the open kitchen door, they heard the phone ringing.

"I'll get it." Dallas sprinted into the house and picked up on the fifth ring, just as the answering machine began to record.

"Dallas, hey, it's Grant." He paused. "Dallas?"

"Yes. Hi. Hold on while I turn off the machine." She did so. "Okay. I'm back."

"How are the dogs adjusting to their new home?"

"Terrific. You'd never know that they've only been here for a few days. Ally follows Berry around as if they've been together for years, and Cody and Fleur are inseparable."

"Great. I'm glad it's still a go for you all."

"It's definitely a go."

There was a silence, which he finally broke. "So I was wondering if you'd decided yet."

"Decided what?"

"Decided where you'd like to go to dinner tonight. I was thinking somewhere outside of town, maybe, so you could escape the scrutiny of everyone in St. Dennis who goes out to dinner on Friday night. Which is just about everyone in town."

"I'm sorry." Dallas frowned. "Did we make plans for tonight? If so, I'm afraid I've forgotten."

"Really? I'm crushed, Dallas. That's like an arrow straight to my heart." He paused, then said, "Okay, we didn't exactly make plans. I did ask you if you wanted to have dinner with me and you didn't respond. So I thought I'd take that as a yes and see where that got me."

Dallas recalled their reintroduction and handshake the other day.

"I thought you were kidding," she told him. "I'm sorry. I thought you were just joking around."

"No joke. So, should I try again?" Another pause. "Or did you already make other plans?"

"Well, no, but . . ."

"Great. What time can I stop for you?"

"Really, Grant, I don't know if this is such a good idea . . ."

"I think it's a great idea. Hey, we're old friends, right? It'll be fun to catch up after all these years. And it'll be just like old times. Me living here, you visiting, although briefly this time, I suppose."

"Not so brief," she told him. "We'll be here till just after Labor Day."

"Really?" He took a moment to digest the news. "I hadn't heard that."

"Cody's having a great time. This trip has done him a world of good. And I'm getting some work done, so I thought we might as well stay for the rest of the summer."

"You could tell me about it over dinner."

For a moment, Dallas felt like a cartoon character with a little tiny angel on each shoulder. *Go. Have fun. Think of what it could lead to!* the bad angel whispered, hinting that a hot time might be had before the night was over. *Tell him no.* The good angel tugged on her earlobe to get her attention. *Think of what it could lead to!*

When she hadn't answered, Grant said, "How 'bout I pick you up around seven and we drive up to Cameron? There's a great place there, right on the water. Picnic benches outside where they cover the tables in brown paper and dump your crabs directly onto it. Messy, but fun. And they have music on Friday nights."

"You know, it does sounds like fun." Dallas smiled. "And it sounds like maybe I should toss a spare T-shirt into my bag. When it comes to neatness, I'm afraid my crab-eating technique hasn't improved a whole lot over the years."

"You're just out of practice. I'll see you at seven . . ."

The drive to Cameron seemed to take forever.

"I should have picked you up earlier," Grant told her when they'd finally made it through the traffic onto Route 50. "I wasn't thinking about how much traffic we get around here on Friday nights."

"It's not that far to Cameron, though. At least, I don't remember it being that far."

"True enough." He ejected a CD from the player and slipped it into its case. "There are some CDs in a box under your seat," he told her. "See if there's anything in there that you like."

"What did you just take out?" She reached under the seat, found the box, and picked it up.

"Audiobook. The latest Harlan Coben. I never have time to read anymore, but I hate to miss any of his books, so I listen to them while I drive. It takes me longer to get through the book this way, but it's better than missing out all together."

"I know exactly what you mean. I used to love to read." She thumbed through the box. "I've been so busy these past few years, it seems I've had no time to myself. I'm making up for it this summer at Berry's, though."

"Barbara's made sure everyone at Book 'Em knows whenever you come into her shop." Grant grinned. "We all know what you've bought and whether you've given it a thumbs-up or a thumbs-down."

"Well, I have been in there a lot lately, so she's had a lot to talk about."

"So what did you read that's been good?"

She handed him the Eagles' *Hell Freezes Over*, and while he slipped the CD into the dash, she told him about *Pretty Maids* and her plans for turning the book into a film.

"That's what I've been working on this past week," she confided. "Premature on my part, I admit, but I can't seem to get the story out of my head."

"What's it about?"

"It's about two women, grandmother, granddaughter, both of whom have dark secrets in their pasts that are coming back to haunt them now, and how they help each other survive." Dallas went on to explain the plot.

"It sounds very complex," Grant noted, "but you're right. It would make a really interesting movie."

"With the right actors, it could be golden." She hastened to add, "Not me, but the role of the younger woman would be perfect for a friend of mine. And only Berry could play the part of the older woman."

"I thought Berry was permanently retired."

"She is, but maybe I could talk her into doing this one last project. I haven't discussed it with her, but I will when the time comes. And it occurred to me yesterday morning that it would be an excellent vehicle for Jason Milhouse's music. Haunting melodies, those electric guitars, the horns and strings." She beamed just thinking about it. "Gorgeous—and perfect."

"Sounds like you have it all planned."

"All but having the rights to the book and the backing to make it. Otherwise, yeah, I've got it all planned."

"I hope it works out for you," he said softly. "You obviously want it badly."

Dallas nodded. "I haven't wanted anything this badly—anything professional, anyway—since I first auditioned for my first film role."

"*Rose Everlasting.*"

Her jaw dropped. "You saw that movie? I didn't think anyone saw that movie."

"I admit I didn't see it when it first came out. I caught it a few years later on tape."

"I'm stunned. How did you even know about that film?"

He hesitated for a moment. "Okay, here's the truth. I knew that it was your dream to go to Hollywood and make movies, but it never occurred to me that you did it. Not that I didn't think you weren't beautiful enough or talented enough," he hastened to add. "It's just one of those things that you never think about someone you know actually doing."

"So someone here in St. Dennis told you that I was in some films?"

"No." Grant shook his head. "Some guys I lived with when I was in vet school were going to the movies one night and asked me if I wanted to come along, but I had a test first thing in the morning so I passed on the invite. The next day they were talking about this girl who was in the movie, going on and on about her, and I'm half listening, you know? And then one of them mentioned your name. I said, wait, is this girl blond, like really light blond . . . ?"

The expression on his face as he re-created the conversation made her laugh out loud. It was so incredulous.

"So I figured out it was you. I mean, *Dallas MacGregor*. How many beautiful blondes with that name could there be in Hollywood? So that night, I went to the movies to see for myself."

"Did you drag your buddies back with you?"

"No. Actually, I went alone, and sat in the back row of the theater." He appeared somewhat sheepish at the admission. "And then the movie started and there you were. It was surreal. My jaw just dropped. All I could think of was, 'She did it. She really did it. Just like she said she'd do.'"

"Which movie was that?" Dallas smiled with no small amount of satisfaction that he had noticed, that he had been impressed. That he'd remembered her dreams. "That first one that you saw in the theater?"

"Dear Olivia."

"My first speaking role. I had five whole lines." Dallas leaned back against the seat. "No one was more surprised than I was to have landed in that film."

"Well, except possibly me. After that, I had to go back and check out all your movies, starting with *Rose Everlasting*. And I never missed one after that." He slowed the car and made a right turn into the parking lot, which was overflowing. "Maybe we'll get lucky and someone will be leaving."

Two turns through the parking lot later, he drove back

onto the road. "Guess we'll have to park out here. Do you mind?"

"Of course not. This is fine."

Grant parked along the marshy area where red-winged blackbirds sat on cattails that swayed in the breeze and marked their respective territories with song. Beyond the marsh lay the Bay, where the big bridge rose like a steel rainbow.

They walked to the restaurant through the parking lot and entered through a side door. Dallas kept her dark glasses on even as they waited for the hostess.

"How many? Just you two?" The young woman wore printed shorts and a brightly colored T-shirt and held a clipboard in her hand.

Grant nodded.

"Bar, dining room, or deck?"

"Feel like eating outside?" Grant asked, and Dallas nodded.

"Five minutes," the woman told them. "You might want to grab something from the bar and listen to the band. They're just setting up but they should start soon."

"Sounds good." Grant took Dallas's hand and led her to the bar, where they ordered beers. They'd just been served when the hostess tapped Grant on the shoulder to let him know that their table was available.

"You're lucky," she said as she led them outside. "We don't have that many tables for two."

They walked past the bandstand, where the musicians were just beginning to play, and the marina, where several dozen boats were tied up. Their table was the last one in the row, and overlooked the water.

"This is really cool." Dallas nodded and looked around. "I like the vibe here."

"Me, too," he told her from across the table.

"So you folks ready for some crabs?" The waiter appeared out of nowhere.

"Sure. A dozen jumbo jimmies to start," Grant told him.

"Coming up." Their server pointed to their half-empty glasses. "Another beer?"

"With the crabs?" Grant asked Dallas, and she nodded.

"I'll send someone out with them." The server smiled down at Dallas, then looked at her more intently. She put her head down and kept her glasses on.

"So. We've talked about my plans," she said after the waiter left their table. "Let's talk about yours."

"Build up my practice in St. Dennis. Finish renovating my house. Find a home for all the homeless animals that cross my path. And of course, most important, raise my daughter to be a happy, well-adjusted, responsible human being." He counted them off on his fingers. "You can probably figure out which of those is proving to be the most challenging."

Dallas nodded. "Parenting under the best of circumstances is just flat-out hard. Tougher still if you're doing the job of both mother and father."

"Krista—that's my ex-wife—is a really good mother. I can't complain about her, except that . . ."

Dallas raised a questioning eyebrow, wondering if he'd finish the sentence.

He did. "Except that I'd rather have Paige with me all the time. I'm grateful to have her for the whole

239

summer, don't misunderstand, and we get weekends and holidays together during the school year, but . . ." Grant shrugged.

"But you'd rather she stay with you full-time."

"I can't stand not having her around. I'm selfish that way."

"It's not being selfish. You love your daughter. You want to spend time with her. I totally understand. I don't know what I'd do if Emilio tried to win custody from me."

"After the last few weeks, I think the possibility of him getting custody of Cody is pretty slim. I doubt that you have much to worry about."

The waiter approached with a basket full of cooked crabs.

"Here you go, folks." He dumped the contents of the basket on the table, handed them each a pick and a pair of crackers, and left the empty basket for the discards. "Enjoy."

Dallas perched her sunglasses on top of her head, picked up a crab, and took the back of the shell off with one twist of her wrist. Grant whistled appreciatively.

"I thought you said you were out of practice."

"*You* said I was out of practice. *I* said I was still messy." She dug out a hunk of crabmeat and popped it into her mouth. "Berry was teaching Cody her technique and I'm not ashamed to say that I eavesdropped."

"I'm impressed. Damn." He shook his head. "You can take the girl out of St. Dennis . . ."

Dallas grinned. "The girl is glad to be back."

"The girl is not the only one."

She decided it best not to comment further. She was still debating the wisdom of having listened to the bad angel and accepted Grant's offer of dinner. The tone had been casual, a sort of let's-catch-up between old friends, definitely nonthreatening, definitely easy. But hadn't that always been part of Grant's charm? The easy smile, the gentle humor, the feeling you always had when you were in his company that the entire world was as laid-back as he was, there was no chaos or strife, and that everything would always turn out all right?

"So how's Wade?" Grant pulled her out of her reverie.

"I guess he's okay." Dallas shrugged. "I've left several messages for him to call me—as has Berry—but we haven't heard from him. I'm starting to get concerned. It's been a while since I talked to him, and I haven't seen him since Christmas."

"I've seen him more recently than that. He was here for Beck's wedding," Grant told her.

"Berry did mention that. She said he didn't stay over, though. That he was here for the ceremony in the afternoon and for most of the reception, but that he left before it was over."

"Yeah, Steffie was pretty pissed off about that."

"Steffie?" Dallas frowned. "Why would she care about what time he left?"

"Hot and heavy on the dance floor." Grant wiggled his eyebrows.

"Really?" Dallas put down the crab leg she was working on. *Wade and Steffie?*

Grant nodded. "She's always had a thing for him, didn't you know?"

She shook her head. "No. I had no idea. Wow. Wade and Steffie . . ." She pondered the possibility. "I could see that, though, you know? He needs someone who's strong enough to not take his guff. Someone who could kick his butt. And Steffie is one tough cookie. Yeah. I can see the attraction."

"Well, for the love of all that's holy, don't let her know I told you."

"Afraid of your little sister, Grant?"

"You betcha."

Dallas laughed again. *And that's why I came with him tonight*, she told herself. *Because no one, ever, has made me laugh the way Grant Wyler does. Not back then, not in all the years between, not now. No one has ever made me completely forget myself the way he did—and still does.*

Dallas wasn't sure how she felt about that. It made Grant dangerous in a way that no one else was.

"Dallas?" Grant reached across the table and touched her arm. She was vaguely aware of a flash from somewhere off to her left. "All of a sudden there are a lot of people staring at us."

"Shit." She slid her glasses back down onto her face.

"Oh, good move," he deadpanned. "Now they'll never know it's really you."

"I wasn't thinking. I should have left them on," she said, referring to the glasses.

"To tell you the truth, I don't know that they do all that much to disguise you. At first, yeah, you could be any beautiful blonde walking by. But even with the dark glasses, anyone who looks at you for more than a minute is going to realize it's you." He took a swallow of beer from the mug he'd been holding, then put it down quietly. "Would you like to leave?"

"How bad is it? I don't want to look around."

"It's ... well, it's pretty much spreading like wildfire, from where I sit. Lots of whispering, then people turning to look this way. Of course, we are sitting at the last table on this side, so maybe they're looking at something behind me. Or maybe they all just recognized me." He lowered his voice. "Hey, you think it's easy being the Dog Rescuer? It's the same everywhere I go. The whispers. The cameras. Everyone wants a piece of me."

"I'm sure that must be it."

He used one of the wet wipes to wash the Old Bay from the crabs off his fingers. "So what do you think? Want to split?"

"I think I want one of those wet things to clean my hands. I smell like ... well, like crabs." She busied herself wiping off both hands. When she finished, she said, "Are you sure you wouldn't mind? Are you finished ...?" She pointed to the few crabs that remained uneaten.

"I'm fine. I don't want you to be uncomfortable."

"All right then, as long as you—"

"Don't say it. Just smile, stand up, and walk out as if you are not aware that you've suddenly become the main attraction."

She tossed the wipe onto the table and stood, grabbed her bag from the deck near her feet, and waited for Grant, who, having signaled the waiter, handed over enough cash to cover the check and the tip. Then he took her hand and casually led her to the exit. Several times she was stopped and asked for her autograph, and each time she politely complied.

"Is it always like that?" Grant asked when they got to

the car. "People gawking and taking your picture and stopping you every time you go out?"

"Not so much in L.A.," she replied. "People there are more used to seeing film people. In St. Dennis, people mostly leave me alone, and even the tourists are very considerate. Most of the time, I'm not bothered by anyone. Tonight . . . I guess one person pulling out their camera just encouraged everyone else to do the same."

"I'm sorry your dinner was ruined."

"My dinner wasn't ruined," she protested. "It was delicious. Was your dinner ruined?"

"Well, no, not really."

"It's no big deal unless it bothered you."

"I thought I toughed it out pretty well."

"You did. You were very brave." She patted him on the shoulder and buckled her seat belt.

"Yeah, well, you know, like I said, I have to deal with this sort of thing all the time, so I'm used to it."

"That's what happens when everyone knows your name, pal. It's the price you have to pay for your fame."

"So what do you think?" He turned the key in the ignition. "We head back to St. Dennis?"

"Sure."

"We can stop for ice cream if you want dessert. I heard my sister made something today with raspberries and fudge."

Dallas groaned. "Your sister is going to be the death of me. And as tempted as I am, I'm trying to limit my visits to Scoop to three per week. I was just there yesterday."

"Stef's got a good thing going." Grant waited for a car to pass before pulling onto the roadway. "She's worked really hard to get her business off the ground. I'm really proud of her."

"You should be proud. She's got a great product and she's in the right location." Dallas added, "I'm sure your folks are proud, too."

"They are. I think they feel a lot better about leaving St. Dennis now that Scoop is doing so well. I think they were worried for a while that she wasn't going to be able to support herself selling ice cream."

"Where did they go?"

"They moved to Havre de Grace a couple of years ago. You know my dad was a waterman, like his dad, and his dad before that. But with the Bay having gotten so polluted there for a while and the crab and oyster catch falling off every year, he figured out that he'd need to find something else to do. So he went back to school and majored in environmental studies, got a job with a new outfit that was studying the Bay and how best to bring it back from the brink. One of the areas he's working on is the Susquehanna watershed. The water that flows down through Pennsylvania into the Bay has been bringing pollutants, farm waste, insecticides, chemical fertilizers—" He stopped. "Sorry. I could go on and on. As you can guess, my dad's pretty militant on the subject."

"No need to apologize. The Bay is ... well, it's the Chesapeake. I remember times when we were kids that the water was cloudy and Berry didn't want us to go swimming."

"It's improved a lot over the past few years. There have been a lot of new regulations and real efforts to clean it up, and from what my dad tells me, the efforts are paying off.

This spring the population of blue crabs increased pretty dramatically."

"So your dad went from catching the blues to saving them."

"That's exactly what he says. He's pretty happy that he made the switch when he did. He loves the Bay, loves everything about it. He said that the Chesapeake took care of our family for the past two hundred years, it was time we started taking care of it."

"I'm surprised they'd sell the house. I seem to recall it had been in your family for a long time."

"They didn't sell it. They rented it out. My mom has all intentions of coming back here someday." Grant shook his head. "They'd never sell that house. Too many memories, you know?"

"I'm surprised you or Steffie didn't rent from them."

"Stef already had her place, and I hadn't made the decision to move back here when they were looking for a renter."

Dallas shifted in her seat to better see Grant's face. "Didn't you have a practice already established somewhere else?"

"I did. In Ohio, where we were living, but this just seemed like the right move. I never felt like I belonged in Camden Lakes, the town we settled in. I guess I always knew I'd be back here someday; at least that was always my goal. When my marriage broke up, it seemed like the right time."

"Is your ex-wife living in Ohio?"

"Yes. She grew up in Camden Lakes. Her whole family is there. There was no question that she'd stay and I'd go."

246

He shrugged. "Besides, there was no way I was ever going to feel comfortable being around that situation after some other guy moved into my house."

"Ouch."

"Yeah. How 'bout it?"

"She's remarried?"

He nodded. "Last fall. He's not a bad guy. I think it would have been easier if I hadn't liked him as a person. But once I got over the shock that Krista had found a replacement for me—before I knew she was even looking for one—well, I had to admit he was a nice guy, a good guy. I think he cares a lot more about her than I did, to be truthful. And he's a good stepfather to Paige. Never tries to come between us, never tries to override me, which I appreciate. So I guess it could be worse."

"Still, that couldn't have been easy. I mean, I know what it feels like to have your spouse betray you."

"Well, she had her reasons, and I can't say that I blame her."

"Were you . . ."

"Cheating on her?" He shook his head. "No. I don't believe in it. I figure, if the relationship is broken to the point where you want to look for someone else, you make a clean break before you start looking. I think we just sort of outgrew each other and I guess she thought there was no other place for her to go but to someone else."

Dallas wasn't sure how to respond. *I'm sorry?* Or maybe, *That's a really mature way to look at it?* Either of which was better than her first inclination, which had been, *At least the press didn't have a field day with it.*

She decided that this might be one of those times when

she was better off saying nothing at all. She turned up the music. The Eagles CD was still playing as they arrived in St. Dennis.

"It's so early," he noted. "Are you sure I can't talk you into ice cream? Or a drink down at Captain Walt's or maybe at Lola's?"

She shook her head. "No, thanks. But if you'd like to come in, I can offer you a cup of coffee or a glass of wine. Sorry we don't have any beer to replace the one you left on the table, though."

"You can buy me a beer some other time." He made the turn onto Berry's road, then moments later, into her driveway. "Do you think your aunt is still up? I have some information on the fencing she asked about."

Dallas stared up at the house. "Her bedroom light is still on. She turns in early, but she's still awake."

He stopped the car and they got out. By the time they'd arrived at the front door, Berry was there to open it.

"I wondered who was pulling in the drive and then I remembered that you were out for the evening," Berry told Dallas. "Hello, Grant. It's awfully early to call it a night, don't you think?"

"We had to leave the restaurant." Dallas led the way into the house. "There were too many gapers."

"That's too bad, dear. Next time try a dark wig." Berry closed the door behind them.

"Miss B, I have the names of several contractors who have been recommended to me for fence installation. You might want to make some calls and get a few estimates." Grant took a folded piece of paper from his back pocket and handed it over. "The one with the asterisk is Rexana's brother-in-law."

"Oh?" Berry unfolded the paper to take a look. "Married to Rexana's sister Marsha, no doubt. I believe I may have met him a time or two down at Captain Walt's. The other names . . ." She scanned them quickly. "None of them ring a bell. Thank you, Grant. I'll make some calls in the morning."

Berry started toward the stairwell.

"Berry, want to join us in the kitchen? The choices are wine or coffee." Dallas stood in the doorway leading to the back of the house.

"Thank you but no. I'm reading and enjoying a cup of herbal tea. Mint always does so much to soothe, you know."

"I thought that was chamomile," Dallas said.

"Highly overrated." Berry wrinkled her nose. "I never cared much for the smell."

"I'll see you in the morning, then." Dallas turned to Grant. "Have you decided what you want?"

"I believe I have," he said softly.

Dallas backed into the kitchen. "The only choices right now are coffee or wine."

"What will the choices be later?"

"Stop it." She laughed and opened the refrigerator and took out the bottle of pinot grigio she and Berry had opened at dinner the night before. "From the Friuli region of Italy. It's quite good."

"I'm game."

Grant went to the back door and unlocked it. He went out onto the porch and disappeared from view. Dallas poured two glasses of wine and took them to the door.

"Grant, would you . . ." She started to ask him to open the door, but he did so before she finished her sentence. She handed him one of the glasses and said, "Thanks for grabbing the door. Would you like to sit up here on the porch?"

"We did that the other night. Let's go on down to the river, see what fish are jumping tonight." He took her free hand.

"We don't get too many jumping fish out this way." She walked down the steps slightly behind him. When they reached the bottom step, she asked, "Berry had a spotlight installed last summer. Want me to turn it on so you can see where you're going?"

"I can see. Besides, it's more romantic with just the lights from the house."

"I thought this was supposed to be a just-friends dinner."

"It was. But dinner's over." He led her down to the dock and they walked to the end of the pier just as a boat came around the river's bend at a leisurely pace. When Grant waved, the driver sped up and went past them, the wake sloshing against the sides of the dock.

"Do you know that person?" Dallas asked.

"No, but I think I know the boat, so I guess it was just a reflex. Old Carter Harwell was in a few weeks ago with his greyhound and he mentioned his kids didn't think he should be driving anymore and they talked him into hanging up the keys to the car as well as the boat. He has a property that he rents out, about a half mile upriver from here, and he was thinking about including the boat with the house so the renters could use it. Said he just couldn't bring himself to sell it. It had been an anniversary gift from his wife, who passed away last year."

"Maybe that was the renter."

"Maybe." Grant took a deep breath of the air that was perfumed with the scent of the lilies that grew in Berry's garden. "Beautiful night."

"Mm-hmm." She took a sip of wine and swallowed hard. There was such an air of anticipation about them both, she could hardly stand it. Someone, she told herself, was in deep denial—probably both of them—for thinking that they could be nothing more than friends.

She knew before he turned her face up to his that a kiss was coming that was going to turn her world upside down, and she tried to brace herself for it. When he found her lips with his, for a split second, she was sixteen again, kissing him for the first time. Back then, she'd waited for weeks for him to make that move. This time, so many years later, the thrill was just as new, the kiss just as perfect. She eased her body into his and he pulled her closer, then closer still. His breath was fragrant with the wine, and his lips were warm and demanding, and when he parted her lips with his tongue, she invited him in just as eagerly as she had that first time. He teased the corners of her mouth and she couldn't stop herself from pressing into him, wanting as much of him as she could have in a few brief moments. When he broke from her, it was to take her glass from her hand.

He placed both glasses on the deck, then backed her up against one of the pilings, and she braced herself, leaning back and reaching up for him. Winding her arms around his neck, she pulled him toward her, meeting his lips halfway. She felt him all through her body, as if every vibrating cell remembered him, remembered other nights like this, and responded the only way they knew.

"Grant," she whispered as reason began to trickle back into her consciousness. "I think—"

"No, no. That's the worst possible thing you could be doing right now." His lips traveled to her chin, then the side of her face, then to her neck. "And besides, didn't you hear? Thinking's banned in St. Dennis on Thursdays."

"Today is Friday," she reminded him.

"Then, too." When his lips began to trail down the V of her dress, she forced herself to break away.

"Grant, I really think we need to stop and . . . and think about what's going on here." She pushed him slightly from her, hoping to gain a little breathing room. "All things considered, this isn't a good idea."

He sighed deeply, and a moment later asked, "What things are being considered?"

"We haven't seen or spoken to each other in twenty years. We don't know each other anymore." She stepped back another step and his arms caught her.

"You're, ah, a little close to the edge, there," he pointed out.

Dallas looked down into the water that was less than three feet away.

"Well, that would have added a bit of drama, wouldn't it? Me going off the end of the pier into the river?"

He laughed. "Look, you're right on one thing. It's been twenty years since we've been together. But I don't agree that we don't know each other anymore. I'm still the same guy I was back then. Older, hopefully a bit wiser, but I really haven't changed a whole lot. I doubt you have, either."

A breeze off the river tossed her hair around her face, and he tucked it back behind her ear.

"I think regardless of the fact that you are now a famous and highly celebrated star, you're still the same girl who came to St. Dennis every summer. I'd be willing to bet that inside, you haven't changed a whole lot. At least, I hope you haven't."

"It's not as easy as that."

"Sure it is. I'll bet you still walk barefoot as often as possible, get pissed off every time you see someone drop trash on the sidewalk, and you still eat your burgers rare. Though never from a fast-food place."

She laughed. "Yes, but—"

He continued. "These days, the beef is from pastured cattle that have never been injected with hormones or antibiotics and all of your food comes from a market that only sells organics. In your garage back in California, you have a hybrid SUV and a bicycle that you never ride. You still blush when people gush over you and you still don't have a whole lot of girlfriends because most women are jealous of you and you sense that and so you pick your friends very carefully."

"Where did that come from?" Dallas frowned. "That last part?"

"From the week I spent at your place in New Jersey. It was very obvious that you only had one or two friends. Equally obvious that the other girls in that summer theater group didn't like you a whole lot but for no reason other than the fact that you were prettier and had such clear and amazing natural talent."

"What was obvious? What made you think that?"

"When you were onstage, rehearsing, I sat in the audience, remember? With the cast members who were waiting to be called up to rehearse their lines?"

She nodded slowly.

"Well, there was always a group of girls who sat behind me who talked about how you ..." He froze, apparently realizing this was not a good idea. "How you hadn't been in summer stage there the other years but that you just walked in the first time and got the biggest role. That sort of stuff. You know."

"And you didn't think to tell me that back then?"

"I didn't think it would be a good idea." He bit his bottom lip. "Probably about as bad an idea as it was just now."

His discomfort was endearing, and Dallas knew there'd been more discussed among that group of girls than he was letting on. She'd heard it from someone else that summer. Still, the fact that he'd hidden it from her back then to spare her feelings only served to remind her of how sweet a guy he'd been at eighteen.

"My only point is that some things never change. There was something between us back then that was one of those things. I know it's still there because I feel it, and you still feel it, too. That pull—whatever it is, I'm not going to try to put a name on it—is still there."

She nodded slowly. "I need to think this through, Grant. I don't know where this could go."

He rested his forehead on hers. "Where do you want it to go?"

"I don't know that, either, and until I do, I think we need to slow this train down . . ."

Chapter 14

MAN, you are so smooth. Grant mocked himself as he drove home, his head still buzzing from that last goodnight kiss. *You sure do know how to play it cool, keep a woman guessing . . .*

Idiot.

Earlier that night, before he picked up Dallas, he'd had a pretty stern talk with himself. Reminded himself that he needed to stick to the plan, to keep everything friendly and to not even try to make romance a part of the equation. Things had ended badly for him the last time around, slamming him with the greatest heartache he'd ever known, and only a fool would step up to that plate again. And yet there he was, his arms around her, his lips on hers, drinking her in like a man who'd just come to an oasis after walking across the Sahara.

Couldn't keep your hands to yourself, could you? Moron.

She's leaving at the end of the summer, just like last time, he reminded himself. *And she's going to leave you hurting—just like last time.*

She'd said that come September, she was going to go back to her own life. He considered what that life might be like. By the time he pulled into his driveway, he mentally envisioned Dallas on the arm of some high-powered star—hadn't he heard just last week that Chase Winston was getting divorced? He and Dallas had made several movies together, one of which had a pretty spicy love scene. Yeah, she'll probably hook up with Winston or someone just like him—someone equally famous and wealthy and great-looking—and it'll be another twenty years before she's back in St. Dennis.

And sucker that you are, twenty years from now, you'd do the same thing all over again, because the truth is, you never really loved anyone but her. Never really felt complete with anyone but her. Never dreamed of happily ever after, except with her.

Yeah, well, we know how that worked out, don't we?

The dogs in the shelter began to bark when he slammed his car door, and by the time he got around to the front door, the dogs he and Paige had adopted eagerly spilled out of the house to welcome him home, their geriatric tails wagging, their grayed heads butting against his legs for attention.

"Okay, guys, I'm glad to see you, too." He patted each dog's head. "All right. As you were, fellas."

One by the one, the dogs drifted away, and it was then that Grant noticed that all the downstairs lights were on. He was certain he hadn't turned on any of them before he left the house, except one in the front hall. Just then, Paige came out of the kitchen, her feet bare, a large cookie in one hand.

"Hi, Daddy," she said with somewhat exaggerated nonchalance.

Grant stood in the hallway. "I thought you were at Quinn's house for a sleepover."

"I was. I came home." She walked past him and went into the living room and flopped on the sofa. "A bunch of boys came over and everyone was acting so lame." She made a face.

"How'd you get home?" He sat on the arm of an over-stuffed chair. "Did Quinn's mother drive you?"

"She wasn't there"—Paige continued to feign indifference—"so I walked."

"Whoa. Back up there. What do you mean, her mother wasn't home?" The no-big-deal posturing was beginning to make sense. "You told me she was going to be there."

"Quinn said she would be. I guess she decided to go out at the last minute or something." Paige finished the cookie, wiped her hands on a napkin, and got up to leave the room.

"Not so fast, kiddo." Grant motioned for her to return to the sofa. "Go back to the part where you walked home from Quinn's."

"Yeah. I already told you that part."

"I didn't hear the part where you said who walked with you."

"No one walked with me."

"You walked all the way home from Quinn's by your-self?" Grant's eyebrows rose. "In the dark?"

"It's no big deal, Dad. It's only a couple of blocks."

"It's four blocks, and it is a big deal." He couldn't even bear to think of what could happen to a young girl alone in the dark. "Why didn't you call me?"

Paige shrugged.

Grant knew what she was thinking: this was his fault

for not calling Quinn's mother himself. That's what Krista would have done. If anything had happened to Paige . . .

"Next time something like that happens, you call me to come pick you up, understand? You don't do that again, okay?"

Paige made a face. "You sound like Mom."

Well, I suppose that's a good sign, he told himself.

"So did you have fun?" she asked.

"Yes, I did. But don't try to change the subject. You shouldn't have been here alone, Paige."

"Dad," Paige said with infinite patience, "this is St. Dennis. Safe place, remember? That's what you always tell Mom, anyway."

"It's summer. Who knows who's in town these days?"

"I have the dogs to protect me," she said as the old rottweiler collapsed at her feet. "See? Schultz loves me. He wouldn't let anyone hurt me."

"Schultz has doggie Alzheimer's and has hardly any teeth," he reminded her.

"But he's got a really big bark."

"Paige . . ."

"All right. Next time I'll call you. Promise." She crossed her heart, then paused for a moment. "Dad, are you still going to take us to Baltimore to see the *American Idol* concert tomorrow night?"

"I said I would."

"Thanks, Daddy. We're all so excited about it."

"So who's the best dad?"

"You're the best dad *ever.*" Paige stepped over the dog that had begun to snore loudly. She kissed her father on

259

the cheek and started to run up the steps. She'd gone halfway up when she stopped and turned back.

"Dad?" She grinned conspiratorially. "I won't tell Mom about tonight if you won't."

Before he could reply, she scampered up the steps to the second floor and disappeared into her room. Grant sighed and checked to make sure all the doors were locked, then turned off all but the porch lights. He'd certainly had an interesting evening, he mused as he went upstairs, one that ran the gamut of emotions, from feeling like an eighteen-year-old romancing the girl of his dreams to feeling like the hundred-year-old single father of an almost-teenage girl. He wasn't sure he'd handled either situation particularly well, but, hey, no harm, no foul, right?

"There's always tomorrow, Scarlett," he muttered as he went into his room.

It didn't occur to him until later, when he'd almost fallen asleep, that he'd only have until the end of the summer with both Paige and Dallas. By the first week in September, they'd both be gone, both off to lives that didn't include him. The unhappy truth kept him awake for most of the night.

"Dallas, did I remember to tell you that I was taking Cody and Logan to Ballard today?" Berry poked her head into the office the next morning, drawing Dallas from a day-dream in which she and Grant had been engaged in activities that might have shocked Berry, had she known. Then again, probably not, Dallas thought as she sat up. No one could say that Berry hadn't *lived*.

"You mentioned that you were going to take Cody to

a movie, but I don't remember that you were taking Logan. Not that it matters, of course, as long as you're up to it."

"Of course, I'm up to it. It's the film adaptation of one of the books they read at the library last week, and they're both excited about it. And after the movie—assuming they behave while in the theater—we'll stop and have pizza on the way home. Then, if there's still time and they haven't stuffed themselves to the point of illness, we'll make a stop at Scoop for dessert."

"Sounds like a pretty full afternoon."

"I'm looking forward to it. The boys are such fun. They're both so smart and so polite. It's a pleasure to take them places."

"That's nice to hear."

"That's what Brooke said, too, when she called last night," Berry went on. "How nice it was to hear good things about your children. I've never had my own, of course, but I always took pride in the manners that you and Wade showed." She paused. "Well, Wade . . . perhaps not always. He did go through a spell. But you were always well mannered."

"Thanks, Berry." Dallas tapped her pen on the side of her laptop.

Ally began to bark at the front windows. Fleur flew down the steps to join in.

"Oh, that must be Brooke's car I hear. She asked if she could drop off Logan around eleven while on her way to Annapolis. A cousin's wedding, I believe she said. I told her to go and enjoy herself and not worry about her boy, that I'd give him dinner and will drop him off later this evening . . ." Berry's voice faded as she drifted toward the front door.

Dallas got up from the desk and closed the office door. The last person she wanted to see—or hear—was Brooke. She forced her attention back to the scene and the dialogue she'd been working on before Berry stopped in. Soon the voices from the front hall faded, and she was lost in *Pretty Maids* once again.

"Mommy, Aunt Berry's taking me and Logan to the movies and for pizza, and if we're good, we get to go to Scoop!" Cody bounded into the library with Logan and Fleur at his heels.

"Well, I suppose that means you will both be very good at the movies and at the pizza place." She swung the chair around and stood. "Come give me a hug before you go."

Cody wrapped himself around her legs. "Logan, you gotta hug my mom, too."

Logan quietly joined Cody and gave Dallas a half-hearted hug.

"Thank you, boys." She patted them both on their heads. "Now don't keep Aunt Berry waiting. And remember to behave."

"We will," the two boys cried in unison, and raced out of the library.

"Would you like the door closed, dear?" Berry asked from the doorway.

"No, you can leave it open." Dallas glanced at the door as she sat back at the desk. "My, aren't we looking fine today. Not to mention stylish."

Berry smoothed the short-sleeved white linen jacket over her hips. She wore a matching calf-length linen skirt and a hot pink tank, and flat leather sandals that looked like snakeskin. Dallas didn't ask if they were real: Berry never went for faux anything.

"One never knows who one might run into." Berry slid her dark glasses down onto her face and repositioned the straps of her shoulder bag. "Come, boys. We're off for an afternoon of fun."

The house was eerily quiet once the three had departed, and after trying to work through a section of dialogue that she just couldn't get to ring true—even after speaking all the parts aloud—Dallas went into the kitchen. She'd eaten little at breakfast and hadn't had lunch, so hunger might be the cause. Low blood sugar, she told herself as she poked around in the refrigerator. She found the last bit of Anita's chicken salad and some fruit salad from yesterday's lunch, and ate both standing next to the table, looking out the window.

The sound of an approaching boat drew her attention, and she watched the bowrider slowly pass their pier as it headed out to the Bay. *Well, if that's the same boat we saw last night, at least the driver has its speed under control today*, she thought as she polished off the cantaloupe. She thought the boat might be having engine trouble, as it appeared to be idling on the river when she went out the back door with the dogs a few minutes later. But as she drew closer to the trees, the boat resumed its journey.

Dallas found the red ball on the grass and tossed it to Fleur, who chased it merrily while Ally rested herself in the shade.

"These young kids, eh, Ally? All sass and energy, right?" Dallas took the ball from the returning Fleur and gave it one more toss. When the dog brought it back, she called them both into the house with her. After giving them each one of the organic treats she'd picked up at Bowwows and Meows and making sure there was fresh cool water in their bowls, Dallas went back into the library to work.

"'I really can't bear to think about this right now.'" She read off the line she'd written for Charlotte, then revised it. "'I don't think I can bear to talk about this right now.'"

She pondered both before making her selection, and moving on to the next line, then the next. She'd finished the first draft of the scene and was reading the lines aloud when the dogs began to bark. A moment later, the doorbell rang several times in quick succession. Dallas glanced at her watch on the way to the foyer. It was 4:20.

Through the glass panels, Dallas could see Brooke on the other side of the door. When she reached for the bell to give it another ring, Dallas opened the door.

"What do you want, Brooke?" Dallas made no effort toward civility.

"I know I'm early to pick up Logan, but I wanted to have a few minutes to talk to you alone, before the boys got back with your aunt. May I come in?"

"Why? Did you find another sleazy little tabloid story that you want to make sure I don't miss?"

"It wasn't meant like that. I mean, yes, I wanted you to see it, but—"

"All right. You showed me. I saw it." Dallas started to close the door.

"You don't understand . . ."

"You're absolutely right. I don't understand." Dallas's temper was ready to blow. "I don't understand why you'd do something so cruel. Frankly, I don't care why you'd want to hurt me. But do not ever—ever—bring such trash around here where my son might see it. Cody's father is what he is, and Cody's still trying to make sense of it all. You have a lot of nerve, coming here, after—"

"I understand why you're angry, but if you'd give me five minutes to explain. This is a total misunderstanding."

Dallas snorted. "Did I miss something? Was that Brooke's evil twin who waved that tabloid in my face?"

"Please? Just five minutes?"

Dallas leaned against the doorjamb and looked at her watch. "Five minutes, Brooke. Starting now."

"I saw the paper in the market," Brooke began. "I knew that you were in town and I was pretty sure that you wouldn't want Cody to see it. So I bought the papers and I put them in the trunk of my car. I just wanted you to—"

"Wait a minute. You bought them?" Dallas frowned. "How many did you buy?"

"All of them."

"You bought *all* of the papers in the market?" Dallas asked incredulously. "Why?"

"To hide them. Or burn them. So that no one else would see."

"Why would you do that?"

"Look, I know I wasn't very nice to you back when we were kids." Brooke sighed deeply.

"That's putting it mildly."

"I know, I know. I did everything I could to make you hate St. Dennis so that you'd go away and never come back. I was not the nicest kid in my class. I admit it. But that was twenty years ago. I've grown up a lot since then."

"So what's this got to do with that gossip rag?"

"I didn't know if you'd seen it . . ."

"I hadn't."

". . . and I thought you should know what was being said, that's all. I just wanted you to know that this was making the rounds here in St. Dennis in case someone said something to Cody. I thought you should be prepared."

Dallas stared at Brooke. Kindness from Brooke? Consideration from the girl who once made her life a living hell? This was one of the last things she'd expected.

Dallas stepped back and held the door open. "Would you like to come in and finish this conversation inside over a glass of iced tea?"

Brooke nodded. "I would. Thank you."

As they walked to the back of the house, Brooke said, "I know it sounds pretty stupid now. But I wanted to clear the air between us, and I thought that might be a start. I haven't been back in St. Dennis for very long, and it seems like everyone I know is married or has moved away."

Except Grant, Dallas thought, wondering if there was any truth to the speculation that Brooke had come back to St. Dennis because she was hoping to catch his eye.

"I thought . . . I don't know, I guess I thought maybe we could be friends. Logan likes Cody so much, and they seem to be such good friends. It's been hard on him, too, these past few years. Losing his dad, then moving from our home in Florida to Myrtle Beach to stay with my mom after both my dad and my husband died. It took Logan a while to get settled there and to make friends. I guess to him, it seems he had no sooner gotten comfortable there than we moved again." Brooke swallowed what must have been an enormous lump in her throat. "He was all loose ends this summer, until Cody started coming to the library story hours. Cody's friendship means so much to him. I wouldn't do anything to spoil that."

"Nor would I." Dallas pulled a chair out from the table and offered it to Brooke. "Please," she said, "have a seat."

Brooke sat and looked around the room while Dallas found glasses and took the pitcher of iced tea from the fridge.

"I've driven past this old house a thousand times over the years, and I always wondered what it looked like inside. It's really beautiful. I love that all the old wood is still natural and the moldings are all so ornate."

"Thank you. Berry's done a fabulous job in maintaining it. It's her pride and joy," Dallas said.

"And you have this wonderful view of the river." Brooke turned her head and stretched her neck to see out the window. "You must love coming back here."

"I do." Dallas poured their tea and took both glasses to the table. "I haven't been here in a long time—not to spend any significant time, that is—but I'm glad we're here now."

"Logan said Cody told him he was staying for the rest of the summer." Brooke took a sip of tea. "He said until September seventh, as if that was some magical date."

"I guess for Cody it is." Dallas laughed. "He memorized it so he could tell everyone. He was so happy when I told him. He was having a hard time of things back in L.A., and he was so glad to leave and come here. I think

267

he would have been happier anyplace than in L.A. But for the record, I'm equally pleased that he found such a nice friend in Logan. He's a really nice boy."

"I appreciate that. Thank you. He's so much nicer than I ever was as a kid," Brooke said matter-of-factly. "Don't bother trying to think of something nice to say. It's the truth. I was an obnoxious child, and a mean girl in high school. You have no idea of the number of things I regret having said or done back then."

"Is there anyone who doesn't look back sometimes and think, 'I wish I hadn't . . .'?"

"Oh, but I took it to the extreme. Take you, for example. I really disliked you from the first day you arrived. There was just something about you . . ." Brooke shook her head. "Not that you did or said anything, but even back then, I knew that you were going to be trouble in my life."

Dallas laughed.

"Seriously. You were such a thorn in my side. And it used to kill me that you just didn't seem to be aware of it, that you just didn't care."

"I knew. I cared," Dallas said softly, remembering the years of snubs and whispers behind the hands of the girls who hung around with Brooke. "I just didn't know what to do about it. I didn't really know how to make friends with any of you."

"Except for Grant."

"He was the first person who was nice to me. Actually, now that I think about it, he was the only person who was nice to me."

"That's because he was in love with you."

268

"Not when we were eleven," Dallas said.

"Yes, starting when we were eleven. That's why all the girls hated to see you arrive back in town, didn't you know that? Everyone had a crush on him. During the school year, things would be great. We all went out with him at one time or another. Parties, football games, dances." Brooke rested her arms on the table. "Then every year, June would come around, and there'd be no more Grant until September. And all the other guys would sort of hang around, hoping you'd get tired of Grant and give them a chance."

"Gee, this makes me feel swell."

"I'm sorry. It was a lifetime ago. I shouldn't have said anything."

Ally came into the room from her living-room perch where she watched for Berry, and went to the back door.

"Want out, girl?" Dallas walked to the door and opened it. "Stay right where I can see you."

She turned to Brooke. "I can't believe I talk to this dog as if she's a person. But if Berry came home and her dog was missing . . . yowzer."

"Is that one of the dogs you got from Grant?" Brooke asked.

Dallas nodded.

"He mentioned it the other night, that he'd found a dog for your aunt and one for your son. Of course, now Logan *must* have a dog, too, and Grant would be happy if we took one, but I don't know if I want to take on a dog right now. I'm still geting used to being in St. Dennis again. It's very odd, coming back to the place where you were a child, living in the same house you grew up in."

"I'm sure." Ally scratched at the door and Dallas got up to let her back in. She gave the dog a treat, as she always did, and Ally took it into the front room. "So, are you seeing Grant, now that you're back?"

She tried to sound nonchalant but wasn't sure she succeeded.

"I see him a lot, yes." Brooke nodded. "Regardless of how much the population grows from May to September with all the summer people and the tourists, this is still very much a small town, you know? You see everyone." She started to raise her glass to her lips. "Oh. You mean, am I *seeing* Grant? As in dating?" Brooke shook her head.

"I know that's the rumor that's going around, but it isn't what people think. Once I got past the indisputable fact that Grant was never going to like me in that way." She smiled wryly. "When he came back after visiting you that last summer and told everyone you'd broken up for good, I thought, wow, here's my big chance. As it turned out, it was my big chance to prove what a good friend I was by letting him cry on my shoulder every waking minute until I left for college. We've been friends ever since." Her voice dropped. "I know that everyone is saying that I came back to St. Dennis because of Grant, and in a way, it's true. After my husband died, I needed a friend. Grant wrote to me after he heard about Eric, and it was very comforting to know that someone I hadn't seen or thought about in a long time remembered me and cared enough to reach out to me. He's let me take my turn crying on his shoulder, and I appreciate that a great deal."

"I'm so sorry for what you must have gone through."

Dallas realized how that sounded, and amended it by adding, "What you're still going through."

"Thank you. It's been a living nightmare, the kind you never wake up from." She shook her head from side to side as tears welled in her eyes. "I wish you'd met him. I can't even begin to tell you what he was like. Eric was the absolute best, most wonderful guy in the world. There could never be anyone else like him." She opened her bag and rummaged for a moment, then brought out a small leather volume. Opening it, she passed it to Dallas. "This is Eric, on our wedding day. Did you ever see a more handsome guy?"

"Wow. What a gorgeous bride you were. And yeah, he just might be the handsomest groom I ever saw. He certainly did justice to that tux."

"I know, right? He was . . . everything good. We were going to do so many things together." She pulled a tissue from her bag and wiped her eyes. "Logan was an accident. We'd decided we weren't going to start a family until Eric's last tour of duty was over. We were going to find a great place to settle and have three or four kids. But you know what they say: man plans, God laughs."

She smiled at what might have been a memory. "Not that either of us was ever sorry about Logan. Surprised, yes, but sorry, never. And so happy. Eric was so proud of his son." She began to cry. "It just kills me to know that Logan will never know just how good a man his father was."

"He'll know." Dallas got up and put an arm around Brooke. "You'll tell him. You'll make sure he knows."

Brooke nodded. "It's not the same . . ."

"Of course it isn't. But he'll know his father through you and the stories you'll tell him."

"Most times, I can't even bring myself to speak his name," Brooke confessed. "It just hurts too much to talk about him. I don't know why I'm talking about him now." She choked on a sob and Dallas got a glass of water for her. "I'm just so lonely with him gone, I don't know what to do with myself. I thought maybe if I came back home here, I'd feel better, you know? Maybe things would be better."

"Has it been?"

"In some ways, yes. Being in a place that's familiar, with people I've known all my life, has been good. And it's been wonderful for Logan to be able to spend some time with my brother. And my mom's here with us and we're all staying out at the farm, which my brother took over when my dad gave it up." She smiled. "He's been terrific about letting us stay with him, but I know it's putting a big-time damper on his social life, with his mother, his sister, and his six-year-old nephew underfoot all the time."

"I'm sure he's happy to have you there."

"He says he is, but he's been known to lie to be polite in the past." Brooke sighed. "I'm so sorry. I didn't intend for this to turn into a weep-fest. I was just feeling so blue, coming back from the wedding. The last time we were all together was at my wedding eight years ago, and today everyone was remembering Eric and offering their sympathy."

"It must have been a rough day."

"Yeah."

"And you came here to apologize and I did everything

but kick your butt down the front steps." Dallas frowned. "I'm really sorry. I'm embarrassed that I was so rude."

Brooke waved a hand dismissively. "It was a misunderstanding, that's all. Besides, after the way I used to treat you, I figure you owe me a boatload of rude."

Dallas extended her right hand. "Friends?"

"Friends. Absolutely, yes. Friends." Brooke shook Dallas's hand. "Thank you."

"So now that we're friends, I need to ask you something."

"Anything."

"Are you really studying to be a veterinary assistant?"

"Are you kidding? The first time someone brought in a sick animal, I'd lose it." Brooke laughed. "No, I'm taking business courses now. I left college after my third year, but I've always regretted it. My brother suggested that I enroll at Chesapeake College and get the credits I need for a bachelor's. I needed an elective, so I signed up for animal husbandry. I grew up on a farm, so I figured it would be an easy course for me. So the next thing I knew, Logan was telling everyone that I was going to be a vet and work for Grant. I guess that's the leap his little mind made, because he'd love for me to be a vet so that he could be around the animals all the time, and the only vet he knows is Grant. But the story going around—the one that has me planning to go to work for Grant so that I can seduce him? Totally not true."

"Good to know." Dallas nodded. "So, what do you want to do after you finish school?"

"Cupcakes."

"You mean a bakery? I think there is a fairly new

bakery in town, but Berry said it wasn't great. Maybe you'll—"

"Uh-uh." Brooke cut her off. "Not a bakery. No breads. No doughnuts. No cakes, pies, or cookies. Just cupcakes."

"I've seen shops that only sell cupcakes in just about every major city I've been in over the past two years or so."

"No shop." Brooke shook her head. "I want to go mobile. Sort of like a hot-dog vendor, but without the hot dogs. Just cupcakes." She took another sip of tea. "I read about a woman who has a van that she takes around the city where she lives, and makes several stops every morning, sells out, then she's home by noon. That's what I want. I can sell in the middle of town, I can sell down on the dock and at the marina."

"Do you need a permit for that?"

Brooke nodded. "I already spoke with the mayor but she said there's no precedent, and there's no law against it. I imagine there will be something put in force now that I've raised the issue, but I don't expect a problem with it. The important thing is that I'll have time with Logan after school, we can have dinner together, and I can put him to bed. That's my priority these days."

"I think it's a very clever idea. I like it."

"Thanks for the vote of confidence."

Ally began to bark at the side windows and soon was joined by Fleur. Dallas looked out and saw Berry parking near the back porch. The boys tumbled out of the car, and Dallas opened the door to let the excited dogs out.

"Be prepared for a bit of pandemonium," Dallas

warned Brooke. "The dogs make for quite a welcoming committee."

"So I see."

Moments later, Berry came into the kitchen with Ally at her side, and Fleur bouncing merrily between Cody and Logan.

"Did you have a fun time?" Dallas asked, ignoring Berry's raised eyebrow at seeing her niece and Brooke obviously enjoying a tête-à-tête at the kitchen table.

"Yes!" both boys yelled.

"The movie was so fun. It was just like I pictured it in my head, Mom," Cody said.

"And we had pizza," Logan told his mother. "Pizza with lots of cheese on it."

"Mom, Aunt Berry had figs on her pizza!"

"Fig Newton pizza!" Logan shouted, and the two boys fell over each other laughing.

"You might want to let those two run off some of their excitement for a bit," Berry told the boys' mothers. "Not to mention the sugar from the ice cream we just had at Scoop."

Dallas rolled her eyes.

"Well, I did make them drink water instead of soda with their pizza. You could thank me for that."

"I thank you for including Logan in your fun," Brooke told her.

"You're welcome, dear. He's no trouble at all, and certainly much more Cody's speed than I am."

"Come on, Logan. Let's play with Fleur." Cody tugged at his friend's arm, and they raced out the back door with the dog.

"I think I'd like to go upstairs and change out of these clothes. I swear, it must have been a hundred degrees in that theater." Berry started toward the hall.

"Thank you again for taking Logan today," Brooke said.

"My pleasure, dear." Berry turned and called her dog, and Ally followed her up the stairs.

Brooke turned to Dallas and said, "Since we're friends . . . now it's my turn to ask something of you."

"Shoot."

"It's a favor."

"All right."

"If you don't care about Grant as much as he cares about you, please don't go out with him again, don't spend time with him. Please don't let him think for one minute that this time it will end differently." Brooke set her glass on the table. "Please don't hurt him this time around."

"I don't have any intention of hurting him."

"Good. Then we're all on the same page as far as Grant is concerned." Brooke stood. "I should get Logan and go on home. I'm sure my mother is wondering what happened to us."

"How much do I owe you for all those newspapers you bought?" Dallas asked as they walked outside.

"How about a cup of coffee one day?"

"I'll go all out and spring for lunch."

"Lunch is tough." Brooke shook her head. "I have classes every day and mid-terms are coming up. But my first class isn't until eleven, so I'm good any morning after exams."

"Give me a call when the smoke clears and we'll get together."

"You're on."

"Want to meet at Cuppachino? I'm getting addicted to their iced lattes," Dallas confessed.

"My favorite place," Brooke agreed.

"Great. You just let me know when you're free."

Dallas stood back with Cody as Brooke backed her car around Berry's, and waved as they disappeared down the driveway and onto River Road.

Who'd have thought this day would ever come? Dallas mused as she walked back into the house. Brooke Madison and Dallas MacGregor—BFFs, Berry would say. The Apolcalypse must be near.

Chapter 15

THE morning had begun so peacefully. Dallas had joined Cody and Berry for tai chi, and then breakfast, which had been on the dock at Cody's insistence. But she and Cody had taken a walk down the path that ran behind the houses along the river, intending to go as far as the bridge about a mile upstream, and they'd startled a snake that had been sunning itself in the middle of the walk. When it rose up and began hissing, mother and child turned tail and ran back to the safety of Berry's yard.

"Aunt Berry, there was a snake! It was really big!" Cody shouted as they ran across the lawn. He pulled up short in front of the chair where she was reading the morning paper and held out his arms to show her just how big it was. "The biggest snake I ever saw! And it was almost going to bite us! It opened its mouth like this."

He demonstrated the snake's wide-open mouth.

"Was its head slightly triangular in shape?" Berry adjusted her glasses upon her nose.

Cody turned to his mother and asked, "Was it?"

"Maybe. I was too busy screaming to notice." Dallas bent over and rested her hands on her knees and tried to catch her breath. "It had sort of a tip on the end of its nose, but we didn't wait around to notice much else."

"Most likely a hognose, dear." Berry patted Cody on the back. "They play a tough game, but they're perfectly harmless."

"No, he was going to bite us, he was. He made a sound like . . ." Cody hissed.

"All part of the bluff," Berry assured him, "but you were wise to just walk away. There are copperheads in the area, and we want to avoid them. They can deliver a very nasty bite. You're more apt to see a water snake, though. There are plenty of those around."

"Like the one me and Logan saw in the river last week?" Cody asked.

"Exactly. We give them a wide berth but they won't bite unless they are threatened. I was always told that they aren't poisonous, though some believe they are."

"There was a snake in the river last week?" Dallas frowned.

"Of course. There are always snakes in the river, don't you remember?" Berry folded the paper and dropped it to the ground.

"I guess I blocked it out," Dallas admitted. "It's the one thing Indiana Jones and I have in common: We both hate snakes. I don't even like thinking about snakes."

"Well, they do a job, and they do it well," Berry told her.

"What job do they do, Aunt Berry?" Cody sat on the arm of the wooden chair.

"They eat rats and frogs and mice," Berry explained. "Why, we'd be positively overrun with rats were it not for the snakes."

"Ah, that's another thought I try to avoid." Dallas shuddered. "Being overrun with rats."

"I don't remember you being quite so skittish when you were younger." Berry trained her eyes on Dallas.

"I didn't know any better then." Dallas picked up the paper. "Oh, the *Gazette*. Grace's paper, right? Anything in here I should know about?"

"Not really. It's basically the same every week: what new shops have opened, who's having sales, the calendar of upcoming events. Oh, but there is a rather nice article about the town festival," Berry pointed out.

"What town festival?" Dallas scanned the front page.

"Discover St. Dennis, dear."

"I discovered St. Dennis years ago, Berry."

"No, that's the name of the festival. They used to call it Founders Day, but someone wisely thought that sounded all too ho-hum. We needed something a bit more distinct. Several years ago, the Chamber of Commerce adopted 'Discover St. Dennis' as our town motto. I'm sure you've seen it on everything from T-shirts and aprons to tote bags and mugs. Anyway, someone proposed that we rename Founders Day as 'Discover St. Dennis.' I think it works quite nicely."

"What do they do on Discover day?" Cody asked.

"What don't they do? And it isn't just a day, it's the entire weekend, Friday through Sunday. There are sailboat races, a big picnic down in the park, and there are house tours in the historic district down around the square in the morning. There's a race through town early in the morning for those who run, and there are footraces for children after the parade."

"There's a parade?" Cody asked, wide-eyed.

"Oh, yes. They block off the side streets for that." Berry stood and stretched. "It's quite the weekend."

"It all sounds like fun and I'm glad we'll be here for it this year." Dallas finished skimming the paper and refolded it.

"Me, too." Cody nodded enthusiastically. "I love parades."

"So do I." Berry glanced at her watch. "Time to get ready for story hour, Cody. Run inside and wash your hands and find the book you took out of the library last week. We'll want to take it back and get a new one ..."

"Ah, bliss," Dallas murmured as she booted up her laptop, having seen Cody and Berry off for the library. Yesterday she'd worked on *Pretty Maids* for hours, until Berry suggested that the three of them take a walk to a neighbor's house where they'd been invited for an afternoon barbecue. Dallas had reluctantly shut down her computer, but later had to admit that she'd enjoyed the company of Berry's friends and the stories they'd told about their days growing up in St. Dennis. Dallas mentally tucked much of it away, thinking that now would be a great time for Berry to start on her memoir. Dallas had suggested the idea as they walked home, but Berry had appeared horrified at the very idea.

"I don't think so, dear." Berry had shaken her head.

"Oh, but what tales you must have to tell."

"There are some tales that weren't meant to be told."

"You've lived a fabulous life, Berry." Dallas had slipped a hand through her aunt's arm.

"Oh, indeed I have." Berry smiled. "But that doesn't mean the rest of the world has to know about it."

Dallas had let it drop for the time being, but resolved to work on Berry again before the end of the summer.

She reached for the photo of Berry and the mystery man that she'd left standing against the desk lamp, but realized it wasn't there. She moved all her papers around, picked up the laptop, and looked around the floor, but the picture was nowhere to be found. She reached for the photo album where she'd found it, thinking perhaps Berry had returned it there, but no luck. Her cell phone rang as she finished flipping through the pages. Caller ID announced that Norma was on the other end.

"You're up early for a California gal," Dallas said by way of a greeting.

"Well, when you have good news—as in, I have good news, and I have good news—why wait to share?" Norma replied. "Besides, it's not so very early. It's eight thirty. So. First the good news: I have to be in court at ten on someone else's case but wanted to give you a heads-up. Your divorce hearing is scheduled for one this afternoon, West Coast time. The judge's clerk called a few minutes ago, wanting to postpone the hearing because they thought it might go on too long. I assured them this would be quick and dirty because we've come to an amicable agreement that all parties have signed and we just needed to have the judge sign off on it."

"You mean, that's it?"

"You signed and returned the papers I overnighted to you the other day, and Emilio's attorney took them to the rehab center for his signature. Everyone's signed on their respective dotted lines, so unless Emilio's attorney comes up with something half-assed at the last minute, yes. That's it. You'll officially be a single girl again and you can put that whole nasty business behind you."

Before Dallas could respond, Norma said, "And now for the other good news. I spent most of yesterday on a conference call with Victoria Seymour and her agent." She chuckled. "I thought Kathy Eagan—the agent—was going to have a stroke trying to keep Victoria quiet. The author is thrilled to death that you loved her work, and was willing to almost *give* the rights to you. I promised her she would be well compensated, but she was so excited. Suffice it to say that Kathy had to all but put a muzzle on her to make her stop talking and to hang up so that we could negotiate the deal."

"So we have the rights?" Dallas held her breath.

"Of course. I could have taken advantage of them and paid half of what you're going to, but I gave her what you wanted to offer, so everyone's happy." Norma paused. "You *are* happy, aren't you? You're awfully quiet."

"I'm delirious. I'm just stunned that you were able to work it out so quickly."

"Victoria is a huge fan of yours—she was almost hyperventilating on the phone—but I have to tell you she was disappointed when I told her you wouldn't be starring in the movie. Any chance you'll change your mind about that? It might help to sell the project."

"I have someone in mind for the role."

"Well, in any event, the film rights for *Pretty Maids* are yours. Or will be, once the contract is signed."

"Can you start working on that?"

"Dallas, you wound me." Norma sighed. "I have my assistant typing the first draft even as we speak. The finished product will be on Kathy Eagan's desk late this afternoon. As soon as we have the signed contract back from her, we'll send it on to you."

"Wonderful. You really are full of good news today."

"Well, I still have to get the divorce decree signed, and you need to get that screenplay finished. And we have to get backing. But leave that to me. I don't expect that to be a problem. With your name attached to it, we should be fine." Norma paused again, then asked, "What are the chances you'll be able to talk your aunt into returning to the screen one more time?"

"I haven't discussed that with her. I wanted to wait until I knew I had the rights."

"If I could tell potential backers that Beryl Townsend was coming out of retirement to play Rosemarie, and that you were writing and directing, that could seal the deal."

Dallas thought it over. "I'll toss it out there and we'll see if she bites."

After Dallas ended the call, she sat back in the chair and reflected on the news. If all went well, her marriage to Emilio would be officially over in a matter of hours. Regardless of how it had ended, she'd gone into the relationship with stars in her eyes, determined that she and Emilio would beat the statistical odds. She knew that the majority of Hollywood marriages didn't last, but she'd been sure that hers would be the exception, that they would live happily ever after. She had been so happy on their wedding day, so certain that their life together would be wonderful and that their love would overcome any obstacle. Her optimism had lasted longer than Emilio's resolve to keep his vows. She had endured years of emotional pain and betrayal, and it was hard to believe it was really coming to an end. Still, even when a marriage is bad, it's often hard to put aside. She couldn't help but feel sad that they'd come to this, after starting out with such high hopes.

Life can only get better, she thought, then realized that it already had: *Pretty Maids* was going to be a film, and she was going to make it.

She wanted to shout. Dance. Celebrate. She wanted to lift a glass and toast herself, but she'd never been one to drink alone. Restless, she wandered around the downstairs. The dogs heard her footsteps and came to investigate, then proceeded to follow her from room to room.

"You are great pups and I'm very fond of both of you," she announced as she unlocked the back door to let them out. "But, Ally, you don't dance and, Fleur, you're way too young to drink."

She checked the time and knew that Berry would still be in the library with Cody, so she couldn't call her. She couldn't call any of her friends in California because she didn't want the word out until she had the signed contract in her hands, lest someone else decide to buy the book out from under her.

Damn, she thought. All this good news and no one to share it with. Even her new friend, Brooke, would be in class.

Oh, who are you kidding? she chided herself. *You know there's really only one person you want to celebrate with.*

She went back into the library and searched her wallet for the card she'd tucked away, and dialed the number before she lost her nerve.

The call went right to voice mail.

"Grant, it's Dallas." She paused, not sure what she wanted to say next. She settled for, "Would you give me a call when you get this?" She left her cell number and hung up.

So, she told herself. *That's that.* What came next, who could know? All celebratory activity would have to wait. There was still work to be done.

She brought the dogs in and went back to the library. The photo album was still on her desk. She returned it to the shelf, then grabbed the next one from the stack, thinking maybe the picture had gotten placed in a different book. She went through it, page by page, but there was no photo of Berry and her mystery guy.

On to the next album, and the one after that. In the fifth book she found a different snapshot of Berry with the same man. She took it to the window to get a better look. The camera had caught them in a private moment, one in which they were gazing into each other's eyes and smiling secret smiles. Dallas was so absorbed in their expressions that she didn't immediately notice the background, but when she did, she took the photo out onto the back porch. *There,* she told herself, *there's the tree, but in the photo it's much smaller.* The vines that now climbed the carriage house walls were missing, and the dock was much shorter, but clearly, the picture had been taken there at the house.

"Someone knows who this man is," she murmured as she went back inside.

She slipped the photo into her bag and smiled with satisfaction. If Berry wouldn't tell her, Dallas would find someone who would. And she had a pretty good idea of where to start. She grabbed her sunglasses and the keys to her rental car, and headed into town.

She parked out back of Simmons Spirits and went inside. Ten minutes later, she was on her way back to River Road with a magnum of Moët & Chandon that she planned on putting directly into the refrigerator to chill. On her way back through town, she stopped at the *Gazette* office.

"I was wondering if I might speak with Grace Sinclair, if she's available," Dallas said to the woman at the front desk.

"You just missed her by about ten minutes," the woman told her. "She ran over to Bites to grab lunch. You can probably catch her there. Or if you'd rather leave a message, I can take one."

"I'll go across the street, thanks."

Bites, the soup-and-sandwich spot where many local folks gathered for a quick lunch, was directly across the street from the *St. Dennis Gazette*'s building. Dallas ordered an iced tea at the counter, then made her way to the side of the room where Grace Sinclair sat at a table for two, looking over the latest edition of her weekly paper. She glanced up when Dallas's shadow fell across the table.

"Well, what a nice surprise. I had a note on my things-to-do list today to call you later," Grace told her. "Would you like to sit . . . ?" She began to clear her purse and a shopping bag from the other chair. "Did you order lunch? Are you by yourself?" Grace looked around to see who Dallas's companion might be.

"No, I'll be having lunch at home when Berry and

Cody get back from the library, and yes, I'm alone. I don't want to interrupt your lunch. I just wanted to say hi."

"Sit, dear, if you have a moment." Grace pulled the chair out halfway from the table, and Dallas turned it so she could sit facing the older woman.

"I stopped at your office to see if you had a minute to spare and they told me you were here. There's something I wanted to ask you."

"Oh?" Grace put down the half sandwich she'd been holding.

"It's about Aunt Berry," Dallas began. "You've known her for a long time, haven't you?"

"Of course. We both grew up here. Now, keep in mind, she is ten years older than I am, but we've had a number of mutual friends over the years. Is there something wrong?"

"No, no. I just found this photo of her, and she seemed evasive when I asked her about the man who's with her." Dallas opened her bag and looked for the picture. "Actually, this is the second picture I found of her with this same man. I showed her the first one, but she more or less blew me off and the photo disappeared. I didn't show her this one."

Dallas placed the photo on the table between them.

"The background looks like the back of Berry's property, so I thought there might be a chance he was from this area. And I figured if he was from around here, you'd most likely recognize him."

Grace put on her glasses and held up the photo, then smiled.

"It's Archer Callahan."

"You know him." Dallas couldn't help but grin. She'd figured right.

"Of course." Grace looked up from the photograph. "He's my cousin."

"He's your cousin?" Dallas's eyes widened. She'd expected that Grace would be able to identify the man, but hadn't expected this bit of news.

Grace nodded. "On my mother's side."

"So what was the story here?" Dallas tapped the photo. "I'm thinking there must have been a story."

"Oh, yes, indeed, there was. Archer and Berry circled around each other from the time they were about fifteen. Even after she left for Hollywood and he left for college, they were still an item. He never really discussed it with me, but when he finished law school, I think he expected Berry to put her career behind her and come back to St. Dennis and marry him and settle down. Obviously things didn't work out that way, and she stayed in California. It wasn't too much longer after that, he married someone else."

"What happened to him? Where is he now? Is he still alive?"

"Still alive and kicking. His goal was to become a judge, and he did, eventually. Retired from the bench last year. I was speaking with his sister last month and she said he was selling the house in Annapolis to his oldest son."

"He has a family?"

"Oh, yes. He and Mary Claire, his wife, had four children, and did a fine job raising them." Grace stared at the photo for a while. "He was something, Archer was. Handsome, arrogant, brilliant—the perfect counterpart to

Berry. He adored her, and it appeared she adored him in return. You can even see it here, in their faces." Grace turned the photo to Dallas, who nodded in agreement. She'd thought that very thing.

"Everyone was shocked when Berry left that last time to go back to California," Grace continued, "and shocked even more a few months later when Archer brought Mary Claire home and announced they were getting married. She was very quiet, reserved, just the opposite of him, and she couldn't have been more unlike Berry if she'd tried."

"Did you say she *was* quiet . . . ?"

"Mary Claire passed on about a year and a half ago."

"So, he's a widower, then . . ." Dallas thought aloud.

"Yes, he's . . ." Grace's eyebrow rose slowly as if she'd read Dallas's mind. She smiled. "Yes, indeed, he is."

"I wonder if Berry knows that."

"I imagine she does."

"It's a wonder they haven't run into each other. St. Dennis is such a small town."

Grace shook her head. "No, dear, he rarely comes back to town. Only for special occasions."

"I suppose there are no special occasions coming up." Dallas frowned.

"Well, perhaps there might be," Grace said. "Perhaps . . ."

Dallas watched the woman's face and studied the smile that grew and spread from side to side. "Yes, I believe there might be something special coming along quite soon."

"Good." Dallas nodded. "That would be good."

"I'll think on that," Grace assured her. "Give me a few days to work things out."

"Take all the time you need." Dallas glanced at Grace's unfinished sandwich. "I'll let you get back to your lunch now. I've already taken too much of your time."

"Not to worry, dear. And as I said, I was going to give you a call. We have the festival this weekend, which will bring thousands of people into town and just generally create havoc. But perhaps you could pencil me in for one day next week. Perhaps Wednesday?"

"Wednesday of next week would be fine," Dallas agreed.

"Does eight in the morning at Cuppachino work for you? The breakfast crowd will have moved out by then, but if it's still buzzing, we can take a walk down to the marina and chat on one of the benches near the water."

"I like that idea." Dallas leaned over and gave the woman a peck on the cheek.

"I'll see what I can do about that other matter," Grace told her.

"Great. Thanks. I'll see you later . . ."

Berry and Cody were already home when Dallas returned with her bottle of champagne, which went right into the refrigerator. She chatted with Cody about the book they'd read at story hour that morning, then, after lunch, went back to work after sharing her news with Berry. Dallas wasn't sure which bit of news—that of the imminent divorce or obtaining the rights to the book—had pleased her aunt more. For her part, it was all Dallas could do not to spill what she'd learned about Berry's mystery man, or at the very least, use the word "archer" in a sentence, but since nothing fit into the conversation, she went into the library and returned to work.

It's going to be mine, she gleefully reminded herself as she opened the last file she'd worked on. *Pretty Maids is going to be mine, all mine . . . and what a glorious film it's going to make.*

Dallas's phone rang later in the afternoon, shaking her out of her work zone. She found the phone in her pocket and checked the caller ID. Page One Animal Rescue Shelter flashed on the screen.

"Hi, Grant. Thanks for calling me back." She forced a casual note.

"Hey, is everything all right? The dogs are both okay?" He sounded concerned.

"Yes, they're fine. Sorry, I should have said that there was no emergency."

"Glad to hear it. I got a little worried when I got your message." He paused. "So what's up?"

Dallas took a deep breath.

"I was wondering if you might be free this evening."

"Depends on what you've got in mind. Flight to Paris might be tough—I have a full book tomorrow. On the other hand, I might be able to fit in hot monkey sex."

"Could you fit in something that falls somewhere between the two?"

"Hmm. An entire range of possibilities . . ."

Dallas laughed. "I have a bottle of champagne that needs to be shared, and I thought if you weren't busy . . ." She let the thought trail off.

"Oh? Special occasion?"

"Two special occasions, actually." She spun a paper clip around on the end of her pen. "One, my divorce is supposed to be finalized today. And two, my offer for the film rights to *Pretty Maids* was accepted."

292

"Wow. Doubleheader. Good for you." He sounded impressed. "I'm not sure which one I should ask about first. And do I say 'congratulations'? Is that the appropriate response?"

"We can talk about both, if you're free tonight."

"Ahh, actually . . ." Grant hesitated, and her heart sank.

"It's okay if you're tied up," she hastened to say, and tried to keep it light and casual, as if it didn't really matter. "We can get together another time. I'll be here all summer."

"Here's the thing: I have some dogs that are being brought in from a kill shelter down south. I expect them around seven, and once they arrive, they'll need to be walked and watered, and I'd like to examine them before I bring them inside and pen them alongside the dogs that are already here."

"Well, as I said, we can get together another night."

"Dallas," he said with greatly exaggerated patience, "this is where you're supposed to say, 'Is there anything I can do to help?'"

"Oh. Sure. Is there something I can do?"

"Now that you ask, yes, there is. You can walk the dogs when they're let out of their crates. Paige usually gets that duty, but she's working with Steffie tonight. There was some big group in town today and my sister couldn't keep up with the crowd, so she called Paige in to help. They're open till eleven, so Stef will drive her home after they close. Paige loves working at Scoop, but it means I'm shorthanded with the dogs. So what do you say? You've had some time to perfect your dog-walking skills."

"If I were more of a cynic, I'd say that's one hell of a

line you've got there, Dr. Wyler." She lowered her voice. "'Want to come over and walk my rescue dogs?'"

"Yeah, I know. It hasn't worked very well in the past, but since you haven't said no yet, maybe things are looking up."

"What time do you want me?"

"Anytime you can come over would be fine. I'll be seeing patients right up until around seven, so I'll be cutting it close if they're on time. Which they usually are not."

"I'll see you later, then."

"Great. Yeah. I'll see you then."

For the second time that day, Dallas hung up from a call with a smile on her face. She was going to celebrate her happy day with Grant, and who knew where that could lead?

Chapter 16

"IT looks like flea baths for everyone," Grant announced to no one in particular.

"What?" Dallas stood in the doorway, holding a young beagle on a leash. "Flea baths?"

"Yeah." He nodded and flashed her a smile. "We'll start with you."

Dallas crossed her arms over her chest.

"Kidding," he told her. "I was referring to the dogs. One in the bunch had fleas, they'll all have fleas. If we don't knock that out right now, every dog in the shelter will be scratching by the weekend. Anyone know where Janelle is?"

"She went to pick up a pizza," Mimi Ryan, one of Grant's assistants, told him.

"No eating on the job. I thought we had posted that in the kitchen."

"Ha ha. Good one, boss." Mimi whispered something to the dog Grant was examining, and patted its head.

"I get no respect. I'm thinking about changing my name to . . ." He looked over at Dallas. "That comedian who got no respect. What was his name?"

"Rodney Dangerfield," Dallas replied.

"Yeah, him." Grant continued his exam of the grey-hound. "What do you think, Dallas? Rodney Wyler?"

Dallas offered a thumbs-down.

"I had a feeling you were going to say that." Grant ran his hands along the dog's back. "You're looking good, Champ. Take a walk with Mimi and she'll give you a bath."

"How come I have to do all the flea baths?" Mimi complained.

"Because it's in your job description."

"No, it isn't."

"It is now."

Mimi laughed good-naturedly and walked off with the greyhound.

"So tell us, Dallas MacGregor, international superstar. How did you celebrate the outstandingly good news you received all on one day?"

Grant waved on Janelle, who walked in with a pizza box in one hand and a tan mixed-breed pup in the other arm. She handed the pup to Grant, who stood it on an examining table. "'Well, Oprah, I just totally went to the dogs that night,'" Grant said.

Dallas rolled her eyes. Janelle took the pizza into the kitchen, then came back and took the beagle from Dallas, who traded for the foxhound that was next in line.

When Grant finished with the puppy, he moved on to the beagle while Dallas walked the foxhound.

"I'll bet you can't remember the last time you had this much fun," Grant said to her when she came back into the barn after walking the dog.

"Actually, I can," Dallas deadpanned. "August 2001.

The *Tarzan* remake. Up to my chin in quicksand. Well, actually, it wasn't *real* quicksand, but it felt like it."

"Because you know what real quicksand feels like," he scoffed.

"If it's soft and mushy and wet and you're in it up to your chin . . ."

"All right, I'll give you that one." Grant turned and called to Mimi. "If you're done with the greyhound, I have a beagle here that could use a bath."

"You're going to have to hold him for a minute," Mimi called back. "This guy still needs to be dried off."

"I'll take her back." Janelle reached for the beagle and led it to the room off to the side of the barn where the dog bathing was taking place.

"How often do you do this?" Dallas asked Grant.

"As often as someone brings me dogs," he said simply. "When someone in the network gets a call that a bunch of dogs at XYZ shelter are going to be put down, if they can get a volunteer to pick up the dogs quickly enough, they'll drive them north. I take a few, other shelters take a few. We save as many as we can." He looked across the examining table and met her eyes. "These are all good dogs, Dallas. They deserve a chance to have good owners and good homes. Forever homes."

He knelt down to take a look at the foxhound, then smiling up at Dallas, he said, "I don't suppose you'd want to . . ."

She held up one hand and laughed. "Hey, you're two for two. Don't press your luck."

"No harm in asking." He examined the foxhound, who licked his chin. "Nice girl here. Beautiful dog. Yes, you're a pretty thing, aren't you? And young." He checked her teeth. "Maybe eight, ten months at the most. And so well behaved. We're going to find a good home for you, baby girl, and someone is going to thank me."

Grant had been charming and fun on Friday night, but the Grant who calmly and gently examined each dog, speaking softly and with affection, was the Grant who Dallas knew she'd be unable to resist. She thought of the champagne that she'd brought with her and that Grant had placed in the ice maker in the old refrigerator in the shelter's kitchen, and wondered if resistance was going to be an issue.

When he'd looked over the last dog and handed it off for its bath, he wiped his hands on his lab coat, which had long since ceased being white, and told Dallas, "Give me ten minutes to grab a quick shower. I'm really pretty doggie. Do you mind waiting?"

"Not at all. Oh. The champagne ..." She dashed into the kitchen, and returned with the bottle.

"Good call." He nodded and started for the back room. "I'm just going to check in with Mimi and Janelle, see if they need anything before I leave."

"I can help them if they want," Dallas offered.

"Nah. Your job was to walk dogs, and you did that quite admirably. But flea bathing ... ah, that's an acquired skill. But thanks for offering." He went into the back room and moments later emerged. "They're almost finished and will lock up, so I'd say our work here is done."

He reached for her hand, and they walked across the yard to the house.

"Beautiful night," Grant noted. "Not too hot, not too cool. Stars overhead. Nice bright moon on the rise there." He took a deep breath. "Nice to be alive on a night like this."

She smiled and allowed herself to be led up the brick walk to his front door. It was nice to be with someone who noticed such things.

When he opened the door, three large dogs spilled out, all wagging their tails and making a fuss over Grant. He introduced Dallas, telling her, "These are the old folks, the dogs that got kicked out of their homes because they were too old to keep around. This is Schultz. Everyone expects rottweilers to be tough, but he's a lamb. Probably because he's forgotten he's a rottweiler." Grant gave the dog a scratch behind the ears.

"This is Sailor." He pointed to a wizened bloodhound. "He has arthritis in his back legs and doesn't move very fast these days, but he's a good old soul. And this is Mamie, my number one girl. After Paige, that is. Oh, and you, of course." He looked up from the dog and smiled. "Mamie is part retriever, and part shepherd, and all love. She must have been a sassy girl when she was younger."

He leaned over and kissed Dallas on the mouth, a quick meeting of lips that was just enough to promise more later. "The dogs will keep you company while I'm in the shower. I won't be long." He handed her the remote control for the TV. "In case you get bored."

"I won't get bored." Mamie followed Dallas to the sofa and gave her a good sniffing. "Grant, is there a powder room where I can wash my hands? I'm a little doggie myself."

"Right through this door, through the kitchen, door on the left."

"Thanks."

Grant disappeared into the hall and she heard him take the steps, two at a time, to the second floor. She found her way to the powder room, where she washed up. She took her time on the way back to the living room, wanting to see where he lived, what things were important enough for him to have in his home. She'd always believed you could learn a lot about a person by the things they keep near.

She found the kitchen to be quite old-fashioned, with wooden cabinets painted white, a worn linoleum floor, and ancient wallpaper with random bunches of cherries, the background of which had probably once been white but was now yellowed. The appliances were new, though, and she suspected that his renovations hadn't gotten as far as the kitchen yet. A glass filled with cornflowers and Queen Anne's lace was placed in the center of a wooden table in the bay window—Paige's contribution to the decor, she guessed—and near the open door that led to a back porch stood three bowls of water for the dogs.

She went back into the living room, the furniture of which was new, but the wallpaper as antiquated as that in the kitchen. On the floor was a large oval multicolored rag rug and in one corner was an old rolltop desk that appeared to be authentic rather than a reproduction. Paintings on the walls were mostly of boats and the Bay. A closer examination revealed they were all painted by the same hand and signed A. Clanton. Most were of skipjacks or skiffs, the Bay's hardworking boats, but there were a few of sailboats and one of a schooner. She walked around the room to study each.

"Not bad for someone who never had a lesson, don't you think?" Dallas hadn't heard Grant come down the steps, and was startled at the sound of his voice.

"Who's the artist?" she asked.

"My mom's mother did those. She raised nine children on a waterman's income, and when the last of her kids left the house, she went back to school, got a GED, and decided she was going to be an artist."

"I'd say she succeeded. These are lovely." She turned to him. His dark hair was still wet and his cotton shirt was partially unbuttoned and clung to him in places that were still damp, and his feet were bare. Dallas thought she'd never seen a sexier man in her life.

"You should see the landscapes," he went on. "They were split between my older sister, Evie, and Steffie. Most of the cousins got one or two, but we got the most because Gramma was living with my parents when she passed away and she gave them all to my mom."

"I keep forgetting you had an older sister. Where is Evie these days?"

"She and her husband moved to Iowa about three years ago. That's where he's from originally, and he wanted to go back, work the family farm. Evie was okay with that— she's into organic gardening—so off they went. Stef calls them Mr. and Mrs. BOR-ing, but they're happy and doing their own thing, so I say good for them." He stood and just stared at her for a long moment. "So. Champagne."

He went into the kitchen and returned with the bottle in one hand, two wineglasses in the other, and a towel over his shoulder.

"I'm afraid we're out of flutes this week." He set the glasses and the bottle on the coffee table, where a brochure for a conference sponsored by the Veterinary Emergency and Critical Care Society sat atop a copy of *Small Animal Internal Medicine*, which sat crosswise on a pet supply catalog, and a copy of *Kirk's Current Veterinary Therapy*. "Let me just move this stuff . . ."

He stacked the books and papers on the floor, then proceeded to open the bottle. The cork flew out and was caught in the towel he'd draped over the top of the bottle.

"Which of your good fortunes should we toast first?" he asked as he poured into both glasses.

"I think my divorce first, because that's a solemn thing and it closes a door," she said thoughtfully. "Then we'll celebrate me getting the film rights to my favorite book, because that's a door that is just starting to open."

"That's what we'll do, then." Grant lifted both glasses, handing one to Dallas. "Here's to closing some doors and opening others."

"I like that." She nodded.

They touched glasses and each took a sip.

"Let's hope those doors that are opening for you will lead to better things." He sat next to her on the sofa. "Now, which do you want to tell me about first?"

Dallas shrugged. "There's not so much to say about Emilio that you couldn't read in any tabloid or celebrity magazine."

"I don't bother with that stuff. The raciest thing I've

had time to read lately was *The Manual of Equine Reproduction.*"

Dallas laughed. "Really, there's not too much to tell— you already know the story. I guess I was hoping for Cody's sake that things would turn around, but they never did." She leaned back against his arm, which was draped over the back of the sofa. His skin was warm and comforting through her knit dress. "In retrospect, I was totally stupid through the whole tawdry thing. I should have divorced him when I realized that he hadn't married me for the right reasons, but for a while it was easier to just go on pretending that things were just skippy."

"So now it's done."

Dallas nodded. "Now it's done. Norma, my attorney, called late this afternoon to tell me that the judge had approved the property distribution that we'd all signed off on, so yes. It's done." She took another sip of champagne. "I guess I could have moved this along more quickly and it would have been official before now, but I was in a rut, I suppose." She smiled. "You know what they say about the path of least resistance."

"But now on to happy things. You're going to make a movie."

"Well, I'm not going to make the movie," she corrected him. "I'm going to write the screenplay, and I would like to direct, assuming I get financial backing for it. That's an involved process but Norma thinks it won't be difficult to get a studio on board. Especially if I can talk Berry into playing one of the roles. I haven't discussed it with her yet, but I plan on doing that tomorrow."

"That would make a difference?"

"A gigantic difference. Berry was a big box office draw for a long time, and she hasn't made a film in almost fifteen years. She's always being offered parts, but she just hasn't wanted to. If she'd do it for this one, though, it could be huge."

"What if you don't get the backing?"

"I guess I'd have to consider financing it myself. I hadn't thought seriously about that, but I'd do it." She thought for another moment, then added, "A lot of independent films have done very well; there's no reason why this one wouldn't. Especially if Berry were signed on as a lead."

"I've seen her movies," he told her. "My parents had them all on video. I had yours—I think I told you that? Video tapes first, then DVDs."

"You had both?"

"All of 'em." He nodded somewhat shyly. "I probably shouldn't have told you that. Does that make me sound like a stalker?"

"Not as long as you didn't sit in a dark room, all by yourself, while you were watching."

Grant looked at the ceiling.

"Tell me you didn't . . ."

"No, I didn't. And mostly I just wanted to see you, to see how you were doing. It always felt so strange, to see your face there on the TV screen. As time went on, and we both got older, it was more to see how you were—" He stopped abruptly.

"How I was . . ." She gestured for him to continue. "How I was what?"

"I was going to say 'aging' but I don't think that would be wise." He frowned. "It's probably not the right word."

"You could probably find a better one," she agreed, laughing in spite of herself.

"How about, I wanted to see how you changed over the years? Does that sound better?"

"It'll do." She nodded. "So, have I changed all that much?"

"Not so much." Grant shook his head. "Your face looks surprisingly like it did when you were a kid, but better." He paused. "Not that you didn't look really great when you were in your teens. I didn't mean . . ."

"I didn't think you did." She couldn't help but smile. He was trying so hard not to offend her.

"My mom would say that you grew into your looks. Actually, my mom did say that about you."

"She did?"

"She saw one of those award shows where they do the red carpet thing, and told me about it the next day. She said you had on a really pretty long dress and that you looked really big-time Hollywood but she could tell it was you, all grown up." The hand that had rested on the back of the sofa reached out and touched the back of her neck, his fingers tracing a circle. "I guess that's a really different way of life, your life out there, as compared to here."

"As different as night and day in some respects, not so very much in others. When I first moved out there, I was dying to be part of it, you know? I couldn't wait to get dressed up in fabulous designer gowns and jewelry and be interviewed on the red carpet. And the first few times, it was a lot of fun, I won't deny it. But as time went on, and I had Cody, I wanted to be around the house more and more. I came to look upon the roles I played as nothing more than that: roles I played because it was my job. I enjoy doing it—I love doing it—I really believe this was what I was born to do. But it's my job, not my life. I care more about the films that I make than I do for the rest of it—the parties and the gossip and the chatter—who's been seen with whom and who does your hair and who's your stylist and who's your personal trainer and how many houses do you own and—" She stopped. "Sorry. I'm sorry. It's just that the trappings grow old, if you're smart enough to let them. I'm getting to the age where the best roles are going to be offered to actors who are younger than I, so there aren't quite as many parts as there were ten years ago. I've made enough money that I can pick and choose among those that do come my way. I can honestly say that working on this screenplay has given me a renewed interest in the business, but from a different perspective."

"Do you think you'd want to do more screenplays?"

"Absolutely. I have an idea for one, an original story, that I want to work on as soon as this one is finished. And I'm hoping—"

"Dad?" The front door flew open and Paige bounded in. The dogs, roused from sleeping in the kitchen, sauntered in to greet her, tails wagging furiously. "Can I sleep at Steffie's? She wants me to work in the morning so she can show me how to make . . ."

Paige's forward motion stopped at the living-room door.

"Oh," she said when she saw her father and Dallas seated on the sofa.

"Hey, Paige." Grant turned around.

"Hi, Paige," Dallas said.

"Hey, guys." Steffie stopped to give each dog its due, then followed Paige into the room. Where Paige had looked flummoxed, Steffie appeared amused. "Oooh, champagne. What's the occasion?" She picked up the bottle and looked at the label. "Nice. Must be something big."

"Dallas met a few milestones today," Grant said.

"Anything you can talk about in front of the *c-h-i-l-d*?" Steffie asked.

"Very funny." Paige made a face at her aunt.

"I made an offer for some film rights on a book I read and fell in love with, and the offer was accepted." Dallas thought perhaps the short version was best. "And my divorce was granted."

"Swell," Paige muttered, then plunked herself down on the end of the sofa.

"Paige, run and get your stuff," Steffie told her. "We're going to have an early morning and a long day. I'm doing a new flavor tomorrow and that always takes me longer, so if you want to learn the ropes, you're going to have to be up bright and early. The plan is up at five, in the shop by six."

"Maybe I changed my mind about staying over," Paige said. "Maybe I'll come over in the morning."

"Maybe you'll get your butt upstairs and get your things, or maybe I'll have someone else work instead of you tomorrow, which means that someone else will be earning all those lovely dollars that could have been yours and learning my secret formulas."

"You only boss me around because I'm a kid." Paige got up and stomped into the hall and up the steps.

307

"I pay you the same as I pay everyone else, which gives me the right to equally boss everyone who works for me," Steffie called after her. "I even let you have a share in the tips today, so don't overplay your hand, missy."

"I'm going," Paige called from the second floor.

"So, you're celebrating." Steffie sat on the sofa arm that Paige had vacated.

Dallas nodded.

"Thanks for letting Paige work with you, Stef." Grant turned and looked at his younger sister.

"It's the least I can do." Steffie leaned around him to ask Dallas, "So what's the book about?"

Dallas proceeded to outline the story. She'd just finished when Paige came down the steps, a canvas bag over her shoulder.

"Got everything?" Grant asked, and she nodded. "Give the old man a kiss and say good night to Dallas."

Paige leaned over the back of the sofa and kissed her father on the cheek. "Good night, Dallas."

"Good night, Paige. Maybe we'll see you tomorrow at Scoop. I'm not sure I've met my weekly allotment of fat and calories yet," Dallas told her.

"I have a new flavor I'm trying tomorrow." Steffie picked up the champagne bottle again. "I wonder how champagne ice cream would taste?"

"I think the alcohol might interfere with the freezing process, but I'm not a chemist, so I could be wrong," Grant said.

"But the flavor of the champagne ... hmm, maybe with some peach ... or cherry ..." Steffie's eyes narrowed. "I'll have to work on that."

"See you both tomorrow." Grant rose and walked them to the door.

"See you, Dallas." Steffie waved.

"Good night, Stef," Dallas called back.

As Grant was closing the door behind them, he heard Paige ask Steffie, "Do you think they're going to have sex? I think they're going to have sex . . ."

Grant laughed self-consciously and sat back down on the couch.

"Where were we?" he asked.

"Well, according to Paige, apparently . . ."

"Oh, you did hear her. I was hoping . . . Well, you never know what's going to come out of your kid's—"

Dallas reached over and pulled his arm to bring him closer, then met his mouth with hers, brushing his bottom lip with hers. His hand went to the back of her head and drew her to him, his tongue teasing her top lip. She wrapped her arms around his neck and tilted her head, inviting him to kiss her more deeply. This was what she had wanted, what she'd been missing, what she needed, and she was done with trying to convince herself that things could ever be other than this between them. His tongue darted from one side of her mouth to the other, stoking a fire that had been dormant for a long time, and she felt the heat all through her body. His hands were on either side of her face, holding her as if he was afraid she'd disappear if he let go, and kissing her as if his life depended on it. Her head spun and her breath caught in her throat and she was sure she was drowning. The need to have him closer, closer, was overwhelming, and she lay back on the sofa and took him with her.

The weight of his body was both familiar and strange. They seemed to fit together in much the same way they once had, but now he was leaner, harder, more muscular, than he'd been at eighteen. His hands found her breasts and stroked her through the knitted fabric of her dress until she couldn't wait any longer to have those hands on her skin. She tugged at the dress and he slipped a hand under it, stroking her skin from her knee to her breast and back again. His lips made a trail from her mouth to the side of her face, to her chin and her throat, her neck to her collarbone. She struggled to get the dress up higher, then when she started to pull it over her head, Grant cleared his throat and said, "Shades. Should . . . pull them. Maybe hit that light . . ." and for a moment, he was gone. She heard the shades being drawn, saw the hall light go out, and the room darkened a bit when he turned off the overhead light.

"Not very romantic," he explained as he came back to the sofa, unbuttoning his shirt and unzipping his jeans. He lowered himself to her and kissed her as he slipped the straps from her bra over her shoulders, and she reached behind her to unhook it.

"Pretty," he said as he tossed the lacy garment over his shoulder. "I always liked that you wore lacy things."

And then his mouth and hands were at work again, and she arched eagerly at his touch. When his lips settled on her breast, she gasped and ran her fingers through his hair, and begged him to take more of her, to take all of her. His tongue flicked at her skin without mercy and shot a steady bolt of fire to her core, and she mindlessly ground against him and urged him on by wrapping her legs around him and drawing him in. She moaned softly when he entered her and raised her hips to meet his. He let her set the pace and she knew she should slow it down, take her time, but she was powerless to stop the wave that had begun to roll through her and took them down along a long spiral path that shattered them both and left them breathless.

"Holy . . ." Grant gasped.

"Amen." She put her head back and fought for breath.

He rested his head on her shoulder for a moment, then turned them both so that they were side by side, Dallas resting against him. He held her to him, one hand running up and down her arm, for a long, quiet time. There was so much to be said, and yet no words would come. She told herself to be content to be there with him in a way she never dreamed she'd ever be again, to take what they'd been given and not risk breaking the spell by speaking.

Determined to savor every second, she closed her eyes, and let herself drift away with him. The memories were there, and she remembered the sweetness of the first time as well as the bittersweet of the last time—but none of the memories were quite as good as this time. No matter what the future would bring, tonight was magic, and she was going to make it last.

Chapter 17

DALLAS wasn't sure what time of day or night it was when she first woke, but she thought it might still be dark out. She opened her eyes and found, not Grant, but a large dog looming over her. She remembered where she was and who the rottweiler belonged to right before she opened her mouth to scream.

"You are one scary-looking dog," she muttered.

At some point during the night, Grant had tossed a sheet over them, and there was a pillow under her head, though she didn't remember how it got there, and Grant was nowhere to be seen. The dog sniffed at her shoulder, then nuzzled her arm.

"All right, Schultz." She yawned and reached out to pet the dog's head. "Good morning to you, too."

"Are you a must-have-coffee-first-thing person, or do you prefer breakfast first?" Grant came into the room, already dressed for his day, and leaned down to kiss her.

"What time is it?" she asked. "How long have you been up?"

"I believe I had the first question this morning, Ms. MacGregor. You must answer before you get to ask, and you may only ask one at a time." He kissed her again, then sat down on the edge of the sofa cushion.

"Coffee first. So now you have to answer. What time, and how long . . ."

"Five thirty and for about thirty minutes."

"Shit. I spent the night."

"So you did."

"I need to get home." She pulled the sheet up as far as her chin, and sat up. "Why are you up and I'm not? Why didn't you wake me?"

"The dogs are early risers and I heard them shuffling about in the kitchen. I didn't think there was a reason to wake you, so I thought I'd let you have a few extra minutes. Why don't you get dressed and come into the kitchen and I'll have your coffee ready. I need to go find Mamie. She sometimes forgets where she lives, and I don't like her to roam too far."

"Deal. If you have to look for her, I'll help."

Dallas sat up, and with the sheet still wrapped around her, set about the task of finding her clothes. When she'd gathered up everything that she'd worn the night before, she made her way to the powder room at the back of the house. Through the partially opened window she could hear Grant calling his dog. She dressed quickly in case he needed her to help, but just as she pulled the dress over her head, she heard him crooning, "Good girl, Mamie. Good girl. Come on in now, girl . . ."

With her fingers, Dallas smoothed her hair as best she could, then slipped her feet into her sandals and went into the kitchen, where Grant was pouring coffee into two cups.

"No matching china," he said without turning around. "Krista kept that. I keep meaning to go out and buy something, but I just never seem to get to it."

313

"It isn't a priority," she told him. She slipped her arms around his waist from behind. "You've got your priorities just right. Your daughter, your clinic, your dogs . . ."

"And you?" he asked softly. "Do you fit in there somewhere?"

"Let's not go there this morning." She rested her head against his back. "Let's just be so happy for what we have right now."

"Are you happy this morning?"

"I am." She smiled. "Are you?"

He nodded.

"Good, then," she told him. "Let's just leave it there for now."

"All right." He turned in her arms and handed her a cup of coffee. "Leaving it there, handing off the morning brew."

"Thank you." She took a sip. "It's really good."

"Don't tell Carlo, but I'm thinking of opening my own coffee spot. I'm thinking I'll call it Cuppachino Too. Or T-w-o, I can't decide which."

"Either would probably get you sued," she noted.

"Good point. Maybe I'll stick with the clinic for a while."

"That might be best." She leaned against the counter and glanced at the clock. "What time do your employees start arriving?"

"Most of the time, Janelle gets in around eight, Mimi rolls in at nine."

"I should probably go." She nibbled on her bottom lip pensively. "I hope no one was looking for me last night."

"If your son got up in the middle of the night and you weren't there, what would he do?"

"If he needed something, he'd go to Berry. But Cody never wakes up once he's asleep unless he's sick. At home, we have Elena, who lives with us and takes care of Cody when I'm away, so it isn't as if he'd panic that I wasn't there. On the other hand, if Berry missed me, she'd assume I'm still here with you and she'll be wearing a very self-satisfied smile when I get home."

"Why's that?"

"Are you kidding? The woman thinks you walk on water. She adores you. She'd like nothing more than for me to—" She caught herself. "For me to spend more time with you."

"That Berry, she's a wise, wise woman. I say, let's make the old girl happy."

Dallas finished her coffee without comment, and rinsed out her cup. "I should go. I don't think it would be smart for me to let people see me leaving here."

"Are you embarrassed that you spent the night here?"

She shook her head. "Of course not. Not at all. But all these years, all the time Emilio was doing what he was doing, there has never been any gossip about me, because I never gave anyone anything to talk about. I don't want talk to start now. I have a good reputation and a son to protect. You have a daughter, and a reputation of your own."

"I understand." He nodded. "Come on, I'll walk you out to your car."

He kissed her good-bye inside the front door before he opened it. "Just so I know, Dallas. Are we going to pretend that this never happened? Or are we going to have to wipe this from the slate along with the past?"

"I suppose I set myself up for that." She leaned back against the door and sighed. "There's no wiping the slate, Grant. You were right. What was between us was very special. It still is, even after all these years. So maybe you're right, maybe it's always going to be there. But where we go from here . . ." She shrugged. "Neither of us can answer that right now. So let's be grateful that we had last night, and let's let the rest of the summer unfold as it will. Sometimes things are best left on their own."

"I won't back away from this, Dallas." He tucked a loose strand of hair behind her ear.

"Neither will I. I just don't want to put a name on it or stare too long at it or think too hard about what happened last night. It's been a long time since we were together, and a lot of things have happened in both our lives during that time. I don't want either of us to think this is something that maybe it isn't."

"Something like what?"

"Maybe something driven by sentiment, I don't know."

"I do know, Dallas, and that's not it."

"Maybe you're right. But let's give ourselves time to find out."

He nodded, kissed her one last time, unlocked the front door, and along with the dogs, walked her out to her car.

Grant stood in the drive and waved one last time, then watched her car disappear around the corner. Down on

316

the street, the last bits of early morning fog had yet to burn off, and tufts of mist scattered as cars drove through them. He called the dogs to him and went back into the house.

He paused to straighten the sofa cushions and to fold the sheet Dallas had left over the arm, then took it and the pillow upstairs. When he came back down, he picked up the wineglasses and the half-empty bottle of champagne, and took them into the kitchen and placed the glasses on the counter. He poured the rest of the champagne into the sink muttering, "Pity," then placed the bottle in the recycling bin. He added the glasses and her coffee cup to the dishwasher and closed it, then poured himself another cup.

He'd wanted to say, *Just give me the rest of the summer, Dallas. Just one more summer and I won't ask for more than that* ... but the words had stuck in his throat. Besides, he knew that last part was a lie. How could he say he wouldn't ask for more when he knew he wasn't going to be satisfied with just one more month of having her in his life again?

On the one hand, he could kick himself for letting last night happen. On the other, he couldn't believe that it *had* happened, it had been that unbelievably good between them, that right, that natural. It had been just as he'd remembered, only better. Magical. Every single minute of last night had been magical. Just as it had always been.

He looked at the calendar and counted the days until September 7, and knew there wasn't time enough. There'd never be time enough, not when he knew as sure as the sun was rising over the Bay that she'd be leaving him, just as she'd left him before, and who knew how long it would be before she'd be back, if ever?

His rational self told him that it would be better if he backed off, let go now, before things got any more complicated. Barring that, if he were wise, he'd make every effort to keep things casual between them. He could see her for dinner now and then, or stop out to see how Miss B was doing with the dogs, but no more nights like last night. In the long run, it probably would be better. But it wasn't likely to play out that way.

He knew that anytime she wanted him, he'd be there for her, no questions asked. She'd always been his girl, and she always would be. Damn the consequences. It was just the way it was.

So much for the opinion of his rational self.

There'd be no backing off. No pretending that it didn't matter. Hell, even she knew it mattered, and that admission on her part had buoyed his spirits and gotten his hopes high. He knew there was no way to make her stay, that there was every chance he'd crash and burn again at the end of the summer, but he didn't care. There were some things in life that were worth the risk. If he ended up looking like a fool, well, he'd been there before and survived. The truth of the matter was that last night he'd felt complete, at peace, for the first time in a very long time.

He heard Janelle's car and checked the time. There were dogs to be fed and exercised, and with Paige at Steffie's, he'd have double duty at both the shelter and the clinic this morning. He checked to make sure his own dogs had water and treats, then went out the back door to start his workday. With any luck, he'd be able to keep his feet on the ground and his head out of the clouds, but he wasn't counting on it.

Chapter 18

WHY do I feel like a sixteen-year-old sneaking in after curfew?

Dallas drove slowly up the long drive to Berry's house, and debated whether to go in through the front or the back door.

The back door, she reminded herself, was the farthest from Berry's room and she could go up the back steps from the kitchen and slip into her room. Just like she used to do when she *was* sixteen and she *was* sneaking in after curfew. She parked the car and got out, closing the door as quietly as she could. She climbed the back steps and paused at the top to take in the always breathtaking view of the sun rising over the river, then into the house and up the back steps on tiptoes—*Ridiculous! I'll be thirty-eight in a few weeks!*—straight to Cody's room. Her son slept on his side, one arm looped around the dog that thus far had shown absolutely no interest in the dog bed that they'd bought for her.

"You know a good thing when you see it, don't you, girl." Dallas whispered and patted the dog's head.

Dallas left the room as silently as she'd crept in. She went into her bedroom and sat on the edge of the bed, but she knew it was futile to try to sleep. Already wide-awake, thanks to a strong cup of coffee at Grant's and a tangle of conflicted feelings she wasn't ready to sort out, she went into the shower, then dressed and went back downstairs as quietly as she'd gone up. She'd make a pot of coffee and go directly into the library to try to get some work done, her theory being that the more she focused on work, the less she'd try to analyze the night she'd spent in Grant's bed. She'd just started to pour water into the coffeemaker when she heard the shuffle of slippered feet in the hall.

"My, my," Berry said as she came into the kitchen. "Aren't we the early bird today?"

Dallas tried to think of a quick and clever retort, but couldn't manage either on so little sleep.

"Please don't even try to pretend that you haven't just gotten home. I wasn't born yesterday, you know." Berry swept past her and went to the refrigerator for half-and-half.

Dallas was still trying to come up with a cleverly vague retort, but she had nothing. She felt her face flush and went about making coffee.

"Cat got your tongue, dear?"

"I didn't expect to ... I hadn't planned on ... that is, I ..."

Berry waved away her attempts to explain. "You don't owe me any explanations. I know how these things go. Besides, you're an adult."

She was smiling smugly when she added, "So, was it as good as you remembered?"

"Berry!" Dallas scolded.

"Just making conversation." Berry was still smiling. "I imagine it was, or you wouldn't have stayed the night."

"You're impossible," Dallas muttered. "It wasn't supposed to happen that way. It was supposed to be a friendly celebration, nothing more than that. I never expected—"

"Please, it's your Aunt Berry you're talking to."

Dallas measured coffee into the filter, then finished pouring in the water.

"I'm not trying to be coy," she told Berry. "I really hadn't thought that far ahead. Of course, in retrospect, maybe that was deliberate on my part."

"The not-thinking part?"

Dallas nodded. "I always feel confused about Grant, except when I'm with him."

"How do you feel then?"

"Comfortable. Like everything's the way it's supposed to be."

Berry sat at the table, her chair turned slightly so she could see the new day outside as well as her grand-niece.

"Perhaps it's a good time to stop thinking about it and just let go, see what happens, where it goes on its own," Berry said thoughtfully. "Sometimes we think too much about things that are really quite simple."

"Maybe. That's pretty much what I told Grant." Dallas got out two of the new "Discover St. Dennis" mugs that Berry had bought at Cuppachino a few days earlier. "What would you do?"

"I very rarely give you advice, Dallas." Berry sat with her hands folded on the edge of the table. "But since you asked . . ."

Dallas poured the coffee and brought both mugs to the table.

"Sometimes we make decisions that we don't totally think through, decisions that are perhaps based on what we think we want at that particular moment, rather than on what we really need and what we want for the long run. Sometimes those decisions turn out to be more final than we'd planned." Berry's eyes grew moist. "It's very rare to get a second chance. Not everyone does, you know."

Dallas sat next to Berry and studied the older woman's face, and tried to recall the last time she'd seen Berry near tears.

"Was there something you wished you'd had a second chance at?" Dallas asked softly.

"Water over the dam, dear." Berry took a deep breath, and tried unsuccessfully to force a smile. "Water over the dam. And we were talking about you, not me."

"Grant thought I'd dumped him, back then," Dallas confessed. "He thought I just left to go home that last summer and didn't intend on coming back. He specifically said 'dumped,' as if I'd meant to hurt him."

"That bothers you."

"It does. I never thought of it that way."

"What were you thinking?"

"I was thinking about the letter I'd gotten from the drama coach. I was thinking about trying out for the fall semester play," Dallas replied sheepishly. "It sounds so lame now, but Grant never understood how much acting meant to me. Even back then, I knew what I wanted, Berry. I wanted to be a movie star. I wanted to be just like you."

"And it appears you are." Berry sighed. "In more ways than you know."

"I wanted that more than anything. Grant and I ..." Dallas sought the words. "We were too young, Berry. We hadn't really tested ourselves or found our own way back then. I never said good-bye to him, because I never really thought I was going." She smiled wryly. "Until I went, that is."

Dallas looked up across the table at Berry. "I guess I thought it would all work out. I thought I was coming back, do you remember?"

"For some reason, your mother chose that time to try to bond with you." Berry added drily, "Who knows why."

"I think she wanted to ... to try to make up for not having been better than she was. She fell apart after my dad died, and she just couldn't seem to put herself back together again. I felt sorry for her."

"Darling girl, you were eleven years old." Berry reached for Dallas's hand and gave it a squeeze. "You were the one who needed consoling. That's why I insisted on you and Wade spending that summer here with me. I knew that Roberta simply wasn't up to comforting anyone other than herself."

"That was your idea?"

"You were so stoic at the funeral, both of you were, that you frightened me. I couldn't very well leave you there. Your mother was a very dependent sort. Before too long, she'd be looking to you to carry her emotionally. You were far too young for that. I thought you needed to be able to act like children who were grieving the loss of their father, not children who were trying to hold up their mother, so I told Roberta that she needed to pack your things and bring you and Wade here." Berry seemed to be studying Dallas's face. "Was that the wrong thing to have done?"

"No. You're absolutely right about Mom. She was always dependent on Dad, and after he passed, she became dependent on me. It's just that all these years, I thought Mom sent us away because she didn't want to be bothered with us." Dallas smiled weakly. "I suppose in a sense, I was right."

"Roberta has a way of sucking the life out of things." Berry frowned. "I'm very sorry if this offends you, but if the truth were to be told, I was against their marriage from the start. Of course, Ned didn't give a fig for what I thought, and I'm glad he ignored me, because you and Wade mean everything to me."

"You loved my dad very much, didn't you?"

Berry smiled. "He was a delightful child and a wonderful man. Yes, I loved him very much."

"More than the other kids?"

"Oh, much more. Just as I've always loved you and Wade more than any of your cousins," Berry told her. "My sister's other children never meant the same to me. Sad, but true."

"Why do you suppose that was, Berry?" Dallas tasted her coffee and found it had gone cold, but she didn't want to break the conversation right then to refill her cup.

Berry didn't answer immediately, but rather appeared to be weighing her answer. Finally, she merely said, "Chemistry, I suppose."

"I wish my dad had been around to see me make even one movie. He would have been proud of how hard I worked."

325

"Oh, he sees, I suppose, from wherever it is that souls go when they leave this dimension. I'm sure he knows, and if human emotions survive this life into the next, I'm positive that he's very, very proud of you."

"He was proud of you, that's for sure. He always managed to slip into conversations with new people that Beryl Townsend was his aunt."

"Oh, I know he was, the dear boy." Berry smiled. "When he was younger, I'd fly him out to California on his school holidays and take him around with me, and he'd just nearly burst with pride."

"I didn't know that," Dallas said. "That he spent so much time with you when he was a child."

"Oh my, yes. We had some grand times when he was a boy. He was very clever and smart and quick, and yet very sweet, too. Cody reminds me very much of Ned."

"I'm surprised Grandmother Sylvie let him go away so much. I remember her as being very skittish about things. One time my dad's sister, Tess, told me that neither she nor her sister had bikes when they were little because their mother was afraid they'd fall off and break an arm or a leg."

"My sister was a nutcase about some things, it's true enough." Berry paused. "You do remember that Sylvie and I were identical twins, don't you?"

Dallas nodded.

"Identical in appearance only. She was always very tentative about everything. Me?" Berry smiled. "Not so much. Tessa and Patsy were more like their mother, but Ned was more adventurous, so it was natural that he and I would hit it off. Duncan, your grandfather, never really paid much attention to his children. In their world, the mother raised the children and the father went off to work to support them all. Things are different now, but that's how it was in that generation." Berry smiled again. "But Ned did so get a kick out of telling his friends about his aunt who was in the movies."

Dallas thought she heard opportunity knocking right about then.

"Berry, do you ever think about making another film?" she asked.

"No. I'm not the sort to retire, then unretire. Retire, unretire." Berry flipped her hand back and forth. "Tiring for everyone, and yes, lest you ask, the pun was intended."

"But what if a fabulous role was offered to you? Would you consider it?"

"I doubt it. How many fabulous roles do you think there are for a woman of my . . ." Berry paused before adding, "Experience?"

"But what if there was one . . . ? What if there was a role that was so fabulous that no one but you could play it? Hypothetically."

Berry narrowed her eyes. "What role are we talking about? Hypothetically."

"Rosemarie."

"Pretty Maids' Rosemarie?"

Dallas nodded, not trusting herself to speak.

"Are you asking me if I'd take the role if it were to be offered to me?"

"Yes."

"I haven't worked in a very long time, and when I left Hollywood, it was with the intention of never going back." Berry tapped her fingers on the side of her cup and gazed out the window. "Have you changed your mind, Dallas? About playing Charlotte, I mean."

"No. As much as you are Rosemarie, I am decidedly not Charlotte. Besides, I have someone else in mind for that part."

"May I ask who?"

"Laura Fielding."

"Laura Fielding?" Berry frowned. "That little bleached-blond tart who can't seem to keep her clothes on? *That* Laura Fielding? The one who made all those films where she—"

"She's not a 'tart,' Berry." Dallas sighed. She supposed "tart" was preferable to the increasingly popular "ho," which seemed to pop up just about everywhere these days. "Laura's been badly cast for years, but she has great talent. I worked with her early on, and I think she'd be perfect as Charlotte."

"But she has such a dreary reputation."

"So because she made some career mistakes in the past—and don't get me wrong, I agree, she's made some beauts—she should never be given the chance to show what she's capable of doing?"

"You really believe in her that strongly?"

"I do."

"I suppose then you should ask her to read for the part, when the time comes."

"Will you read for Rosemarie?" Dallas held her breath.

"I don't know. Suppose I've lost my touch?" Berry shuddered at the thought. "I'd hate to be one of those has-beens who makes an effort at a comeback, falls flat on their face, and has everyone shaking their heads and saying things like, 'Dear me, and she used to be so great,' or, 'She should have stayed in retirement,' or ... well, you know the things that are said. I don't want such talk going around about me."

"Impossible. That could never happen to you. You haven't lost a thing."

"I just don't know. It isn't something I've thought about. I realize that's not the answer you want, but it's the only one I can give you right now."

"Fair enough. But I would ask you to do me a favor and give real consideration to the idea. Promise?"

"All right. I'll think about it. I'll consider it."

"That's all I'm asking." Dallas stood and kissed her great-aunt on the forehead. "More coffee, Berry?"

"A spot to warm this up would be nice."

Dallas took both cups to the counter, where the coffeepot stood. After she refilled both and returned to the table, Berry said, "May I ask how you left things with Grant? Or is that intrusive?"

"I don't know how we left it. Not really. I don't know how I feel." Dallas sat and took a sip of her coffee.

"Of course you do." Berry waved a dismissive hand.

"Look, Berry, there goes your great blue heron." Dallas directed Berry's gaze out toward the river.

"Lovely. Don't change the subject."

"What if we got involved again and it didn't work out again? What if he thought I dumped him again? What if—"

Berry cut her off. "What if you both manned up—pardon the expression—and admitted how you feel about each other?"

"What if one of us cares more about the other?" Dallas said slowly. "What if someone gets hurt again?"

"Oh, for crying out loud, Dallas, what if Godzilla rises out of the Bay and plays 'terrorize the tourists' at the festival this weekend?" Berry threw up her hands. "What if aliens landed next door on the roof of the Considines' barn?"

"I see you're not taking this very seriously."

"I'm not the one thinking up knuckleheaded reasons for not taking advantage of this most precious opportunity. You and Grant lost out once before. Now, in all fairness, you were very young, but from what I can see, neither of you ever really got over it. Excuses are for cowards, dear. Be brave enough to go for it."

"Well, I guess you told me."

"I suppose I did." Berry sat back with a satisfied smile.

"Since you're such a brave soul, let me ask you something." Dallas rested both arms on the table. "Suppose you got another chance at ... at whatever it was that you passed up on before. Would you take it?"

"What makes you think there's something—" Berry chose that moment to stir her coffee.

"Please." Dallas rolled her eyes. "Don't play that game with me. I know you all too well. So answer the question, please. If you were to have a second chance at—"

"I hardly think that's relevant." Berry sniffed and picked up her cup, more to keep herself from fidgeting, Dallas suspected.

"Oh, it's not relevant to your situation—whatever that might be—but it's relevant to mine."

"Some things are too far in the past to do over."

Dallas made a *buc-buc-buc* sound. "Chicken."

"Don't be ridiculous. And stop that. You sound like a ..." Berry started to laugh. "Well, you sound nothing like a chicken."

"Answer the question, Ms. Eberle." Dallas wasn't going to let her off the hook. "If you had that second chance you didn't have ... whenever ... would you take it, if you had it now?"

Berry put her cup down and appeared to think it over, and for a moment, Dallas thought she was going to plead the fifth. Instead, she looked out across the Bay and whispered, "I've never considered the possibility, because it never occurred to me that there'd be another chance." She glanced back at Dallas. "Would I take it? I don't know ..."

Berry was still pondering that question all through tai chi when she should have been channeling her better, deeper, innermost self. The only time she was distracted and stopped thinking about it was later in the morning when Louis from the marina pulled up in his pickup with an aluminum rowboat in the bed.

"What's that you've got there, Louis?" Berry called from the back porch, where she'd been reading *Pretty Maids* and trying to see herself as Rosemarie.

"Got you a new lightweight boat." Louis hopped down out of the cab with as much grace as an arthritic seventy-five-year-old man could muster.

"Where's the boat you picked up here the other day?" she asked.

"Berry, there was no hope for that boat. She had the dry rot so bad, there was nothing I could do for her. Now,

331

I know you wanted something for your boy there, and I thought maybe this might work."

"Well then, let's take a look." Berry turned to Cody and said, "Go get your momma and tell her to come on out here and take a look at what Mr. Small brought us."

"The oars are nice and light, too," Louis pointed out.

"This will probably come as no surprise to you, but I won't be rowing that boat. That's going to fall to my grand-niece, so she's the one who has to be happy with it." Berry turned to the house, where Dallas was coming down the steps behind Cody, who was running excitedly with both dogs at his heels.

"Dallas, this is Louis Small from the marina. He picked up that old boat of Wade's the other day and took it down there to see what he could do with it."

"There weren't nothing to be done with it," Louis told Dallas. "It was just dry-rotted near everywhere I looked. We just got this in and I thought maybe you'd like to try 'er out. See what you think of it."

"It's been years since I've rowed, but sure, I'll give her a spin. Thank you. It was nice of you to think of an alternative." Dallas smiled and walked around the boat. "It's nice and small . . . smaller than the wooden one we had. What's it made out of?"

"It's a composite. It's the lightest boat on the market right now. Weighs less than sixty pounds."

"Sounds good. Let's get her down to the river and put her in."

"Me, too! I want to go, too!" Cody jumped up and down.

Dallas lifted one side of the boat, and Louis lifted the

other. "Cody, come see if you're strong enough to lift one side. We won't always have Mr. Small here to help us."

Cody came around the back of the boat to where Dallas stood, and with a nod to Louis, she let her side down. Cody picked it up with both hands, though it was a struggle for him.

"I can help, see?" he said happily.

"I see. I think we'd be able to manage it." Dallas nodded. "All right, then. Let's see how she moves on the water."

Berry followed behind while Dallas and Louis, assisted by Cody, carried the boat to the river's edge, where Dallas kicked off her sandals and stepped into the water.

"Cody, take off your sneakers and take Mr. Small's side of the boat so he doesn't get his shoes wet," Berry directed, and Cody complied immediately.

"I best get those oars for you," Louis said as he returned to the truck.

"Lift the boat just a little more," Dallas told Cody, "so we can get her far enough into the water that she floats."

"Why do they call boats 'she'?" he asked.

"I don't really know, but that might be something you and Berry might want to look up when you're at the library." Dallas pulled the boat farther into the river as Louis brought the oars out to her and placed them in the boat.

"We'll do that this very morning," Berry called back to them.

"I want to get in with you, Mom." Cody was watching Dallas climb over the side of the boat.

"Berry," Dallas called to her, "I don't suppose there are any of those old life jackets around?"

Berry shook her head. "I haven't seen those in years. We'll have to pick up some new ones."

"This one time." Dallas held a hand out to Cody. "But from now on, you do not get into a boat—any boat—without a life jacket on."

"Perhaps they sell them at the marina." Berry walked to the water's edge to watch.

"We got all sizes down there."

"Wonderful. We'll stop there after the library and we'll pick one up," Berry told them.

"Can we pick up two?" Cody asked. "That way Logan can ride with us."

"All right. Two it is. And perhaps one for your mother as well," Berry replied.

"Not a bad idea, though we certainly won't be taking this little thing into deep water."

"You never know, Dallas."

"You're right, Berry. We should all have life preservers if we're going into a boat," Dallas repeated for Cody's benefit. "Now, let me show you how the oars work."

She slid the oars into the rests and locked them in. With Cody sitting next to her, Dallas began to row.

"Why do you need two oars?" he asked.

"Well, let's see what happens when we only use one." Dallas slid one oar out of the water, then rowed with the other.

"Hey, we're going in circles," Cody noted.

"That's right. And that's why you need two oars, so you can keep the boat straight, and steer it where you want to go." She grabbed the other oar, straightened out the boat, and rowed a little farther into the river.

"Teach me!" Cody demanded. "I want to row, too."

"Let's see if you're strong enough . . ." Dallas let him take the oar on his side of the seat and showed him how to row.

For a scant moment, Berry thought she was looking into the past, watching herself teach Wade how to row the day she'd bought him the rowboat. She blinked, and the vision—if that was what it had been—was gone.

"You made yourself a sale, Louis," Berry said. "We'll take it . . ."

"I'll go on back to the marina and I'll get an invoice made up for you, toss in a couple of life jackets," her old friend told her.

"We'll be in later this afternoon. And thank you, Louis. I appreciate it."

"No worries, Berry." He returned to his truck. "Happy it worked out."

Louis drove off, and Berry sat in one of the Adirondack chairs to watch the rowing lesson.

"Boy, am I out of shape for that exercise," Dallas told Berry after they finished and she'd tied up the boat. "I used muscles I'd forgotten I even had."

"Cody did quite well," Berry noted. "For his first time at the oar."

Dallas nodded. "I was surprised at how well he did, frankly."

"I recall how you and Wade both loved to take that little boat of his out. I'm so sorry we weren't able to have it repaired. I did ask Louis to take another look at it and see if there isn't some way he could salvage it."

"This one is so much lighter than the wooden one," Dallas commented. She turned to look for Cody, and when she found him on the pier, ready to step into the rowboat, she called him.

"What, Mom?"

"There are going to be rules, and the rules will be followed," Dallas told him, "or there will be no more boat, understand?"

He nodded.

"You don't get into the boat without a life jacket. And you don't take that boat out by yourself, not ever. It isn't a toy, son."

"I know." He scuffed his toes in the grass.

"Having a boat is a big responsibility. It can be very dangerous under the wrong circumstances." She tilted his chin so that he was looking into her eyes. "Got it?"

"Got it, Mom."

"Good. Now come on in and get ready to go to the library."

"Wait till I tell Logan!" Cody shot off toward the house.

"There goes one extremely happy boy." Dallas put an arm around Berry's shoulders as they followed him. "Thank you, Berry."

"It's my pleasure, dear." Berry patted Dallas's hand where it rested on her shoulder.

The summer was turning out so well for them, Berry reflected while she waited for Cody to gather his things for the library. Dallas was happily at work on her screenplay, and with luck, she should be able to get the backing she'd need. Cody was having the time of his life. And she, Berry, was having more good days than bad, the uncertain nature of her mortality put aside for now. Not that there was any urgency, but at her age, one did think about such things from time to time. The problem was that before Dallas and Cody arrived, Berry was thinking about it almost nonstop. Since their arrival, she'd barely considered it at all.

All the more reason to want them to stay for as long as possible, she thought. *That's one way to keep my mind off eternity and focused on the here and now.*

Ally met her halfway to the back porch, and Berry smiled just to see the happy way the dog ran to join her, as if she were the most important and wonderful person in the world.

Well, to her, I suppose I am. How nice to be so important to someone. Something, she reminded herself, dogs not being people, which to Berry's mind was strictly a matter of opinion, now that she had a dog. Ally was just one more happy by-product of Dallas's decision to spend the summer in St. Dennis.

If Berry had her way, Dallas would jump at that second chance with Grant and find a way to make it work. Any idiot could see they belonged together. One of Berry's greatest dreads was that Dallas would make the same mistakes she herself had made, and drive the man she loved into the arms of someone else because she was too preoccupied with her own ambition to compromise.

And oh, Berry had loved that man with all her heart. Even now, the memory kept her awake sometimes at night, when the might-have-beens and the what-ifs tortured her soul.

A second chance? Not going to happen—even though

in her heart of hearts, she knew she'd walk over hot coals for the opportunity. When a man said he'd never forgive, most likely he knew what he was talking about. And Archer Callahan had never been a man to toss words around carelessly, whether words of love or words that wounded. No, there'd be no second chance for her. Not because she wouldn't consider it, but because the last words Archer had spoken to her, those many years ago, still rang in her ears.

"I'll never forgive you, Berry, and I hope to God I never see you again."

She'd never forgotten, and she was pretty damned sure he'd never forgiven.

"Berry, are you coming in?" Dallas called from the porch.

"I'm on my way."

Berry picked up her bag and a magazine she'd dropped on the ground next to her chair and walked toward the house, where Dallas and Cody waited. They, along with Wade—and now Ally—were all she had. They'd see her to the end of her days. She didn't figure she had the right to ask for anything more than that.

Diary ~

Well, what a week this has been. I've been working around the clock—well, not really but close enough—to get all the ads lined up and all the articles written about the upcoming Discover St. Dennis weekend. So much to do—so little time! I think the grand marshal this year is going to be not only a big surprise, but a huge hit! I'm so glad I thought of it, frankly, and should pat myself on the back. And I will, as soon as I have a few moments to indulge myself.

But a curious thing—Dallas came to me with a photo she'd found of her great-aunt and wanted to know if I knew who the man in the picture was. Well, of course I knew—it was Archer. Dallas says she's never heard of him. Now, how odd is that? Berry and Archer were best friends from the time they were children, lovers for a long time after that. Everyone assumed they'd marry, but, no. So how is it that Berry has never spoken his name to her closest living relative? Unless the loss was so great that she cannot speak of it—the thought of which set my little wheels in motion.

To intervene—or not to intervene? That is the dilemma . . .

~ Grace ~

Chapter 19

IT took a great deal of willpower on Grant's part not to call Dallas that afternoon. Wasn't there some rule about how soon was too soon to call? He'd been out of the dating scene for just long enough to have heard that there was such a rule, but he wasn't sure what it was. He'd hesitated several times between patients, then finally, muttering, "Who makes up these rules, anyway?" gave in and dialed her cell number. He was sorely disappointed when it went to voice mail, but was determined not to hang up until he had his say.

"Hi. It's Grant." Like she wasn't going to know that. *Moron.* "Just called to say hi. And see how you're doing today. And . . . well, I guess that's really all. You can call me if you want. I'll be at Paige's softball game tonight, but you could call my cell or just leave a message or . . . well, or I guess I could call you tomorrow." He paused. "Maybe we could have lunch tomorrow. Just something quick. We don't have to go anywhere special. I just like to look at you."

Figuring he'd already sounded about as lame as a man could possibly sound, he topped it off with, "I guess I'll see you."

Anything else he might have said would have been cut off anyway, so he just left it at that.

He was neutering a borzoi when he felt his phone vibrate in his pocket. There was no way he was going to get to the call, so he simply let it go to voice mail. Of course, he suspected it might have been Dallas, and of course, as luck would have it, it was.

"Just to let you know I got your message," he heard her say when he played it back. "I . . . ah, I'm sorry I missed your call." Pause. "I'd love to grab lunch tomorrow. I'll stop at the clinic for you at noon, unless I hear from you with other plans." Pause. "Tell Paige I said good luck tonight." Another pause. "I . . . ah, I like to look at you, too."

He played the message back three times, smiling through each recitation, before returning her call.

"Damn, I hate voice mail," he grumbled as he was forced to leave another message. "Dallas, noon tomorrow would be great. I'll see you then."

He pocketed the phone, and went back to work.

He couldn't decide if it was easier, or harder, this time around. On the one hand, the expectations were different, or at the very least, he tried to convince himself that they were. Actually, what he wanted to do was to convince himself that he had no expectations of her or of their relationship, but he'd heard a little voice inside singing, *Liar, liar, pants on fire*, every time he repeated the phrase "no expectations." The truth was that this time, he wanted it all. He wanted her to love him again, he wanted them to be so happy together that the past would no longer matter, and he wanted her to stay in St. Dennis and live happily ever after with him. Just thinking about it being a possibility made him happy . . . until he remembered that the odds of any of this happening were pretty damned slim, which of course meant it really wasn't a possibility after all.

She's having lunch with me tomorrow and that's a start, he told himself. After reflecting, he corrected himself. *Last night was the start. This phase*—date me, fall in love with me again—*this is phase two*. The solution seemed pretty simple once he'd broken it down. He just had to keep Dallas in St. Dennis for as long as possible, and spend as much time with her as he could. That was his only shot at winning her back, and he was going for it. He knew there was risk involved—knew exactly what he was risking—but he couldn't dwell on that. Once he acknowledged that there *was* a risk, he banned himself from thinking about it. Why confuse the present situation with facts?

He tried compartmentalizing her, but it didn't work. However hard he might focus on other things—his daughter, his patients, the dogs in the shelter who needed homes—sooner or later, his thoughts went back to her. How she'd looked when she came into the shelter the night before, what a good sport she'd been, helping with the dogs, how the night had progressed so unexpectedly. How she'd looked sleeping next to him. How he couldn't stop looking, which accounted for the fact that he'd gotten no sleep at all the night before.

His daughter had gone for the jugular when she called that morning.

"So, Dad, did you get lucky?"

"Paige, that's an entirely inappropriate—"

Paige had giggled. "Aunt Steffie just said you were

342

going to say that." Paige had lowered her voice and mimicked his indignant tone. "'Paige, that's an entirely inappropriate—'"

"Paige, I don't think you're funny. We're going to have a talk about this. Now put your aunt on the phone." Grant was not amused.

"Yes?" Stef took the phone from Paige.

"I know you think it's funny, but she's only eleven years old, Stef. I don't appreciate you encouraging her."

"I didn't encourage her. That was all hers. But I'd be remiss if I didn't remind you that she's not a baby. She's almost twelve. She knows a lot more than I knew at her age. She understands—"

"She'd better not."

He heard gulls screaming in the background, a sure sign that Steffie had walked outside.

"So, did you?" she asked.

"None of your business."

"That means yes. Good for you. I'm going back to work now. Toodles."

The worst part of it was that Grant knew that his sister was probably right. Kids knew so much more now than they did when he was growing up, and they say that girls grow up faster than boys. He tried to remember what he was like at her age, how much he knew. Throw into the mix the fact that Paige was pretty damned precocious, and he shuddered.

"It's all that stuff on TV," he muttered as he went into his office. "Krista lets her watch anything she wants. MTV. All those movies. The reality shows. The music they listen to. The language. Anything goes."

"So, Dr. Fuddy Duddy, you ready for your next patient?" Mimi stuck her head into the office.

"Do I sound like a—"

"Yep. Cocker spaniel with thorns in his paw, exam room one." Mimi disappeared, and Grant put his phone on vibrate once again before going into the exam room.

"Just wait until you have kids," he called after her.

"We're off to the dedication of the new children's library wing this morning," Berry reminded Dallas on Thursday morning after they'd finished their tai chi. "Would you like to join us?"

"What time does it begin?" Dallas slipped her feet into her flip-flops, which she'd left at the end of the dock.

"It starts at eleven, but we need to leave at ten. Cody signed up to bring refreshments."

"What are you taking?"

They walked to the house, taking a detour past Berry's flower garden.

"I ordered some of those chocolate-dipped strawberries from the sweetshop in town." Berry stopped to deadhead one of her lilies.

"That's a pretty sophisticated snack for a bunch of little kids," Dallas noted.

"Really? Well, it's never too early." Berry dismissed the comment. "Logan said he's bringing cupcakes, so I suppose all will be well."

"I'll bet Brooke made them." Dallas thought aloud. "She said she'd like to have a business making cupcakes someday."

"Really? And here all the talk is about her becoming a vet's assistant or some such thing."

"Not true. Got it straight from the source, so the next time you hear that rumor, you may feel free to put an arrow through its heart."

"Will do." Berry linked her arm through Dallas's. "And I'll be sure to check out those cupcakes."

"I'll stop over at the library later," Dallas told her. "I need to get gas in the car." She paused. "And I'm having lunch with Grant today. I'm picking him up at noon."

Berry appeared pleased, as Dallas had known she would be, though she kept her thoughts to herself.

After Berry and Cody left the house, Dallas showered, dressed, and headed to the lone gas station on the outskirts of town. It was strictly pump your own, and when she finished filling the tank, she grabbed a wet wipe from a stand next to the pump to wash the smell of gas from her hands.

Nice they thought of that, she was thinking as she walked to the trash can near the office door to toss the used towelette. Inside, opposite the glass door, newspaper boxes were lined up against the wall. First in line was a tabloid that, Dallas could see even from the other side of the door, bore her photograph dead center. She couldn't read the headline, but wanted to see what she might have done that would have been considered newsworthy by someone. She opened the door, and stepped inside.

DALLAS MACGREGOR'S SECRET LOVER! BETRAYED ACTRESS SEEKS CONSOLATION WITH HER FIRST LOVE! RETREATS TO CHILDHOOD HOME AS DIVORCE FROM DISGRACED DIRECTOR BECOMES FINAL!

The headlines screamed across her face in bold type. She leaned closer to get a better look. In the center photo, she was on her way out of Scoop, one hand behind her closing the door, the other hand holding a cup of ice cream. She wore a light-colored tank dress and sunglasses, her hair pulled back in a ponytail, and realized it had been taken earlier in the week. But it was the photo next to it that held her attention. She and Grant stood on the dock behind Berry's house, their arms around each other, their gaze on something near the river.

The boat, she recalled. The photo had apparently been taken from the boat that had slowed the night she and Grant had been on the dock. What night had that been? Friday? She recalled that Grant thought he might have known the owner. As much as she hated to do it, she bought the paper and stuck it in her bag, obscuring the smaller headline WHO IS DALLAS'S MYSTERY LOVER?

"Really? It says that?" Grant opened the paper after Dallas handed it to him a few hours later. He stared at the picture. "Damn. They didn't get my good side."

"Grant . . ."

"Sorry. I know. Intrusive. This would have been Friday night, right?"

"I'm thinking that boat that went by . . ."

"And slowed down, yeah." He nodded. "That must have been it."

"You thought you might know the person who owned it," she reminded him.

"Yes, but I don't. His son was in yesterday with one of their cats. He said his father didn't sell the boat after all. Backed out of the deal at the last minute. But remember, there are several marinas up river, so the boat could have

346

come from one of those. Or maybe it was someone who came into the river hoping they'd get lucky—which they did."

"That means that someone told someone else that the first house off the Bay is Berry's." Dallas frowned. So much for anonymity.

"Well, at least they didn't catch us doing anything kinky," he noted.

"True enough." She tossed the paper into the nearest trash can. "So where would you like to go for lunch?"

"Are you sure you want to be seen in public with me?" He paused dramatically. "'Dallas Dines on Sushi with New Guy.'"

"I hate sushi."

"So do I. Let's splurge and go to Lola's. Celebrate having been publicly outed." He took her hand. "And we'll walk, if it's okay with you."

"It's fine."

"So, are you upset?" he asked as they walked down the long drive.

"About the paper? I don't know. On the one hand, I'm surprised. I was feeling so anonymous here. But on the other, I'm not. People have been snapping pictures with their cameras and cell phones for the past few weeks. I'm thinking that maybe the picture of me coming out of Scoop—nice publicity for Stef—could have been taken by a tourist who decided to sell it. The sale might have drawn the pro back to St. Dennis. But I'm not embarrassed to have people know that we're seeing each other." They stopped at the curb to let a car pass. "Or that we saw each other."

That sounded awkward.

"I liked 'seeing each other' better," Grant said.

"Me, too."

They walked to the corner of Cherry Street and crossed.

"So where are you with the movie you want to make?" he asked as they strolled along.

"Nowhere, right now. My lawyer is taking meetings this week and hopefully there will be some interest."

"If not? Not trying to be negative, but I believe in contingencies."

"So do I. If I have to, I'll find a way to put the money together myself."

He looked at her hand, where red ink in the shape of a dog had been stamped.

"Tattoo?" he asked.

"They were stamping hands at the new children's library this morning. I got the dog. Berry got the Cheshire cat."

"That seems apropos, somehow," he noted.

Dallas grinned. "Cody got a Wild Thing."

Grant's eyebrows rose.

"From the book. *Where the Wild Things Are*. It's a classic, and one of his favorites." They crossed Charles Street at the light. "Mine, too."

"I remember that one. The kid in the boat who sails off and lands on an island where there are monsters—"

"Wild things," she corrected him.

"Right. And they made him king, right?"

Dallas nodded. "King of the Wild Things."

"Paige liked that one a lot, too. I'll bet she still has her copy somewhere." He added, "Somewhere at her mother's house."

Dallas stepped aside while Grant opened the door to Lola's Café.

"Dr. Grant, we're filled," the host told him. "We've been jammed for the past hour." He lowered his voice and added, "It's all these people who've come to town for the Discover Days. Bunch came in a day or two early. But I can probably fit you in at the bar."

"That's fine with me," Dallas told him.

They'd been seated for ten minutes when Dallas felt a touch on her arm. She turned and found Grace Sinclair at her elbow.

"I thought I saw you come in. My, but business is really booming, isn't it? I'd stopped at Captain Walt's but there was an hour wait for a table. Can you imagine?" Grace was clearly pleased. "We'll have a lot of happy folks in St. Dennis when this weekend is over and they tally up their receipts."

"It's good for business, that's for sure," Grant agreed.

"Now, I'm expecting both of you at the cocktail party tonight," Grace told them.

"It's on my calendar," Grant said.

"What cocktail party?" Dallas asked.

"The big shindig we have every year to kick off the big weekend. It's a fund-raiser that benefits the community— this year the money will go to the new children's park—and we announce the name of the parade grand marshal." Grace patted Dallas on the back. "You'll want to be there."

"Berry hasn't mentioned it," Dallas said.

"You be sure to remind her, then. It's important that she's there."

"I'll remind her. Do we need to buy the tickets in advance?" Dallas asked.

"Berry's already purchased several. I'm counting on you to get her there."

"I'll do my best," Dallas promised.

"And be early, if possible," Grace added.

"If it's a cocktail party, I suppose children aren't included."

"Strictly adults, Dallas," Grace replied.

"I'll have to find a sitter for Cody," Dallas noted after Grace had gone on her way.

"Paige will probably be available. Want me to call her now to ask?"

Dallas nodded. "That would be great. I don't know anyone else to ask."

Paige was available, and as soon as lunch was over, Dallas and Grant walked back to the clinic. He showed her around, then kissed her in his office before letting her go. Dallas left the clinic and was on the phone to Berry before she even got back to her car.

"Berry, do you have something on the calendar for tonight?" she asked.

"Not that I know of."

"Want to take a look?"

"I'm fairly certain I'd remember . . ." Berry fell silent for a moment. "Oh, the cocktail party. Well, we don't have to go. I purchased the tickets to be supportive."

"No, we want to go." Dallas corrected herself: "*I* want to go."

"But Cody—" Berry began.

"Will be here with Paige. I've already arranged it. So we can go."

"Wonderful. Well, I must go see what I can wear." Berry paused. "Did you bring anything suitable?"

"How dressy do people usually get for this?"

"A few steps this side of fancy," Berry told her.

"In that case, I think I'll pop in to Bling right now and see if Vanessa has something."

"I'm sure she will."

Vanessa did have just the thing—a white strapless knee-length dress that had small black dots and a full skirt.

"With that dress, you need these shoes"—Vanessa pointed out a pair of high strappy heels—"and this bag."

She held up a black clutch that was totally covered by a red chiffon flower.

"I like it." Dallas nodded. "Wrap it up."

Vanessa smiled, happy to have made a great sale.

"So how's your guy?" Dallas asked as she searched in her bag for her wallet. "I'm assuming he got back from his trip safely."

"Grady is great, thank you. He'll be there tonight, so you can ask him about his camping trip." She rolled her eyes. "Guys think the damnedest things are fun."

Dallas laughed and handed over her credit card.

The bell at the door rang and Dallas turned to see four women enter. Vanessa greeted them and pointed out several items they might want to check out. When they'd moved to the back of the store, she whispered, "A few more weeks like this one's been and I'll be paying off my mortgage early."

"That good, is it?"

"The sales have been crazy. I have to keep ordering new things in." Vanessa grinned. "This has been my best week ever. I'd thought about closing a little early tonight because of the cocktail party, but ended up bringing someone in to work for me so I don't lose the business."

"That's terrific." Dallas took back her card and returned it to her wallet, well aware that Vanessa's customers were now staring at her and whispering in the back of the store. "I'm glad you're doing so well. You and Steffie are setting the world on fire here."

"We sure are. Anything else I can get for you?"

"No. I'll leave you to your customers."

"I'll see you later, then."

Dallas took her bags and went out the door, but hadn't gotten as far as her car when one of the women from Bling followed her out and asked for an autograph, which Dallas gave. She walked a little faster to her car and got in before she was stopped again. Seeing her face on the front of the tabloid earlier in the day had reminded her that as good as the people of St. Dennis had been about shielding her from unnecessary intrusion, the tourists had no such loyalty.

She and Berry had time for a light dinner with Cody before getting ready for the cocktail party. It was almost seven when Grant rang the doorbell to drop off Paige.

"Wow. Look at you!" Grant wolf-whistled when Berry opened the door. "You look . . . like an A-list super-star, Miss B."

"Flattery will get you anywhere, Grant." Berry smiled.

"She does look fabulous, doesn't she?" Dallas came down the steps.

"She does." Grant's face lit up as she walked toward him. "And you look . . . you look . . ."

"You look real pretty, Dallas," Paige chimed in.

"Thank you, Paige."

"Real pretty." Grant smiled. "I couldn't have said it better myself."

"You didn't." Paige punched him playfully on the arm. "Where's Cody?"

"He's on the back porch, waiting for you. Maybe you could bring him in so we could go over last-minute instructions," Dallas told her. "This is the first time he's had a babysitter since we arrived in St. Dennis, and I think we need to lay some ground rules."

"Okay." Paige went off in search of her charge.

"We should all go together," Grant said. "Since we're all going to the same place. I'll drop you off afterward and pick up Paige at the same time." He turned to Berry. "That is, if you don't mind riding in a Jeep to the Inn."

"A Jeep?" Berry walked to the front door and craned her neck to look at his vehicle. "I don't know that I've ever ridden in a Jeep. Let's do it."

"I'll be back in a minute," Dallas said. "I hear the kids in the kitchen."

Dallas gave Paige and Cody the rundown: They and the dogs would stay in the house—doors locked—until the adults returned. No one in, no one out. No opening the door for anyone for any reason. If anyone called for her or for Berry, she wasn't to say that they weren't at home, just that they were unavailable to take the call right at that moment. Dallas posted her cell-phone number on a sticky note on the refrigerator door, then returned to the front hall with both kids.

"I brought some books to read to Cody." Paige opened the backpack she'd dropped near the door when she arrived and took out several books. "See? *Treasure Island. Pippi Longstocking.* I thought Cody might like stories about adventures."

"He does. He'll love both of those books. Good call, Paige." Dallas picked up her bag from the hall table. "Call me if anything comes up. Anything at all."

"Will do." Paige adopted a very adult demeanor.

"And you know how to get me," Grant told her as they were preparing to leave. "If you have to call—"

"Got it, Dad," Paige said.

Dallas showed her how to lock the door, then followed Berry and Grant out to the car.

"Blue certainly is your color, Miss B," Grant told her as he opened the front passenger's-side door for her.

"Thank you, Grant. Fortunately I did have something to wear tonight. I'd completely forgotten until Dallas reminded me." She paused. "I'd prefer the backseat, if you don't mind, dear. I like to spread out a bit."

"Whatever makes you happy." Grant opened the back door and helped Berry into the seat.

Dallas got into the front seat and buckled her seat belt. Grant slid behind the wheel and backed the car out of the drive onto River Road.

"This will all be blocked off on Saturday morning," Berry said to no one in particular. "What a mess it will be in town."

"What time does the parade begin?" Dallas turned in her seat to ask.

"Nine A.M.," Berry replied. "It's always such a fun thing. I didn't go last year, but I'm looking forward to this one."

"Why didn't you go last year?"

Berry shrugged. "I guess I just didn't feel up to it."

"Were you sick and you didn't tell me?" Dallas asked.

"Not sick. Just . . . oh, bored, perhaps. But not this year." Berry smiled. "No time for boredom this time around."

They arrived at the Inn at Sinclair's Point and Grant turned the car over to the valet. With Berry on one arm and Dallas on the other, he led the women through the lobby and into the ballroom.

"Oh, it's all been redecorated since the last time I was here!" Dallas exclaimed. "It's beautiful."

"Glad you approve." Miss Grace appeared and kissed each of them on the cheek. "Daniel had the entire Inn redone several years ago, right before he lost his wife. I keep telling him it might be time to redo a little here and there, but that boy of mine is a stubborn cuss."

"He's also a very busy cuss." Daniel Sinclair approached the group, one arm outstretched to hug Berry, the other to shake Grant's hand. "And this is Dallas. Good to have you back with us again."

"It's good to be here, thank you, Daniel," Dallas replied.

"The party has already started, so please go on in, have a glass of wine and some hors d'oeuvres."

The threesome did exactly that. They enjoyed the hors d'oeuvres while they chatted with neighbors and old friends. Dallas met many of Berry's contemporaries and former classmates of Grant's, many of whom swore they'd known her "back then," but she had no memory of all but one or two. The evening's finale—the naming of the parade's grand marshal—was announced with much fanfare by the mayor, accompanied by the president of the town council and the county's district attorney.

"Attention, everyone. May I have your attention please?" Mayor Christina Forbes stood on the podium, a microphone in her hand. "The moment I know you've all been waiting for is here. As you know, the grand marshal is selected by the Committee for St. Dennis, composed of the members of the town council—and of course, me—along with the president of the Chamber of Commerce and the chief of police. The selection has to be unanimous, and I can tell you there have been years when we've had to vote over and over and over and ... well, you get the idea."

Laughter from the audience.

"This year, however, we nailed it on the first vote. I'm so pleased to announce that, by unanimous vote, the grand marshal of the 2010 Discover St. Dennis parade is ... Beryl Eberle!"

Applause erupted from every corner of the room.

"Oh, for the love of all that's holy ..." Berry's hand flew to her mouth. "Is that woman serious?"

"Miss B, you know the rules." Grant leaned over her shoulder. "If elected, you must serve. There is no saying no when it comes to leading the parade."

A momentarily flustered Berry was led to the podium and handed the microphone. She took a moment to collect herself, then said, "This was totally unexpected, but I know it's a great honor. I'm delighted. Thank you all for this privilege. I promise to fulfill my duty to the best of my ability, and to wave royally"—she demonstrated—"and will toss candy to the children on *both* sides of the car along the parade route."

There was light laughter, then applause once again as Berry returned the microphone to Christina.

Berry was handed a glass of wine and was congratulated with pats on the back and fond smiles as she made her way back to Dallas and Grant.

"Well, there'll be no skipping the parade this year," Dallas told her.

"Give me five more minutes to be gracious, then we are out of here," Berry whispered. "I will need my beauty rest tonight and tomorrow night if I'm to be up at the very crack of Saturday. Hmm. What shall I wear? I expect it will be hot ... of course, a hat; that goes without saying. One with a wide brim. And perhaps a dress of a very lightweight fabric. Something gauzy. And sleeveless, of course. Thank God, I still have the arms for it ..."

Twenty minutes later, in the car on the way back to the house, Dallas asked, "So what's the deal for Saturday? What exactly does the grand marshal do?"

"I ride in a convertible—top down, of course, otherwise, why bother with a convertible?—the very first car in the parade. I wave grandly, I throw sweets, I smile. I'm photographed for posterity. I give the signal to start the boat races, and I ... well, there may be another little thing or two. I'm sure someone will tell me."

"I'm sure you'll be very good at all that," Grant noted.

"Please, dear. I've played several queens in the past. I have the royal demeanor down pat."

"I thought the title was grand marshal, not grand empress," Dallas said.

"Same thing." Berry waved a hand. "I'm sure a wee bit of drama is to be expected of me."

"And I'm sure you'll deliver, Berry," Dallas murmured, and Grant smiled.

The entire downstairs was lit up when they arrived at Berry's, lights on in each room.

"Hi, Mom," Cody greeted them at the front door excitedly. "We've had so much fun! Paige and I have been reading. She let me read some of the pages and helped me with the words. Look, Mom! Pirates buried a treasure on this island!"

An animated Fleur gaily danced around the group in the front hall.

"I remember reading that book a long time ago." Dallas ran a hand through her son's hair. "There might still be a copy in the library here."

"Can we find it?"

"We'll look for it in the morning." Dallas held out her wrist and pointed to her watch. "Way past the bedtime, bud."

"I know, but we were having so much fun reading." Cody wrapped his arms around Paige. "Paige is the best reader ever. Even better than the library lady."

Paige smiled and hugged him.

"Well, we all have things to do tomorrow. Paige has dogs to walk, Dallas has work on her screenplay, I have animals to tend to, Cody has story hour, and Miss B has to get her glorious self ready for Saturday." Grant took his daughter by the arm.

Dallas paid Paige for babysitting and everyone said their good nights. Dallas accompanied the departing father and daughter outside.

"I have a couple of surgeries lined up for tomorrow, and another for tomorrow evening, so I'm pretty much MIA until Saturday morning," Grant told Dallas.

She stood at the foot of the front porch steps. Ahead, in the dark, Paige ambled to the car.

"I do have to work on my screenplay, you were spot-on there." Dallas nodded. "Especially since I suspect Saturday will be spent in town, watching herself wave to the peons as she travels through the heart of St. Dennis."

Grant laughed softly. "She'll be fabulous."

"She always is," Dallas agreed.

"Dad, the mosquitoes are getting me," Paige whined.

He raised Dallas's hands to his lips and pressed a kiss in each palm. "I'll be over on Saturday to walk down to the parade route with you and Cody."

She nodded. "I'll see you then."

She stood with her arms folded over her chest, and watched the car disappear behind the trees that lined River Road. After the taillights disappeared around the bend, she went back inside to close up the house for the night and tuck her son into bed.

Chapter 20

"I WISH I had better news, but so far, no one's been interested in this deal unless you and Berry star in the film together," Norma told Dallas on Friday morning. "Personally, I feel it's a form of blackmail to get you and Berry in the same film, which of course would be box office dynamite."

Dallas sighed. "We've gone over this."

"Yes, we have. And I respect the fact that you've made up your mind, and believe me, I've been very supportive of that decision at each of these meetings. Frankly, the feeling that I'm getting is that everyone thinks you're holding out for astronomical bucks and a huge percentage to do the film."

"That's nonsense."

"That's Hollywood," Norma corrected her. "But not to despair. I have another meeting in about an hour, another at four this afternoon, and another tomorrow morning— actually, that's a lunch meeting. So we just need to wait and see. Personally, I think these people are all crazy because the film is going to be a blockbuster and everyone who's passed it by is going to be kicking themselves in the ass later."

"Well, let's see what your other meetings bring. Thanks, Norma. I hope you have some good news soon."

"So do I." Norma hung up, and Dallas began to pace.

She wasn't at all surprised that the studio and production people Norma had met with believed that Dallas was holding out. Games were played every hour of every day. It was part of the business, though definitely not her favorite part. She'd long since grown tired of it.

"So far, two girls and one boy," Grant greeted her when he called a little while later.

"What are you talking about?"

"I'm talking about the litter of Great Danes I'm delivering. Three pups so far. Two of one, one of the other. All brindles. Cute as can be."

"Do you usually assist at deliveries?"

"Not as a general rule, but her owner brought her in this morning because she was—get this—'acting strangely.' She was looking for a place to have her pups, but they didn't recognize the behavior until she started delivering in the waiting room out front. And how's your day going?"

"I spoke with my lawyer earlier. No one's feeling the love for *Pretty Maids* unless Berry and I are in it."

"Sounds like a form of extortion to me."

"That's what Norma and I think, too. I may end up having to put my money where my mouth is, but we'll see. I'm just going to keep working on the screenplay."

"Atta girl. Don't let the bastards get you down."

"How's everything else going for you today?" She walked to the window and looked out. Berry had just returned from the library with Cody and they were walking across the lawn, a much-animated Cody telling something to Berry, who was smiling broadly.

"All right. Surgery day. I just popped into the kitchen to grab some lunch."

"I hope you washed your hands."

"Ha ha. I'm hanging up now and going back to work." There was humor in his voice, and a natural warmth that she'd always found irresistible.

"What time do you think you'll be by tomorrow? Berry has to be at the parade staging location at eight thirty, and I'd like to go with her."

"I can meet you there. Where does the parade begin?"

"The corner of Andrews and Charles. Just look for the first car."

"What fancy vehicle did they find to transport Miss B?"

"No idea what she'll be riding in." She lowered her voice as Berry and Cody came in through the front door. "She's really quite taken with this whole thing, you know. There's going to be no living with her for a while after this."

Grant laughed. "She'll wring every bit of fun from the entire day. She'll have a ball."

"I'm sure she will."

"Oops, number four is on its way out. I'll see you in the morning."

"See you in ..." she began, then realized he'd hung up.

"Who are you speaking to?" Berry peeked into Dallas's office.

"I was talking with Grant but we've hung up. He's going to meet us in the morning at the staging place."

"Good. I'm sure Paige and Cody will enjoy the parade. As will we all." Berry started to close the door, then stopped and poked her head back into the room. "If you have a free moment later, perhaps you could help me decide between two possible outfits."

"I'd love to. But you know, whatever you wear, you're going to look fabulous."

"Goes without saying." Berry closed the door and left Dallas to her work.

Saturday morning was clear and beautiful and blessedly free of the humidity that had plagued St. Dennis on and off for the past several weeks. Dallas was up and dressed and ready to go by eight, in case Berry needed help with anything. This was going to be a big day for her, Dallas knew, being honored by her hometown. Berry had tried on several outfits the night before with all the enthusiasm of a teenager trying on prom dresses.

"What do you think, Dallas?" Berry had sashayed out of her room in a lime green dress and a white hat with lime green and yellow flowers.

"Not your best color." Dallas shook her head. "Not bad, but you can do better. What else do you have?"

Berry disappeared into her room and came back to the landing ten minutes later in a white dress of gauzy fabric that had colorful embroidery around its scoop neck.

"I haven't yet found the right hat, but I know I have one," Berry explained.

"That's it," Dallas told her. "Look no further. That's a perfect dress and it looks super on you. Shows off your still-girlish figure quite nicely."

"I thought so, too"—Berry grinned—"but I didn't want to be the one to say it."

"Take it off, hang it up before one of the dogs jumps up on you, and go find your hat."

"I'm on my way …" Berry's voice trailed off as she swept down the hall.

Breakfast had been at seven thirty, which gave Berry about forty-five minutes to dress. She'd taken every one of them, but Dallas had to admit it had been worth it. Berry *did* look fabulous, and Dallas told her so.

"You'll turn a lot of heads today, Berry."

"Yes, everyone muttering, 'She doesn't look too bad for an old broad.'" Berry flashed a look at Dallas. "Which is not to say that I see myself as an old broad. I do, however, believe there are some who might."

"Misguided fools."

Berry smiled. "Indeed."

Dallas packed a canvas bag with several bottles of water for Berry to take in the car with her to sip on during the parade. The August sun could be unmerciful, and while Berry wouldn't admit to feeling the effects of her age, Dallas knew that dehydration was no friend to the elderly. She sent Cody to get the dogs inside and went out back to pull her car around to the front of the house for Berry, telling her, "There's no point in arriving at the parade sweaty and hot. We'll drive, and I'll find a place to leave the car."

"All right, dear." Berry poked her in the back. "But some of us don't sweat."

"Right." Dallas picked up her bag from the kitchen table. "You glow."

The drive took all of five minutes, because they ran into roadblock after roadblock due to the parade route. They arrived at the designated corner, and Dallas let Berry out of the car while she looked for a place to park. When Dallas made her way back, she saw a most elegant vehicle at the head of the parade.

Wow, she thought. *A white Bentley convertible. Berry must be beside herself.*

As Dallas drew closer to the car, she realized that Berry was more than simply beside herself.

"Surely this wasn't your idea." Berry was addressing a tall, good-looking man with white hair who leaned on the passenger-side door with a certain amount of proprietary interest.

Dallas couldn't hear the man's response, but when Berry saw her niece approaching, he turned to follow her gaze, and Dallas knew exactly who he was and who had somehow managed to get him there.

"Hello," Dallas said, extending her hand to him. "I'm Dallas, Berry's niece—well, grand-niece, but we usually drop the 'grand.'"

"Archer Callahan." His smile was charming, his eyes crystal blue.

No wonder Berry had fallen.

"Is this your car?" Dallas pretended not to have noticed Berry's glare.

"Yes," he replied. "An oldie but a goodie, as they say."

"It's beautiful. Are you loaning it for the parade?"

"Well, I'm driving it, but yes, we're using her in the parade today." He turned to Berry. "That is, if the guest of honor will *get in.*"

"Of course she'll get in." Dallas smiled. "Why wouldn't she?" She turned to Berry. "I have water for you to take in the car. Where would you like me to put it?"

"I can think of a place, but Cody's standing right behind you." Berry was looking at Archer, not Dallas.

"Berry, are you ready to lead us onward?" Grace appeared at Dallas's elbow. "Oh my, don't you look ... well, 'beautiful' hardly does you justice today, Berry. Archer, doesn't Berry look lovely?"

"She certainly does. I'd have told her myself if she'd stop biting my head off long enough for me to get the words out." Archer stood with his hands on his hips, his gaze challenging Berry.

Oh, this is good. Dallas suppressed a grin. *This is really good. Berry, caught off guard? And now speechless?*

She stole a glance at Grace, who winked.

Gracie! You little devil, you ...

"Well, we need to get on with the parade. We're already seven minutes behind schedule and we have a very full day. Berry, if you'll just get in, we can tell Beck we're ready to roll." Grace took Berry by the arm and turned her toward the car. "He's got Hal out there detouring traffic until after the parade finishes up, but traffic is building, as I'm sure you can imagine." Berry hadn't moved. "What?" Grace asked.

"This was your doing," Berry said under her breath. "Don't even try to deny it. You arranged for this car."

"Well, of course I did. Henry Wagner was supposed to drive his old Cadillac as the lead car, but it has some mechanical problem, I forget what he said it was. We only just found out about it late yesterday. Well, the only suitable car I could think of on such short notice was Archer's." Grace patted Berry on the arm and led her one step closer to the Bentley. "The only other convertible would have been Hal's old Buick, but he never did get that body cancer taken care of, so there are those rusty spots." She lowered her voice. "We didn't think that was quite the thing."

Grace got Berry as far as the car door.

"Aunt Berry, you're going to get to drive in this really cool car!" Cody was leaning over the side to look at the interior. "Lucky duck!"

For a moment, Berry appeared to be indecisive.

"Who owns this car, Aunt Berry?" he asked.

"Mr. Callahan owns the car," she told him.

"Would you like to see the inside, son?" Archer asked.

Cody nodded vigorously.

"Come on over here and take a quick look." Archer beckoned him. "The parade has to start." He glanced over at Berry. "Are you ready, Grand Marshal Eberle?"

"As ready as I'll ever be, Mr. Callahan." Berry entered the car regally, and settled into the passenger seat. Dallas handed her the chilled bottles of water and called Cody to her side.

"The cars are going to start now," Dallas told him. "We need to find Paige and Dr. Wyler."

"I'll see you at the end of the parade route," Berry called over her shoulder as the car began to glide toward the center of town. "The marina, I believe."

"We'll be there," Dallas called back.

After the car had rolled away, Dallas turned to Grace and asked, "How did you make that happen?"

"Oh, a little luck, perhaps a bit of magic." A little smile played at the corners of Grace's mouth.

"What did you do, wave your magic wand?" Dallas laughed.

"Nothing quite that dramatic. Besides, wands are so passé." Grace patted Dallas on the back as she made her way toward the back of the line. "Now it's out of our hands and in theirs."

"Come on, Cody, let's look for . . . oh, there's Grant." Dallas waved to him, and he cut between the cars to join them on the opposite side of the street.

"Where's Paige?" Cody asked.

"Her aunt is crazy busy at Scoop already this morning, so she asked if Paige would come in and help out," Grant told them. "I guess you're stuck with me and your mom for now."

"That's okay." Cody looked around. "Will we see the whole parade from here?"

"No, we're going to walk up to the center of town," Dallas said.

Grant took her hand, and she took Cody's, and they quickened their steps to get ahead of the parade. Four blocks up, they ran into Brooke, her mother, Logan, and Brooke's brother, Clay, all standing in front of Sips, the beverage-only shop in the very heart of town. Brooke introduced Dallas and Cody to Clay. They'd already met her mother at Bowwows and Meows.

"I'm thirsty," Cody said. "All that running up the street in the hot sun."

"Yeah, me, too," Logan complained.

"Come on, you two." Clay tapped them each on the head. "And we'll get something cold to drink. Anyone else want something?"

There were no takers, so Clay cut through the crowd with the two boys, Dallas watching anxiously.

"What's the matter?" Grant leaned down to ask.

"There are so many people here," she said. "I hope Cody doesn't get separated from Logan and Clay."

"Don't worry about it. He knows where he is, and he knows where we're going. Even if he got separated, he knows where to go." Grant grinned. "He'd head right for Scoop."

Dallas laughed. "You're probably right."

They could hear the high whine of the bagpipes that had been hired to accompany the cars filled with local dignitaries, and while they stood on the curb waiting for the parade to reach them, Dallas was aware of the cameras, aware that by tomorrow there would be pictures here, there, and everywhere of her standing in front of Grant, leaning back against him, his hands on her shoulders.

She could write the headlines herself: MEET DALLAS'S LONG-LOST SWEETHEART! IS MARY-LAND VET STILL THE LOVE OF HER LIFE?

She knew there was nothing she could do about it other than lock herself in the house, and she wasn't about to do that, especially today, when Berry was being feted and fussed over—all while in the company of her own lost love. She wondered how that was working out.

The Bentley was moving toward them, and soon was just feet away.

"Aunt Berry!" Cody cried excitedly as he and Logan returned to the curb. "Aunt Berry!"

Berry leaned around Archer to throw a handful of wrapped hard candies to the boys, but others in the crowd beat them to the goodies. Berry frowned and said something to Archer, who nodded and turned to Cody.

"Your aunt would like to know if you'd like to ride down to the marina with us?" Archer asked.

"Can I, Mom?" Cody looked first at his mother, but before she could reply, he ran to the car. "Can Logan come, too?"

"If it's all right with Logan's mother and with Mr. Callahan, it's certainly all right with me," Berry told him.

"Mom, can I? Can I go?" Logan begged.

When Brooke and Dallas both hesitated, Berry told them, "They'll be with us. You can join us down at the marina in a few minutes. There's a hospitality tent there. We can tell them to expect you."

"All right." Both mothers nodded.

Archer put the car in park and helped the boys to climb in.

"Cool car!" Logan called to his Uncle Clay.

"Darn cool car." Clay nodded appreciatively.

"Mom, we're in the parade!" Cody yelled as the car began to move again and made a left on Kelly's Point Drive to take the parade down to the marina and the park.

"I shudder to think what's going to happen when this crowd starts down Kelly's Point," Grant commented. "I'll bet the line into Scoop is going to come all the way back up here to Charles Street."

"I hope Steffie made a lot of ice cream this morning," Dallas said.

"I don't think she has enough to feed this crowd," he told her. "I'll bet she's sold out and closed by two this afternoon."

"At least she'll get to enjoy the day. What comes after the parade?" Dallas asked.

"The boat races begin. They'll go on all day. First the speedboats, then the sailboats."

They applauded the local high school marching band and numerous social and civic organizations before the parade came to an end. As Grant had predicted, the crowd followed the last marchers down Kelly's Point Drive, past the municipal building and to the marina. On the grassy area behind Captain Walt's, a green-and-white-striped tent had been erected, and it was there that Grant and Dallas headed. They met up with the two boys, and Berry, who was busy playing belle of the ball until she was tapped to kick off the boat races.

"What do we do now?" Dallas asked.

"I suggest we get the boys and go stand near the dais, where Berry will announce that the races are to commence. Then someone sets off a flare from the end of the pier, and the boats will be off," Grant explained.

"Where do they go?" Cody asked.

"The speedboats go out to Goat Island." Grant pointed off to their right. "See it out there, past where the river comes into the Bay?"

"Do goats live there?" Logan asked.

"No one lives there. It isn't much of an island," Grant said, "but it's the turning point for the race, so all the boats have to go around it and come back to the starting line. See them all lining up out there?"

The boys nodded.

"Can we go closer to watch?" Cody asked.

"I think you'd better stay here with us." Dallas looked around at the crowd. "It would be very easy to get lost here today."

"We couldn't get lost, Mom," Cody told her. "We know where we are."

"Still, there are just too many people. I think I'd rather have you—"

"There's my mom and my uncle and my gramma!" Logan pointed. "They're going closer. Can we go with them?"

"Sure, but go now, while I can watch you."

"Thanks, Mom." Cody scooted off.

"Stay with Logan's family, Cody," Dallas shouted after him, but they were gone. She watched anxiously until the boys caught up with Brooke, who paused to listen to something the boys were telling her, and who then turned around and gave Dallas a thumbs-up.

"See?" Grant massaged her shoulders. "You don't have to worry. There are three adults there. The boys are fine."

"I know they are. I can't help myself. I'm that kind of mother." Dallas shrugged somewhat apologetically. "I probably should get him one of those children's cell phones. Logan has one. It only has the capacity to store a few numbers but it would be handy to have if you were in a crowd and became separated."

Grant started to say something, but the mayor was testing the microphone, then proceeded to welcome the visitors as well as the residents. She handed the mike over to Berry to read the official opening speech—which never changed from year to year—and to drop the red handkerchief that would signal that the first boat race was about

372

to begin. Berry read her lines flawlessly—of course—and dropped the handkerchief with aplomb. The flares were lit, and the first of the boats were off toward Goat Island.

"How many races are there?" Dallas asked Grant.

"However many they need to give all the entrants a spot. They can only run four at a time. Otherwise, it gets too dangerous rounding the island. Then they run off the winners of each leg to get a winner in this category," he told her. "Then, when the speedboats are finished, the sailboats begin. They don't go to the island, though. They head off in the opposite direction, toward a buoy in the middle of the bay."

"So this goes all day long."

"Pretty much, yeah." Grant nodded and craned his neck to see which boat was taking the lead.

The sun grew in intensity as the morning progressed. By noon, Dallas was looking for shelter.

"If you can wait until the first sailboat race gets under way, I'll walk you down to Stef's and we'll see if she has anything left."

Dallas nodded and raised a hand to her forehead to shield her eyes. She scanned the crowd, searching for Brooke and her family, but they were nowhere in sight. She turned to look in the opposite direction, but there was no sign of Brooke or her brother, or either of the boys.

"I wonder where they went," Dallas murmured.

"Where who went?" Grant was watching the sailboats line up.

"Cody and Logan."

"They were with Brooke and her family, right?"

Dallas nodded.

"They're probably at the other end of the marina. Clay used to sail in this race, so he might have wanted to get a little closer."

"Maybe." It made sense but she still felt uneasy, not having seen her son for over an hour. She trusted Brooke—of course she did—but she wasn't used to having him go off with anyone when they were out at events such as this. Then again, she reminded herself, he'd never really had a friend like Logan before, one he did everything with and played with on a steady basis. Grant was right. They were probably with Clay to watch the sailboat race that was about to start.

"I sure hope the storm holds off." Grant pointed toward the west, where dark clouds had only just started to gather. "The weather forecast called for a storm this afternoon. I hope they get all the races in."

Dallas nodded somewhat absently, still searching the crowd for a glimpse of her son.

"Seen enough? Want to head over to Stef's?" She nodded and Grant took her hand. "You're worried about Cody."

"I can't help it."

"I wouldn't be surprised if we walked into Scoop and found the two boys in there sucking down a cone."

"I doubt either of them have any money on them."

"Like that would stop Stef or Paige from giving them what they wanted. Come on, let's take a walk."

Dallas's eyes went from face to face and to every child she saw who was close to Cody's height and weight, without success.

Grant's probably right, she reminded herself. *The two boys are probably with Clay watching the races. You know how Cody loves boats. Or he talked Paige into giving them ice cream.*

374

"My mom will pay you when she gets here," Dallas could imagine him saying.

There were several hundred people between Scoop and the Bay, but the boys weren't among them. Dallas followed Grant into the small building, grateful to be out of the hot sun, and looked around. No boys, no Brooke, or any of her family.

"Hi, Daddy," Paige called from behind the counter.

"Hi, sweetie. How's it going?"

Paige rolled her eyes. "It's been crazy here. Steffie made a ton of ice cream last night and she was up early this morning again to make more, and she had stuff in the freezer that she was making for the past two weeks to get ready for today. But it's almost all gone." She grinned. "She said when it's gone we have to close."

"You know you can leave anytime you want," Steffie told her as she moved to the cash register.

"I like working here," her niece insisted. "I don't want to leave."

"I don't want to get arrested for violating the child labor laws," Stef told Grant. "I send her in the back every so often to rest, but I think she spends the time straightening shelves and sweeping the floor."

"I love Scoop. It's my favorite place."

"Paige, have the boys been in?" Dallas moved closer to the display case. "Cody and his friend Logan?"

Paige shook her head. "I haven't seen them."

Steffie looked up from the cold case where she was busy constructing a three-layer cone. "They haven't been in."

Dallas turned to Grant. "Let's take a walk down to the end of the pier."

375

"Do you want something to take with you, Dallas?" Steffie asked.

"Maybe a bottle of water."

Paige went to the back room and came out with two plastic bottles and gave one to Dallas and the other to Grant.

"Grant? Can I get something for you before you leave?" Stef asked. "It's now or not again until tomorrow. This stuff is going quickly."

"The water's fine. Thanks." He reached for his wallet and his sister waved him away.

"Thanks, Stef," he said as he led Dallas to the exit.

She nodded and continued to serve her customer.

"So we'll head over to the pier?" he asked, and she nodded.

"I suspect Cody is ready to eat something," she told him. "It's well after one."

They made their way to the end of the pier, where they found Clay sitting on one of the pilings.

"Hey." He waved. "Did you see that last race?"

"No, we just came from Scoop," Grant told him.

"It was tight. Jack Hollenbach's son—"

"Excuse me, Clay," Dallas interrupted him, "but where are the boys?"

"They walked up to Charles Street with Brooke, I think. I heard someone say something about lunch," Clay replied.

"Thanks." Dallas turned to Grant. "I'm going to walk up to look for them. You can stay to watch the rest of the races if you want."

"I'll go with you." He took her hand. "We'll look together."

They stopped at the green-and-white-striped tent, where Berry was holding court, but she hadn't seen the boys since the end of the parade when Archer let them out of the car.

"Should I be worried, Dallas?" Berry frowned.

"No, no. Clay said they were with Brooke," Dallas assured her.

On their way up Kelly's Point Drive, Dallas and Grant surveyed the throng on either side, but there was no sign of Brooke, her mother, or the two boys. They checked Sips, but had no luck there. When they arrived at Cuppachino, they stepped inside to take a quick look around. Dallas walked up to the counter and caught the owner's eye.

"Carlo, have you seen either Mrs. Madison or Brooke . . . ?"

He shook his head as he made an iced latte for a customer. "Not since earlier in the week. If they come in, you want me to tell them you're looking for them?"

"Yes, thank you."

Dallas turned to Grant. "Maybe Sips—oh, wait. There's Brooke . . ." She stepped off the curb to get Brooke's attention.

"Where are the boys?" Dallas called.

"They're in Sips." Brooke wiped perspiration from her forehead. "It is so blazing hot out here. Mom had to open the store at eleven, so we walked her up, and they wanted to get a drink, so I gave them money—"

"We just came from there. They aren't there." Dallas felt the first wisp of panic begin to spread through her.

"They aren't?" Brooke frowned. "I told them not to leave. They have to be there."

Brooke took off across the street, and Dallas followed. They went back into Sips, but as Dallas had said, the boys were not there.

"Then they must have gone back down to the marina to watch the rest of the races," Brooke said. "They were having fun watching with Clay."

"Does your brother have a cell phone on him?" Grant asked.

Brooke nodded, took her phone from her bag, and speed-dialed the number.

"Clay, did the boys come back down there with you?" She looked up toward the sky, an anxious look on her face. "Well, would you mind looking around the pier and the dock area? Check out that area on the grass where the tent's been set up? Call me back the minute you find them, okay?"

She disconnected the call and slid the phone into the pocket of her shorts.

"I know this is St. Dennis and the boys know the town pretty well, but still, it's disconcerting to not know where they are." Brooke spoke as if trying to calm herself. "I'm sure they're fine, and we'll find them."

"Hey, guys, are you enjoying the festivities?" Beck pulled his patrol car to the curb and leaned across the passenger seat.

"Not right at this moment," Grant told him. "We seem to have lost track of Dallas's and Brooke's sons."

"Where were they?" Beck put the car in park.

"They walked up to Charles Street with me and my mom, then went across to Sips to get cold drinks," Brooke told him.

378

"How long ago was that?" Beck asked.

"Maybe thirty minutes. I walked up to Mom's shop with her, and there'd been a delivery at the back door, so I helped her bring the boxes in." Brooke leaned against the car door. "I just called Clay, thinking maybe they wandered back down to the pier. He's looking for them down there."

"Does Logan have his phone with him?" Dallas asked.

Brooke shook her head. "The pockets in the shorts he wore today were too small for it to fit."

"Did you check any of the other shops?"

"Only Scoop and Cuppachino," Dallas told him as she approached the cruiser.

"Why don't you three split up and start checking the shops here on Charles Street," Beck suggested. "Meanwhile, I'll ask Hal to go down Kelly's Point and give Clay a hand. Maybe see if anyone else is in the area who can take a look around. I'll drive around and see if I can spot them, give you a call if I find them."

"Thanks, Beck. We appreciate it." Dallas and Brooke spoke at the same time.

"Hey, what else does a small-town cop have to do on a day like this? The crowd's been well behaved and we haven't had one fender bender since the weekend began. Knock on wood."

He drove off slowly and made a right onto the first side street.

"I'll take the opposite side of the street," Grant told the two women. "You two split up this side. Keep in touch." He crossed and went into Petals and Posies, the florist on the corner of Kelly's Point and Charles.

379

"I'll start with Bling," Dallas told Brooke. "You take the next shop and we'll go every other one until we run out of stores."

Brooke nodded and the two women took off. When they met up in the parking lot next to the market twenty minutes later, they were both obviously distressed.

"No one's seen them." Dallas had to bite her lip to keep from crying when Grant crossed the street to join them.

"No luck here, either," he told them. "All right, let's think like six-year-olds for a moment. Where would you go on a day like today, and why?"

"I can't think," Brooke told him. "I feel like stopping people on the street and asking them if they've seen two little boys."

"There are so many kids in town today." Dallas pointed across the street. "There are five little boys who look to be around six right over there.

"Maybe they went to the library," Dallas thought out loud.

"It's closed today," Brooke told her. "But maybe the park . . ."

The three took off at a trot, back across Charles, down Kelly's Point, across the parking lot. When they got to the park, they were out of breath. They split up, each taking a section, but the boys were nowhere to be seen.

"Sir, have you seen two boys around this tall?" Dallas asked one older gentleman who sat on a folding chair watching a softball game.

"You gotta be kidding, lady." He laughed. "You know how many kids 'that tall' have gone past here in the past hour alone? Kids are everywhere today."

"Thanks," she muttered.

The boys were not in the park, nor were they down at the dock. They saw Beck's car pull into the municipal building's parking lot and ran to see if he'd had any luck, but he got out of the car shaking his head.

"No luck, guys," he told them. "But Hal and Mia are both out looking for them by car now. There's always the chance that I missed them somehow. I've called everyone on duty and asked them to check whatever area they're in and report back. The whole town is covered now, so we should start hearing back soon. Why don't you come in and wait for—"

"I can't," Dallas told him, the tears she'd been holding back finally starting to flow. "I need to keep looking."

"Me, too." Brooke nodded.

"Let's check the house," Grant suggested. "Maybe they went back there for some reason."

"Bathroom, maybe?" Brooke guessed.

"Could be. Brooke, why don't we get Clay up here to drive back to the farm, see if they headed out there for some reason."

"All right." She dug the phone from her pocket and walked toward the road as if she couldn't stand still.

"Let's get my car and drive up to River Road," Grant told Dallas.

"You drive up, I'll walk," she said. "Maybe I'll see something along the way that we'd miss if we were both in the car."

"You want to drive and I'll walk?"

She shook her head and backed toward the road. "I want to walk. I'll meet you there."

Dallas all but ran back to Charles Street and all the way to River Road. At some point, Grant must have passed her, but she didn't notice, just as she was unaware of the darkening sky and the distant rumble of thunder. She broke into a trot when River came in sight, her eyes darting back and forth across the sidewalk. She didn't know what she thought she'd find, but it was the only thing she could think of to do. When she reached the edge of Berry's property, she ran across the lawn, unable to wait until she reached the drive. Grant was on the front porch when she got there. The look on his face made it clear that he'd seen no sign of the missing children.

"Does Cody have a house key on him?" Grant asked.

"No. But he knows where Berry keeps a spare." She ran around to the basement entrance and moved a rock that was near the flower bed. "It's still here."

"Maybe he used it, went inside, used the bathroom or got a snack, locked up the house—"

"Put the key back under the rock?" Dallas finished the sentence, then shook her head. "If he'd come home, and if he'd gotten the key, he'd have left it inside, and probably left the front door open."

She started toward the back of the house. "Maybe they're out back . . ."

They called both boys, but there was no response. The dogs were barking inside and Dallas used her own key to let them out. She ran through the house, calling their names, from the basement to the third floor, but the house was silent.

She went outside and sat on the steps when her legs

gave out on her. Her head in her hands, and shaking all over, she began to weep.

Grant came up the stairs and sat next to her, his arms around her, and rocked her slowly.

"Someone's taken them," she said through her sobs. "Someone has them, right now. It's the only explanation I can think of."

"Dallas, let's not—"

"I know my son, Grant. There's no way he'd disappear like this on his own, and not for this long a time, unless something or someone was stopping him. If he'd gotten separated from Brooke, he'd have gone back to the tented area. He'd go where he knew someone he knows would be. If he didn't find us, he'd have gone to Berry, or if he couldn't find her, he'd have gone to Scoop. At the very least, they'd have gone back to Clay." She shook her head, her voice breaking. "I think someone has them. I think they've been kidnapped . . ."

Chapter 21

DALLAS sat still as a stone on a chair in the living room. Her heart had been racing since the moment she realized that Cody and Logan were not with anyone they should have been with. That had been seven hours ago. Since then, Beck had closed off all roads leading in or out of town, and had set up a checkpoint where the backseats and the trunks of all vehicles leaving St. Dennis were checked. Hal viewed the surveillance tapes from every shop on Charles Street, and Clay Madison and his buddies had gone up and down every street in town calling for the boys.

There'd been no sign of either boy.

Beck had called the FBI and requested their assistance, and several agents had already arrived in St. Dennis. Agents in Arizona had been dispatched to the rehab center where Emilio was staying, and while no one was saying he was a suspect, after informing him that his son was missing, they requested and received a list of everyone who'd visited him since he signed himself in.

"You don't really think he'd kidnap his own son, do you?" Dallas asked when she'd been told.

"It's not unusual for noncustodial parents to take off with their kids, or hire someone to do it for them," explained Beck's wife, Mia, who as a former FBI special agent had been involved in several such investigations.

Dallas had shaken her head. "He wouldn't want to be bothered on a full-time basis. Believe me, I know this man. And he'd never have taken Logan, too. Uh-uh," she'd said softly. "Emilio is capable of many things, but this isn't one of them."

Her head pounded and her throat was raw, and the hole in the bottom of her stomach just kept getting bigger and bigger as time passed with no word from or of the boys. Her hands shook when she tried to lift the glass of water or the cup of coffee that Grant brought her from time to time, and her legs were like rubber when she tried to stand. She sat next to a traumatized Berry and held her hand, and tried to keep herself in check for her aunt's sake. Dallas knew that it would take next to nothing to put either of them over the edge at that point, so she focused on giving the illusion of remaining calm and rational, when inside, she knew she was neither.

Brooke was at her family farm with her mother and the FBI agents who were busy searching the fields and the marsh across the road from the property, but there'd been no sign that the boys had ventured that far out of town. So far, three agents had gone through Berry's house from the attic to the basement, and had covered every inch of the carriage house.

Outside, the storm that had been threatening all day had unleashed a furious wind and a torrent of rain that hit the living-room windows unrelentingly. Lightning split the sky over the Bay and thunder clapped overhead.

"If he's out there, he's cold and he's wet and he's scared to death," Dallas said mostly to herself.

Grant had held her as she sobbed and done his best to keep both Dallas and Berry grounded, holding their hands and reminding them that the search had begun immediately once the boys were determined to be missing. He answered the questions that the agents had about the festival and who had been where at what time, and all the while he was sick inside at the thought that something really bad had happened to the two boys.

Every time the phone rang, Dallas jumped, afraid to answer it, and afraid not to. She'd been instructed by the agent in charge what to do if the call was from someone claiming to have the boys—what questions to ask, what not to say while the agents attempted to trace the call. But the only calls she received were from Paige, who'd heard that the boys were missing, and who, with Steffie, was on the way to River Road, and from Emilio, who was on his way east and demanded to know how Dallas could have been so neglectful that some pervert had been able to walk away with his son.

"Hey." Grant had taken her chin in his hand and forced her to look into his eyes. "Emilio is an ass. You know it and I know it. His opinion isn't worth shit. Don't let him put this on you."

"It is on me," she'd said quietly. "I should have kept a closer eye on him. I shouldn't have let him and Logan go off alone."

"They weren't alone," he'd reminded her. "They were with Clay, and then they were with Brooke. And I'm not pointing the finger at either of them, Dallas, but you can't be with a child every second of every day. And they still could turn up."

"The FBI is here," she reminded him. "They've put a tap on my phone and they have agents crawling all over St. Dennis. They apparently don't think the boys will just 'turn up.'"

"That's their job. They're doing what they do whenever there's a report of a missing child," he told her. "They have a protocol to follow and that's what they're doing."

"Miss MacGregor." The agent in charge of the investigation, Vic Turner, stepped into the living room. "If we could just go over a few things with you again . . ."

"Certainly." She nodded.

"You've said there'd been no strange phone calls, no suspicious cars in the area, no one hanging around the property . . ." He was going back over her previous statement.

"That's correct. I haven't noticed anything like that since we arrived in St. Dennis," she told him.

"Dallas, there was the boat early in the week," Grant reminded her.

"What boat?" the agent turned to him to ask.

"We were out on the dock one night and a boat came into the river off the Bay and slowed for a moment, then took off downriver," Grant said.

"Had either of you seen this boat before?"

Dallas and Berry both nodded. "It's been around for the past few weeks," Dallas replied. "And now that I think about it, it has seemed to slow down then speed up again."

"But that's the boat that took the photos," Grant said.

"What photos?" the agent asked.

Dallas explained about the pictures in the tabloids several days earlier.

"Do you have the paper?" Turner asked.

"No," Dallas said, "but there might still be a few at the store."

"What kind of boat was this?"

Grant described it. "As a matter of fact, it was almost identical to a boat owned by a gentleman in town. I can get the specifications on it, if you'd like."

"Please." Turner nodded.

Grant went into the kitchen to make the call to Carter Harwell.

"Miss MacGregor, can you think of anything else?" Turner sat on the edge of a nearby chair.

"I can't. I've gone over every minute since we arrived, and I can't think of any time when anything happened that set off any alarms." She turned to Berry. "Have you thought of anything, Berry?"

Berry shook her head. "I can't think of anyone who'd want to harm that dear boy." She corrected herself: "Those two dear boys."

Grant came back into the room with a description of the boat, which he handed to the agent, telling him, "There are several marinas upriver. If the boat is docked on the New River, someone will know about it."

The doorbell rang and everyone jumped, but when the agent answered the door, Steffie and a white-faced Paige were on the porch. They came in carrying several bags from Scoop. After hugs all around and some tears, Stef said, "We brought ice cream. We figured no one would be eating dinner and maybe you'd want something later. I'll just put it in the freezer. Unless you want some now?"

When everyone shook their head, Dallas took the bags and went into the kitchen, followed by Steffie.

"This was nice, Stef, thanks," Dallas told her.

"We didn't know what to do," Stef admitted. "So as soon as the shop cleared out, we grabbed some stuff out of the cooler and locked the door and jumped in the car. I'm afraid I'm not much help. I don't know what to say or do."

"Neither do I," Dallas admitted, tears in her eyes. "On the one hand, I feel that if something horrible has happened to Cody, I'd know, wouldn't I? I'm his mother. I should know if something bad . . ." She choked back a sob. "On the other hand, if nothing's happened to him . . . where the hell is he? Why isn't he here?"

Steffie shook her head.

No one slept except Paige, who curled up on a Victorian love seat around midnight.

"She must be exhausted," Berry observed. "That's the most uncomfortable piece of furniture in the house."

Though the worst of the storm passed during the night, rain was still coming down in the morning and the wind was only beginning to die down. At eight A.M., the doorbell rang, and Agent Turner answered it. There was muffled conversation in the foyer, then Emilio blasted into the room.

"I shouldn't have let you take him," he shouted at Dallas. "I should have fought for custody. You—"

"You traded him for a beach house in Malibu, a cabin at Lake Tahoe, and a fake Italian palazzo in the Hollywood Hills."

389

"Agent Turner, please have this man removed from my house," Berry said calmly. "He isn't welcome here."

"You crazy old bat, you're just as much to blame as she is," he continued to rant.

Grant stood. "That's enough. You have ten seconds to turn around and start for the door."

"Or what?" Emilio smirked. "Oh, wait. You're the boyfriend." He looked around Grant to address Dallas. "Too busy with the boyfriend to keep an eye on your son?"

"Eight, nine . . ." Grant counted.

"Sir, if I could ask you to step outside?" Agent Turner came into the room and took Emilio by the arm.

"And who are you?" Emilio shook him off.

"Special Agent Turner, FBI." Turner held up his ID.

Emilio nodded. "Good. The FBI has been called in. At least you did one thing right, Dallas."

"Sir, if you'd come this way?" Turner looked as if he'd heard enough.

"I want you to know I'm going for custody when this is over. When they find him." As he went to the door, he said, over his shoulder, "If they find him."

Turner's hand was on Emilio's arm, steering him toward the door.

"I'm going to kill that man," Berry announced loud enough to be heard in the entry.

"Did you hear that, Agent Turner? The old lady just threatened me!" Emilio yelled as the agent closed the door behind them.

"Dallas, I used to think that man was obnoxious," Berry told her. "Now I believe he's the very spawn of the devil himself."

"He's upset about Cody," Dallas said wearily.

"We're all upset about Cody," Berry snapped. "He's going to play this for all it's worth, you wait and see. He'll be setting up for a press conference before the day is over."

Emilio's press conference took place approximately thirty minutes later, at the top of Berry's driveway, early enough to make the morning news back in L.A.

"Press whore." Berry sniffed. "Who wants coffee?"

She slowly made her way into the kitchen.

"I can't stand sitting here any longer," Dallas told Grant. "I want to go out and look for my son."

"You can't leave, Dallas. You have to stay in case some-one calls."

Dallas's eyes followed Berry. She turned to Grant and said, "I've never seen Berry look ... well, old, but she's added twenty years since last night. Cody means more to her than ..." She bit her lip to keep from crying again.

Grant took her hands and held them. "Come on. Let's get some coffee."

They were seated at the kitchen table when Agent Turner came in.

"I've advised your ex-husband to remain off the prem-ises," he told Dallas. "I've instructed Agent Hawkins to physically remove him if he returns."

"Where are you going?" she asked.

"They've found a boy's bike in the marsh across from the Madison farm. I'm going up to take a look."

"Neither Cody nor Logan had their bikes yesterday," Dallas told him.

"Mrs. Bowers has identified the bike as belonging to her son. We need to check it out."

Dallas nodded. After he left, Dallas got up and began to pace.

"Why would Logan's bike be in the marsh?" she muttered. "Though I suppose there's a chance that they walked to the farm yesterday, then for some reason got Logan's bike ... but that doesn't make any sense to me."

"I think it's more likely that Logan left the bike there before yesterday, and they're just realizing it now. With all that rain last night, they probably couldn't have searched the marsh very well," Grant pointed out.

"That seems logical, Grant," Berry said wearily.

"Berry, why don't you go upstairs and lie down," Dallas suggested. "You look so tired."

"I'm fine, dear. I couldn't sleep anyway. Not until we know something." Berry gazed out the window.

Everyone fell silent again.

Paige came into the kitchen a few minutes later with several books in her hands. She sat at the table and began to page through them sadly.

"What do you have there, Paige?" her father asked.

She held up one of the books. "I brought these for Cody the other night when I babysat for him. He loved these stories. I read them over and over and we talked about them." She tried to smile. "He said he wished he could have an adventure like Max or Pippi did."

Grant stared at his daughter, then looked out the window. After a long moment, he turned to Dallas.

"Dallas, did you say something the other day about Cody getting a boat?"

She nodded. "A rowboat. Berry wanted to have Wade's old one refurbished for him, but there was too much dry rot, so she bought him a new one. It's his pride and joy."

"Where is it?" he asked.

"It's tied up at the dock." She pointed out the window. "See there, the rope on the last piling?"

He got up and went outside. From the kitchen window, Dallas saw him lean over the side of the dock, then stand and take his phone from his pocket and make a call. When he finished it, he held the phone in his hand, slapping his palm with it as if impatient. Moments later, the phone was at his ear again. He turned and made his way back to the house.

"What's up?" Dallas asked when he came into the kitchen.

"Cody's boat isn't out there," he told her.

"But the rope—"

"Whoever untied it, did so from the wrong end."

"You mean from the boat instead of the dock?"

He nodded. "I think Cody and Logan took the boat and went off in search of an adventure yesterday."

Her face drained of what little color it had left. "But if they were out there during the storm . . ." She couldn't bring herself to finish the thought.

"I called Beck to pass the idea by him, and he tried to call Agent Turner. But if he's still in the marsh, he's in a dead zone, because the calls failed." Grant knelt down in front of Dallas. "Beck is borrowing Hal's boat, and we're going to go see . . . if there's anything to be seen. If they had the boat out and the storm came up, they could have gotten caught in the current and they could be up around the bend somewhere."

"Or they could have capsized or they could have lost their oars, or the boat could have been swamped ..." Dallas began to shake again. Up until this moment, "lost" had not been narrowed to any specific danger. Now the possibility that the boys had gone into the Bay in a storm made her light-headed, and for a moment, she thought she might pass out. If they'd gone into the Bay during the storm, they might well have drowned.

"Oh, dear God ..." She stood on weak legs. "I'm going with you."

Grant took her by both arms. "You can't go with us. There's a chance we're wrong, and there still might be a phone call. Agent Turner said if there was going to be a ransom call, it most likely would come today." He eased her back into the chair. "You stay here with Berry."

"I could go ..." Paige began, her eyes beginning to fill, her bottom lip quivering. "If Cody went to have an adventure because I brought him these books, it's my fault. I read the books to him. I made him think—"

Dallas reached out to her. "It's not your fault."

"But I told him how fun it would be to be like Max and sail off to an island ..." Paige began to wail.

"Island," Grant repeated almost imperceptively.

They heard the sound of a boat's engine drawing near.

Grant looked out the window. Hal's boat, the *Shady Lady*, was idling near the end of the dock.

"Hal and Beck are here. We'll be back." He kissed her mouth. "Say a prayer."

He unlocked the back door. "All of you, say a prayer ..."

The Bay was choppy and the waves higher than normal, but the *Shady Lady* cut through them with ease, though they weren't able to pick up too much speed because visibility wasn't the best.

"Stay as close to the shoreline as you can without scraping bottom," Grant told Hal, "so Beck and I can keep an eye on the beach."

"He had one of those lightweight little rowboats, you say?" Hal had one hand on the steering wheel and the other wrapped around a travel mug of coffee. "Beck, toss Grant one of those parkas with the hood on it. He's going to be soaked to the skin before we make it to the mouth of the river."

Beck disappeared into the cabin and moments later returned with a yellow parka, which he tossed in Grant's direction.

"Thanks." Grant pulled the parka over his head and pulled up the hood.

"You know, it's entirely possible that the wind tore the rope from the boat back there at the dock," Beck tried to shout over the wind. "He and Logan may not have taken it out."

"I guess that could have happened, but my gut is telling me they went off in search of an adventure. They wouldn't have thought about the weather. They're six years old, both of them." Grant paused for a moment to think. "Hal, head over toward Goat Island."

"Goat Island?" Hal frowned. "You think they could have gone that far?"

"Cody was real curious about it when I mentioned it the other day."

"If they set out for Goat Island yesterday, the boaters would have seen them," Beck pointed out. "The boats all had to do a pass around it. They'd have been sure to notice a couple of six-year-olds in a rowboat in their path."

"The speedboats went around Goat, but the sailboats went off in the opposite direction when the speedboats were finished. They watched the speedboat races with Clay. It wasn't until the sailboat races began that Brooke took them up to Charles Street."

"I guess it's possible, but how could two kids that small row a boat into the Bay?" Beck still wasn't convinced.

"Dallas said the oars are super light, and that Cody was actually pretty good with them. I don't know about Logan," Grant said.

"I called Clay right before we picked you up to let him know what we were doing," Beck told him. "I wanted him to be prepared in case ... well, in case the boys did what you think they might have done. Anyway, he mentioned that Logan knows how to row. Clay took him out a couple of times on the river in a dinghy."

The *Shady Lady* rode through the wake of a passing cabin cruiser and headed off to the right. In the distance they could see the outline of the trees on Goat Island. The spray blew in their eyes and they hunched inside their parkas and prayed for the wind to die down.

As they neared the island, Grant called to Hal, "Is there a light on the front of this boat?"

Hal nodded.

Grant pointed to the left. "There's something there, near the beach, but I can't tell what it is. Can't even tell if it's on the beach or in the ... yes, that's it, there." He raised a hand to try to keep the spray out of his eyes. "I think it could be the boat. That could be them."

Beck joined him at the rail.

"I don't know. I just see a shape," he told Grant.

"Hal, do you have a dinghy?" Grant asked.

Hal nodded. "Back of the boat."

Grant turned and saw the dinghy tied to the back. "Oars?"

"Under the seat there on the left." Hal pointed. "But you're not thinking to . . ."

Grant found the oars.

"Grant, this is nuts," Beck told him. "At least wait until the wind dies down before you go out there."

"If the kids are there, we need to know." He began to untie the dinghy.

"I'll go with you. If you're stupid enough to do this, at least don't be stupid enough to go alone." Beck began to follow him, but Grant was already in the dinghy and had shoved off.

"The dinghy's not big enough for two men and two boys," he called back over his shoulder.

"You've lost your mind," Beck shouted. "Look, it's going to be bad enough if I have to go back there and tell Dallas we couldn't find Cody, but if I have to tell her we lost you, too . . ."

"You won't. Hey, champion swimmer, remember?" Grant began to row the dinghy through the choppy sea. They were only twenty-five feet from the shoreline, but in the storm, it seemed like ten times that much; still he made it to the shore. Dragging the dinghy with him lest it blow away, he put his head down and made for the

397

rowboat that was farther down the beach since he'd been blown so far off course.

As he drew nearer, he realized the boat was overturned, which meant one of two things. Either it had flipped over in the storm and the boys had been washed away, or . . .

He lifted the end of the boat. There, huddled together against the cold, were two very frightened little boys.

"Dr. Wyler!" Their faces lit with surprise. "You found us!"

Chapter 22

DALLAS stood in the midst of the crowd gathered on the dock in anticipation of the *Shady Lady*'s arrival. She could barely stand still.

"You're fidgeting unmercifully," Berry had noted. "Stop it before I shove you into the river."

"I can't help it. I'm so anxious to see Cody," Dallas had replied.

"Patience, dear. And please note that Brooke is every bit as anxious to see her son, and she's standing perfectly still."

"Brooke hasn't come out of her catatonic state yet, Miz Eberle," Brooke told them. "She isn't moving because she's frozen to the spot."

Berry rolled her eyes at both of them.

"This is a joyous time, girls. The boys have been found, they're fine, they're on their way home," Berry reminded them.

"We know that. We just need to see them to make sure." Dallas raised a hand to her eyes and scanned the horizon. "There's a boat coming toward the mouth of the river. See? Is that Hal's boat? I don't know what it looks like."

"Hal has a—oh my God, that *is* him!" Brooke cried. "Oh, and there's Grant on the deck. Or is that Beck?"

"It's Grant," Dallas said breathlessly. "It's Grant."

Was there ever a sight as wonderful as that of Grant, standing on the bow of the boat, between two small figures, both of whom were jumping up and down as the boat neared the dock? Was there ever a man braver, more fearless, more selfless ... more beautiful, than Grant Wyler? Too choked up to speak, Dallas moved to the end of the pier as the boat pulled up alongside.

Clay Madison stepped up and reached out with both arms to lift the shivering boys as Grant handed them out of the boat.

"Mom, we had an adventure!" Cody cried as he ran to his mother. "Me and Logan went to the island like Rob'son Caruso but we lost the oars and it started to rain and we hid under the boat when the thunder started and we had to wait until the rain stopped so we could come home but Dr. Wyler found us and he gave us his sweatshirt 'cause we were cold and we both put it on together and we were like one big person ..."

Dallas hugged him and held on even as he babbled on about his adventure.

"Sweetie, you're cold ..."

"Yeah, but it got dark last night and it kept raining so we couldn't go to look for berries and we didn't have dinner." He held up his hand, three fingers pointing skyward. "We missed lunch and dinner and breakfast and lunch again." He raised his pinkie. "Four times we didn't eat."

"Well, you can come in the house and get warm and eat something right now," Berry told him. "But first come give your old Aunt Berry a hug."

"There were lots of bugs on Goat Island. Me and Logan called it Bug Island and not Goat Island because there were no goats but lots of bugs." He struggled to get loose from Dallas's arms and held up his own to show off his many insect bites, then turned to give Berry a quick hug.

"Why is everybody crying?" he asked.

"Because we were afraid for you and Logan," Dallas told him.

"Why?" Logan pushed away from his mother.

"Because you've been lost since yesterday, and it was storming . . ." Brooke began.

Cody and Logan exchanged a puzzled look.

"We weren't lost," Logan told her. "We knew where we were."

"Well, unfortunately, no one else did," Brooke replied.

"Boys, we are going to have to have a talk about going off and not telling anyone where you're going, and taking the boat out without an adult. You scared the life out of everyone."

"But we wore our life jackets." Cody pointed to the orange vest that he still wore. "Just like you said."

"And that was very good and very smart of you. But the fact remains that you had no business leaving Charles Street without telling Logan's mother. And, Cody, I told you not to take the boat out alone."

"But I wasn't alone," he protested. "Logan was with me."

"Logan isn't a grown-up. Sorry, but there will be consequences," Dallas told them both. Now that the boys were back and they knew that no harm had come to them, there were other matters to be dealt with.

401

"What are 'consequences'?" Logan asked.

"It's when you do something bad and your mother finds out and you're going to get punished for it," Cody explained.

"Nonsense." Emilio stormed down the pier like a freight train, pushing the Madison family out of the way. "There's no need to punish him. He was just being a boy. Come here, son, and let Daddy hug you."

Cody froze at the sight of his father.

"I've missed you so much, son." Emilio lifted the boy off his feet, apparently not noticing that his son was stiff in his arms.

Cody looked over his father's shoulder to his mother, his face white and his eyes wide with uncertainty. When Emilio started to carry him toward the front yard and the gathering of reporters near the end of the drive, Cody's uncertainty turned to fear.

"Emilio, put him down," Dallas said softly. "You're frightening him."

"Don't be ridiculous, Dallas," Emilio called over his shoulder. "He's just surprised to see me, aren't you, Cody?"

"Put me down," Cody begged. "Put me down, *please.*"

Emilio stopped, hesitated, then lowered Cody to the ground. Cody broke the grip his father had on him and ran to his mother.

"He isn't a thing to be paraded around to the press, Emilio. He's a little boy." Dallas unconsciously smoothed back Cody's wet hair from his forehead.

"He's *my* little boy, Dallas. I was just as panicked as you were when he went missing. I have as much right to be here as you do."

"Actually, no, you don't." A tall dark-haired woman came through the crowd that had gone silent on the dock as the drama had begun to play out.

"What the hell are you doing here?" Emilio looked at the woman as if she were a bug to be stepped on.

Norma Bradshaw positioned herself between Emilio and Dallas. "As Dallas's friend, I took the first flight I could get out of L.A. to give her emotional support. As her attorney, I had a feeling you were going to show up as well and thought perhaps I should be on hand to remind you of the way things stand. You signed an agreement very recently in which you gave full custody of your son to your ex-wife. That would be Dallas. So no, you don't have every right. Actually, you have very few rights here." She paused as if considering, then added, "Probably none."

"I am entitled to see my son," Emilio protested. "My God, you don't know what it's like to find out that your only child has gone missing, that he's been lost—"

"Cut the drama. Spare everyone." Norma lowered her voice so that Cody couldn't hear her words. "Holding on to your properties was more important to you than holding on to your son."

"Cody, say good-bye to your father for now," Dallas told him before more words could be exchanged. "You may see him later, if you wish, but only if you wish. Right now, I want you to go into the house with Berry and get warm and cleaned up and get something to eat. I'll be in very shortly."

"Come along, Cody. You must be starving after not having anything to eat since yesterday morning." Berry held out her hand, and he took it.

"We had something to eat. We had peppermints."

"Peppermints?" Dallas frowned.

He let go of Berry's hand and stuck it into the pocket of his shorts. "See? The ones Aunt Berry threw to us from the parade car."

"Say good-bye to your father, child." Berry's eyes had misted.

"Good-bye," Cody muttered. He had still to look Emilio in the eyes.

Paige came out onto the back porch, and the dogs followed her.

"Fleur!" Cody took off across the lawn, all else seemingly forgotten.

"You've turned him against me," Emilio said angrily. "You've alienated his affection."

"Oh, please. You've never had time for Cody. You totally underestimated how your behavior affected your son," Dallas told him. "He's having a problem forgiving you."

"He's too young to have known about . . . any of that." His eyes narrowed. "Unless you told him. I'll bet you showed him all those stories to turn him against me." He looked at Norma and added, "You'll be hearing from my lawyer. I'm going to go to court and ask that my rights be restored."

"I don't think you want to do that, Emilio," Norma told him. "You'll only end up looking worse than you do now."

He waved a hand as if to dismiss her. "There was only that one incident. Anyone can make a mistake."

"We both know there was more than one video," Norma said meaningfully.

"What are you talking about?" He frowned.

"Oh, I think you know."

He eyed her suspiciously.

"I represent a lot of people in your world, Emilio. You'd be very surprised if you saw the names on my client list. Some of whom you know." She paused. "Intimately."

He tried to stare Norma down.

"So don't even try to sell me that 'only one video' bullshit. I know there are many more than one." She chuckled. "Actually, I own more than one. I suspect I could make a nice chunk of change if I put them up for pay-per-view on the Internet."

When his face went white, she added, "Trust me when I tell you that my clients owe a much greater allegiance to me than they do to you."

"Are you blackmailing me, Norma?" he asked.

Norma shook her head. "Not at all. But I am suggesting that now is a good time to walk away. Leave Dallas and Cody alone. When—if—your son wants to see you, I guarantee that Dallas will certainly permit him to do so. Otherwise, stay out of the picture. You'll be much better off if you do."

Emilio took two steps backward, then turned and walked swiftly up the drive.

Dallas turned to Norma. "Do you really have more tapes?"

"No." She shrugged. "But I figured if he was stupid enough to have made one, he'd have been stupid enough to have made others."

"Way to bluff." Dallas hugged her.

"I think Cody's body language spoke volumes," Norma said. "He clearly was uncomfortable when he saw Emilio and didn't seem to have anything to say to him."

"I almost hate to say this—all things considered—but I'm sad about that. I had a great relationship with my dad, and it hurts me to know that Cody doesn't have that."

"It's Emilio's fault, not yours, that his son doesn't seem to have much affection for him. Emilio is a classic narcissist." She pointed toward the street, where at that moment Emilio was addressing the crowd that had gathered. "Even now, it's all about him. He's using this to get good press, Dallas. It's his platform to try to salvage his sunken career and rehabilitate himself in the public's eye. Look, someday, maybe he and Cody will be able to have a decent relationship, but that's up to Cody. He's a smart boy. He'll let you know when he's ready, and you'll permit him to make that decision on his own."

Dallas nodded and turned back to the crowd that was still celebrating the boys' return. Grant was speaking with Agent Turner, and when he looked her way, he smiled. She all but ran to him, threw her arms around his neck, and kissed him soundly on the mouth.

"I haven't thanked you yet," she said, kissing him again.

"I'll let you thank me later. Right now, Agent Turner is chewing me out, and I don't think he's quite finished," Grant told her.

"It was reckless of you," Turner said. "Instead of this great reunion, we could just as easily be trolling the Bay to recover your body right now."

"With all due respect, I'm not stupid, Agent Turner. I was pretty sure I could row from Hal's boat to the shore and make it. I rowed in high school and I rowed in college. I've rowed in storms every bit as bad as the one we had last night," Grant explained, "and I've been a very strong swimmer all my life."

"Still, you should have left it to us."

"We did try to call you." Beck stepped up. "The calls weren't getting through, and we had no way of knowing how much longer you'd be down in the marsh. The agent you left here with Dallas was tied up with her ex-husband and the entourage of press he brought along with him. Once Dr. Wyler figured out where the boys might have gone, we needed to go immediately in case the storm got any worse. I made the decision to go, Agent Turner. I take full responsibility for making that call."

"Would you have taken responsibility if Dr. Wyler had drowned?"

"Yes." Beck nodded without hesitation. "I would have."

Mia came up behind the agent, with whom she'd worked on several cases when she was still with the Bureau, and poked him in the back. "Lighten up, Vic," she whispered. "All's well that ends well."

"You know I'm going to have to speak with both of the boys before I leave." The agent did his best to ignore her.

Mia held up her left hand, using her thumb and forefinger to form an O.

407

Vic Turner shook his head, rolled his eyes, and walked away.

When the agent reached the end of the drive, Beck turned to Grant. "That really was one hell of a stupid thing to have done."

"Hey, you just said—"

"That was because the FBI was standing there, ready to read you the riot act." Beck stood with his hands on his hips. "If anyone's going to ream you out, it'll be me."

The two men stared at each other.

"Frankly, we were afraid you weren't going to make it," Beck said.

"I appreciate that," Grant told him. "But you have to understand that there was no way I wasn't going to try."

"You should have let me come with you," Beck said.

"So we both could have drowned?" Grant shook his head no. He hastened to add, "Not that I really thought that was going to happen."

"It was really that bad out there?" Dallas put her arms around his waist.

"Nah." Grant shook his head. "Everyone likes a little drama. Even Beck."

"Let's bring everyone inside and see if Berry has a bottle or two of champagne to open to celebrate everyone's safe return. I plan on spending the rest of the afternoon hugging my son."

"Good luck with that," Grant told her. "Cody and Logan are feeling like pretty big boys right about now. The way they see it, they had a pretty damned great adventure. Sailed out in a storm, got shipwrecked on a deserted island, slept out in the great wild with only the rowboat for shelter.

Lived on peppermint candies. They'll have a hell of a great story to tell when they get back to school next month."

"Well, good for Cody, but his mother is still a quivering mass and needs to hug her boy," Dallas said.

"I think the press would like a statement." Steffie came across the yard and threw herself on her brother. "The story is all over the news. They're all calling you a hero, you big knucklehead."

Before he could protest, Dallas said, "My hero." She linked her arm through his. "I always wanted to be able to say that to someone in real life . . ."

The celebration lasted until both exhausted boys suddenly and simultaneously fell asleep on the living-room floor. Clay Madison lifted his sleeping nephew and carried him to their car. Dallas hugged Brooke and her mother, then she and Grant walked them to the car. There was still a cluster of reporters gathered on the sidewalk, but Clay drove past them without comment.

Seeing Dallas in the driveway, they called to her, hoping for a quote to go along with their coverage of the story that had a happy ending rather than the worst, as had been expected.

"Dallas, can we have a minute?"

"Dallas, how's Cody?" At this, she gave them a thumbs-up, and someone snapped a picture.

"You should go speak with them," Dallas told Grant. "You're the story here."

"Not my style." He shook his head and took her hand and together they went up the steps and into the house.

"The phone is still ringing off the hook," Berry told Dallas when they went into the kitchen. "I've been letting it go to messages but then I heard Wade's voice but couldn't get to the phone in time to answer it and he hung up. And now I can't get him to pick up. Infuriating."

"Did he leave a message?" Dallas went to the machine to play it back.

"I'm afraid I inadvertently hit erase while I was trying to get the call before he stopped talking." Berry was clearly exasperated. "But he said something about coming home soon and that he had a surprise and we needed to brace ourselves."

Dallas laughed. "We always have to brace ourselves when it comes to Wade. I can't imagine anything he'd do that could that would cause more than a lift of the eyebrows at this point."

"Well, I suppose we'll see soon enough." Berry yawned. "Steffie, would you like another glass of champagne? Some tea, perhaps?"

"No, thank you, Miss B." Steffie seemed suddenly subdued. "I should get back to the shop. Paige, are you going to work for me this afternoon?"

Paige shook her head. "I think I want to wait until Cody wakes up." She turned to Dallas. "If it's okay with you ..."

"Of course," Dallas told her, knowing how much Paige had worried about her little friend.

"I guess I'll see you in the morning, then." Steffie tapped Paige on the top of the head. "Eight o'clock. Don't be late."

Grant turned to Dallas and said, "I need to take a hot shower and get into some dry clothes. And I probably have a bunch of appointments to make up as well."

"There is no way I can ever thank you for what you did today. You saved my son." Dallas took his face in both her hands and looked deeply into his eyes. "No matter what happens, I will never forget that you risked your life for Cody. I will be indebted to you for the rest of my life."

He kissed her, then turned and walked out the door.

"Have you calmed down enough to talk a little business?" Norma asked Dallas when the two of them were the last in the kitchen, Berry having gone upstairs to take a nap.

"Sure. Let's take our coffee into the library." Dallas stood to lead the way. "I've appropriated it for an office. It's a wonderful space to work in."

She opened the door for Norma to precede her into the room.

"I can see why you like to work here," Norma said as she seated herself in one of the oversize leather chairs. "Great light, great atmosphere. And very comfy chairs."

Dallas nodded. "I spend the better part of every day in here. My screenplay is almost finished."

"That's what I wanted to talk to you about."

"I figured as much." Dallas took a sip of coffee, then placed her cup on the table that stood between her and Norma's chairs.

"I'm not having much luck getting backing for your project. I'll tell you flat out that if you were starring in it, and someone else directing, it would have been sold last week for numbers that would make your head spin. As it is, everyone thinks you're playing with them."

"I'm not trying to force the price up. I swear, I'm not."

"I know that. But I just can't get that through to anyone."

"Who have you spoken with so far?" Dallas asked.

Norma went into the hall and returned with her bag. She opened it and took out a small notebook. She thumbed through it until she came to the page she was looking for, then she handed it to Dallas.

"Here's the list along with their comments. Abbreviated comments, but you'll get the gist."

"Would it help if I met with some of these people directly?" Dallas studied the list.

"It might." Norma smiled weakly. "It couldn't hurt."

"See what you can set up for me. The sooner the better."

"I'll see what I can do." Norma finished the last bit of coffee in her cup. "So. Couldn't help but notice that's some guy you've got there."

"He's . . . amazing. He's . . ." Dallas sighed. "He's the guy I fell in love with when I was sixteen years old, except that now he's all grown up."

"Not too many like him around. Oh, sure, lots of pretty faces in Hollywood, but how many of them would risk their life to save a child? A child that isn't even his."

"Not many, I suppose."

"Damned few, if you ask me. I'd hold on to that one, honey."

"He has his business here," Dallas told her. "My business is on the opposite coast."

"Too bad." Norma shrugged, then went on to something else. "So, when do you think you'll be coming back to L.A. for good?"

"Cody and I planned on September seventh. The day after Labor Day. I figured that would give me two weeks to get Cody situated to go back to school." She inspected a fingernail and found she'd bitten it without even realizing.

"Cody seems like a different kid here," Norma remarked.

"Doesn't he?" Dallas smiled. "He's been really happy here. He has a best friend—a real best friend—for the first time ever."

"Logan. His partner in yesterday's crime."

Dallas nodded. "Every kid needs that kind of playmate. Not that I want them to do that again. I just mean—"

"I know what you mean. Hell, I've stayed in Laguna Beach for five years longer than I'd have liked to because my daughter has such a strong social network there. I figure it helps to make up for the fact that I'm a single parent and she's an only child. She has lots of friends on our street and has gone to the same school forever. I'd like to move from that house, but I know it's better for Elisabeth if we stay there for a few more years. I keep telling myself that once she leaves for college, I can live anyplace I want." Norma's phone chirped, announcing a text message. "Excuse me, Dallas, I need to take a look at this. I've been expecting . . . yeah, that's what I've been waiting for." She looked up at Dallas. "Mind if I excuse myself to make a call?"

"Not at all. Go right ahead."

413

Dallas lifted her feet and rested them on the big round ottoman that sat next to her chair. She hadn't realized how tired she was until she sat down and started to relax. She yawned and closed her eyes, and wished that she'd gone back to Grant's when he did, but she didn't want to leave Cody until she'd gotten used to the fact that he'd survived his ordeal and was back home again, safe and sound, when the outcome could have been so very different. Could *easily* have been much different, had it not been for Grant. There were so many awful stories in the news, so many terrible things happening to innocent children—other people's children—that she could scarcely believe that her child had been spared, that her son had not been one of the stories that would cause every other parent to slap a hand over their mouth in horror.

The last thought she had before falling off to sleep was that leaving St. Dennis at the end of the summer was going to be much harder than she'd ever imagined it could be.

Chapter 23

WHEN Dallas called Grant the following morning and asked him to have lunch with her, he wasn't quite sure what to expect. But he hadn't expected what she had to say.

"Norma's set up meetings for me for this week. Four of them. We're hoping that I can talk someone into putting up the money for *Pretty Maids*. So far, everyone's turned her down," she told him over pizza at Ferrari's Pizza. "Everyone seems to think I'm jockeying for someone to put up superbucks for me to star in the film, which I'm not doing, and frankly, I am a little disappointed that some people I've known for years and have worked with before would think I'd play such games, but there it is."

"I'm assuming the meetings are on the West Coast." All he could think of was he wished he'd chosen a different place for lunch. It was noisy and crowded and not the type of place where you'd toss your heart onto the table. But he was good at improvising. He'd go with what he had. Apparently, he wasn't going to get another chance before she left. He was going to have to make this time count, speak his mind, and get it all out there, once and for all.

Dallas nodded. "I'm flying out tonight. God, I hope I can sell someone on this. It means the world to me to be able to make this film."

He forced a smile. "I can't imagine anyone turning you down, once you tell them about it the way you've told me. They'll be fighting over each other to give you the money to make it."

She reached across the table and touched two of his fingers with hers.

"It means a lot to me that you believe in me. I have so much to thank you for . . . not just for saving Cody's life, but that's certainly in the number one spot."

"Do me a favor, Dallas." He put down the slice of pizza he'd been about to bite into. "Don't tell me again how grateful you are."

"I *am* grateful to you." She put down the paper cup of water she'd been drinking. "From what Beck and Hal have told me, you could have been killed out there in the Bay on Sunday morning. They said you could have been tossed overboard from that dinghy you were in, that at one point they thought you *had* been tossed into the Bay. Beck said there was no way they could have gotten to you because the water was too shallow for Hal's boat to get any closer to the beach." Her eyes filled with tears. "You risked everything to save Cody. Do you think I could ever forget that?"

"I didn't do it because I wanted your eternal gratitude, and I don't want to be Cody's savior. Of course I'm glad that everyone made it home all right and the worst thing that came out of it was Logan's cold, which according to Clay is minor. But I don't want to be your hero, Dallas. I want to be ..." He struggled for the right words, then gave up. "I want to be your guy."

She reached across the table and touched his face. "You'll always be my guy, Grant."

She stared at him for a long moment, then said, "I know you think that I'm not coming back, but you're wrong. I'll take care of my business and I'll be back by the end of the week. I promise."

He could have said—wanted to say—*Yeah, well, I've heard those words before. I think we both know how that turned out.*

But he couldn't bring himself to burst the bubble of the illusion that she would come back to him, or ask how long she'd stay this time. So instead, in the midst of the commotion of a children's birthday party and a rowdy bunch of tourists, he said, "Here's the thing, flat out. I didn't choose to fall in love with you. I didn't want to, this time around—I really didn't—but I couldn't help myself. And once I realized what was happening, I just said the hell with it and let myself fall. If I have to pick myself up, I can do that. I did it once before. I survived then. I can make it again."

She started to speak, but he silenced her by saying, "No, this is my turn. If I stop, I'll probably run out of nerve. So here it is: I don't want your eternal gratitude. I don't want you coming back here to be with me because you feel *indebted*. That's the word you used the other day. I went after Cody because I thought I knew where he and Logan might have gone, and knowing it and not going for them—well, that's not the way I'm wired. But the last thing I want is for you to be *indebted* to me. Don't come

417

back if that's all you feel, Dallas. Please stay in L.A. if that's all we're talking about here."

He glanced at his watch. He was already ten minutes late for a surgery he'd scheduled.

"I gotta go." He pushed back his chair. "Got a schnauzer with a cancerous growth on his liver that we're going to try to remove."

He leaned across the table and kissed the side of her face. "Good luck with getting your film made," he whispered. "I hope they give you everything you want, and more."

"I'll be back by the weekend," she said softly.

He forced another smile. "Sure. I'll see you then."

He left her sitting at the table because he couldn't bear the thought of watching her leave, didn't want to see the back of her as she walked away. He could have asked her to drop him off at the clinic but he needed the time to walk off the hurt and to try to clear his head. She always did have a way of clouding his head.

He had no doubt that she'd get whatever it was she was going out there for, and he'd be happy for her because it meant so damned much to her. She'd make her film and it would be great and probably win her all kinds of awards and her life would be firmly entrenched on the West Coast again. But he also had no doubt that he'd been a fool to let this go beyond friendship again. He should have known—oh, hell, he *had* known—what was going to happen. Same story all over again. Dallas here for the summer, Dallas gone come September to chase her dreams. Grant stuck in his own life.

Had he really not changed all that much since he was eighteen?

He hadn't given her much of a chance to talk, but really, what could she say? He'd heard the "I'll be back" line before, and sure, she probably meant it when she said it. If she didn't intend to come back, she'd have told him. Dallas was honest, he'd give her that.

He walked along the hot sidewalk, and with each stride, he saw the rest of his life spreading out before him in chunks of June-July-August, just as it had long ago. She'd leave in September, and when Cody finished school in June, she'd be back. And he'd be waiting, counting the days, until she got there.

The sad, simple fact of my life at age thirty-eight is is that I love her. I always have, and I probably always will. Not much different than things were when I was eighteen—that's the sad part. The simple part? That's the part about loving her. I can't not love her. I tried. It didn't work.

"Took the cure but it failed," he muttered as he crossed the road in front of his clinic and went in through the front door.

You are one pathetic chump, he told himself. *One big, sorry . . .*

"Dr. Wyler, the Fosters are here with Mika and she's been prepped for surgery." Mimi met him at the door that led back to the operating room.

"I'll be right there."

Grant went into the back and prepared for the operation on the schnauzer. Feeling sorry for himself was going to have to wait. He pushed all thoughts of Dallas to the back of his mind, then went in to do the job of trying to save the dog's life. Dallas had her priorities, and he had his.

419

"That went well," Dallas said sarcastically as she slid into the passenger seat of Norma's Jaguar sedan. "They couldn't have been more annoying if they'd tried."

Norma passed a tip to the valet and snapped on her seat belt as the door closed quietly. "I told you they think you're playing with them."

"Why would they think that? I've worked with Adam Kessinger before. He knows me. He knows what I'm like. Why would he think I'd be playing him? If I wanted more, I'd have asked for it point-blank. Why would he think I'd be playing him?"

"Because everyone else in town does it?" Norma shrugged. "I did warn you . . ."

"Yes, you did." Dallas leaned her head against the headrest and sighed. This had been her third turndown in as many days.

"Everyone expects that you will agree to star in the film if and when the price is right."

"Damn it, that makes me so mad." She felt like punching something. "I'm wondering if there's any point in meeting with Helga Graham tomorrow. She never liked me very much anyway."

"It's up to you. I have no problem canceling out on her." Norma smiled as she made a left. "She never liked me much, either."

"I guess I'm going to have to go to the alternate plan," Dallas said.

"Which is?"

"Finance it myself. That is, if I can afford to." She made a face. "I don't even want to know how much of my assets Emilio walked off with."

"Oh, I know the exact number," Norma told her. "That would be zero."

"What?" Dallas frowned. "That can't be right. California law—"

"Dallas, you're as bad as Emilio. Apparently neither of you read the fine print."

"What fine print?"

"In the marital settlement agreement. The part where both parties agreed that all community property would go to Emilio and both of you would keep your personal assets."

"So all the money I made . . ." Dallas thought aloud.

"Is yours. And all the money he made . . . is his."

"I made a whole lot more than he did."

"No fooling." Norma's smile spread from ear to ear.

"Didn't his lawyer catch that?" Dallas was still wide-eyed that Norma had managed to protect her earnings.

"He did. But since I gave Emilio twenty-four hours to sign the agreement before I pulled it off the table, he wasn't about to take a chance of losing millions of dollars in real estate."

"So my investments . . . my bank accounts . . . the art-work I bought before we were married . . ."

"All yours, darlin'."

"I can do it." Dallas sat straight up. "I can finance the film. I can make this movie on my own."

"That's going to take a chunk of it. Not to mention that it's going to be a lot of work."

"Not if I hire the right people."

"First you have to find the right people," Norma reminded her. "Really good people are not that easy to find."

Dallas grinned. "Hey, I found you, didn't I?"

"Poor Cody is exhausted, but I never saw a child fight sleep the way he did tonight. He just couldn't hug that dog of his enough," Berry said. "And he's never come into a room specifically to hug me as he did not once, but three times since you arrived."

"He missed Fleur terribly when we were in California, and you, too, of course," Dallas told her. "He couldn't wait to get back here. I think that, deep inside, he was afraid that we wouldn't come back. He took a whole stack of photos of the dog to share with Elena. I know he was happy to see her. She's been with us since he was born, you know. She stayed with him when I had to travel, she keeps house, she cooks, she hires the landscapers . . . she's like the perfect wife. Everyone should have one."

"Well, now that Cody's tucked into bed, tell me why you decided not to meet with Helga Graham." Berry sat at the kitchen table, Ally at her feet.

"I decided it was a waste of my time." Dallas explained why she'd been turned down over and over.

"The nerve of them all. If I didn't know better, I'd think it was a conspiracy," Berry said haughtily. "Well, the hell with them. We'll think of someone else. We'll go to Plan B." She leaned forward and asked, "Is there a Plan B?"

"River Road Productions." Dallas sat across the table from Berry and stretched her legs out in front of her. "I'm putting up my own money to make the film. If I can't make it the right way, there's no point in making it at all. I'm not Charlotte. Laura Fielding—she's Charlotte, and she's going to be incredible." Dallas smiled smugly. "Everyone who ever discounted her as an actor is going to be kicking themselves when they see how fabulous she is as Charlotte."

"How can you be so sure ...?"

"I had her read the part for me yesterday morning. Berry, you are going to fall in love with her, I promise you. Please trust me on this. She's going to be the perfect Charlotte to your perfect Rosemarie."

"But putting up your own money, dear." Berry shook her head. "That's much too great a risk for one person to take."

"I'm willing to take it."

"You believe in this that strongly?"

"If you're willing to be Rosemarie, then yes, I'll believe in this project with my whole heart and I'll put everything I have into it."

"You have a son to consider. You can't take the chance of bankrupting yourself and jeopardizing your future—and his—for the sake of one film."

"I don't believe I'm going to lose," Dallas said adamantly.

Berry stared out the window for a few moments.

"Then here's the deal. I'm in for fifty percent." Berry added, "No need to change the name of the company."

"Berry, you'd put your money into this? It's going to take a whole lot of cash."

"I made a lot in my day, spent a lot but invested more. My investments have done reasonably well in spite of the economy. And there are all those videos and DVDs and whatnot, a steady stream of dollars into the old bank account. What else should I do with the money, Dallas? Sit back and see how much of it the next recession eats up? I'm your Rosemarie, but only if you let me in for half."

"You drive a hard bargain, lady." Dallas jumped up and hugged her. "You will not be sorry, Berry, I promise you." She danced around and repeated, "I *promise* you."

Ally scooted closer to Berry to get out of the way of Dallas's dancing feet.

"Yesterday I signed an agreement of sale on a condo in L.A. I figured we'd need a place to stay while we're out there making the film."

"Good thinking," Berry said absently, then fell silent.

"What?" Dallas asked after a few quiet minutes had passed. "What are you thinking?"

"I'm wondering why we have to make the film in L.A."

"Where else would we make it?"

"We could make it here," Berry suggested.

"There's no studio here," Dallas reminded her.

"But there could be."

"Where?" Dallas was intrigued. "Where would we all work, where would we film?"

"Hal Garrity owns several warehouses down along the river, at the end of River Road. Last I heard, he doesn't know what he wants to do with them." Berry smiled. "You could set up a lot of the technical work right in there. And as for shooting, for heaven's sake, the story takes place in a small town. Hello, Dallas. St. Dennis?"

"We'd need people . . ."

"Who'd bring revenue to our town. And keep in mind there are many talented people in New York. L.A. isn't the center of everyone's universe, you know. People move around all the time to work on these things, dear. Why not here?"

"It could work." Dallas thought it through. "I think it could work."

"Oh my, won't Cody be thrilled. He wants so badly to stay in St. Dennis."

"There's no question he's much happier here. All the time we were in L.A. he kept asking when we were coming back. It was only four days, but to him I suppose it seemed like weeks. It would definitely be the best thing in the world for him." *And in the long run, the best thing in the world for me, too. Won't Grant be surprised?* "Cody will be beside himself when we tell him that he can go to school here. He even asked me if Logan could move to L.A. with him so they could go to the same school."

"Shall I call Hal in the morning?"

Dallas nodded. "First thing. We'll talk to him first thing." She paused to reconsider. "On second thought, better make that the second thing . . ."

At five thirty the following morning, Dallas was sitting on Grant's back porch steps, drinking her first cup of coffee and nibbling on a croissant. When he let the dogs out—which he had to do because they were barking like maniacs at the back door even though he kept telling them it was probably just a raccoon or a stray cat—he all but fell over her.

"Coffee?" She held the cardboard take-out cup up to him.

"Thanks." He took the coffee and sat down next to her, looking puzzled. "You're back."

"Don't look so surprised. I told you I would be."

"You're up early."

"I set the alarm for four thirty," she told him, "so I could be here when you let the guys out."

"You could have knocked. Or called." He lifted the lid on the cup and took a sip. "Cuppachino's finest organic blend. My favorite."

"Carlo said it was."

"So. You're back. You're really back."

She handed him a paper bag. "Doughnut or cruller?"

"Doughnut. Definitely." He looked inside. "Peach. Oh, yeah. I guess Carlo told you about the doughnut, too."

She nodded and watched him take a bite.

"So I guess you want to know about my trip," she said. She leaned back against the porch railing and slipped her feet out of her sandals. Her right foot reached out to his left, and her toes stroked his instep slowly.

"I do. Great doughnut, by the way." He pulled a napkin from the bag and wiped the corners of his mouth. "How was your trip?"

"It was fabulous, thanks for asking."

"I guess you accomplished what you wanted?"

"Oh, yeah. You could say that." She smiled and watched him try to ignore the fact that his foot was starting to twitch.

"Got the backing you needed?"

"The money for the film is there."

"So. I guess it's all a go, then, huh?" He looked as if he

were trying hard to look happy for her. "I'm glad. I know it means a lot to you."

"It does mean a lot."

"So who's backing it?"

"River Road Productions." She watched his face. For a moment, nothing seemed to register.

"River Road. That's some coincidence."

"How 'bout it?" She'd try to play it cool, but she couldn't keep from grinning. "It's me. Me and Berry. We're River Road."

"Well, that's cool. That's a good name." He reached down and grabbed her foot to stop its movement on his.

Just another reason to make her smile. She knew she was getting to him.

"It's River Road not just because that's where the family home is, and not just because it's our money that's going to finance the whole thing." She turned so she could look him full in the face. "It's River Road because that's where the studio is going to be. Well, it will be, if Hal sells us the warehouses."

Grant put the coffee down.

"What are you talking about?"

"Hal owns some warehouses at the other end of River Road, right along the river. Berry thinks they could be converted into space we could use to make the film, like our own studio, where film could be edited and scenes could be constructed. She's going to talk to him this morning about selling the buildings to us."

"You mean, you'd . . ."

"Set up shop here in St. Dennis, yes." She was grinning again. "Making films right here. At least, the first one. If it does well, we'll go on to another one. Baby steps, you see. One picture at a time."

"That means you . . ." He appeared to be afraid to say the words, so she filled in the blank.

". . . will be staying in St. Dennis, yes. That's exactly what it means. Actually, we're going to live here. Home and business in the same place. This place. I hear lots of people work from their homes. It's a trend."

When he didn't react, she reached over and turned his face toward hers. "Grant? Did you hear what I said?"

"For a moment, I thought you said you were staying in St. Dennis." He reached for the coffee and raised it to his lips again.

"I did." She reached for his free hand and held it.

"Seriously?"

"Seriously. When I finally stopped to think about it, I realized there was every reason to do it here, and none that I could think of for doing it in California." She smiled. "Except for the fact that there are studios already built out there. Other than that, everything and everyone I love is here. Berry. You."

"Don't say things just because you feel grateful." She could feel him starting to pull away. She wasn't going to let him.

"I was—am—grateful to you. That has nothing to do with the fact that I love you. I can feel more than one thing at the same time." She raised her left hand, palm side up and open. "See? Gratitude." She raised the right hand in a similar fashion. "Love. Two emotions. Both very real. One not dependent upon the other.

"I had a lot of time to think over the past week. Mostly

428

while I was on the plane, or when I should have been sleeping. There was so much going on in my head. I went out there because, hey, it's where you go to talk to people when you want to make a movie. But I didn't want to be there. It didn't feel like home anymore. I felt more at home here. I wanted to be here with you. When Berry suggested we look into buying Hal's old warehouses, it was as if a light went on inside my head, and it all fell into place. Of course it felt right. It *is* right. I spent most of last night kicking myself for not having thought of it sooner."

"You could have come over here and spent the night kicking me. I'd have let you in. Go back to the part where you said you loved me and say it again."

"I do love you. I've always loved you." She smiled. "I want you to be my guy."

"God, I can't believe I actually said that to you." He ran a hand through his hair and laughed self-consciously. "That was so *lame*."

"I thought it was darling. I thought it was the sweetest thing anyone ever said to me." She slid herself onto his lap. "I kept thinking about it all the time I was in L.A. That you're my guy." She kissed him on the lips. "I want to be your girl."

He cupped the side of her face, then kissed her, a long lingering kiss etched with the promise of many, many more to come.

"You are my girl. You've always been my girl, always will be."

"Always," she repeated.

"I can hardly believe this. I've waited for twenty years

to hear you say those words." He frowned, and momentarily his hand on her foot went still. "Does that make me sound like an idiot?"

She shook her head. "Twenty years ago, we were too young. We both had places to go, things to do. Right person, wrong time. Now we're both here, in the same place at the same time."

"Right place, right time. Right person."

She nodded. "Maybe this is the way it was supposed to be all along, I don't know, but I think we should make the most of this second chance."

"You know, they say love's better the second time around."

"I've heard that, too."

She leaned in to kiss him. The back door swung open and hit the side of the house with a bang.

"Dad, your answering service is on the phone and—" Paige stopped short. "Oh."

"Dallas just stopped over to let us know that she and Cody are staying in St. Dennis," Grant told her. "Isn't that great news?"

"Staying, like, for good? Like, moving here?"

Dallas nodded.

"Why does everyone get to stay here but me?" Paige demanded. "Why am I the only one who has to leave?" She stormed into the house and slammed the door.

Grant sighed heavily and ran a hand over his face.

"Go inside and talk to her," Dallas said. "She needs you right now."

"So much for our romantic early morning reunion," he said.

"That'll make our reunion later tonight even sweeter. How 'bout dinner at Lola's and a movie back here?"

"Paige . . ."

"Can babysit for Cody." She thought for a moment. "Which means a 'movie' here first and dinner later."

"I don't know." He leaned against the railing. "I don't know that I want to do a 'movie' without some sort of commitment from you."

"What kind of commitment? What are you talking about?"

"I'm talking about the fact that you committed to your film when you decided to bankroll it yourself. You made a commitment to St. Dennis when you decided to make this the home of your production company. You made a commitment to Berry when you talked her into being in your movie, and you made a commitment to Cody when you decided to move here permanently." Grant crossed his arms over his chest. "What kind of commitment are you willing to make to me?"

"What kind of commitment do you want, Grant?" she asked softly.

"The permanent kind," he told her. "Of course, the fine print is open to negotiation. The wheres and the whens, that sort of thing."

"Should I call Norma?" Dallas pretended to ponder. "She does all my negotiating for me."

"Sorry. This time you're on your own."

She moved closer and rested her elbow on his knee. "First, we need to define 'permanent.' What does that mean to you?"

"It means forever. It means always."

"All right." She nodded. "We're in agreement there. My commitment to you will be forever. For always. But you have to reciprocate."

"Goes without saying." He smiled. "We're going to have to formalize this, which I believe usually requires a ceremony of some sort."

"And a party. A glorious party." She moved closer. "I'd like to propose the Inn at Sinclair Point."

"Agreed." He smiled and took her hand. "You know, there's really nothing to this negotiating stuff. I don't see why lawyers charge so much to do it."

"You understand that, when I'm working," she said, her eyes serious now, "I may have to go away for several weeks at a time."

"I promise not to whine." He crossed his heart with his index finger. "We can even write that into our vows."

"Where will we live?" she asked thoughtfully.

"We could live here." He pointed behind him at the old house he was renovating. "Unless you want something bigger. I know it's not Hollywood style."

"I like this house. It's a good family house. It's plenty big enough." She looked over her shoulder at the house. "But I should warn you. I will want a new kitchen."

"I'll add that to your list of demands." He sat up and pulled her to him, and kissed her. "There. That seals the deal. There's no backing out now."

He traced her bottom lip with his index finger. "You sure about this? Do you need time to think it over?"

Dallas shook her head. "I think I spent more time trying not to think about where we were going because this is where I wanted us to end up, and I was afraid we'd never get here." Dallas touched his face. "How 'bout you?"

"I've always been sure," he said simply. "It's always been you."

"Seal the deal again." She leaned in to kiss him.

"Dad!" Paige yelled from an upstairs window. "The answering service is on the phone again."

Grant sighed.

"Go on in and take the call. I'll see you tonight."

"I don't want you to leave now. I was just getting warmed up."

"Save it." She kissed his lips softly. "We have the rest of our lives . . ."

Berry poured her second cup of coffee and walked out onto the back porch. She held the door for Ally to follow, then closed it quietly. Cody was still sleeping off his jet lag. He hadn't even joined her for tai chi that morning, but no surprise there. The boy was exhausted.

No surprise, either, that Dallas's car wasn't there. Berry knew where she'd have gone. Well, knew where she, Berry, would have gone, if she'd been in Dallas's shoes.

Well, you had been in her shoes, once upon a time, a tiny voice reminded her, *but you chose a different direction*.

"Thanks for the reminder," she muttered aloud drily.

As if she needed a reminder of her own folly, so many, many years ago.

"Water over the dam," she said. But if she had to do it over—if the choice were hers to make again—would she have chosen her dreams over love?

Not just love, but the love of her life. Had she realized

at the time that she'd never love another? That her future would be defined by the day she'd turned her back and returned to the coast to make yet another movie?

"*The Firebrand*," she murmured. "Worst film I ever made. Tanked big-time, almost ruined my career. That should have told me something."

Secretly, she'd thought he'd been bluffing, thought that despite his angry words, he'd be waiting for her when she came back, whenever that would be. He'd wanted a wife who'd be there for him, wanted children, wanted holidays with his family, he'd said. She hadn't believed him. She'd really believed that he wanted her more than he'd wanted those things, that all that talk was just to get his way and make her give up her career and marry him.

But there'd been no bluff. He'd wanted what he wanted, and he'd wanted it with her, but she'd been too foolish to see beyond her own nose, to see anything other than her own dreams of stardom. And before too long, he'd stopped returning her calls, and the next thing she knew, she was hearing rumors from St. Dennis that Archer Callahan was getting married.

She really didn't think he'd go through with it, thought it was a ruse to get her to come running back.

Seeing him on Saturday had been such a shock. Spending the day in his company had done little but make her heart hurt at the reminder of what she'd lost, what she'd left behind. Had it not been for Cody's great adventure, as they now referred to it, she would have wallowed all weekend in anguish.

You can't turn back the clock, she'd been reminding herself. *You had a good life. Could it have been better? Who's to say?*

434

And yet in spite of her denial, she knew in her heart that she'd made the wrong choice. Regrets were a bitch.

"Well, when you screw up, Berry, you screw up big-time."

She went down the steps to the lawn, and made herself comfortable in one of the big wooden chairs that looked out toward the Bay. With Ally, she sat and watched the gulls circling around something on the beach across the river. She smiled when the great blue heron flew by on its morning run, and wondered where its nest was, if it had a mate. If so, perhaps there'd be fledglings, and more herons to ride the air above the surface of the river this time next year.

Ally began to growl, a deep, low rumble, before she exploded with a bark. Standing behind Berry's chair, she took a stand. Berry turned to see what had caused the dog to go on alert, and her heart stopped in her chest.

Walking toward her, a large spray of pale-colored roses in his arms, was Archer Callahan. For a moment, he looked as he had so long ago, straight and tall and blond, his athletic stride eating up the distance between them. Then she blinked, and saw him as he was, older now, white-haired, the athletic build gone a little soft, not quite as tall with the weight of the years, but she couldn't help but think that he was still the most beautiful man she'd ever seen.

"I heard you were an early riser," he was saying as he approached. "I'm an early riser, too, so I thought I'd stop by. I hope you don't mind that I took the liberty . . . ?"

"I don't mind," she told him as she stood. "I don't mind at all. I was just watching the day begin."

"It's a beautiful morning, isn't it?" He handed her the roses. "I saw these yesterday in the window of the flower shop up on Charles Street, and they made me think of you. I remembered how you loved those pale pink roses. So light they were almost white. Took me all night to build up the courage to bring them over."

She reached her arms out to take them and buried her face in their scent, recalling other such bouquets.

"They're beautiful, Archer," she said softly. "Perfect. How nice that you remembered."

"Some things you never forget," he said simply. "Some things just stay with you."

She was so moved, she couldn't speak. Finally, she said the only thing she could think of.

"Would you like to come in and have a cup of coffee with me?"

"I can't think of anything I'd rather do."

"Neither can I." Berry took his arm and started for the house, Ally trotting by her side.

"Nice dog, Berry," Archer said. "I always liked a golden retriever myself."

"She's a lovely dog, Archer. Let me tell you how I found her. That is, of course, if you have the time."

"I have time," Archer assured her. "I have all the time in the world."

Diary ~

*Well, if this hasn't been the summer of second chances, I don't
know what is! I can't recall when I've ever seen so many old
lovers reunited! Dallas and Grant are everywhere together these
days—you rarely see one without the other—and Berry tells
me in the strictest confidence that she expects big news from
them soon. Certainly not cohabitating—Dallas would never,
because of Cody—but Berry suspects an engagement could be
imminent. And how lovely would that be! Another wedding at
the Inn, perhaps?*

*I finally did interview Dallas last week—my piece will run
in the next issue—and my, what plans that girl has for our
humble little community! She's formed her own movie
production company, bought Hal Garrity's old warehouses to
build—wait for it now!—her own movie studio! In St.
Dennis! Imagine! She tells me she's already drawn up the
plans for the warehouses to be fitted to suit the needs of her
newly formed production company and she's currently
interviewing contractors. She plans to start the work
immediately upon finding the right person. Well, I don't have
to tell you what a boost this will be for our town ... though
some are already complaining that, if built, the studio will
bring too many people to St. Dennis. I say, tell the people who
own shops up on Charles Street that they'll have too many
patrons for their businesses! Ha! Believe me when I say the
merchants in town are solidly behind Dallas and her venture.
Of course, I'd personally support just about anything that
would keep that girl and her boy here in town, if for no other
reason than it makes Berry happier than I've seen her in years.*

Dallas tells me that Berry has agreed to star in the first movie that will be made here, Pretty Maids. *I assumed that Dallas would be starring with her great-aunt (the very thought gives me goose bumps!), in Berry's return to the silver screen after all these years, but no. She has someone else to play the part of the younger woman, someone she says will surprise absolutely everyone, so I can't wait to see who it is. The important thing, Dallas tells me, is that she'll be able to spend most of her time here in St. Dennis with Berry and Cody, and of course, with Grant.*

Oh, and speaking of old lovers reunited—Berry and Archer have picked up where they left off more years ago than I can count. I don't think I'd be surprised if Berry actually beat Dallas to the altar. Wouldn't that be one for the books! Berry Eberle, a bride, after all these years?! It simply boggles the mind. But true love, like truth, always will out . . .

Speaking of truth outing, everyone in town is buzzing about Wade MacGregor's return to St. Dennis! Berry had mentioned that he was coming home, and that he had a big surprise for them. I'd say that surprise hardly tells the tale! Berry said that she and Dallas were both caught totally off guard and were completely shocked—well, who would ever have guessed that? Everyone wants to ask, but no one has the nerve! After watching Wade and Steffie Wyler carry on at Beck and Mia's wedding, I'd thought they were an item for sure. But apparently not. The latest rumor has it that he's back to stay!

I hear Steffie is just fit to be tied at the news . . .

~ Grace ~